The Unfairest Cape

Cyril Fox

Author of **The Life and Times of Esther Cronjé**
and **Upper Shit Creek** (Australian short stories)

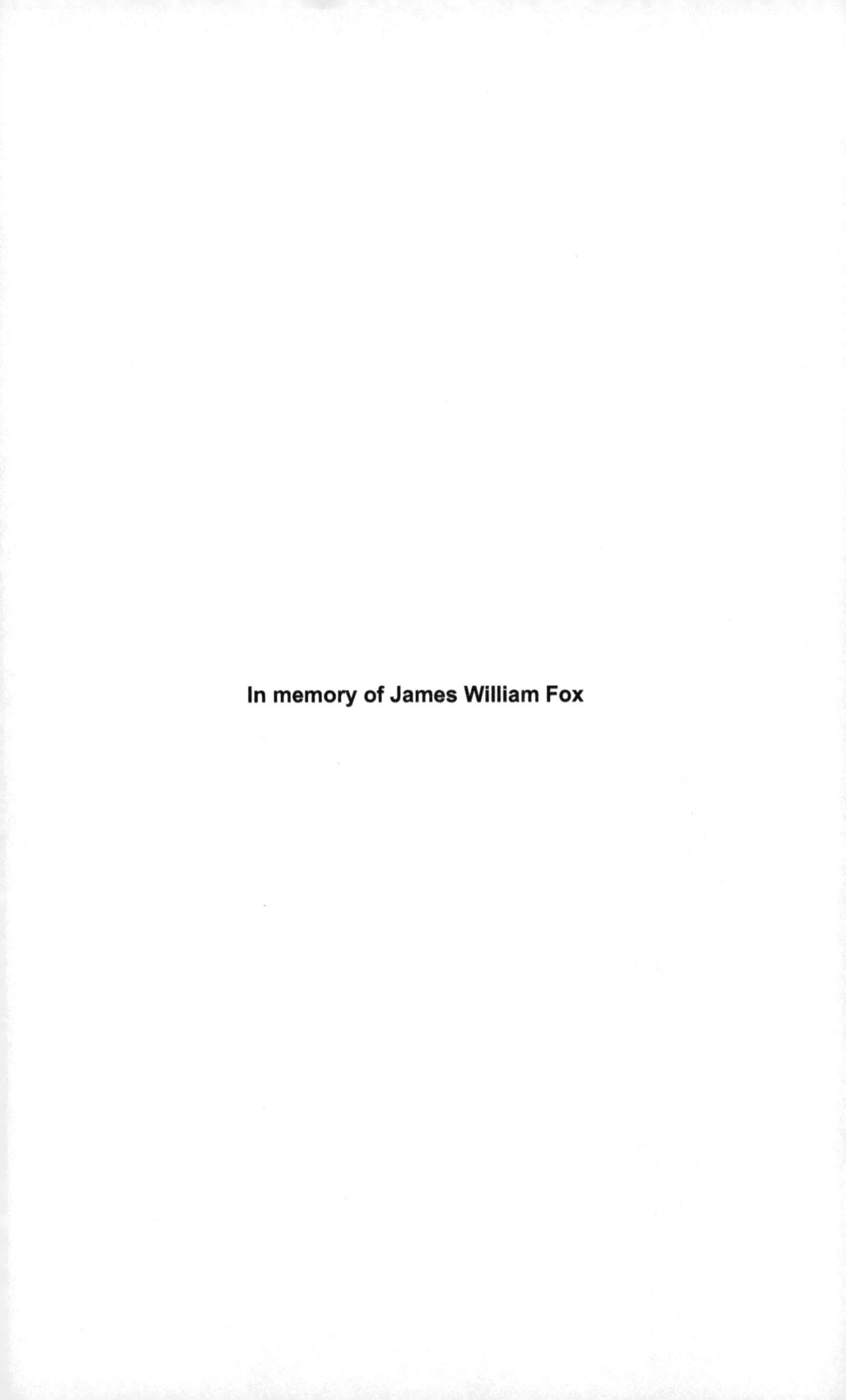

In memory of James William Fox

Important Notice

A number of terms used in this text which are today considered offensive were in common usage in the era in which this novel is set, often to the extent that these terms were even used in official records. In the author's opinion any attempt to sanitise the language of the text will serve only to water down to a tasteless tale the authenticity of the narrative.

The commentary about race and racial relations scattered throughout this novel does not reflect the personal views of the author but rather provides an historical backdrop to the never-ending discussion about race, culture and ethnicity in Southern Africa.

Similarly, observations made through the voices and reflections of the characters in his text do not represent the author's views about sexuality, gender roles, prostitution, tradition, religion, or anything else. The world, at the height of colonial dominance at the turn of the 20th century, was then a very different place, and it is through this lens that this text should be viewed.

A glossary of outmoded, colloquial, and other language words and phrases is included at the end of the text for the assistance of readers.

INTRODUCTION

While researching the Fox family tree I discovered that the late police constable James William Fox, stationed on Robben Island more than a century ago, is my third cousin, as we have great-great-grandparents in common. The fact that he was stationed on the infamous Robben Island, a place with a long and vicious history, immediately captured my interest, and added another avenue of inquiry into my ancestral connections with the Cape of Good Hope. Everyone with a little general knowledge of South African history knows that it was on Robben Island where Nelson Mandela and his fellow 'terrorists' were imprisoned for their 'treasonous' acts; this story is not about those times but predates Mandela's era by more than half a century.

James was born at Rondebosch, Cape Town, in December of 1884, one of the twelve children of John Palmer Fox and Eva Fox.

In my research I uncovered some curious facts and some head-scratching missing links concerning both James and his mother, Eva. This situation has led me to conclude that some of the omissions in the historical record, i.e. the unknown facts, may have been an inconvenience to the family had they been known at the time.

I have set about writing this fictional account to fill out the sparse historical evidence, and to weave a story to replace the lost history of my forebears at the Cape of Good Hope.

Obviously, I never knew any of these ancestors or their contemporaries and, for this reason, I disclaim here any responsibility for distorting their memory with any of the living descendants. The events described in this text are almost entirely imaginary, while the real people portrayed in this novel, that is, those who are named in the historical record, those who once breathed and walked on this earth, merely form a focal point for the story and an anchor to the time and place.

I wish to thank Doug Green of Victoria, Canada, for generously sharing his research into the descendants of John Fox of Great Ellingham, Norfolk (1761 -1842) and to Esmari du Toit of Oudtshoorn, South Africa, for freely giving me her time and expertise with genealogical research.

I also wish to thank Dirkie de Wet of Dirkie's Art Studio for permission to use a monochrome of one of his Table Mountain paintings to construct the backdrop of the front cover design.

Finally, for the benefit of the inquisitive reader I have included a brief postscript detailing a little more information about some of the real people featured in this text.

Cyril Fox

Melbourne, September 2022

Contents

Chapter 1 – The Hanging

Sometime during the night of 23rd to 24th November 1910, Gina hanged herself in the coal shed of Chief Warder Steenkamp's house on Robben Island.

This happened six months after the formation of the Union of South Africa and just one week after Gina's release from Valkenberg Asylum.

The reaction of the local women - mind you, not the lunatics nor the lepers - but the wives and the mothers and the sisters of the warders and the assistant warders, also the nurses at the asylum and at the leprosarium, was near-audible applause that the little wench, that object of temptation, was dead.

Female opinion was virtually unanimous that Gina's death was no loss to the world.

Male opinion was a lot more uncertain.

Dr Ernest Moon, the on-call doctor, and Constable James Fox of the Cape Mounted Police, were summoned to the coal shed to view the body and the scene of death. Moon, intense and tempered by years of toil, and not unaccustomed to suicide on the island, had no hesitation completing the death certificate, noting 'Death by Suicide" and on the advice of the householders recording the name of the deceased as Rainha da Cunha, a coloured person, born approximately 1892. Making her eighteen years old, or thereabouts.

Constable Fox noted in his diary that the noose was a belt strap, described to him by Mrs Steenkamp as a *riemstrop* belonging to Mr Steenkamp, the chief warder. The policeman noted, too, with the help of a sketch, the approximate size and extent of the coal shed and he dutifully recorded a list of the meagre contents of that outbuilding. Something which his senior, Sgt. Boyce, drilled into James was the importance of being thorough, detailed and factual. After all, was not sloppy note-taking the main cause of sloppy policing?

Later, back at the police station, James Fox would file his detailed report and discuss the apparent suicide with Boyce. The sergeant, a man as sharp and hard-edged as a woodsman's axe, would have questions, of course. He always did.

And a particular question on Boyce's mind would be looking for an answer. Did Gina really commit suicide or was her death made to look like suicide? There were, after all, a number of people on the island who may have wanted her dead.

Later that day Constable James Fox was feeling curiously unwell, but he put this down to witnessing the horror of the seeing the strangulated body of the girl in the coal shed. He shrugged off the feeling as a passing sensation.

No doubt he would feel better tomorrow.

Chapter 2 – The Foxes of Harrow

'There's a registered letter for you, James,' father declares as I walk into the kitchen, 'looks very official if I may say so.'

Always quick to shoot with my tongue, I answer, 'Why, Father, I thought that before now you'd have steamed the letter open to discover the contents?'

'Be gone with you,' grumbles the old man, 'as if I would stoop to do such a thing. If I wanted to know about the letter, I'd have asked your mother to tell me, her being clairvoyant and all.'

Mother looks across at me from where she stands emptying the coal scuttle into the stove, 'I see a sudden death descending on your father's head and I see the headlines in tomorrow's Cape Argus, *Rondebosch resident has his brain scuttled by wife.*'

Father chuckles at mother's remark, raises his teacup, and announces solemnly, 'Then, dear family, I'll drink to my life, and I'll declare that once I loved my wife.'

Louisa and Emma now joined the fray, Emma remarking, 'Father, you're not allowed to die, at least not until you tell me where you have hidden the gold sovereigns you've so carefully squirreled away over the years...'

'You mistake me for someone else,' interrupts the father, 'I am John Palmer Fox, railway gatekeeper, not Cecil John Rhodes, who owned half the wealth of South Africa. I've quite forgotten what a sovereign looks like, not having seen one in so many years.'

'Well, James, 'queries Louisa, 'are you going to open the letter or not? If not, let's just watch it burn in the stove...'

'Whatever you say, sweet sister, pass the letter this way if you don't mind.'

Taking the letter, I string out everyone's anticipation by carefully examining both the front and the back, exaggeratedly squinting at the typewritten characters. The mode of address is odd, you could say back to front:

Fox, James William – Constable
"Harrow"
Main Road
Rondebosch - C.o.G.H.

The return address offers me the next clue:

Office of the Inspector
Cape Mounted Police
P.O. Maitland – C.o.G.H.

Enough of this game! I tear open the envelope and remove a single sheet of paper.

The letter, on the embossed letterhead of the Cape Mounted Police, is clear and concise:

...you are to report to Sgt.John Boyce, O.I.C., at the police station, Robben Island, before ten hundred hours on the morning of the 13th day of December, 1909. To ensure your timely arrival, you are instructed to sail on the vessel, Tiger, departing from Dock Basin at eight hundred hours...

Well, that's unexpected! One day after my twenty-fifth birthday and at least a month earlier than I expected to receive the notification of my posting. I thought they would wait until after Christmas, and after the new year but, no, it is not to be.

After resigning – at father's insistence – from the Cape Government Railways, I enlisted with the Cape Mounted Police and underwent my training at the Maitland training ground. Ordinarily I wouldn't have been accepted as I knew nothing about horses, to the extent of having trouble telling the front of a horse from the back, but my brother Bayes (his first name was George, but we all called him 'Bayes,' his middle name) – well, Bayes was engaged to the daughter of a high-ranking police officer, a captain no less, and one thing following another, I secured a recommendation for the constabulary on the proviso that I learnt to ride a horse before the commencement of training.

. . . .

My parents, John Palmer Fox and Eva Fox (born Christoffel), were hardy, humble people, but not entirely ordinary.

My grandparents, along with father and his siblings – common labouring folk from Norfolk in England - arrived in Cape Town, I believe sometime around 1860, and I seem to recall hearing as a child from kitchen table conversations, that the Fox family arrived on board a vessel called the *Roxburgh Castle* which was en route to Sydney in Australia.

The Foxes had dreamt - and dared to undertake - the escape from the gloom and grind of England to the better climate and improved prospects at the Cape of Good Hope. Seemingly the prospects matched their expectations as, within a few days of disembarking in Table Bay, both John Fox senior and his son, John Palmer Fox – my father – found employment as gatekeepers with the Cape Government Railways.

Father was stationed at the Kenilworth railway gates and there he worked for over forty years, manning the gates at the busy road crossing. It was a position of trust requiring the steadiness of perfect attendance, punctuality and sobriety. Although my father was a man with little formal education, he had all the needed qualities of a reliable gatekeeper, and he placed great value on the security and predictably of regulating his life with the railway timetable and his treasured Waltham pocket watch.

In May of 1867 he married my mother, Eva, in circumstances which I only discovered when I was nearly grown up. They were an odd match. Father was always entirely predictable and beholden to duty and responsibility, while my dear mother can probably most kindly be described as a gypsy. Although father bought her nice clothes and small articles of tasteful jewellery, she chose to present herself in an odd assortment of threadbare garments, saving her better garments for rare special occasions such as weddings and christenings. Some days, when perhaps she ought to have been attending to her duties as a mother and a wife, she would sit herself in a cane rocking chair in the darkened sitting room, with its curtains tightly drawn, and attempt to commune with the world of spirits and angels and, then, at the most unexpected times she would rouse herself from this dreamlike state and, out of the blue, foretell an event, often an event which she had no way of imagining at the time. One such prediction particularly stuck in my memory. In the first week of November of 1903, mother handed me - with the instruction to 'wait and see' - a folded scrap of paper on which she had penciled, 'Pembroke R.I.P.' At that moment the name was meaningless but, just a week later, the iron barque, *County of Pembroke*, was shipwrecked near Port Elizabeth with all lives lost. Make of it what you will.

By 1878 my parents had, by frugal living, saved £75 and they found for sale in Main Road, Rondebosch, a stone cottage, which came with the name *Harrow*, on which they put down their savings as the deposit with the balance to be paid off at £2 per month. In among the neglected rose bushes dotted about the front yard of our home, was scattered a curious and slightly macabre display of several dozen bleached whale bones, keepsakes abandoned there by a previous owner.

Father often told of how he would rise at four in the morning for six days a week, pick up from the kitchen table his lunch pail, packed the evening before with bread and cheese and sliced onion or sometimes with buttered bread and polony, and head out onto Main Road in the pre-dawn, blanketed in his greatcoat and armed with a hurricane lamp, to walk the three miles to Kenilworth.

In the years 1868 to 1884, my mother gave birth to twelve children; among the large brood my sisters, Harriet, Emma and Louisa, and my brothers Albert, Charles, 'Bayes' (George Bayes) and, in 1884, yours truly - James William. Thankfully both my parents insisted that I should be called James rather than Jim or Jimmy, and for this I remain eternally grateful. When friends or acquaintances would knock at the door and ask for Jim or Jimmy, the standard response was, 'There's no Jim here, but if it be James you're after...'

The cottage was full to bursting point with humanity, and there was never any 'spare cash,' so we made our own soap, used charcoal paste to brush our teeth, and passed many days and evenings close to the coal stove as there wasn't enough fuel for the fireplace in the lounge room. Our clothes were mended, and re-mended, and handed down and oddly matched, but we were happy enough. Occasionally, by a word-of-mouth recommendation, mother would be called upon to read tarot cards, which she'd do for a fee of five shillings and five pence. The five pence went straight into a jar which mother labelled her 'coffin fund.'

Then, taking some of the remaining shiny coins and pressing them into the nearest child's hand, she'd command the offspring to 'buy cake for all.' And, needless to say, the appointed child could not run fast enough to the bakery to buy a huge bag of cream cakes!

Father was a predictable man, as predictable as the cycles of the moon, and as steady as his Waltham pocket watch, his most prized possession.

He worked from Monday to Saturday, attended mass every Sunday morning at St.Michael's and on Sunday afternoons loved nothing better than a picnic and a meander on Rondebosch Common. It was his expectation, unspoken but clearly understood, that all his children needed to attend with him both the mass and the open-air frolic on the common. Searching for the single word best to describe my father, I will settle on 'patient'. I don't recall his ever saying an angry word to anyone, not even to my mother who had an unfortunate habit of testing his forbearance at times.

Mother refused to attend mass, proclaiming that religion is a crutch for weak-minded and fearful people who are unable to face the prospect of their mortality without something or someone to lean on. She enjoyed denouncing Christians as lame ducks and 'bobbin heads;' a term I have never fully understood. Her carryings-on about religion clearly pained her husband, but she would persist with them anyway.

Claiming that the sun would darken her skin and make her look like a *hotnot,* she also declined coming along to the Common, preferring the company of her friend, Mabel, ten or more years her junior, for afternoon tea at home.

There are several curious incidents concerning my mother which hide in the shadows of my boyhood memories.

The first such incident concerns Father Kelly, a wild-eyed Irishman, our parish priest at St.Michael's. Never without his favourite Biblical quote (from Romans 6:23) that, '...the wages of sin is death...,' our agent of God was ever ready with a pointed admonition. One memorable Sunday, he stood in the pulpit and denounced, in a sermon powerful enough to rouse the long-dead crusaders, his condemnation of the wicked example of parents who fail to lead their children to the catechism of the True Church. Father Kelly's righteous rage stopped just a cat's whisker short of mentioning my dear mother by name.

A second incident happened in 1899 when I was just fourteen years old. Father enrolled me at Rondebosch Boys' High School, which had only opened a year or two earlier. He saw in me a liking for books and study and, more than anything else, he wanted me to be the best I could be, possibly even a 'man of profession.' Father himself is by no means an unintelligent man but he never had the opportunity of a decent education and, so, like so many parents before and since, he wanted me to live out the dreams he'd never dared to hold for himself.

One day, several months after starting at my new school, there was a fire in the school building and the headmaster, Mr Ramage, dismissed us early for the day, cautioning us to 'take heed' to head straight home. *Harrow* is just a few blocks from the school and, arriving home a couple of hours earlier than usual, I thought it best to take myself around to the backyard and let myself in the kitchen door, which was never locked, just in case I would disturb mother in one of her 'trancing' sessions.

The door swung open silently and I tiptoed into the kitchen. At first, all I could hear was the tick-tock of the mantel clock as it measured off little moments from eternity but, as my hearing grew more attentive to the silence, I thought I could hear a low moaning noise. From somewhere within.

Entering the hallway, I picked up on a curious smell, a smell I can only describe as acidic, a little like recently heated charcoal. What was it?

Another moan, then a voice - lower than mother's voice - from the sitting room. With my senses now tensioned, I glided closer and closer to the source of the sound.

The door was ajar, and I nudged it.

Opening silently, the door obeyed my nudge, and I gave wordless thanks to father for oiling the hinges every month; for his inability to put up with things which squeak and scrape around the house.

I felt a presence, an indescribable presence, even before I saw what I saw in the gloom.

Mother was sitting in her customary chair, slightly slumped and seemingly asleep, but maybe she was not asleep because she was reciting something in a low voice and behind her was an exceedingly faint blue light, like a lamp in the fog.

Seconds later the glow simply disappeared, as if turned off, and mother opened her eyes. And slowly her focus fixed onto me, and we just looked at each other, looked momentarily without seeing, without comprehension, I think both of us unsure what needed to be said, until she blinked hard several times and made to rouse herself.

'James!' she exclaimed in a strained voice, 'what are you doing here?'

I took a moment to marshal my words before answering. 'Mr Ramage dismissed us early...'

Without allowing me to finish, mother interjected, seemingly irritated by my intrusion. 'Doesn't that fellow care about your education? Fancy letting you go early! Just you wait, I'll be having a word with that little cockroach.'

'Mother, I'm so sorry for disturbing you. There was a fire at school, you see, and it really wasn't Mr Ramage's fault.'

My parent looked me carefully up and down and, detecting no trace of guile or deception in my manner, she appeared to calm herself while holding a minute's silence.

I gathered my courage to ask, 'What were you doing, Mother? I thought I saw a strange light in here.'

'It was my projection, James. You know, it's when you disconnect your spirit from your body.'

Emboldened now by her unusual willingness to talk and intrigued by what I'd just witnessed, I was brave enough to comment. 'Father Kelly told us the Bible says that it's wrong to communicate with the world of spirits. Are you not afraid, Mother?'

'Father Kelly is a fool who fills your head with rubbish. No doubt he is quoting from the book of Leviticus, a book which sets out rules for rabbis and Levites. Now tell me, child, do I look like a rabbi or a Levite?'

'No, mother,' I said, astonished by her quick and detailed response. I never imagined her knowing the contents of the Holy Book, perhaps even knowing more than Father Kelly.

She was speaking again, 'Years ago when I was a young girl, in a different place, among different people, knowledge of things spiritual was quite commonplace.' Then, standing up, she dismissed me. 'Now I must attend to other matters.'

Her words, 'in a different place,' kept ringing in my mind. What different place would that be?

. . . .

Curiously, a year or so after the incident of the spirit encounter, an unannounced visitor – a young woman, dark-faced like a Malay or an Indian – turned up on our doorstep. She came asking for mother.

Mother let her in and, without introduction to those of us who were present, she promptly ushered the caller into the sitting room and closed the door. They were in there for a long, long time and this did nothing other than to kindle our curiosity. Who was this woman - this mysterious person whom we had never seen before – and how was it that mother seemed to know her?

Well, of course, mother and the visitor did eventually appear from the sitting room and, at last, a slight introduction was forthcoming, with mother declaring, 'This is Maria. She will be staying a while and sharing a room with Emma.'

The year being 1900, and with the Anglo-Boer War at a point where there were heavy British casualties, my sister, Louisa, was away and working as a nurse aboard the hospital ship, *SS Maine* (a vessel which had been donated to the Royal Navy to help with the evacuation of serious injured Empire combatants from South Africa.)

What struck me about Maria was her remarkable resemblance to mother. Yes, she is darker - and prettier – than my parent (who takes little care with her appearance), but the features seemed to be chiselled by the same Sculptor attempting to craft the identical image.

Like younger siblings the world over, my sister, Emma, can at times be so annoying, so immature, so exasperating, but she scores full marks for sheer craftiness. When the competition is bigger and better provisioned, well, then you are reduced to been craftier in order to get your fair share of the spoils, aren't you? And our Emma is the ultimate in craftiness. A true Fox!

Emma soon befriended the mysterious Maria, took her to Simonstown for a day in the open air, to Wynberg for an afternoon of window-shopping, and before you knew it, they were exchanging secrets, those intimate secrets which all young women seem to have. But tricky Emma wasn't looking for confessions about trysts and skinny-dipping and stolen kisses. No, not at all, Emma wanted the story behind the story and, after a week of spooning out honey to Maria, the mysterious guest confessed.

Maria Christoffel is mother's little sister, a *laatlammetjie,* literally the last little lamb in the flock.

Their father, Gabriel Christoffel, is a Rhenish missionary, from somewhere in Germany or Austria, and he was a member of a group which set up a mission church in a place which they named Rehoboth, in an untamed and unclaimed part of southern Africa (an area which is today German South West Africa.) Gabriel Christoffel married a local woman, Susannah Jacobz, a *baster,* herself baked from an exotic and well-spiced dough of Malay, Indian and Khoi antecedents. Gabriel and Susannah had three daughters: our mother, Eva; Christa, the middle child; and Maria, the last little lamb.

At age eleven, Christa was abducted by a group of passing herdsmen. Her survival remained undiscovered until decades later.

Maria revealed to Emma that her mother, Susannah, died when giving birth to her, and that she was raised by foster parents, fellow adherents of the Rhenish Missionary Society.

When Susannah died during childbirth, our mother, Eva Christoffel, was thirteen or fourteen years old and, almost before her mother was cold in the grave, Erwin proclaimed to his flock that the Lord was directing him to populate the sparse community, to take his daughter, Eva, as his new wife and to make many children with her.

Eva, strong and independent even as a youngster, wanted no part of Erwin's plan for her and she promptly ran away, at times disguising herself as a boy, and over the next month made her way eight hundred miles southwards to Cape Town, to seek refuge in the home of her auntie who lived in Woodstock.

Well, Aunt Salomé did take her in and, immediately and without question, young Eva was required to earn her keep. Times were tough and there was no free ride for an able-bodied child; Eva had to keep house and, whenever paid work was available, she had to clean homes for white people to bring a few shillings to the household budget.

Salomé herself had regular employment at the fish market in Salt River. The pay was exceedingly poor but the big benefit in that line of work was that she had easy access to quantities of fishy off-cuts, heads and tails and roe and edible bits of innards. Now, mind you, Eva's aunt was not unkind, but as an almost toothless *baster* widow, she was battling from week to week to keep her head above water, no easy matter in the heaving tide of unfortunates inhabiting the threadbare areas of Cape Town.

Several years later, sometime around 1873 or in the early part of 1874, Eva – my mother – was sent to a Rondebosch address, for the performance of some housekeeping duties. Her work was apparently satisfactory to her employer, and she refrained from pilfering his possessions, with the result that soon enough she secured regular work, laundering and scrubbing and even cooking meals, at that Rondebosch address, for a young bachelor, an *engelsman,* and an employee of the Cape Government Railways.

Well, in time the bachelor and his young house servant became better acquainted, in fact, so much better acquainted that they were married in July of 1874.

That bachelor was, of course, my father, John Palmer Fox.

Now things were falling into place for me! Now I understood how my mother came to have a detailed knowledge of the scriptures; something to be wholly expected for the intelligent daughter of a missionary. And I also understood now her antipathy towards Christianity; was it not the Christian preacher at the behest of the Christian God who wanted her to make babies with her own father? For the first time in my life I began to understand, too, the secrecy surrounding my mother's origins; even her pretense that she was just a dark-haired white person. And I understood her wanting to minimise her exposure to sunlight was clearly an attempt, which she occasionally verbalised, to avoid looking like a *hotnot.*

The secret was out. How did it make me feel? Well, my mother was still my mother and, if anything, I felt closer to her knowing why she was at times so odd; I felt a deep sadness for the violation of her childhood and I could not begin to imagine those terrible times which led up to her eventual escape from the clutch of poverty and impending abuse. Her marriage to an immigrant railwayman raised her from the sewer into the relative comfort and security of the European working class. Such uplifting was both a rare and wonderful thing and went a long way towards explaining mother's reluctance to talk about her past; in case, somehow, she would be pointed out in the street and told to go back to 'her people.'

What Maria did not know and was therefore unable to tell Emma was where my mother had developed an interest in clairvoyance and spirit communication. I could only speculate that it came about sometime after her flight from Rehoboth, and I made a mental note to ask her one day, one day when the time was right.

What was Maria doing in Cape Town, such a long way from Rehoboth? This was now the compelling question which was desperately looking for an answer.

Even Emma had trouble prising open that secret.

Another month passed. Then quite unexpectedly all was revealed - by the cheval mirror in the bedroom which Emma and Maria were sharing.

Maria was at the mirror, doing whatever women do in front of a mirror. and she was quite unaware that Emma, seemingly preoccupied with reading *Jude the Obscure,* was watching her closely. And it was then when Emma, sharp-eyed Emma, noticed the bulge, an undeniable bulge, protruding from Maria's belly.

Emma, always direct and to the point, just had to come right out and say aloud, 'Why, Maria, why did you not just tell me you're pregnant? It's not as if you are the first or the last woman in your situation.'

'I'm not...'

'Don't lie, girl, remember you're talking to Emma, so please don't insult me with a fairy tale. Now spill the beans.'

Maria was silent for a minute. Then, looking up with tears in her eyes, she said simply, 'Yes, I'm pregnant.'

'I know that! Where and when and, most of all, why? Why are you in this predicament, and how long did you expect to keep the secret?' Now there was no stopping the onslaught from Emma; Maria would not be allowed to walk out of that room until she had confessed. And. not just confessed but delivered up every little detail.

And so, at first hesitatingly, Maria told her story. Then, faster and faster, the facts and the tears flowed from the young woman from where she sat on the hardness of the floor and, rocking back and forth while clasping her knees, she told her story. The whole story.

Although Maria's sisters, Christa and Eva, also disappeared from Rehoboth, Maria's circumstances were different, although the common factor in the departure of the sisters from their childhood home was undoubtedly the unequal power of armed and brazen men over vulnerable *baster* women in a lawless land.

Rehoboth is a very remote place and this remoteness (as isolation has often permitted throughout history) allowed for unrestrained wrongdoing at the hands of the strongest and the most brutal of humankind and so it came about that, late one morning, two bushy-bearded Afrikaner men armed with hunting rifles and accompanied by pair of full-grown ridgebacks rode into Rehoboth, ostensibly prospecting for *blink klippies* but when no gemstones could be found or extracted from the local people, the riders took six donkeys and a Cape cart from the Mission.

And they also took Maria.

She had no chance to escape the rifles and the ridgebacks and, to maximise her degradation, they tied her down facing backwards on one of the stolen donkeys, and that is the way they left – unchallenged – into the wild country along the Oanob River.

Maria knew that she was not going along for sightseeing. On the donkey's back, securely trussed like a freshly hunted impala, Maria struggled just to breathe, to remain conscious, as the party trekked most of the day through the thin scrub, in a land where rain often forgot to come from one season to the next. Other than for the breathing of the animals and an occasional clearing of the throat by the two men, the only sound in the vast land was the rising and falling chorus of the cicadas dancing to the silent pulse of the afternoon sun.

About an hour before sunset, the party stopped and set up camp in the centre of a clump of mopane trees on some flat ground near the river.

They unstrapped Maria from the donkey and tied her to a wheel of the Cape cart and she was allowed to sit half under the cart. One the ridgebacks came over, had a sniff, and promptly peed against the wheel, catching Maria in the splatter.

Then, as the sun descended from the day and spread itself along the horizon, the song and dance began. Like a couple of house cats with a mouse, the men wanted to play, to torment their prey, to watch their victim squirm and plead and beg for mercy.

The men's game started out in a low-key way, without any dramatics, almost as if they were just a couple of regular chaps – you know, fellows engaging in a little horseplay and mischief – like when a brother hides his sister's shoes in the coal box or drops a dead spider into her underwear drawer.

The younger Afrikaner, a squint-eyed man whom Maria referred to as *Daai Skeeloog,* a beast with hands the size of dinnerplates, swaggered over to the cart carrying a tin cup filled to the brim with water.

'*Haai meidjie,* you like a nice cup of fresh river water, hey?'

Maria nodded.

When he was just two or three steps away, Skeeloog stumbled – in the way known as 'accidentally on purpose' – and he spilled the entire contents of the cup into the dirt, and he made a great big show of being sorry. *'Jammer, jammer, jammer!* How clumsy of me! You must be so thiiiiiirsty! I'll ask Gert here if he'll make you a nice cup of sweet tea…'

The bastards laughed their heads off, slapping their thighs and play-punching each other on the shoulder.

'Stop! For chrissakes stop!' pleaded the older man. 'I must get the kettle boiling for the lady's tea. Now fuck off!'

Maria so wished she could block her ears, but with her hands tied to the cartwheel she could barely move.

A short while later, Skeeloog wandered over towards Maria until he was just two steps away, and standing before her in mock humility, in imitation of a personal servant, he observed, 'Well, *baie jammer,* madam, looks like we had ourselves a little accident, but never you worry yourself because we, that's Gert and me, we're going to make very sure of your pleasure and happiness while you're travelling with us, while you're guiding us through this valley of temptation. Now isn't that what the Bible says?'

Maria wasn't at all sure what Skeeloog was rambling on about; all she was sure about was a deep sense of foreboding. Nothing good would come of this encounter. Maybe she would be just lucky enough to escape with her life.

Skeeloog was speaking again; 'Now, while Gert is boiling some water for your tea, maybe we'll check out the dinner menu together. I'm sure you'd like to see the delights in store for you this very evening,' and as he uttered these words he stood squarely in front of Maria and proceeded to unbutton his fly.

He reached inside his trousers, appeared to grab hold of his peter – at which moment Maria firmly shut her eyes in expectation of God-only-knows-what.

Half a minute later, nothing having happened, Maria's unblocked ears detected a sound like water trickling onto sand and, daring to open her eyes for a millisecond, she spied Skeeloog facing away from her and pissing on the dirt. Her relief was immense but at the same time she was furious, shamed and still petrified at the prospect of what would surely happen to her later.

Gert chided, 'What's the matter, Klaas?' - his real name now revealed - 'Is little Peter not standing up for the lady today?'

'Fok jou!' growled Klaas – Skeeloog - as he stomped off to look for something in his saddlebag. In due course, he extracted a stick of *biltong,* sat himself down on a nearby rock and gnawed away in silence.

Even in her terror Maria sensed a certain tension between the men. What was it? Could they be reluctant, maybe out of some twisted sense of Calvinistic propriety, reluctant to violate her within each other's view? Or could it be that they wanted her exclusively, like two boys not wanting to share a toy truck? Whatever the underlying cause of this tension, there was no mistaking it.

Seemingly the game-playing was done for now and a grimness settled on the camp.

Maria noticed that, after feeding the dogs a couple of chunks of unidentifiable meat, the men proceeded to tie them up to an ancient tree stump. Presumably they would not want the ridgebacks wandering off into the night and being confronted by a lion or a pack of hyenas.

The men ate biltong and biscuits and eventually gave Maria a couple of biscuits and the long-awaited cup of water - but clearly evil was lurking just beyond the circle of light from the campfire. Several times eyes glowed from the shade and depths of the night, watching and waiting; and occasionally little animal noises scurried about in the surrounding brush.

Then without notice Gert stood up. Stretched. And announced, quite matter-of-factly, 'I'm taking the girl for a walk. And maybe we'll just hold hands under the stars, hey? So, you stay here, Klaas, and look after the fire.'

Klaas said nothing, just sucked on the pipe he was smoking.

Gert untied her and led her away. Like a chicken to the chopping block.

Obviously a creature of habit, he brought his rifle and hat, almost as if he was planning to pot a bird or a rabbit for dinner and, as for Maria, her little attempt at resistance was futile; the man's huge hand clamped unrelentIngly around her neck, to the point where she could hardly breathe, much less resist.

He led her through a clump of mopane and down to the river's edge, to a flat patch almost next to the water. There the river glistened in the light of the rising moon, and the water gurgled softly and the only other sounds in the world were an awakening chorus of crickets and the croaking somewhere of a solitary frog. The moon itself, almost full and glowing with a dull and sickly pallor against the inky canvas of the sky, looked on impassively at the young woman and her predicament.

Unceremoniously and without a word, Gert pushed Maria down, down onto her back on the sand and, using his left hand to maintain the grip around her throat, with his right hand he fumbled with his belt and his trousers, and he tore away her underwear, and then he lowered his weight onto her while pinning her legs apart. Maria closed her eyes and, for the first time in several years, she prayed. Prayed for it to be over, prayed to get through this night.

She would not remember anything else until she felt his great weight lift from her and, seeing him stagger to his feet, she watched as his bulk rose, with his trousers around his ankles, silhouetted against the moon.

It was at that moment when the instinct for survival awoke sharply within her and while his trousers were still down below his knees and encircling his ankles, she kicked against his legs with the strength of a wounded wildebeest and knocked him flat to the ground and, then, with a quick sweep of her arm as she uncoiled her body from the ground, she picked up his rifle and ran. Ran along the river and into the night.

. . . .

She knew they would track her, two horsemen with a pair of hunting dogs, hunt her down in the darkness like a pack of hyenas chasing a solitary goat. Unless she could - with the skill and cunning of the *Khoi* ancestors - evade her pursuers, the chase would be over in less than ten minutes.

The fact that Maria had Gert's rifle would hopefully slow the trackers down as they simplyhad no way of knowing whether she knew how to use the rifle, that she really had no inkling beyond pointing it vaguely in the direction of the target and pulling on the trigger in the hope that it would fire.

For a minute or two she ran like her feet were on fire and then, finding an open access point to the river, she waded in and moved upstream in the water as fast as she could in the moonlight. She remembered, from a story she had once heard, that the only chance for a fugitive in this situation to elude the hunting dogs is to flush away the scent of the trail by moving through water. This is what Maria did; she thought that if she could move far enough in the stream then with a bit of luck the dogs would not pick up her scent again.

Soon enough she could hear her pursuers, rapidly getting closer and closer and in minutes they drew level with her; any moment now they might spot her out in the stream, so she moved quickly mid-stream to a group of rocky channels and there she lay herself down, as flat as possible, and as best she could to blend herself in with the riverine terrain.

Hastily she settled herself in among the rocks, her body more or less submerged. And waited.

Sure enough, within moments the horsemen and their canines were right there on the bank, probably not twenty yards away. As fortune would have it though, in their rush to chase down the girl, the men had neglected to bring their hurricane lamps, and the moonlight was simply not luminous enough to identify her prone body, nestled where it was mid-stream among the rocks. For the moment Maria was safe.

The men and dogs moved upstream and, when they were gone, Maria emerged from the river, and promptly moved downstream, putting distance between herself and the trackers, and for added insurance she criss-crossed the stream several times, to break up and erase her scent. She still carried the rifle; and even though it was waterlogged and almost certainly unserviceable, it would make anyone think twice before coming too close.

It also occurred to her that in the right place the rifle might have a reasonable barter value.

What was she to do?

She was at least thirty miles from Rehoboth and over a hundred miles from the port of Walvis Bay. The men would almost certainly return to Rehoboth to look for her and, if they caught her, her fate was certain. They would break her apart and hang her to die in the nearest tree.

Maria considered going south overland to Cape Town, to find Eva, but how would she cross the eight hundred miles with a war going on in South Africa? She had heard the talk about the Border Scouts shutting down all movement south of the Orange River, all the way from the east coast to the southern edge of the Kalahari.

The better option seemed to be to go by sea, maybe on a coastal trader from Walvis Bay to Cape Town. Still without a clear plan in mind, she started walking westward towards Erongo and Walvis Bay, all the time keeping a lookout for one of the wagon trails used by traders moving goods from Walvis Bay into the interior.

Fate was on Maria's side. The very next day, in the forenoon, she spied a donkey wagon in the distance and, moving quickly to a concealed spot on the wagon's trajectory, she lay in wait to see who it was moving across the land, but she need not have worried. The wagon, moving westward with a load of animal skins, was being driven by Oubaas and his son, Willem, members of the Lichtenecker family, a well-known and respectable *baster* clan from Rehoboth.

Stepping out onto the track from her place of concealment, Maria stood still, like a sentinel with her rifle, right in the middle of the wagon's path. Poor Oubaas almost had a heart attack when he saw her and he was just beginning to protest that he had nothing worth stealing, when he recognised the tousled apparition standing in his path.

'*Here, meisie! Wat maak jy hier?*'

'It's okay, Oubaas. I'm just looking for a lift to Walvis Bay. If you're going that way?'

And this is how it happened that Maria caught a ride to Walvis Bay with two of her own kind.

Once in Walvis Bay, Maria concealed the rifle in some sacking supplied to her by Oubaas.

Oubaas Lichtenecker, well-known to the seafarers in Walvis Bay, took charge of Maria's situation and, in exchange for one rifle in need of cleaning and oiling, he negotiated a passage as far south as Saldanha Bay for her with Captain Oliveira of the vessel, *MV Vasco da Gama*, a general cargo freighter. And, as she said goodbye to the kindly old man, he slipped a silver crown, money which he could ill afford, into her hand and instructed her to take good care and one day to let him know of her safe arrival in Cape Town.

The resourceful Maria had an uneventful voyage on the long southward passage via Port Nolloth to Saldanha Bay and she even managed to impress Captain Oliveira with her cooking skills, to such an extent that he playfully threatened to have the regular cook walk the plank and to replace him with the young *baster* woman.

From Saldanha Bay Maria made her way easily enough by road for the last one hundred or so miles to Cape Town by hitching rides on sundry carts and wagons going southwards. Southward all the way to the doorstep of her sister's home - our family home - in Rondebosch.

....

All was now revealed, at least all concerning the curious origins of the Christoffel women.

In the early stages of her pregnancy Maria tried unsuccessfully to abort the thing which was growing in her belly. She tried the generally recommended treatment of boiling the seeds of a green pawpaw and drinking the bitter extract mixed in with pineapple juice. It did not work, other than to make Maria extremely bilious. Several months into her pregnancy she had a change of heart about trying to abort the foetus and, rather than take the risk of stabbing the thing to death with needles and aborting the half-formed lump from her belly, she decided to have the baby and let it be taken from her at birth. Maybe there would be a foundling home for it, maybe not; Maria could not bear to think too much about it.

As for Maria herself, well, no one wanted her. Not only was she soiled and devalued as a human being by her unwanted pregnancy but, worse still, she was clearly a *hotnot*, and worse than that, a homeless *hotnot*. The times are changing in Cape Town and, unlike fifty years ago or even twenty-five years ago, race has come to matter, come like a stone wall to divide people, and that is how she has found herself wedged firmly between the world of *witmense*, the Europeans, and her own kind. Except her 'kind' are not really any kind at all, rather nothing more than wrong-colour rejects from the breeding grounds of humanity.

Blood being thicker than water, my mother was adamant that Maria was staying, and to hell with what the fine people of Rondebosch chose to think about it all.

Now mother has taught Maria how to read the tarot and tea leaves, and every Saturday you will find her on the Parade performing readings for anyone willing to part with a few shillings.

Chapter 3 - The Flower Seller

It is on a dreadful Cape Town winter's day - a July Saturday in 1902 - when I first see her.

The Anglo-Boer War is not long done and Imperial troops are still funneling through Cape Town on their way home to England, Australia, New Zealand and Canada. There is a shadow across the land, the grim aftermath of war, and there arises a realisation in the consciousness of the population that great numbers of men, women and children have perished or have suffered great hardship for no better reason than the sorry scramble for earthly riches, specifically gold and diamonds. The war is over now and the British Empire is in unquestionable control, a scourge and a shade, seemingly striding the whole world.

It is my habit to accompany Maria on the tram to the city every Saturday and I happily spend several hours in and around the Parade while Maria does her readings. I love the buzz of the open air market where I will buy fresh vegetables and Darjeeling tea for mother, and a shilling's worth each of *mebos* and *tameletjie* as a little weekend treat for the folks at home and, in between shopping, I will allow myself to be entertained by the live auctions for all sorts of goods, articles such as saddles and paraffin lamps and quack medicines (of which *Dr Hommel's Haemotogen* is the one most theatrically marketed by three fellows in black suits and top hats. One day, following a chance encounter with a knackerman, I discover that *Haemotogen* is nothing more than horse blood which is being bottled adjacent to the Paarden Eiland knackery; undoubtedly the same fine quality product previously imported from England.)

I love to wander beneath the walls of the Castle, and to wonder at the exploits of the men of old in their worm-eaten wooden sailing ships who challenged the howling winds and icy seas of the Cape of Good Hope, euphemistically named, 'The Fairest Cape', a long time ago by Sir Francis Drake. And I love to lose myself among the Adderley Street flower sellers, to disappear in the sensory wonderland of colours and perfumes and the divine artistry of the roses and hydrangeas, arum lilies and pin-cushion proteas, Cape Daisies, carnations even prettier than Mr Van Gogh's famous paintings, and the orange-fanned strelitzia which so much resembles the comb of some yet-to-be-classified tropical bird.

That is where I meet Valerie on that Saturday in July. Mind you, quite by chance. But is that not how these things happen?

I am just about at Trafalgar Place when my reverie among the flowers and the colourful calls of the sellers is suddenly and rudely interrupted by shouts of, 'Stop that *blerrie* thief! Stop him!' A young rascal, as lean and fast as a greyhound, is bolting away along the Adderley Street tram line in the direction of the docks and several men are in hot pursuit. The rascal passes within yards of me as another shout goes up, '*Hier kom die dieners!*' and, sure enough, several constables join the pursuit.

Now there are at least six men giving chase and, calculating that there is no point my joining the pursuit, I just observe closely – very closely - and in the space of half a blink of an eye, the thief appears to bump accidentally into a female bystander, before continuing to hurtle away. In that tiny moment of collision, I see the fugitive press something into the hands of the bystander. Fifty yards down the street the pursuers catch their man, and he throws up his empty hands in surrender and protests loudly that he has done nothing wrong; that he merely believes the men are intending to bash him for leering at a pretty flower seller.

As for me, I closely follow the female accomplice and, at a moment when her way is obstructed by a throng of onlookers and shoppers, I take her very firmly by the wrist and lead her briskly to the constables who are still in deep discussion with the empty-handed fugitive. Although I am just seventeen and a half years old, I am already six feet tall and as sturdy as a railway sleeper and there is simply no way the accomplice can dislocate my grasp. She protests shrilly and tries to push a cloth money bag down her bodice, but I am too quick for her and I snatch the bag away with my free hand.

I deliver the female *skelm* over to the policemen with an explanation of what has just taken place between her and the thief, and the upholders of the law promptly place both miscreants under arrest. A moment later a girl in a bright yellow dress approaches, one of the flower sellers, claims her money bag, thanks the constables, then turns to face me.

She is a little breathless, wide-eyed, petite and perfectly sculpted like a fine wood carving. Without ever meeting her before, I know her by instinct. No, I cannot begin to explain the attraction; it is like the destined but unplanned meeting of a flower and a bee in the *veld* of existence.

For a minute she says nothing. I say nothing. We stare hard at each other in surprise, a sensation of the inexplicable *déjà vu* of already knowing each other. What is happening?

No doubt mother will have some head-scratching explanation to offer, along the lines of kindred spirits intersecting on the earthly plain, but I do not pretend to understand such things. I just know that something special has just happened.

She speaks first and there is no mistaking the Malay cadence in her speech, 'Thank you, *meneer!* Those *skollies*…'

I cut her short, 'No need to thank me. I was just in the right place to see what was happening.'

'Well, I want to thank you anyway, *meneer,*' She looks directly into my eyes as if playfully challenging me to contradict her.

My heart is racing, and my mind is racing twice as fast. I do not want to let her go, not yet, not ever. There is no way I can just let her walk away but what am I to say?

I find some words. 'Please don't call me *meneer*. My name is James, so please call me James, or my parents - who thought long and hard about what to call me - will likely be offended.'

She blinks and then, realising that I am teasing her, she laughs merrily, and it occurs to me that I am smitten by this person, this dark little being with the happy eyes. Continuing in my half bantering tone, I ask her, "Why do you call me *meneer* when we are clearly about the same age? And how long are you going to torment me before telling me your name?'

'James...James,' she begins, struggling a little to pronounce such a royal name, 'I am Valerie.' She hesitates before answering my other question, as if looking for the right words, then says what I was not expecting to hear. 'I call you *meneer* because you're a white man, and I'm just a Malay girl and I need to show respect to my betters. There you have it, *meneer*... sorry, James.'

'Valerie,' I begin, taking her hand in mine, 'I hadn't noticed, and I refuse to notice that we are not the same. And, even if I had noticed, what difference does difference make?'

'Notice or not, James, I am what I am.' she answers bitterly. Then she looks away and tries to extract her hand from mine.

'I will know you, Valerie.'

She looks up as if checking whether I am being serious. 'Okay, James, that's good,' she answers with a wry smile. 'Now I must get back to selling flowers or my mother will beat me for bringing home so little money, but before you go, I want to give you a bunch of flowers as a reward. You can give it to your girlfriend...'

'I will take a little bunch of flowers for my mother, if that's okay with you.' She smiles, and I want to put my arms around her, but I stop myself short with my confession. "I don't have a girlfriend and, if you must know, I've never had one. But I intend to change that.'

'How so?' Valerie asks quizzically.

'You will be the first.'

Valerie laughs merrily, pulls a face, and shoves a bouquet of flowers into my hands, 'Here! Be gone with you.' She glances at me before she turns away towards her stall and I know that I am not mistaken about her.

Later, when I catch up with Maria, she is surprised to see me toting a bunch of white Cape anemones.

'Excuse me, James,' she says, while transferring her clairvoyance trappings into a canvas bag, 'I didn't know there is someone in your life.'

'Not yet, Maria, not yet. These are for mother.' And, as some things are best left unsaid, I say no more. In fact, I am very quiet on the way home.

I have Valerie on my mind. Who is this little flower seller who has just walked into my consciousness and taken over my mind?

What is it she said about me being white? Of course, I am aware that in some circles dark-skinned people are seen as inferior, unwashed, possibly even savage, but this is not my perception or experience. In our home, mother and Maria are Christoffels, *basters* from Rehoboth, while my father has never referenced people by colour or race.

How am I, a 'white man' – yet like so many white inhabitants of Southern Africa, not completely white – how am I going to bond with the flower seller? Maybe telling her about Eva and Maria will help? I ponder these questions long and hard.

Mother is touched by the gift of flowers, and I do not tell her how I come to have them but, mother being mother, her intuition or premonition or whatever it really is, informs her that her son is acting out of character, and it takes her less than a day to work out what is going on.

Without notice, as if merely asking the whereabouts of the kitchen broom, my female parent asks me when we are alone the next morning, 'Are you in love, James?'

Attempting to duck the real question I answer lightly, 'Of course, mother, you know I love you dearly.'

'You can fool around all you like later. But now answer my question.'

I know I am not going to flick that question away as easily as brushing a fly from my face, so I tell her. 'Yes, I believe I am in love but please don't ask me to explain how it happened. Because I don't know...'

'If you understand it, James, it isn't love. Love defies the logic of this plus this equals that. Love works on the same plane as belief; that is, the unexplainable plane.'

That's how it comes about that the *clairvoyante* and I have a long discussion about my newfound love and, when the discussion is done, she orders quietly, 'Come with me,' and taking me by the hand she leads me to her dressing table where she proceeds to scratch around in a carved box, cluttered with a trove of ornate and bejeweled objects, from which she extracts two items of silver. One is a dainty silver ring with the metal twisted about like a cord of rope and the other is a delicate pendant shaped like a fluted flower.

'Here, James, have these,' she commands. 'Give her the little ring now, to establish a connection between you. Later, when you know her better, give her the pendant and know that the flute opens and inside the flute you can place a little message for her.' She demonstrates the opening and closing of the flower pendant as she hands it over, then she continues, 'Neither of these items has any great monetary value but love isn't measured in pounds and shillings. The value lies in the intention and the feeling with which these little objects are given and received.'

'Thank you, mother," I reply simply.

'One more thing, James.' Inquiringly I look up at her face, not knowing what to expect next. 'You must arrange to meet her mother, or both her parents if she had a father, which I know she doesn't...'

'How do you know this?'

'Really, son, you ought to know that I just know things. Now I was saying, you must meet her mother or your efforts to know this girl will be doomed from the outset. It's a cultural thing, James, and you have to honour it.'

Armed with two trinkets and the wisdom of my elder, I know what I have to do. Even if I have to crawl all the way from Rondebosch to the city, next Saturday I intend to keep an appointment with my destiny. My destiny, known as Valerie, the flower seller.

She is there, as I expected she would be. Before I approach, I just watch for a while as she bustles about, bunching flowers into bouquets, and I wonder at her elegance, at her slender neck, her tiny deft hands. Surely, she must have a queue of admirers lined up from Camps Bay to Observatory, from Salt River to Simonstown?

But for me there is no turning around, no escape. For better or worse, I am here in Adderley Street for a chat with my destiny.

She is happy, maybe even excited, to see me and lets me briefly squeeze her hand. I waste no time saying the words I have been rehearsing all morning, 'Valerie, I've come back for you. Please, let me walk you home when you have sold all your flowers. I have to meet your mother.'

'Oh, really, James?' (she has remembered my name!), and cheekily she adds, 'Here I am thinking you came here to meet me, not my mother?'

'You have found me out! How do you know it is really her I want to meet? Maybe I'll marry her and be your horrible stepfather...'

'How...how do you know I have no father already?' she asks, a little puzzled.

'I will explain later, but only if you let me walk you home.'

'I live in Leeuwen Street, over near Jordaan Street, not very far from here, so you'll have to explain quickly, hey?'

'Maybe we'll have to walk slowly then,' and, saying this, I touch her hand again

and, to avoid scaring away her customers, I wander off a little distance to wait.

Later, when we are on our way and about to cross Buitengracht Street, Valerie takes hold of my hand and stops.

'We're almost there, James.' I love the way she says James, almost as if my name is 'Jems.'

After a moment to order her thoughts, she continues, 'There are a couple of things which you should not be speaking about with my mother. The first is my father. One day if she wants to tell you about him, she will, but don't ask. Secondly, please don't discuss religion as it is a sensitive subject with her. We are Muslims, but mother feels abandoned by her faith. In good time, she may explain that to you as well, but it's not a topic for today.'

'Any other instructions?' I dare to ask.

'No,' she replies. 'I'll tell you though that we live with my uncle and auntie who own a small haberdashery shop in the Malay Quarter. Mother keeps house for them and occasionally helps out in the shop but mostly I support us by selling flowers for a big grower in Mamre.'

Forewarned and forearmed, I am ready for the meeting and anxious as hell to make a good impression. Now it is also dawning on me that there will be obstacles, more obstacles than I can imagine at this moment, to having Valerie.

Aminah is an older version of Valerie, still beautiful but a little battered by life. They share the same hazel eyes, the same dusky complexion, but Aminah's face is mapped with the many roads she has travelled and here and there some grey hairs hide unsuccessfully in her crown of abundant black hair which is half concealed by a finely woven shawl.

'So, James,' Aminah says, 'without wishing to be disrespectful, how is it that a tall white man like you wants to court my little dark daughter? What can you possibly want with her and how do you imagine you can be happy with each other?'

'Aminah,' I answer, 'I think your daughter is truly beautiful' - did I just say that? – 'and I doubt you'll disagree with me on that point. For you to understand fully why I have no issue with courting a Malay girl, you need to meet Eva, my mother, and Maria, my auntie.'

'Really? Why?' Aminah looks puzzled.

'For the moment I'll just tell you that they are from the Rehoboth Mission.'

Aminah relaxed visibly, comprehension tiptoeing into her mind. 'Yes, James, I'd love to meet them.'

I think the meeting went well. My worst fear has not materialised; I have not been told to go away, to *voetsek*, to leave the girl alone. In fact, I have promised to take both Aminah and Valerie to Rondebosch to meet my family. I cannot imagine what they will think, but I am not about to worry about what anyone will think. No, not after coming this far.

The meeting over, Valerie walks with me a little way and we linger a little, unwilling to part for another week. Monday to Friday I am at school, in the last part of my final year at Rondebosch Boys' High School, just a month or two from writing my matriculation exams.

I give Valerie the silver ring and her face lights up with delight. 'I suppose you want a reward now, *Meneer* James?' and, before I could answer, she kisses me on the cheek. It is so quick, so light, that I am not even sure it really happened.

'Thank you,' she says a little huskily, 'see you next week.' And she is gone.

Well, in time Aminah and Valerie do come to Harrow, our not-so-grand family residence in Rondebosch. The women meet for an entire afternoon (I extricate myself from the discussion after the first hour) and when the visitors leave it is obvious that the race problem is solved; solved at least between the families. Mother comments favourably about Valerie, 'What a lively and lithe little nymph you've discovered James. Little did I know that you had so keen an eye for such a fine breeder.' And Maria, perkier than usual, declares, 'As for Aminah, what a fine woman; so strong, so proud. I'm sure we'll be great friends.'

Things are looking up. Without fail I am at the flower market every Saturday, and every week we will talk and walk hand in hand up Government Avenue through the beautiful gardens, pause to feed the squirrels peanuts, pause a little more for a kiss beneath an oak tree or a *ficus* or the sensually twisted and intertwined rubber tree. Or we will catch a tram to Sea Point or Green Point or Camps Bay, buy ice cream, run along the beach, feed some stale bread to the seagulls, and lose ourselves in the bright outdoors.

Mostly people ignored us and let us be, but there would be the occasional, *Sies!*, at the sight of a seemingly white man courting a dark girl. By all accounts the old Cape Town, in the time before I was born, was a colour blind place, a place where intermarriage was widely practised and accepted. This tolerance stemmed from the early days when there were not enough women to go around and the European settlers would marry slave girls or local *Khoi* or hottentot women. In this way there are probably few descendants of early settlers who can claim to be fully European, fully white. But the attitudes of superiority, now being imposed on our country by the British ruling classes and some of the Calvinist churches, are reshaping our society, dividing people along lines of race and colour and ethnicity. Some white people are saying, without any evidence or fact, that black people and brown people are morally and intellectually inferior, that they need to be 'protected' by their European masters. In fact, the term 'protectorate' actually appears in the name of some countries, for example, the Bechuanaland Protectorate. Then, too, some of the Calvinist pastors are telling their congregations that black people are the 'descendants of Cain' and are therefore marked for eternity as people of base instincts, little better than domestic animals.

But Valerie and I are happy in each other's company, oblivious to the occasional provocation or contemptuous remark.

In 1902 there is a remarkable spring in Cape Town, a rebirth from the privations of war, and we are too much in love to hold any feeling of resentment or ill feeling towards anyone.

As spring turns to summer though and the days are getting warmer our thoughts and our inclinations turn to being alone together, turn to doing what nature wants young lovers the world over to do and our opportunity shows up in an unexpected way.

Aminah is visiting Rondebosch several times a week. She and Maria have become inseparable, the closest of friends, and the result of Aminah's visits to 'Harrow' is that there are times now when the house in Leeuwen Street is deserted, with Maria out visiting and Valerie's uncle and aunt at their shop.

Valerie chooses the day, a Monday, when she has the day off from selling flowers.

Already the day is hot when I meet her at the tram stop in Buitengracht Street. She's wearing that marigold-yellow dress again, the one she wore the day I met her, and on her feet she's wearing simple leather sandals, no doubt to cope with the rising heat from the cobblestones.

Valerie has her key and lets us in at Leeuwen Street; the house is shuttered to keep the day out. The interior is dim and still and smells of polished wood and scrubbed floors.

At the kitchen tap, Valerie gets us each a glass of water, which we drink silently, then she takes my hand gently but purposefully and leads me down a high-ceilinged passage with long bare walls to the bedroom which she shares with Aminah.

With the shutters closed the room is dim, but not dark; quiet, but not silent. There is a low murmur from passersby in the street and a little shaking of the shutters as they block off the unending push and shove of the southeaster outside. Almost self-consciously we sit on the edge of her bed, an iron bed which is narrow and hard and covered with what looks like a grey hospital blanket.

Valerie is wearing some sort of jasmine fragrance, present but subtle, which is making my head spin, and her hand is cool as she touches my face, before she seductively slips a finger into my mouth in unspoken invitation, at the same time bringing her mouth up close to my ear and whispering, 'Please be gentle with me, James.'

This is how it happens that we, young lovers, discover each other in the dimness of that simple room in Leeuwen Street on that summer's day, and how our lives and dreams flow together like molten metals in the crucible of passion.

Later, I give Valerie the flower pendant, and on a sliver of paper which I place into the flute, in my smallest and neatest handwriting, my message reads: 'Forever yours – James F.'

Chapter 4 – Autumn of 1903

It has been a glorious summer, this summer of 1902-1903.

For me school is over forever and I am on the lookout for employment but the economy has not yet fully recovered from the war and jobs are few and far between. Having been an above average student, possibly because I am a keen reader of every kind of book, I fully expect to get my matriculation exemption, which will allow me to go to university, but university cannot be for me; my family simply cannot afford to support me and to pay for tuition and textbooks.

Father is fond of saying, 'an honest man will find his way in life,' and no doubt he is right. So, I have no expectation of joining the privileged offspring of well to do Cape families by attending the University of Cape Town and, besides, the prospect of working every day of my life indoors and dealing with documents or diseased people has no appeal for me.

I need a job where I can feel the sun and the rain on my face.

Little do I know that I am about to come face to face with a never-even-thought-about opportunity.

One evening my brother, Bayes, calls around (he is now living in Claremont). It is a balmy evening, the twilight taunting the night to come out and get it, and Bayes suggests that he and I take a walk to the Common to discuss, as he puts it, 'some men's business'. Bayes being Bayes, the go-getter in our family, I agree to accompany him as he no doubt has something interesting or important talk about.

Sure enough, before long Bayes shows his hand, 'Am I right in thinking, James, that you're stilling looking for employment?'

'Certainly! I'm sick of being penniless and having to borrow from mother or Maria, a shilling today and a half-crown tomorrow. And, the truth be told, I'm not really borrowing at all because I have no idea when, if ever, I'll be able to pay the money back. It's no way to live, Bayes.' The words were bitter on my tongue.

'In that case, dear brother, I'm your genie. Here to grant you a wish today, and no doubt a couple more in the future.' Bayes looks smug, even more smug than usual.

'There's a job up for the taking at the Harbour Board,' began my brother, 'just the thing for you...'

I interject, 'And you know this how? What is this job?'

'Lightkeeper. Actually, assistant lightkeeper.' He ignores my first question and lets the job title sink in before going on. 'Do you know what a lightkeeper is, James?'

'Of course, somebody who keeps a light.' I can also be smart when I want to be.

Bayes ignores my stupid response. 'In view of a couple of imminent retirements from the Service, there'll soon be a couple of positions for assistant lightkeepers, at Cape Agulhas and at Dassen Island.'

'Not here? Not in Cape Town?'

'No, dear boy, those posts are allocated by seniority. You'll have to start at a remote spot and over several years work your way closer to our fair city.'

'That doesn't work for me!' And I surprise myself with how much feeling I just said that.

Bayes looks at me strangely, even shakes his head. 'What the hell's wrong with you?' he demands, 'this is the chance of a lifetime, a chance for a secure public service job. If you don't screw up, the job's yours for fifty years.'

'But there's Valerie...' I begin, unsure how to say that I don't want to be away from her.

Roughly, Bayes takes a low swipe at me. 'Yes, I've heard about sweet little Valerie. Now I bet she knows how to turn a trick or two, how to leave you lying there as limp as a week-old cabbage, but get with the game, James. She's a passing fancy on your way to manhood.'

'Fuck you, Bayes! If you weren't my brother, I'd knock your block off right here and now. Valerie is everything to me.' Clenching and unclenching my fists, I glare at the bastard.

'James, James, calm down!' Bayes hastily takes a step back in appeasement, almost tripping backwards in the process. 'I didn't know things are that serious...'

'Damn right Valerie and I are serious - as serious as two people have ever been.'

'You're young, James, and in a few years things might look a little different to you. Then there's also something else to consider...'

'What else?' I demand.

'You need to consider your future, James. Hitching up with a Malay girl might not be a smart move, you know.'

'What does that mean? Are you saying there's something wrong with Valerie?' I feel the heat coming back in my face. What stupid remark is Bayes going to parade before me now?

'Where have you been hiding James? Times are changing and what was once considered acceptable, even normal, no longer fits with the mood of the times. For a European to marry a coloured woman is, you know, no longer right. It's the wrong look.'

'No longer, right? What's got into you, Bayes? Dare I say it out loud, our own mother is not a European, and here you are telling me that there's something not right, something sinister, about interracial marriage. Just who have you been listening to?'

I am simmering, near to boiling, damn close to wringing his self-righteous neck. Sometimes it surprises me that Bayes hasn't been smacked in the mouth. Or maybe he has, and I just don't know about it. It is not as if he would announce such a thing to the world, not our I'm-always-right and our just-ask-me Bayes.

'James, I don't dictate the mood of the times, but I do know a lot of people and I have my finger on the pulse of what's going on. But I'm not saying it's right or wrong – after all, aren't right and wrong just relative concepts? – I'm saying that, like it or not, the social make-up of our society is shifting.'

'Well, you know what, Bayes? You do what you want, and I'll do what I want and to hell with the social mood which seems to concern you so greatly. I may as well tell you that I want Valerie and that I intend to marry her just as soon as I can support her.'

Quietly, Bayes replies, 'If you want to support her and yourself, James, then make your way over to the Harbour Board and register your interest to join the Lighthouse Service. It could be a long, long time before another opportunity like this crosses your path.'

We leave the discussion at the Common and make our way back to *Harrow* just as the night overcomes the twilight.

. . . .

I have a lot to think about. The Lighthouse Service? I have no clear idea what is involved. Is there really any more to it than lighting a lamp on the top of a tower and then ensuring that the light stays on all night to warn ships that they are close to the coast? Bayes seems to think there is something noble about being a lightkeeper and maybe Bayes is right. I hate to admit it, but he often is.

. . . .

I am surprised by Valerie's reaction when I tell her. For a brief moment there are tears in her eyes, then she takes a deep breath, composes herself and says, quite matter-of-factly, 'Of course, you should apply for the job, James. There's no question about it.

'But... but, what about us?' I stammer.

'I know you want to spare my feelings, James, but your brother is right. This is a rare opportunity.' She looks me directly in my eyes and, seemingly without sentiment, she declares, 'I'll still be here, James. I'll wait for you. Allah… I mean God; God needs me to be here to provide for Aminah.'

What can I say? I expected… well, what did I expect? She is so composed. So strong.

'Are you sure?' is all I can say.

'Yes, I'm sure.' And that was that.

With my recently arrived matriculation certificate I make my way to the Table Bay Harbour Board – it is Monday, 13th April – to apply as a lightkeeper. Will they take me, I wonder? Maybe they want men with some sort of maritime experience?

But I need not have worried because when they find out that my father is a longstanding employee of the Cape Government Railways and that I have matriculation exemption, nothing less, they immediately accept my application and make favourable comment about my able-bodied appearance. 'Lightkeeping is hard work, you know. Not only must you have your wits about you, but you need to possess the stamina to sleep in the standing position.'

They perform the formality of placing my application before the Board and they waste no time getting back to me. On Thursday afternoon I have their telegram, the message short and compelling:

> *Report to the Table Bay Harbour Board on 22nd instant at ten o'clock for finalisation of your employment in the Lighthouse Service stop By order of the Secretary*

Well, well, that was not so hard, was it? In spite of my initial misgivings about playing around in lighthouses, I am beginning to be quite excited about the prospect of a new adventure, an excursion into the unknown, an escape from my idle existence in Rondebosch. Although I am not thrilled by the prospect of being away for sizeable chunks of time from Valerie, day by day I am learning to accept the necessity for it. After all, as Bayes was at pains to point out, once I have permanent employment, I can set up home and make Valerie my wife. And we can take Aminah in with us. The possibilities are becoming clearer all the time, like fog melting away in the morning sun to reveal cheerful rows of brightly painted houses.

At the Harbour Board I meet Mr O'Dwyer, the head lighthouse keeper. He is businesslike, but not unfriendly. With his wide brow and bushy beard, he looks for all the world like General Cronjé's *doppelgänger,* like your favourite uncle who teaches you how to fish and shoot. Anyhow, here is the imposing Mr O'Dwyer, and he is addressing me; 'Well, Mr Fox, I believe congratulations are in order. You measure up to our strict entrance requirements; now it is up to you to prove yourself in the field, or up a light, so to speak. There'll be days and nights when you'll be lucky to sleep at all and if the sleep deprivation doesn't get you, the cold and the damp will penetrate to your bones. This is not a game for sissies. But after a time you'll acquire the great satisfaction of keeping the light burning, no matter what the weather or the circumstance, and with the knowledge that many lives depend on you, you will feel rightly proud of the essential work you do.'

Here is the pride thing being revealed to me; I cannot quite make sense of it all yet. And lives depending on me? Now there is a novel idea.

Mr O'Dwyer hands me a small book titled, 'Laws and Regulations of the Cape Lighthouse Service' and I am amazed to see that there are hundreds of rules, along the following lines:

Lighthouse keepers are:

> *... forbidden from keeping domestic animals at lighthouses*
> *... prohibited from consuming alcohol while on duty or for 12 hours prior to duty*
> *... not to bring unauthorised persons into a lighthouse, or onto lighthouse quarters*
> *... to report for duty one quarter hour before the rostered commencement time*
> *... forbidden from carrying firearms, swords or other weapons of any description*
> *... to mix paint no more than one hour prior to the intended use thereof*
> *... permitted to carry marine flares for emergency use in the event of the failure of the light*
> *... without delay to provide a detailed written report of any instance of the light being extinguished, for whatever reason, between the hours of dusk and dawn*
> *... required to render all possible assistance to ships and mariners in distress*
> *... prohibited from possessing or cultivating narcotic plants*

And on and on, page after page of regulation, even down to the correct procedure for relighting a lamp. It is a lot to digest, and I wonder will I ever know all this detail? And will I last in the Lighthouse Service, or will I be found wanting and drummed out in disgrace?

'Any questions?' asks my employer, as he fills his pipe from an embossed box.

'Just one,' I dare to ask, 'how long do I remain at the lighthouse for each tour of duty?'

'Theoretically, you are three weeks on and one week off. But you may as well know that there'll be occasions when the weather will put a stop to all movement and there'll be times when, owing to staffing shortages or illness, the planned rotation may be impossible.' I nod and hope that I am not disclosing my dismay. I have no stomach for such long absences. But I am in deep water now. I have to swim. Or sink.

Our meeting almost over, Mr O'Dwyer hands me a slip of paper on which he has written:

Alfred Basin. Noon the 25th. SS Lady Jane

'Here, take this, our supply vessel will take you to Dassen Island, via Saldanha Bay.'

I suppose I look a little lost, possibly even overwhelmed, by this quick turn of events. The older man notices my unease and, in a fatherly way, he rests his large hand reassuringly on my shoulder. 'You'll be fine, young man. When you get to Dassen Island, the chief, Mr Richardson, will explain everything you need to know, and possibly even things you don't need to know. Now, before you go home, you must go to the downstairs basement, to the harbour quartermaster store, and get yourself kitted out with a uniform.'

Mr O'Dwyer offers me his hand. 'Wear the uniform proudly, Mr Fox, and good luck.'

. . . .

That same evening over supper I recount the events of the day, and father is listening attentively, taking in every detail. He is obviously pleased at my good fortune, and he shares the following wisdom with me, 'Be happy, James, a good job is like a good wife. Something to cherish.' Putting down his knife and fork, father continues, 'Tell me you will now marry Valerie, and breed me a flock of grandchildren to amuse me in my old age?'

'Father,' I say, 'why this talk of old age? Yes, I do plan to marry Valerie but I'm not in a position to set us up with a home yet, so I'm afraid both marriage and grandchildren will have to wait a while. Also, as an assistant lightkeeper, I'm not allowed to have a wife with me on the island.'

Never one to speak before thinking, my male parent is quiet for a minute. There is clearly something on his mind, so I give him the room to arrange his thoughts.

'James, do you know what is happening in March next year?'

'Sure,' I reply, 'your birthday is in March.' Where is the old man going with this conversation I wonder?

'Precisely, my boy. Mind you, not just any birthday – my sixty-fifth birthday.' He looks questioningly at me. Am I missing something here?

He sees my lack of comprehension, so father continues, 'Next March I am required to retire, and I will thereafter receive a modest pension from the Railways but I'm very much afraid that I'll be unable to maintain this home in the way we are accustomed. Without wishing to sound self-pitying, James, your mother and I have been unable to set aside any savings all these years.'

I hear myself say, 'What are you saying, Father? Don't you have all of us to take care of you? And for the first time I see my father as an old man. His hair, what remains of it, is as white as snow and his shoulders sag a little from the burden of time. My father a pensioner padding about in slippers? It is hard to imagine. What will happen to his identity as the gatekeeper at Kenilworth? What will he do with his remaining days? And is this a man's reward for a lifetime of honest toil? The reward for showing love and kindness to every person he has ever known? I can hardly bare to think about it.

Mother lifts the mood when she asks, 'Are you gentlemen just going to sit there and mope all night or are you going to sample my trifle?' So, as good trifle cannot be allowed to go to waste, the conversation is promptly packed away for another day.

. . . .

In the following days I do my best to study the little book of lighthouse regulations but, right now, so much of the terminology has no meaning for me. What, for example, is a Fresnel lens? And a glass chimney? Now why would anyone construct a chimney out of glass?

One regulation stuns me though. There it is, as they say, in black and white, on page fourteen, point four, under the heading of 'Professional and Familial Relationships.'

> *In order to maintain and to promote the highest moral standards within the Cape Lighthouse Service, lightkeepers are forbidden from consorting or cohabiting with kaffir women, or dark-skinned women of mixed race or any other race of women of dark complexion.*

Is this what Bayes was talking about?

It is too late for me to turn around, so here and now I resolve to keep my mouth shut about my personal life. I will just do my job and come home.

To Valerie and our future.

Chapter 5 – Dassen Island

Alfred Basin, Table Bay.

Saturday, 25th April.

It is still three quarters of an hour before noon, but I am keen to size things up before sailing away into the great unknown. I could say I am checking the lay of the land, except there is little land to check in the Alfred Basin, only timber wharves set upon mighty trestles and nearby, on solid ground, row upon row of tall warehouses, some of granite and some of brick, the custom house, Günther & Sons Ships' Chandlers, and several victuallers.

The air is filled with the smells of salt, creosote and rotting fish, and seagulls are circling around, assaulting my ears with their cawing cries and scavenging for anything which may be edible in this bustling place.

Like the legs of a great spider, a network of railway tracks runs the length of the wharves and, on these tracks, several dozen goods carriages rest in various stages of loading and unloading. Everywhere alongside the tracks men are bustling about with carts and wagons, moving goods, picking up and setting down. To my untrained eye all this activity appears quite haphazard, quite chaotic, but I am sure there must be a well-tested system at work.

Bollards and coils of rope, drums of lamp oil, wagons, cranes, great crates of who-knows-what; I find myself picking my way through this strange place, this maze of maritime objects.

Today I am wearing my lightkeeper uniform and from several quarters the stevedores and wharf labourers tip their caps in a friendly greeting of *'Môre baas!'*

It is a windless morning, the sun is shining, and all is well. I do not know what to expect but I believe I am looking forward to this adventure.

. . . .

Wearing his cap at a rakish angle, Captain Jacobs, skipper of the *SS Lady Jane* is a bull of a man, with the neck and arms of a wrestler, and a complexion of burnished boot leather. He smiles a missing-tooth smile and extends his hand as I come up the gangway.

'Greetings!' he salutes me as I step aboard. 'You must be the new man for Dassen Island.' he adds by way of a statement rather than a question.

'Yes, James Fox at your service, Captain.'

'Well, well! As they say, another fish for the pot.' His grin widens wickedly and I almost feel in danger of being swallowed alive yet I find the courage to throw out a line for an explanation.

"How so, Captain? Do you mean the mighty Atlantic will wear me down?

'*Ja,* that too. But, no, I'm speaking of the sharks who will get you first. I wish you well, boy, but remember this. Not all is what it seems on Dassen Island. People have died there; others have gone mad there. It's a hard place, *meneer,* so be advised to sleep with one eye open.'

I do not know what to make of the warning. What does this man know?

As if reading my mind, the captain retreats from the subject, just as abruptly as he had advanced towards it. 'I didn't mean to scare you, so please just forget that I said anything at all. I'm known up and down the coast for having a big mouth.'

Somehow not fully reassured, I promise myself to tread carefully, and I change the subject. 'Well, Captain, tell me about yourself and this noble steamer, *Lady Jane.*'

That topic – talking about himself and his vessel – unleashes a detailed history, along with many fishing stories of various lengths and tales of manly exploits with maidens at various ports, and Master Jacobs is so happy to have an attentive listener that he hardly pauses for breath all the way to Saldanha Bay where we need to stop over to load more provisions.

It is late afternoon when I see Dassen Island for the first time. I make out the red and white banded sentinel of the lighthouse before I see the island itself. For some reason I imagined a craggy island rebuffing the onslaught of the ocean with mighty rock cliffs, but the reality is nothing of the sort. What I see instead is an island of little elevation, devoid of any type of tree, with the finger of the lighthouse the only point of note in the landscape. As we get closer, I do make out a group of low buildings below the light station; that seems to be about all there is to the place.

My perception changes again as we sail in closer to the Whale Bay jetty, at the southern end of the island. The island seems more or less barricaded by kelp forests and reefs of dark rock where the breakers beat and swirl and retreat in epic and unending attack. The barricade is incomplete though, parted here and there by stretches of beach. It is not a handsome landscape, but it does own a sort of rugged charm; it is the sort of place you might expect to find in a castaway story, like the tale of *Robinson Crusoe.*

Captain Jacobs tells me that I am lucky; so far today is the calmest day of the year. Yet, even today, I can sense the surge of the deep green surf and the lurking malevolence of submerged rocks. There is a good reason why hundreds of ships have been lost along this coast; it is without doubt one of the most treacherous shipping routes in the world. How brave were those Portuguese navigators who first sailed here four hundred years ago in their little wooden ships? The mariners of today cannot know the marrow-chilling fear of sailing through these seas without charts and in dense fog which may linger for days and days.

Waiting at the jetty are two kaffirs, a grown man and a boy, with an open wagon which is hitched to a single Clydesdale.

The *Lady Jane* is unloaded. Half a dozen barrels of coal oil are manhandled down a broad ramp, followed by a half dozen sacks of mealie meal; sacks of potatoes; a crate of *bokkems*; dried apricots; flour, and numerous other articles.

And, last, James Fox, the new assistant lightkeeper, probably not half as useful as the provisions.

....

Here I am. Not yet eighteen and a half years old but stepping into the world of adults.

I think of Valerie and of my recent initiation into manhood, and I think of mother and father, Maria, Bayes, my other brothers, and my sisters. My life is heading straight into unmapped territory and this brings with it a curious mix of excitement and anxiety. Do I have the character to deal with what is coming my way? I am not at all sure I am cut out for this.

'Baas!' The call of the older kaffir breaks up my daydream. *'Kom baas, ons moet gaan.'*

Obeying the man's request to come, I clamber onto the wagon and we move off along a sandy track through the *fynbos,* the low coastal shrub so common along the Cape coast.

I ask my escorts a few questions, but they seem reluctant to chat, possibly even surprised that the young white fellow wants to talk to them. The boy, possibly fifteen or sixteen years old, says nothing at all, and the grown man, a big strong fellow, is sparing with his words, almost to the point of being downright rude. Without being too obvious about it, I silently survey my companions as the wagon lurches ever so slowly forward over the rough track.

The mature man, whom I later come to know as Diamond, is dressed in what I think might once have been a fine sealskin jacket and he is sporting a curious cap with earflaps, like the ones I have seen in picture books of Siberians and Eskimos. Diamond is driving the wagon and looking straight ahead, as if afraid that if he were to take his eye off the way even for a moment, that we would end up in a ditch or find ourselves sunk into a sandbar. What I first think to be sand of a curious colour and consistency, I soon discover in fact to be tracts of guano packed across the island, the waste of a million penguins and cormorants.

The boy, Isaiah, whom I later discover is the orphaned nephew of Diamond, ignores my attempt at conversation. I wonder, is the boy very shy or very rude? With my unexpressed question unanswered, the wagon strains onward towards a group of low buildings where a man in the lightkeeper uniform, with his arms folded across his chest, is watching us approach. Is this the chief, Mr Richardson, I wonder?

My wondering is cut short when, the moment the wagon creaks to a halt, the man steps briskly forward with his hand outstretched, and in the friendliest tone he introduces himself, 'Pike, Alfred Pike, and you must be James, dare I say a welcome addition to our Dassen Island family?' I feel relieved by the fellow's demeanour, his apparent openhandedness. Was I just being stupid having misgivings about my employment and my future? After all, here I am, standing before Mr Pike and in one hand I have secured myself a position of trust and responsibility, a position with prospects for advancement and, in my other hand, I have the most beautiful woman in the world waiting for me back in Cape Town.

Mr Pike is a least twenty years my senior, but he insists that I call him Alf. He is clean-shaven, but bleary-eyed and turned out in well-crumpled uniform. What do I make of him? To be sure, it is too early to tell. I do wonder though whether it is the privations of the job and life on this remote patch of God's earth which are the sole cause of his sorry appearance?

While the kaffirs unload the wagon, Alf shows me my quarters, one of several small rooms abutting the supply store. The room is spartan, with a small fireplace, an iron bed, a washstand, and a small wardrobe. With a tone of disapproval as his gaze sweeps across my accommodation, Alf comments, 'It can be dreadful lonely and cold in here.' I do not reply; I am too preoccupied with taking in the comforts of my new home.

'You will take your meals at the dining room, which is at the rear of the chief's house,' Alf tells me. 'Our housekeeper-cook is Mrs Andrews, an elderly widow, I think related to Cinderella's stepmother. She breeds the biggest cockroaches on the West Coast, and she knows how to cook fish curry, *potjie, bredie, vetkoek* and mealie *pap.*' Satisfied that I am listening attentively, he continues with my induction. 'You are required to pay Mrs Andrews twelve shillings a week for her cooking and for washing your clothing and bedding; this is the unwritten rule and, whatever you do, do not upset her as she has been known to threaten the removal of the genitals of any man who dares to show her the unforgiveable disrespect of criticising her food, her housekeeping or her personal hygiene.'

I must look shocked as Alf seeks to reassure me, 'Don't worry, James, I can see that you're not the type to be disrespectful,' and naughtily he adds, 'In fact, I suspect Mrs Andrews will take you under her wing as if you were her own son.' The vision of the unhygienic cook drawing me into her bosom like a little boy being embraced by his nursemaid is almost more than I can bear, so, before Alf can go any further, I divert the conversation with a question.

'Tell me, Alf, who lives here on Dassen Island?' A fair enough question I think from the new arrival. Father had told me to ask lots of questions; he said it makes you look more intelligent, before he added that waiting around passively for information is the sure sign of a lazy mind.

'Well now, James. There's Mr Richardson, the chief. Then there's Rex Van Staden and myself, the lightkeepers, and now your good self, the assistant lightkeeper.'

'And Mrs Andrews,' I prompt my informant.

'*Ja*, of course, and Mrs Richardson, the chief's wife.'

'That's it?' I voice my second prompt.

'There's Antonio. Antonio is a salvage diver, the best in the business, but he's only here for six months of the year. Sometimes his woman and young daughter accompany him, sometimes not.'

'What about Diamond and Isaiah. Do they live on the island?'

'Why, yes, they do, but I wasn't counting them because they're only kaffirs. Not one of us.' I can see Alf looking at me somewhat speculatively; is he wondering about my attitude to our dark-skinned residents? If he is, he is does not ask and I am not saying. Not today.

There's a knock at my door. It is Mr Richardson.

After the customary introductions. Alf disappears and I am alone with Mr Richardson. He is a short energetic man with an over-exposed complexion like a sunbaked tomato while his eyes are keen, all-seeing, like the eyes of a meerkat on a stony knoll.

'Welcome, Master Fox! I understand from Mr O'Dwyer that you are well-educated, versed in classics and mathematics?' His question being rhetorical. I allow him to continue. 'Now, heaven knows we're in need of a scholar in our midst, so welcome aboard. Has Alf shown you around?'

'Somewhat,' I respond. 'Alf was just telling me about the arrangements for meals and laundry...'

'Nothing about the job I'll wager?' interjected Mr Richardson.

"Not yet, sir.'

'Come with me, lad, and I'll show you the lighthouse, it being the entire reason why we're here.' And, saying this, he gestures for me to follow him.

The boss begins his lecture while we stride towards the lightstation. 'James, at ninety feet this light is one of the tallest along the Cape coast. Over the centuries several dozen ships have met their watery end around Dassen Island but the one which drew the most attention was the loss of the passenger steamer, SS Windsor Castle, on 19th October 1876. Thankfully without loss of life. The sinking of this vessel was the catalyst for the erection of this lighthouse ten years ago.'

I listen attentively. Mr Richardson clearly loves his lighthouse and knows its secrets.

It is a short walk, and soon we climb the mound on which stands the lightstation, an imposing sentinel banded in rings of red and white.

'Most lighthouses are constructed of brick or rock, 'Mr Richardson informs me as he continues his lecture, 'but the Dassen light is made entirely of cast iron, shipped here and bolted together *in situ*. Come inside, James, and wonder at the engineering of the structure.'

We step inside and immediately my gaze is drawn upwards. Upwards along the helix of the spiral staircase, a twisted marvel of iron bolted to the inside of the cylinder.

'Impressive, isn't it, James?'

Too awed to find words to reply, I nod, and again I allow my gaze to roam up the spiral until it seems to disappear in the dimness high above our heads.

'At one hour before sunset we light the coal-oil burner and trim the flame to the optimum setting in order to vaporise the oil which is used to power the lights in the tower. We allow the extra hour just in case there's a problem.' Mr Richardson keeps talking as we climb the iron rungs into the gloom.

'What sort of problem?' I remember father's advice.

'Well, any number of things can go wrong. There may be an obstruction in the vapour line, or contamination in the oil, or any of a dozen other reasons,' advises my instructor. 'In time you'll learn to deal with all eventualities.'

I am reassured by the obvious experience and skill of Mr Richardson.

At the top of the stairs we enter through a small door into the lantern room, the heart of the lighthouse.

'The lights,' continues my mentor, 'are beamed far across the ocean with the help of these rotating glass prisms. The prisms magnify and scatter the light in every direction.' I continue listening attentively while Mr Richardson goes on with his instruction. 'The prisms are driven by a clockwork mechanism and the prisms slowly rotate in a pool of mercury.' He points to the silvery channel of mercury.

'Why mercury, sir?' I hope it is an intelligent question.

And so it goes with our conversation. I learn about the toxicity of mercury and Mad Hatter's Disease, about the hazard of lead poisoning from the constant repainting of the lighthouse, and about how the long hours of isolation can play tricks on the mind.

'Then, when you've done battle with the lighthouse and the elements, just when you think you can relax a little, you'll find that you'll be contending with the idiosyncrasies of fellow lightkeepers and labourers. In summary, James,' concludes Mr Richardson, 'you'll need to be ever vigilant, to sleep with one eye open.'

Is it my imagination or is this the second time today I have heard this same warning? I wonder, too, about the nature and extent of the 'idiosyncrasies' of those around me.

....

My first supper on the island reveals a little more.

The swearing and blasphemy and general carrying-on of our cook, Mrs Andrews, is a performance of the unholiest kind. If you had told me about it, I would not have believed you but here she is, before my eyes, assaulting my senses like a pirate ship on the high seas.

Where did she learn such language if not in a prison or asylum?

The pork and cabbage stew is tolerable and it fills my belly. After a long day since a couple of slices of buttered bread for breakfast, I am ready to forgive the shortcomings of my hostess, and I tell myself that I may as well become accustomed to the fare since I am hardly in a position to make any complaint. Besides, what was it Alf said about anyone daring to offend the offerings of our cook?

When the dining is done, in exchange for my empty plate I receive an immense mug of over-sweetened tea; this is the apparent signal for some light after dinner conversation.

Both Alf and Rex van Staden, the other lightkeeper, are here this evening and now, with his food in his belly, Van Staden seems ready to acknowledge my presence.

'Want to be a lightkeeper, hey?' he greets me. Before I reply he goes on. 'You look too young to know anything, but you're big enough. Big and stupid and therefore perfect for this job.' Van Staden glares at me, as if daring me to say anything cheeky back to him. I do my best to appear unmoved by his provocation.

Van Staden turns to Alf and questions him with mock formality. 'What do you think, *meneer*? Is the boy ready for a little catechism?'

Alf turns to me. 'Ignore Mr Bigmouth, James. He has already had his last chance in the Lighthouse Service...'

'Shut up! *Fokken moerskont!*' Van Staden turns his head, spits liberally on the floor, reaches into his overcoat pocket, removes a flat flask-shaped bottle of brandy and pours a generous shot into his tea.

I must be staring at this performance because the lightkeeper turns back to me and offers me some real-world advice; 'You'd better learn to unsee and to unhear what happens around here. That is how you'll survive' and turning back to Alf, he growls, And you mind your own business, Alfie darling, and keep your hands to yourself.'

Van Staden rises and looks me up and down. 'Meet me at the light at sunrise, Jamie boy; tomorrow I'm your teacher.'

Alf leaves, too, but I linger a little over my mug of tea and I try to engage my new acquaintance, Mrs Andrews, in a little conversation.

'Well, ma'am,' I begin with a little white lie, 'that was a mighty fine meal. I'm sure my mother would love the recipe.'

'Mighty fine, eh?' I can see she is not displeased - but also not deceived by my compliment.

'Certainly, I'd like you to have the recipe, but it is... how do I say it? A chef's secret. Or maybe some ungrateful bastards will tell you it's a witch's stew. Either way, it's not ready for publication. But tell me, Master James, what are you running away from? A clean looking boy like you has no business in a shithole like this.'

And we get to talking and she pours me another mug of tea which I feel obliged to drink, and I dare to ask her if Van Staden is really as angry as he comes across. I do not imagine people often take the time, or show the interest, to seek her views; I find her happy to talk. Without making any offer in my direction, she pours herself a cup of what looks like madeira from a stone bottle, sits herself down across the table from me and tells me a few things.

'Nothing I tell you you've heard from me,' she begins. 'Having traded all chance for my redemption to Satan a long time ago, I'll caution you to preserve your soul, Master James, if you can, and out of respect for your mother who appears to have done a fine job raising you, I'll share a few things with you if you have the time to listen.'

I lean forward in my chair, lending her my ears. Firstly, she partakes of a fair swig from her cup, pulls a face, takes a deep breath and then she talks. 'With Van Staden, what you see is what you get. Like myself he is one of the rejects of God's creation; he has many faults but, unlike Pike, he isn't into plotting. Or into the commission of acts against nature.'

'What do you mean?' I ask, shocked and surprised.

'Rex says what he thinks – with him nothing is below the surface. You might find it odd what I'm saying, but you can trust Van Staden. He does not tell tales or hide a knife in his coat to stab you in the dark.'

'That's reassuring,' I say, 'but what was Alf saying about Rex's last chance with the Lighthouse Service?'

'In spite of his *kak* attitude Rex van Staden is a very conscientious and experienced lightkeeper, possibly the best lightkeeper in the service. Until two years ago he was the chief lightkeeper at Mouille Point, the most coveted operational posting in the colony.'

Mrs Andrews raises a food-stained sleeve and takes the rest of her madeira (or whatever it is) in one draught, braces her shoulders a little, then continues, 'It's a bit of a long story and some elements of the story are unverified but, for what it's worth, when Rex was a boy, maybe eight or nine years old, his family were living on a farm in the Moorreesburg district, somewhere on the north side, close to the Berg River. On a particular day, young Rex and his older sister, who might've been ten or eleven at the time, went foraging in the veld for the fruit of the *koekemakranka* plant. They reached a point where they were far from the farmhouse and in denser bush alongside the river when, according to Rex, they quite suddenly came across a couple of *hotnots* who were busily digging a hole in a small clearing. Rex and his sister soundlessly concealed themselves in a clump of bushes. In order to spy on the diggers, you understand.'

She pauses, reaches for the bottle and pours another measure of refreshment for herself. 'Well, over the following minutes fascination turned to horror as those kids observed the *hotnots* proceed to dump a headless body into the hole. Overcome with fright and revulsion, and, leaving their harvest of *koekemakrankas* just where they'd dropped it, the kids managed to filter away undetected from the scene and run home. The alarm was raised and a search of the entire Swartland - from Malmesbury to Piketberg, Darling to Riebeek Kasteel - was conducted for the *hotnot* hole-diggers. The curious part of the story is that no one had seen those coloured men lurking around in the district. Nor was anyone reported missing in the district who may have accounted for the headless body and, to cap it all, the grave was never found. The investigation petered out, no one was ever apprehended, and both Rex's father and the police eventually concluded that the children had fabricated the entire story. Rex and his sister - I think her name is Sannie - were spared a whipping only because their mother would not allow it on account of the lack of any evidence to support the big-lie theory. For this reason, their punishment was commuted to a three-month grounding and extra chores around the home.'

'It's a horrible account, Mrs Andrews, but what has all this got to do with the Lighthouse Service?'

Is she rambling, I wonder, or is there a point to the story?

'Patience, Master James, I'll get to the point by and by. Please don't interrupt or I'll likely lose the thread of my account. You know, I used to have a memory as detailed as an almanac but these days I'm struggling to remember my own name.'

I nod.

'The next incident of interest took place four or five years later. Rex and Sannie, both older now, were home alone; their parents over at the *handelshuis* in Moorreesburg with the Cape cart shopping for the monthly provisions. Young Rex was doing some homework in the dining room while Sannie was in the kitchen baking cakes for afternoon tea when Rex heard voices at the kitchen door, to which he initially he didn't pay much attention as it wasn't unusual for one of the farm labourers to come knocking for a cup of sugar or a measure of cooking oil. But as the minutes went by the voices became louder, more insistent, till somewhat reluctantly Rex got up from his chair and moved closer to listen.

At the kitchen door there stood three coloured men, or rather two men and a teenage boy, none of them known to Rex. On the pretext that their mother was unwell they were insisting with Sannie that she accompany them as she was urgently needed to attend to the sick woman. Sannie was not silly and she refused to go, but the more she refused, the more insistent the *hotnot* callers became.

Quickly Rex slipped away, glided into the lounge and took his father's Mauser from the rack next to the fireplace. From the mantel he took half a dozen cartridges, inserted one and closed the bolt. In moments he was back at the kitchen.

There and then, sweating with apprehension, the boy stepped into the kitchen. The tallest of the three men had taken hold of Sannie's arm and he was trying to lead her away.

Piet raised the Mauser. Aimed it at the head of the tall man. Then, in his high-pitched adolescent voice, he ordered the men to leave. And leave they did, like hens being chased by a wild dog. And, for good measure, always being particular to finish things properly, Rex fired a shot over their departing heads.

The boy had suddenly become a man; a man who had no love for the *kleurling* or the kaffir. Isn't it curious, Master James, how we are shaped by the experiences of our childhood? How we judge all by the actions of a few?

Anyway, Rex van Staden joined the Lighthouse Service, worked his way up and down the coast from Cape Agulhas to Cape Point, Saldanha Bay, Robben Island and every light in between. He did a fine job and received good reports and by 1895 or thereabouts he was appointed as chief lightkeeper at Mouille Point. Being such a trusted and respected employee, he was asked one day by the powers that be to attend the lightstation on Robben Island to investigate some suspected irregularities at that location. Apparently, the Table Bay harbour master had received reports from incoming vessels that the light on Robben Island was dark for several nights in a single month, yet there were no reports from the lightstation staff about any issues with the light.

In his usual thorough way Van Staden checked every log, interviewed every Robben Island lightstation employee. He even went to the extent of having some unofficial discussions with other Robben Island residents such as employees of the asylum and the leprosarium, and with the local police. It took two or three weeks of tireless effort but, sure enough, he found the truth.'

For dramatic effect, the cook pauses and douses the flame of her thirst with another slug of madeira. And I am bold enough to enquire, 'The truth, ma'am?'

'Ah, the truth, hey? Buried somewhere between damned lies and more damned lies, we discover the truth, don't we, sir? Well, the truth is often queerer than fiction and this was certainly the case with the Robben Island investigation.

Late at night or in the early hours of the morning, the light would inexplicably extinguish itself and refuse all efforts to relight. The lightkeepers did what lightkeepers do and checked every component of the lantern; they even ran checks on the stored coal oil for combustibility. Not wanting to look like complete dolts for being unable to resolve the problem, the chief and his lightkeepers decided not to say a word, to withhold reporting the incidents of the light being out, at least until they could get to the bottom of the problem. By sheer chance a warder at the asylum, a person who frequently had trouble sleeping at night, maybe on account of the shift work he performed, was wandering about in the vicinity of the lightstation very late one night, when he noticed a dark figure emerge from the lighthouse and quickly disappear down Minto's Hill. Within minutes the light in the tower went out.

The sleepless warder returned on several nights and, sure enough, on the third or fourth occasion, he caught an intruder at the lighthouse. *In flagrante delicto*, as they say.

There he was, one of the kaffir labourers employed at the lightstation. He was decanting sea water into the fuel line near where it enters the burner, doing this while the on duty lightkeeper was fast asleep above in the lantern room without an inkling what was going on under his nose.

Now, Master James, I can hear you thinking; why was this wretched *muntu* fucking up the light?'

Mrs Andrews rose from her seat, stretched, and produced a huge yawn, without making any attempt to cover her near-toothless maw. Then she sat down again and continued her account. 'It turned out that this fellow had over a period of time been influenced by certain black political prisoners with whom he had come into contact on the island, influenced into believing that the white man needed to be driven into the sea, influenced into thinking that the Cape needed to be under the sovereignty of the black man. This man, this lightstation employee, was convinced that it would be the right thing to do to sabotage the colonial power and that a good way to achieve it would be to extinguish the light on Robben Island and allow the white man's ships to smash themselves to bits on the rocky coast and reefs.

The chief lightkeeper and the lightkeepers had nowhere to hide. Sleeping while on duty is a sackable offence and the chief lightkeeper's failure to supervise his keepers to ensure that they are awake and vigilant is an equally serious offence. After all, the entire reason for the lighthouse being there in the first place is to ensure that for three hundred and sixty-five nights a year and for three hundred and sixty-six nights every leap year, the light is illuminated to ensure the safe passage of mariners at the Cape of Good Hope.

But, sir, at this point in proceedings Rex van Staden made a serious error of judgment and screwed up his career.

Being the sort of person he is, he decided not to report the Robben Island lightkeepers but, nevertheless, mightily enraged by the act of sabotage on the part of the *kaffir,* he bustled the black man to the cover of the wattle grove, tied him to a tree, and belted him with a *sjambok* before having the bleeding and unconscious man dragged to the island hospital. In time the story came out, after the man's injuries were reported to the Medical Superintendent of the Cape Colony, and the Lighthouse Service was compelled to take disciplinary action.

Van Staden was demoted, fined two months' pay, and sent here to Dassen Island. Now you see why he is such an angry and bitter man. The headless corpse incident of his childhood, along with the kitchen incident at the farm and, on top of it all, the sabotage of the Robben Island light, have combined to scar this man with a deep hatred for all people of colour and, no doubt, there's also an element of fear and misgiving in Rex's heart, the same sort of fear shown by people who were bitten by a dog when they were kids.

I'm advising you, young James, to hold your tongue when Rex starts ranting on about the blacks and the coloureds; he has no tolerance for them. He also hates Antonio, the salvage diver, because Antonio, who is white and Portuguese, is living with a *baster* woman. Rex cannot – will not - understand how a white man can freely choose to take a *hotnot* woman for his bed partner and breed with her to bring another *hotnot* child into this world.

Now, Master James, you'd best be taking yourself off to bed and be sure to be at the light by sunrise or Rex'll be having your guts for garters and your testicles for appetisers.'

I leave. Promising myself not to utter a word about Valerie. Not to anybody.

If only I could hold her tonight and tell her how much I love her.

Chapter 6 – Valerie's Reflections

I am really missing James. Yet it has only been a week.

The world is such an unfair place. The moment I believed James and I had found perfect bliss; he is taken away from me. Yes, the lightkeeper job has all the makings of a lifelong calling yet, at a certain level, I wish he had never heard about it. The promise of security is compelling. On the one hand we are willing participants in our rush to secure the promise in the craypot but, once we are in the pot, we realise with sudden unease that it is a trap, that there is no way out. In this way we are no smarter than the lowly *kreef*.

I am not about to influence James to abandon his employment; he must take the time to know what is involved and then to make up his own mind. It may sound old-fashioned to you, but I honestly believe it is my role to support him in whatever he does, even if it is not what I would choose for us.

Is it not strange how we humans wish so ardently for something and then, when we have it, we find that it is unbalancing our lives? It reminds me of those stories we read as children about wishes being granted by a genie in gratitude for being released from a bottle and how the granting of the wishes always brings with it an unintended and unwelcome complication.

Mother and I have been to Rondebosch to visit James' family, and we are always so welcome there. Mother and Maria are almost inseparable these days. Mr Fox treats me like another daughter; he is such a kind old man and full of homely wisdom and quaint expressions like saying 'the wind is blowing seven devils' or referring to James as 'his mother's son.' As for Mrs Fox, she is - how shall I say it? – different, even strange, but unfailingly kind to me. She gave me a pair of pearl earrings with the declaration that the pearls would contrast well with my beautiful caramel skin. When she looks at me though, particularly when she thinks I am looking elsewhere, she sometimes has an infinitely sad look in her eyes, almost as if she can sense something which does not give her joy. Of course, James has told me of his mother's clairvoyant abilities and her sometimes bizarre behaviour, so I never feel offended or unwelcome by her demeanour. In fact, she remarked upon the flower pendant which James has given me and says she greatly approves of the choice he has made, that she has seldom seen such a lovely young woman as myself.

Unaccustomed as I am to such high praise, I did not know what to say beyond a simple thank you. If this flattery continues my head will soon be so big that I will be unable to get through the doorway.

I do so love James, but I admit that it is my great fear that he will tire of this little flower seller.

For my part I will take my chance for happiness.

Chapter 7 – Dassen Island Days

It is still dark, maybe a half hour before dawn, when I reach the light.

Rex is not here yet.

A light breeze is blowing and bringing with it the sound of breakers somewhere in the distance. The sky is mostly clear and visibility is good, and the light high above my head, like a titanic glowing finger, is sweeping its circular path through the dusk.

I turn down the wick on my lamp and I stand at the base of the lightstation and allow the chilly air to blanket my senses; how marvellous to be in this place, to smell and hear the mighty Atlantic as it batters the island in that primeval struggle between earth and water.

I am aware that Alf must be in the tower, on nightshift, but I am in no hurry to leave my moment of solitude. I sense that today will be a big day, that I will have much to learn, and that taking a few minutes to clear my mind is a good thing.

I have never had any difficulty keeping my own company, being alone, sometimes with a book and sometimes without. The constant need for people and chatter is not something I want, or even like, but I do wonder how a dozen hours up the tower on my own will be. Will I hear voices, talk to the voices, or merely talk to myself? Will I see ghostly figures in the mist or unexplained lights in the sky? Will I, I wonder, imagine all kinds of plots and double dealings by the people around me? Already Mrs Andrews has filled my head and primed my thoughts with her tales of Mr Rex van Staden and his exploits.

My reverie is broken by an approaching figure. No doubt this is Rex.

. . . .

'*Môre*, James!' he greets me, with no hint of the moodiness from the evening before. 'Are you ready for your education?'

'I have my pencil and my slate, and my shoes are polished, sir,' I reply with a smile. It will likely pay me to preserve the friendly mood.

The door of the lightstation opens and Alf appears before us, in his heavy coat looking like a lost explorer from the Arctic tundra. He blinks, as if trying to find the focus of our images, then without any courtesies he declares, 'She's all yours, boys,' and he shuffles away like a penguin.

'*Poes!*' mutters Van Staden, 'that idiot is supposed to give us a hand over before he pisses off. Then, turning to me, his irritation gone, he asks, 'What is a hand over, James, and why is it important?'

For the next twelve hours Rex drills me in the procedures and the maintenance of the light. I learn how to clean and service the burner, remove and clean the precious prisms, check the lines, how to wind the rotation mechanism. I am shown the right way to keep the log, what needs to be reported, the procedures for documenting the wind speed and the air temperature. Nothing can be overlooked, and Rex frequently reminds me that 'lives depend on us.' I get a firsthand insight into his efficiency and his knowledge of the light and I can appreciate what Mrs Andrews was saying about him likely being the best keeper in the light service.

For my part, I am content to be taught by the best, happy to ask lots of questions and to get all the answers I need.

At lunch time Diamond turns up at the lightstation with a flagon of ginger beer and corned beef sandwiches, compliments of the cook. Without a word being exchanged between him and Rex, the labourer hands over the sustenance, and departs just as quickly as he came.

'Useless kaffir,' Rex informs me. 'Unless you watch the bastard, he'll be asleep at the jetty or stealing penguin eggs.'

I look inquiringly at the lightkeeper. What is he saying and why does it matter if Diamond takes a few penguin eggs? As if reading my mind, Rex goes on, 'The kaffir is supposed to collect the eggs. I have a contract – written, signed, witnessed and sealed – to supply fifty dozen penguin eggs a week to the boer at the Yzerfontein Farm. No doubt the boer sells the eggs in Malmesbury or elsewhere for a nice profit, but that's not my business. My business is to collect the eggs, but when you have lazy kaffirs like the two useless sods on this island, getting enough eggs each week can be a struggle, more so if they eat some of the eggs.'

Unable to say anything by way of reply, I decide to change the subject and ask my mentor a question. '*Meneer,* I sense that you are not on good terms with Mr Pike. Since I have to work with both of you, I think it is only fair that you tell me in your own words the basis of the bad feeling between yourselves.' Father would be most impressed by the way I asked that question so diplomatically.

'*Fok, boet!*' begins Van Staden, 'where do I begin? But don't let it be said that I'm poisoning your impressionable mind. I'm advising you to observe Mr Alfred Pike very carefully; observe where he goes, what he does. Begin your observation, I suggest, by noting who comes and goes from his room. Then broaden your observation by taking note of the quality of his work and, lastly, pay attention to what gets reported and what doesn't get reported to the Lighthouse Service.'

I guess I look unenlightened by the response. Van Staden probably notices this and continues, 'It won't take long for you to see his true colours. Let it not be said that I am saying anything objectionable or libellous. Observe and make up your own mind, Jamie boy. All I will say to you at this point is that it is on your head to ensure that the light is always working; don't be tempted to take any short cuts. While you are here on the island you are married to that light. Take care of her, service her daily, oil her parts, and she will serve you well.'

My new comrade looks me up and down. 'Maybe you will do.'

Seemingly I am measuring up to my teacher's requirements and as the day wears on he becomes more agreeable. Then, out of the blue, he asks me, 'Do you have a girlfriend back home?'

I have rehearsed my response to this question; I knew that sooner or later it would jump on me. And, here it is, sooner rather than later.

As coyly as possible I answer that question. 'I suppose you could say that I have a girlfriend, *meneer,* but I'm only eighteen years old you know.' Answered as if an eighteen-year-old has not yet reached the age of puberty. And there I allow my statement to drift away.

'What does she do?' he asks. I sense though that he is relieved to discover that I am just a regular fellow and, now that he has satisfied his curiosity, he is simply asking another question to be polite.

As offhandedly as possible I hear myself saying, 'She works for a florist some days and spends time looking after her mother.'

'That's nice,' answers my new colleague and mentor. Subject closed.

At supper the chief's wife, Mrs Richardson, pops in. She has heard that there is a new assistant and, like royalty everywhere, she wants to know who has entered her domain. Ever so formally she introduces herself to me and conveys the impression that her approval is hugely important, that she is anything but irrelevant to what goes on here on Dassen Island.

Mrs Richardson is lean, lean in a way sometimes called 'willowy'. Once she must have been a stunningly attractive woman; even now, she is still pleasing on the eye.

So, she has this regal manner about her, erect and superior, and her face is well sculpted, a little weathered but well preserved for someone of perhaps forty years old, while her well- fashioned Roman nose sets off a pair of the deepest green eyes I have ever seen. If you have ever seen green Tiger's Eye, her eyes are precisely that colour.

The introduction complete and protocol duly observed, she disappears just as suddenly as she came, and it is Mrs Andrews who observes, without prompting, 'So, I see the tigress is on the prowl again for prey, I dare say looking for something tasty.'

I am unsure what to make of the cook's statement and I am not bold enough to ask for an explanation. Let it slide, I think; no doubt I shall find out another time.

I notice that Alf has his face in his plate, seemingly unaware of the cook's utterance, while Van Staden is at the light, and the Richardsons are as usual absent from the communal meals, seeming to prefer their own company, above and separate from the hired help.

Cook is at the doorway now handing over tin plates heaped with mashed potato and baked fish to Isaiah, and I wonder to myself where the custom started for the kaffirs to eat apart from the Europeans. Did it have its origins in the days of slavery when dark-skinned people were seen as chattels? In those times when domestic animals and domestic servants had the same status in the household? Or does the fault for our society's negative view of kaffirs lie with the Christian churches who took it upon themselves to judge non-believers (after all, the very word kaffir originally had the meaning of 'non-believer') as inferiors in the sight of God Almighty. Or did the proud European see himself as superior owing to his ability to read, write, perform arithmetical calculations and discuss the sonnets of a certain William Shakespeare of Stratford-upon-Avon? Frequently I have heard the black man being described as stupid and backward but, dare I say it, would the European not be equally stupid and backward if he were never educated or elevated to any position of responsibility? It is a sort of chicken and egg argument, maddeningly circular, without any likely resolution.

Tomorrow I am on with Alf at the light. One lightkeeper works the day shift, performing cleaning and maintenance and equipment checks, sometimes painting, while another keeper works the night shift, ensuring the proper functioning of the light throughout the hours of darkness. The assistant lightkeeper – that is 'my father's son' – fills in for the lightkeepers when they have their week ashore and covers for keepers in the event of sickness or injury. The chief lightkeeper is responsible to supervise the work of the lightkeepers, is answerable to the Lighthouse Service for any outage of the light, and is charged with the accurate maintenance of records, accounts and the ordering of stores. Two labourers are employed to perform any manner of heavy and dirty duties, as directed by the keepers, and as I soon discover, their duties go way beyond what you might expect at a lightstation.

. . . .

At sunrise I am at the light.

Rex is descending the steel rungs from the lantern room when I enter at the base of the lighthouse. There is no sign yet of Alf.

Out of breath when he reaches the bottom rung, Rex curses Alf, *'Fokken skaap! He's always late.'*

'What do you do about such a problem?' I inquire.

'There are those, Jamie boy, who would report him, but I was not brought up that way. I was raised to believe that a man needs to deal with his own snakes and, believe me, I will. One of these days Alfred Pike will get what's coming to him.' Realising that he has probably said more than he wanted to say, Van Staden changes the subject. 'I'm buggered, Jamie, and I desperately need some shut eye. If I head off will you be okay to wait for Pike?'

I nod. Curiously, I am not offending by being called 'Jamie' and 'Jamie boy' by the older man. The use of these names seems quite spontaneous, almost friendly. Also, I am thinking, I am a man now. If I go about my days being upset or unsettled by mere name-calling, or by everyday profanity, or occasional blasphemy, my life will be constantly unsettled. It is time to take my place among men and women. Father says that 'when in Rome, do as the Romans do' – no doubt he is right, as always. Recalling the saying sets me to thinking about Father. In a way he is, and has been throughout my life, like this lighthouse where I am standing now: strong, reliable, steady and enduring; a beacon of stability for us all. I have never known my father to cheat any person or, even when provoked, to raise his hand against anyone. I worry what will become of him when he retires later this year. The crossing in Kenilworth is his identity – who will he be when he is no longer there? Will he sit at the kitchen table and drink cups of tea, or will he don his slippers and doze next to the stove? Will Mother initiate him into the secrets of the séance and the ouija, promoted as 'the wonderful talking board,' the channel to the spirit world? Somehow, I doubt whether my father will take to it. Father Kelly once described communication with spirits as 'intercourse with demons' and I think that, as a good Catholic, my father will continue to subscribe to Father Kelly's views.

I must speak to my father about these things and reassure him that I will do my best to look after him and mother in the twilight of their lives. I owe them more than I can ever repay.

Alf turns up, almost an hour late, and looking as if he has just escaped from the morgue.

'So sorry, James, I've been dreadfully unwell this past night.'

I take his statement at face value, but mindful of Rex's comment that Alf is 'always late,' and I wonder what might be the cause of his lateness.

Alf Pike is not nearly as thorough or as energetic as Rex, and he takes frequent breaks from his toil to smoke his pipe and gaze at the horizon.

A little unsure what to talk about, I take a big step and ask him straight up what he thinks of our colleague, Mr Van Staden.

'I'll grant you that Van Staden is a good lightkeeper, but a sorry human being,' begins Alf, then checks himself a little. 'He has had a hard life, by all accounts his father was liberal with the *sjambok*. He is sore about a lot of things I dare say, not least being posted here to the pile of birdshit.'

I listen attentively and say nothing, so Alf most likely feels obliged to expand a little on his statement. 'You see,' he says, after taking a thoughtful puff on his pipe, 'Rex has a problem with black people, so much so that he has been known to say that the only good kaffir is a dead kaffir.'

'Yes, that's a big statement,' I agree.

'He damn near got himself sacked for whipping a kaffir on Robben Island. He should have let the police deal with the matter but, no, not Rex van Staden. He took matters into his own hands and damn near killed the kaffir.'

Boldly, I ask my next question. 'But why is it, Alf, that Rex seems to have some sort of issue with you?'

'Why, what did he say about me?'

Sidestepping the verbal trap, I answer, 'No, it's nothing he said. It's the almost tangible hostility when you are both in the same place.'

'It's that obvious, is it?' Alf pulls a face.

'More than obvious, like an elephant in a mousetrap, if I may say so.'

'You see, James, I take the time to talk to Diamond and to Isaiah, particularly Isaiah, and Rex doesn't like this. I don't think he likes the idea of a white man speaking to a kaffir in a respectful way, as an equal if you like. He has a bee in his bonnet about it; frankly though, it's his problem, not mine.'

I test Alf a little further. 'Why is it Alf that you are going against general opinion by treating these black men as equal?' and, cheekily I add, 'Don't we all know that they are all savages at heart?'

Mr Alfred Pike clearly has no idea that I am making mischief, so he answers me perfectly seriously that we are all God's children and therefore equal in the sight of God.

And I reply, 'Really?' This really gets him scratching his head and he must be wondering to himself; is this young buck a friend or foe?

....

Alf is nowhere near as knowledgeable or efficient as Rex when it comes to the lightstation procedures, but he does show me some important things, like how to take down and clean the heavy panels of the prism, and how to check and replenish the mercury level. We talk about everyday things such as the treacherous fog which frequently smothers the island, and about how and where best to catch some of the abundant *kreef* lurking in the crevices and caverns of the rock shelves. Clearly Dassen Island is seafood paradise, even though it is, in most other respects, more aligned to the wasteland of Gehenna.

Several times I notice Alf looking at me...how? Speculatively? Puzzled?

I am greatly relieved when Rex reports for nightshift; it seems like days since I have had a meal or a cup of tea, and I make my way directly to supper, to whatever fine cuisine Mrs Andrews has in store for me.

Mrs Andrews is quieter tonight. She serves up inch-thick tranches of corned beef with lashings of mashed potato and my hunger finds no fault with the contents of my plate.

Tomorrow night I am working with Rex to learn the mysteries of the nightshift. During the day I will have the opportunity to explore a little. I imagine I can cover much of the one square mile surface of Ilha Branca, as the early Portuguese navigators named this place, owing to the washed-out complexion of mounds of bird excrement.

After supper I try to engage Mrs Andrews in a little conversation, so I decide to ask her a little about herself. After all, most people – even the grumpy ones – are flattered to be asked about themselves and their interests.

'Tell me, ma'am,' I begin, 'at the risk of coming across as nosey or impertinent, may I ask how you come to find yourself here on Dassen Island?'

She looks at me, possibly unsure whether I am sincere. Several times she shuffles the muscles in her jaw and her jowls, as if about to say something. At last she replies. 'You're a strange one, Master James; the first lightkeeper in years to notice that I am here.' Pointing to various articles about the kitchen, there is a bitter edge in her voice as she continues, 'Yes, sir, I am here, like a tatty old oven mitt, as much part of the kitchen furniture as that kettle and that colander over there. Now you want to know how I came to be here; God alone knows why you want to know this, but I'll tell you anyway.'

'Please do.'

'I come from a farming family in Kaffraria and I'm the eldest daughter of eleven children.

I was born in the Craven District of North Yorkshire, not far from the village of Clapham, in 1836, just a year before my parents migrated to South Africa. Through the good representations of his uncle, a settler from the big 1820 contingent, father secured a grant of one thousand morgen of free land from the Cape government and, in exchange for the grant, he had to agree to occupy, and develop the land within ten years, or it would be forfeited to the Crown.

Against all odds, odds which included an unfamiliar climate, unfriendly snakes and unfriendlier natives, floods, drought and a shortage of funds, our family survived and turned the virgin bush into a more or less productive farm. Here my parents grew mealies, ran merinos, and most years added a new little human to the Lord's flock.

But then, in the summer of 1851, over the course of a single day, the wheels came off the wagon of our humble lives.

On the day in question, owing to the complication known as a breech presentation, my mother died of blood loss while giving birth to her twelfth child. The head of the foetus was trapped, and try as she might, the midwife couldn't dislodge the thing so, in desperation, she cut the cervix, but she cut too much or in the wrong place and ma bled to death while the foetus was suffocating in the birth canal. You may ask, why am I telling you this and how do I know these things?'

'I'm sure there's a reason.'

'I suppose there is, yes, I suppose there is.' The old woman pauses to locate her cup and her madeira before she picks up her account again. 'I know these things because I was at the birth, in that room with the midwife, as the fetcher and carrier. I was fifteen years old, ignorant and impressionable, and I was horrified by what I was seeing. The midwife was a doddery old turkey who had generously dosed both ma and herself with multiple drams of brandy – mind you, for medicinal purposes – to steady the nerves. So, here I was, a hapless teenager in a room with a sozzled midwife and my distraught mother. The nearest doctor was in King William's Town, three or four hours away, so it was no use going for help.

I watched my mother's life drain away and I sat beside her for a long time as her body went cold and hard. I was in a state of shock and to this day I have no idea what the midwife was doing while I sat there. Eventually the sun set outside, and the room went dark and there was no lamp and I just kept sitting there until well into the night. Until they came to take her away from me.

What happened there in that room changed my life. I had the misfortune of being born ugly, big-boned and badly proportioned. What man I ask you, Master James, would want to marry a woman who looks like the back end of a rhinoceros? And, after what I saw that day, I lost all inclination anyway ever to risk the prospect of marriage and childbirth. My decision was made easier by the necessity to take ma's place in caring for my ten siblings; this was my lot and there was no question that things would be any other way.

Father did remarry several years later, and I found my opportunity to escape from the farm. My cousin, Hendrina, who is a few years older than me, was working as a nurse at Somerset Hospital in Cape Town at the time and one day I received a letter from her telling me that the hospital was planning to open a foundling asylum and that there would be a number of positions available. Hendrina believed that with my experience caring for ten siblings I could equally be caring for a group of foundlings, so I wrote to the Somerset Hospital and a month later I had their reply. They offered to employ me as cook for £3 per week, plus full board and lodging and a uniform. And a new life.

The work was hard, and the matron hated me, at least that's the way it seemed. Besides cooking, I was required to scrub the floors, lump the coal, polish the stoves, starch the nurses' uniforms, and perform a hundred other tasks. I often worked sixteen hours a day, usually six days a week. I only had one friend in the place, Ernestine O'Dwyer, a darling girl, who was also Hendrina's friend. Everyone else was horrible to me - the 'ugly farm animal' - as matron was overheard to call me.

Then one day things blew asunder at the asylum. I was preparing to make a *bredie* but from the outset my stew was doomed. The tomatoes were white with fungus and the mutton stank, but when I brought this to matron's attention, she blamed me for not properly storing the provisions, for being wasteful, for cooking disgusting food unfit for dogs, for the decline in morality in Cape Town and for the ill-health of Queen Victoria. It was all too much for my fragile frame of mind. I pelted my tormentor with those rotten tomatoes, threw the mutton into the street for the stray dogs and stomped out of there in a murderous mood.'

'Where did you go?' I prompt the storyteller, who had paused for a refill of madeira.

'Damn me, Master James, for bending your ear so. Can I make you a cup of tea or do you want to take a chance with a drop of my unholy wine? I should caution you though that it's the cheapest plonk money can buy.'

Not wanting to risk my life just yet, I select the tea.

'Now, sir, you ask what happened to me? Well, I was mightily upset at first and to damp the fire in my mind I took a walk to Green Point Common where I walked about in circles for the next hour or two. I knew my time at the asylum was over, and I knew that I was homeless, and I was very much aware that I had savings of something less than £10, barely enough to survive for a week.

I wandered about a while longer then, putting together my shattered confidence and sagging courage, I made my way to Ernestine's home in Sea Point to beg for a safe place to sleep the night.

Ernestine was out, working nightshift at the asylum, but her parents were there.

Mrs O'Dwyer let me in but she did examine me up and down, I imagine taken aback by my bedraggled appearance. She sat me down at the kitchen table and made me a drink of hot cocoa and little by little she prised from me my account of events at the asylum. She was kindly and attentive and allowed me to stay the night, and she voiced no particular comment or judgment about my story.

The following morning when Ernestine got home from her shift, I told the story all over again. Ernestine was, of course, already aware of my unhappy situation at the asylum, so she was not really surprised to learn of the previous day's eruption.

To my great relief Mrs O'Dwyer told me to fetch my belongings and to return to Sea Point, and she directed me to stay until something could be arranged for me.

There would obviously have been much discussion in the O'Dwyer household about my plight, conversation which did not include me. On the second or third day after darkening their doorstep, Mr O'Dwyer, father of the O'Dwyer whom you probably know, Master James, as he is the big chief of the Lighthouse Service...'

'Aah, yes, Mr O'Dwyer!' I interject, 'a fine man. I met him when I joined the service.'

'Well, Mr O'Dwyer senior, in those days the medical superintendent of the Robben Island lunatic asylum – we're going back many years now - summoned me to his study and he came straight to the point. I like that, Master James, a man who, without foreplay or fancy words, comes right to the business. But I'm digressing. This man asks me if I'd like a job, mind you for very little pay, on an island in the Atlantic Ocean. Not exactly a tropical island, he explains, it being devoid of palm trees and coconuts and colourful parrots and white sandy beaches, but nevertheless an island by strict definition.

Well, I guess I must've looked pleased by his proposition because he promptly rose to his feet, shook my hand and congratulated me on my appointment. One week later I arrived on Robben Island, and for the next forty years fed the inmates of the asylum. A very long time, Master James, by anyone's reckoning.

Then one day, out of the blue as they say, I am approached by Mr O'Dwyer junior, whom I know through my lifelong friendship with Ernestine, this being the same O'Dwyer whom you know, and he asks me if I'd like to relocate to Dassen Island, to work for the Lighthouse Service. He explains that it is a new lightstation and that a cook is needed there because the lightstation is really quite unsuitable for families, particularly families with children. A cook is needed he says, to ensure that the men eat properly rather than sustaining themselves on penguin eggs, *perlemoen* and *witblits*.

And that, sir, is how the ugly farm animal came to be here. Here on Dassen Island.'

Chapter 8 – Looking Blackwards

You may wonder how I came to be called Diamond. Actually, I wonder, too.

It is entirely usual, of course, for a *kaffir,* once separated from his *kraal* and his ancestral lands, to find himself attached to a European-sounding name, like Robert or Wellington or Nelson, or to a biblical name such as Moses or Elijah. But, even so, Diamond is a little out of the ordinary.

There is a possibility that my name derives from *die munt,* meaning 'the kaffir,' or *die mond,* meaning 'the mouth'. I have a particularly wide mouth, like the wedge of a watermelon, and this mouth is generously accentuated with prize-winning lips, so I tend to think that the *die mond* theory is the more likely origin of my white-man name.

You may also be curious to know why I hate and distrust white people, except Swedish people.

Begrudgingly, I suppose I must admit that there must be – besides Swedish people – several good white people in the world, but I have yet to know one of them. Maybe the new lightkeeper, the big boy, Mr James Fox, will be the first. He tries to chat to Isaiah and myself in the manner of an equal and he seems uncorrupted so far by the adult Europeans around him. I guess time will tell if he is really any different.

As for the other whites in this place, they are as treacherous as a pit of mambas. Seemingly they are just innocently basking in the sun but, in reality, they are more likely to be tightening their coils to strike.

Before I tell you more about the *umlungu,* the white snakes of Dassen Island, I will tell you a little bit about myself.

I am a Zulu, which places me above the snivelling Xhosa and the cheating Basuto, or it did once. But, now, even the once proud Zulu, the greatest warrior in Africa, is the obedient cur of his white master, his pale-faced *baas.* Clearly the rifle speaks a stronger language than the spear and the shield of hardened cowhide is no defence against the bullet.

In the spring of the twenty-fifth year of the reign of King Mpande, which was about 1865 on the European calendar, I was born in the ancestral *amaZulu* lands among the rising hills in the upper reaches of the Bushman's River. When I turned six or seven I was assigned to help with the herding of the family cattle, to fish, to hunt waterfowl with a little spear, and to work with my father constructing new huts as the termites chewed up the ones erected two or three years earlier.

I was the nineteenth child in my father's *kraal.* My father, Siyanda, cousin of both the lion, Dingaan, and the baboon, Mpande, had five wives and many cattle at the time of my birth. But, just beneath the outward prosperity, life was uneasy. Each year, each month, more and more colonists rode into Zululand and these new arrivals failed to see our people, failed to hear our voices. Or, maybe they did see us but in the way a farmer sees a field of mealies, as something to harvest and to consume. Something to rip from the earth when all has been taken. The intruders were initially satisfied just to graze and water their cattle but, as time went by, they wanted the land for themselves. Our people did not understand the European concept of land ownership. You see, we believe that we are all children of our mother the Earth and that use of the land needs to happen according to ancestral tradition; not in obedience to a piece of paper purporting to be an exclusive right of ownership. The colonists sometimes made a show of buying our land in exchange for whisky or cattle or a few rifles but other times the intruders just took what they wanted without even making any pretense of fair play. Before long, our chiefs realised that the Europeans were never going to leave, never going to share the land and, as the smoke of the white man's trickery gradually cleared away in the breeze of time, our people saw in the redness of the setting sun the vision of the last great battle. This battle, this final reckoning, would be for the control of Zululand, for dominion of the rich land between the Drakensberg, *uKhahlamba,* and the sea.

In the year 1879, the year after I became the *insizwa,* the drums of war were beating with a great rumbling across the land – the white man was coming with a big army, with many guns and horses and wagons. From across the nation, our fearless king, the bull elephant, Cetewayo, called his *impis* together and rallied them to war. I was still too young to join the *impi* so father ordered me to position myself on a nearby hill and if I spied the white army, I was to run and warn the nearby *kraals,* raise the alarm so the women and children could take cover in the dense bush and nearby dongas.

Father gave me a battle spear, saying, 'Here, my son, take this. Keep your spear sharp and ready, for soon you will be a man. The world is full of dangers and treachery - use this spear well.'

Those were the last words my father spoke to me. He left to join the *impi* of Chief Ntshingwayo and, one week later, along with thousands of his fellow warriors, he died on the veld at Isandlwana. Soon the blood of the once mighty *amaZulu* stained the country in every direction; for us it was the beginning of the end.

And soon the invaders descended on our land like locusts from the sky and ate our cattle to fill their stomachs. And everywhere the *kraals* wailed for their fallen men. And my mother, Ayize, the youngest of Siyanda's wives, according to our custom returned to the *kraal* of her family. My little sister, Zenzele, and I, being her youngest children and too young to fend for ourselves, went with her.

Our new home was further down the Bushman's River, towards the mighty Tugela, in the district of a European town which I later came to know as Weenen.

Here was the *kraal* of my mother's people, which included my grandparents, and from the outset our arrival was difficult. There was not enough food for everyone. The cattle, the goats, the chickens, were all gone. The able-bodied men were gone, too, and we were reduced to scouring the veld for anything edible: berries, locusts, flying ants, edible leaves, whatever we could find. People were sick and weak and the little children, with their big unknowing eyes and twiggy limbs, looked like stick insects as they sat in the dust covered in snot and flies.

But destiny was about to step into my life from a most unexpected direction.

One day a Zulu man, dressed in European clothes, came to our village and we wondered at his appearance in our midst. Who was this grand fellow? And where did he come from? And what could he possibly want?

Removing his European hat from his head, the man asked to speak to the elder of the village, this person being my grandfather, Zwelethu, and, as curious as everyone else, I followed the visitor from a respectful distance as he was taken to the ancient fig tree which stands in the centre of the *kraal* next to Zwelethu's hut. The old man was called, probably roused from his afternoon nap, and appeared after a while from his hut.

'*Sawubona!*' The greeting rang clearly from the mouth of the visitor, as he acknowledged the presence of the elder.

Grandfather blinked in the brightness of the day, took a moment or two to focus his vision on the man standing before him. '*Shiboka!*" he responded in his old voice. The visitor took the response as his cue to step forward, which he did, and he extended both hands in greeting to the old man.

After further polite discussion about the state of the village and its inhabitants, the visitor got to the point. He was, he said, an employee of the Persson family, white farmers who came from a country, Sweden, which nobody had ever heard of. In addition to our language, *isiZulu*, this man, Timoteus, spoke both English and Afrikaans. He was a sparrow of a man, obviously no warrior, which probably accounted for his alliance with white people and white culture. He said the Perssons employed him as a translator, messenger, and general factotum, and today he, Timoteus, had brought himself to the *kraal* to inquire whether an able woman and an adolescent boy might be interested in working for the Persson family.

When the request was relayed to the assembled villagers, there was a great silence until, at last, my mother, Ayize, spoke up. 'My children and I have only recently come here to my father's *kraal*. Already there wasn't enough food for everybody, and our arrival has just made things worse. I will work for this these people if I may bring my children.'

My mother's offer was the only offer, so Timoteus, a little exasperated by this single offer of a woman and two children, left the village and promised to return the next day to let Ayize know whether her terms were acceptable to the Persson family.

As soon as Timoteus was out of sight I remonstrated with my mother, something I would not dare to do in front of the assembly. "What are you thinking, Mother, agreeing to work for white people? Are these not the same people who killed my father and destroyed our land? The same people who have taken our cattle. How can you do this?'

And she answered, 'When the lion is hungry, does he ask himself where the antelope comes from? Now that your father has joined the spirits of the great warriors, it is my duty to feed you and Zenzele. Then, one day when I am old and toothless and wrinkled like a sunbaked marula, then, according to our tradition, I will let you take care of me.'

'What would my father say about your agreeing to serve the *umlungu*? Wouldn't he say you are betraying our brave ancestors, Shaka and Dingaan? Wouldn't he say...'

'I don't care what your father, Siyanda, would say,' interrupted my mother sharply. And, bitterly, she added, 'He is dead, he is not coming back, and he is of no use to us. Come now, we must do this and, believe me, if I had a choice, I would choose differently. But hear me now; the clever warrior lives to fight another day. Today it's your turn to be a clever warrior.'

'I'll do as you ask, Mother, and, although you are only a woman, I agree that you know much more about the world than I do. I shall come with you to protect you and Zenzele. I will bring my battle spear.'

'You'll bring no spear. We aren't departing here to make war. Leave the spear here in the hut of your grandfather and, one day, if you need it, come back and get it.'

Timoteus returned and told us that the Perssons agreed that mother could bring both Zenzele and myself. I would be employed as a herd boy, in charge of the cattle, while mother would learn to do housekeeping and cooking, and little Zenzele would be a play companion for the Persson children.

The matter was settled and, after farewelling the people of the *kraal*, we accompanied Timoteus to the Persson farm.

....

At that time, I knew nothing of the habits of Europeans, but it was not long before it became clear to me that the Perssons were different, vastly different from the British invaders, the new masters of Zululand.

The Perssons were very religious people who worshipped a spirit god, Jehovah, and this god had a mortal son called Jesus, and Jesus had an earthmother called Mary. Although Jehovah was the father of Jesus, Mary was actually married to a mortal named Joseph. This man, Joseph, did not seem to mind that he was not the father of little Jesus.

These things were beyond my understanding.

Several years before the British invasion of our country, the Perssons had accompanied to Zululand the evangelist, Otto Witt, from Sweden, a place I am told lies in the cold north of Europe. Reverend Witt tried very hard, but with limited success, to convert the *amaZulu* to Christianity, the big European religion, but the *amaZulu*, for good reason, did not trust the white people or their pale-faced gods, nor did they know that, even though they were white-skinned, the Reverend Witt and his Swedish compatriots were neither empire-builders like the British nor tricksters and thieves like the Afrikaners.

The Perssons looked upon us, their *kaffir* employees, as their equals, as an extension of their own family and, completely out of step with other white people, the Witts had us sit at their dinner table rather than having us wait at the kitchen door for a bowl of *pap* and, when their children, little Elias and Aron, received instruction in English and Afrikaans and arithmetic, Mother, Zenzele and I were always included in the lessons. The Perssons, for being different, were generally avoided by other whites on account of their 'kaffir-loving' ways and the townsfolk of Weenen were heard to remark that it is wrong to spoil a *kaffir* for, one day, the barbarian will steal all your possessions, rape your daughters and embed an *assegaai* in your heart.

I spent the next five years working for the Perssons, five of the happiest years of my life, until my destiny led me on a different path, the path which ultimately led me here to Dassen Island. I have fond memories of endless days herding cattle beneath the big blue skies, and daydreaming about how it came about that the great Unkulunkulu made the earth and the sky and the animals and the plants, and how no detail, however small, was omitted in His great plan.

One day *Herr* Persson (I never called him anything other than 'sir' or '*Herr* Persson') took me aside and confided in me than he and *Fru* Persson and Elias and Aron were returning to Sweden on account of *Fru* Persson suffering greatly from bouts of malaria and no less on account of both he and his wife being terribly homesick. Try as they might, they had found it difficult – no, not difficult, but impossible – to fit in with the people of the district.

Herr Persson went on to say that they were hoping, with our mother's approval, to adopt Zenzele and take her with them to Sweden and, as for mother and me, he was offering us a written recommendation to a well-connected Swedish family in Durban and, hopefully, the Durban family could either offer us employment or help us find suitable positions.

Soon enough mother and I found ourselves in Durban, in the noise and smoke and rush of the harbour city. For us, a couple of country *kaffirs*, this new place, with row after row of imposing buildings and people calling loudly in the streets, had a feel of decadence, of degradation. beyond our prior experience. I hate to admit it, but I was scared. Stopping only occasionally to ask for directions, we kept walking mile after mile until at last we reached the mythical address we were looking for in Berea, on the high ground overlooking the city.

After the residents examined the letter from *Herr* Persson and they were satisfied that we were not wandering vagabonds, they allowed us in and provided us a very welcome meal.

Learning of mother's domestic skills, the Cornelissens (such was the name of the family in Berea) employed my mother, Ayize, on the spot and the very next day Mr Cornelissen took me to the harbourmaster's office to inquire about a labouring job and, when the man at the office - not the harbourmaster himself - saw that I was strong and quick and tireless like a well-trained warrior, I, too, had a job.

Welcome to Durban and to a new life! Now I was herding sacks of mealies, huge hands of bananas, bushels of sugar and rice and every other commodity known to mankind. The work was hard but my back was strong and soon it was remarked by Sebenza, the overseer, that I, Diamond, son of Siyanda, was not your average *muntu,* for not only could I speak English and Afrikaans and perform mental arithmetic with a fair degree of skill but I could also load and unload a ship from sunrise to sunset with hardly a break except to piss, eat a banana and drink some water. Asking nothing in return, Sebenza, saying that every fine warrior deserves a chance for greatness, offered to introduce me to the skipper of the coastal trader. *SS Quirimba*. He, Sebenza, said that he believed I had the skill one day to become a third mate or possibly even a second mate on a merchant vessel.

I never worked out why the overseer was creating this opportunity for me but, believe me, I was most grateful to him. Sebenza is not even his real name since, in *isiZulu*, *'sebenza'* means 'work,' so I suppose he earned this name by constantly yelling 'Sebenza!' at the labourers when they moved too slowly or took too many breaks.

Captain Coelho, half Portuguese and half Sena, skipper of the *SS Quirimba*, a compact trader held together by an abundance of rust and barnacles, was immediately agreeable to taking me on board as a deckhand as he was always in need, he said, of a good worker unaffected by alcohol, syphilis and malaria.

We traded up and down the coast, mostly on the Durban-East London-Port Elizabeth-Cape Town run, but occasionally venturing north, to Lourenço Marques and Beira in Portuguese East Africa. The work was hard but not as hard as on the docks and once I understood the job, I found time to daydream again, to wonder at the mysteries lurking beneath the swell of the Indian Ocean, and to think wistfully of my childhood among the chattering crowd of children and the many huts of my father's *kraal*.

Look at me now, a Zulu boy on the big blue sea, surrounded by strange men with strange customs. In the quieter hours at sea, my shipmates spent their time drinking *vinho,* playing cards and telling incredible stories of lost treasure, memorable fights in bars and romps in perfumed bordellos.

Myself, with no knowledge of these things, said nothing and no doubt my shipmates thought me a little simple, a mere *umfaan* in their midst, a beardless boy unacquainted with the delight of a woman's *isibunu*. But I did not care what they thought, I was happy enough and enjoying the labour, and although Captain Coelho was not a talkative man and not in the habit of praising men for performing the job they were being paid to do, he seemed well satisfied with my work.

Whenever in Cape Town for a few days, usually once every two or three weeks, I roomed at the worker barracks near the docks. The place had a terrible smell about it, and even after the slop buckets were emptied and dosed, the odour of shit and piss and rotten fish never let go its vile grip. But it was a place to sleep, a place to get away from the boat for a spell.

I went for long walks around the city, up Signal Hill, along tree-lined streets with solid white-washed homes, past the bazaars, barbers, saddleries, chandlers, tinkers and tailors of Somerset Road, Chiappini Street, Plein Street, Long Street and a hundred other streets and roads. I got to meet the Malay people, and the Cape *hotnots,* and seafarers from every corner of the world. Mostly the local white people avoided me, often crossing the street rather than risking an encounter with a big *kaffir*, with muscles like a wrestler and a face like a gorilla.

On Dock Road I was frequently propositioned by the local whores, but I knew enough to steer clear from the scourge of syphilis, so I kept my money in my pocket and my *umthondo* securely in my pants.

At first I did not fit in and I had no friends - not until I discovered a little Zulu community in District Six. One day, on one of my walks, I struck up a conversation with a trench digger, Ephraim, where he was working on an excavation outside the Cape Parliament, and immediately he invited me to his place, to eat with him and his brother and his sister, and, that is how - one thing leading to another - the sister, Rebekah, and I soon became more than friends, and I moved into her modest room in their little home in Wicht Street where, whenever I was in Cape Town, we lived as husband and wife. I was glad to be out of the worker barracks, and glad to have the comfort of a woman. How I loved the softness of her bosom pressing against my body and the beating of her heart against my chest as we clung to each other through the chilly Cape Town winter nights. Now I was beginning to feel that I belonged in Cape Town, that I had a connection, a reason to be here.

But, as you know, even the most seaworthy ship will struggle in the swell of a Cape gale and, although I could not feel it yet, the winds were picking up, blowing a surge of change.

Rebekah and I had our first child, a little girl, Thembeka, in 1886, and twin daughters, Unathi and Dulana, in 1887. We tried and tried to find a place of our own, but there was a severe shortage of housing and rents were far beyond the reach of my modest income as a deckhand. Clearly something had to change.

Eventually, after many months of discussion and more than a few tears, we agreed that Rebekah would return to Zululand, to the kraal of her parents and, when circumstances changed for the better, I would come to get her and the girls.

I pleaded with Captain Coelho to allow Rebekah and the infants to voyage to Durban on the *SS Quirimba* as steerage passengers and, even though he generally refused to take passengers, paying or otherwise, the captain made an exception for me, his hardworking Zulu boy, for which I was immeasurably grateful.

From Durban I accompanied Rebekah and the children to the family kraal which lay about twenty miles north of Inanda. I gave her father £10, nearly all my savings, with my instruction to buy a cow and some chickens, as a kind of overdue *lobola,* and I promised to send more money from time to time. That is how it happened that I parted from my little family in March of 1888. I did visit them every month or so until 1893, during which time Rebekah and I had a son whom we named after my great-grandfather, Mageba, an ancestral chief of the *amaZulu.*

But since 1893 I have not been able to get back to Zululand. This I will explain.

In 1890 Captain Coelho accepted a commission as captain of a larger trader, the *SS Ana Chaves,* and he asked me to transfer across as his third mate. This was a great honour for me, and the position came with a welcome increase in pay, though I earned every farthing twice over, as the crew - mostly hard-drinking half-castes of every blend known to mankind - resented the authority of a *kaffir - die fokken aap,* as they called me behind my back. Those were tough days, and I always slept with one eye open in case some hero got the notion to creep up on me and slit my lovely black throat.

In 1892, around October or November I think it was, the master called me to his cabin. This was unusual, as our captain was a man who kept his own company, a sober man with sober habits, a man who read books and wrote letters.

'Diamond,' he commanded, 'today I will ask you to sit down. You see, I have an important matter to discuss with you. After which I also have a proposition which may be of interest to you.'

'Thank you, sir, I'm honoured.'

'Don't be thanking me too quickly, my man. First hear what I have to say.'

I looked at this man, at the greying tracks of hair on his short-cropped head, at the deep lines of seafaring experience baked into his intelligent face. I believe that in a different place and in a different time this man would have made a great and fearless general. There is nothing ordinary about José Coelho, but he has the misfortune to be born a part *kaffir,* his mother a Sena tribeswoman from the Nampula province of Portuguese East Africa. José grew up in the port town of Sofala, where his father, a man of the sea, caught fish and turtles for a living.

Unsurprisingly, having tasted the salt of the ocean and felt the wind on his face from his earliest years, young José, at the tender age of fifteen, joined the crew of his first trader, a small vessel plying the warm waters of the Mozambique Channel.

Now the captain poured himself a cup of coffee, a drink which looked like molasses and smelled like scorched nuts, then he began to tell me what was on his mind. 'This is my fortieth year with the Indian Ocean, and it's been a long marriage, mind you, not without difficult times, not without some shouting, not without a few fights. I could say like any marriage, but I have no experience of marriage since I've never really had the time for it.'

I expected the captain was about to say something really important, so I looked intently into his serious face, and I said nothing. What was in the air?

'So, my fine fellow, here I am, growing old, not far off being scrapped. The week before Christmas I will be fifty-five and I've made the decision to leave the sea, to let her find a younger man. Myself, I'll buy a modest place in Sofala, a place with palm trees and a polished veranda, and I will sit there watching the boats as they tack in and out the *Rio de Sofala*. I will drink fine Brazilian coffee and read adventure books by my favourite authors and, who knows, I might even take a nap during the afternoon heat. Then, rested and refreshed, I may venture out for a long walk down by the shore, down among the local people. I may even meet a lady *bonita, and* I might marry her, buy her shiny bits of jewellery and pretty dresses and have her cook me curried fish and massage my tired feet. You know, if only we believe they can happen, all things are possible.'

I heard myself say, 'But why now, sir, why not five years ago. Or five years from now?'

'Everything – and everyone – has its time. My time to go is now, and it's fair enough to ask me, why now? What has changed you may wonder?' The master sat back in his chair, drew a deep breath, took a large swig of his malodorous drink and continued, 'The owners of the *Ana Chaves* have sold her to a British shipping interest based in Zanzibar. She'll reportedly be assigned to the Zanzibar - Seychelles – Maldives - Ceylon route and the officers and crew will likely be replaced by Zanzibaris under the command of a British captain. Now, at this stage of my life, do I want to compete with younger men for a commission? No, I don't think so. And, even if I do find a pretty young vessel who wants an old-timer like me, do I want to restart with a crew of strangers? No, Diamond, definitely not. It's time for me to go.'

'Sir, I appreciate your telling me this big news, but at the risk of sounding selfish and ungrateful, how does this affect me?' Mentally, I was still chewing the news, clearly not yet digesting the implications.'

The master answered, 'I've just told you that the officers and crew will be replaced by Zanzibaris. That includes you, shipmate. At best you'll be rehired as a deckhand because you should know that the British are dead against allowing a *kaffir*, even a good *kaffir* like you, to hold any position of authority. These people are infinitely superior, at least that is the way they see the world.'

I detected a note of bitterness in Captain Coelho's voice, and I wondered to myself how an island nation with an aging queen could have so much power and influence in the world. Where did their strength come from?

'What I'm saying, Diamond, is that you'll be better off restarting elsewhere. At this stage of your life, you do not want to be a deckhand again.'

'That's easy for you to say, Captain, I answered a little grumpily, 'but, tell me, how will I support my wife and children. The only other thing I know to do is to herd cattle and this is not exactly a calling for an adult man. Anyhow, cattle-herding doesn't even pay a wage...'

'Stop!' ordered the captain, holding up his hand and pulling a face, 'Shut up and listen. I have a proposition for you. If only you'll hold your tongue long enough for me to tell you.'

Acknowledging the man's authority, I looked down, and listened.

'The Cape government is in the process of erecting a new lighthouse on Dassen Island, and at every lighthouse some *kaffir* labourers are employed to do all the shit jobs which the Europeans don't want to do. I understand that, in addition to pay, you will also be given free food and a dry *pondok* where you can rest your head at night. The work is lonely, but I've noticed that you don't seek the company of others and, for that reason, being alone will probably suit you well. Now, I know the Lighthouse Service will surely want a *kaffir* who can speak a little English and Afrikaans, who can work equally hard all day in the sun or in the icy west coast winds, preferably someone who understands the sea. By these measures, you are the right man for the job.'

'I'm honoured by your opinion of me, sir, but how do I find this position?' I was feeling brighter now, like a ship emerging from the fog.

'I know someone who knows someone, and that someone is the man who will be the chief lightkeeper. I will arrange for you to meet him as soon as we berth again in Table Bay.

. . . .

Well, to cut a long story short, I did get the job. Of course, I had no idea what I was getting into, but it was a real job and it paid a real wage. The downside of my new employment was that it was going to be impossible for me to get to Durban and to Inanda, impossible to see Rebekah and my children.

I thought long and hard about it, then, promising myself that I would save every possible penny, I resolved to put away my money and, one day, when I had enough to buy myself a small herd of cattle, and maybe even a bicycle, I would return to Zululand, to my family and to the land of my forefathers.

And I would find my battle spear and I would stand atop a hill somewhere and, in my loudest voice, I would turn in every direction and, over and over, I would shout *'Bayete!'* into the wind, in greeting to the royal spirits of the *amaZulu*.

Chapter 9 – Rips, Currents and Tides

Soon enough the *Lady Jane* shows herself on the horizon and, while I wait for her to berth at the jetty, I review my first three weeks here on Dassen Island.

I have come to know the feathered residents, the entire one million of them, as well as the odd assortment of humanity living here. In a way it feels like I have been on this island for years, yet in a paradoxical way, I may have come here only yesterday. Working shifts as we do, the days and the nights blend into each other like ink and water in a glass, then to end up in an unspecified greyish-blue substance, neither water nor ink, neither clear nor useful.

This is the beginning of my rostered week off, my time to be with Valerie again. And I look forward to presenting myself at *Harrow*, now as the seasoned lightkeeper, the guardian of seafarers venturing past the *Cabo da Boa Esperança*, the name given to this region by the Portuguese king, João II, in a moment of ecstasy after the discovery of the sea route to India. I know my father will be immensely proud of me, his youngest son, now numbered among the ranks of men and occupying a position of great responsibility, and, in her unique way, Mother will also be pleased but, rather than make a fuss about my new occupation, she is more likely to ask me if I have encountered any ghosts or stumbled upon some unmarked graves. As for Bayes, he will be mildly curious about my fellow lightkeepers and the routine of living up a light on an island, while Emma, dear Emma, bless her devious little heart, will want to know immediately about the eligibility of the menfolk.

Captain Jacobs is pleased to see me, looks me up and down inquiringly, and voices what he is thinking, 'Aah, Master Fox, I see you've survived the storms in these parts and you're looking well, that in spite of a diet of penguin eggs and quicksilver.'

Believing his observation to be rhetorical, I just smile and say nothing. Did the captain expect some other outcome for me? He has that knowing look, as if he is the custodian of great secrets, but I am far too excited by the prospect of getting home, of holding Valerie, to let the man's curious comments unsettle me. No, not today. Today I am going home!

You may ask what I have learnt these past three weeks?

I have mastered the mechanics of operating the lightstation, although I have not yet had to struggle on my own to keep the lantern alight in a major gale, But I am confident about the day to day operation, about the endless checking and cleaning, I am much improved now about estimating the position of ships in relation to the rocks and about identifying the type of vessel, whether she is a cutter or a brig, a clipper, or a schooner. Of course, I have a lot left to learn, but I am well satisfied by my progress. Knowing now that I can do this job, and do it well, a certain youthful confidence fills my head. Is it really confidence or just bravado? I am not sure, but does it really matter when I am feeling so good about my employment?

I reckon there is something sinister about Alfred Pike. No one is saying what they know, yet he always has this worse-for-wear appearance about him. On several occasions I have caught him looking intently at me, weighing me up. Why? Want does he want with me?

As for Van Staden, he is a bitter man, scarred by his past and filled with a limitless and unthinking antipathy towards dark-skinned people. I notice though that he is careful in his dealings with Diamond and Isaiah. Yes, he speaks roughly with them, curses them roundly, but he stops short of raising his hand or his *sjambok*. Lightkeeping is Van Staden's life, his very reason for existence, and he is smart enough not to risk his vocation again. No, not on account of a couple of *'fokken kaffers.'*

Then there's dear Mrs Andrews, the one whom the Lord overlooked when he was handing out blessings. She is as rough as old rope, but I have seen, lurking beneath her coarse exterior, the heart of a sad and lonely being. I have discovered that she knows a lot about a lot of things, a lot more than you would expect a cook to know, and she loves nothing better than an after-supper chat washed down with several cups of cheapest madeira.

I am beginning to discover, both by observation and a little questioning, that there is a hidden side to the Richardsons. By no means do I know the entire picture, not yet, but what I have discovered is that Richardson, he who gives the impression of honesty and integrity to his subordinates, in fact, is running an illicit guano-mining venture for his own pocket.

For many years, even decades before the erection of the lighthouse in 1893, the Cape government sold guano-mining rights on Dassen island for the Crown purse. Guano, a malodorous mix of bird shit and seal excrement, has great value as the best fertilizer in the world. Shit it may be, but there is money to be made from the stuff. Our leader, Mr Richardson, is running his own guano-mining venture, quite apart from the approved government concession. He is mining a tract on the windward side of the island, down from Boom Point, and when his 'contractors' (nameless men, apparently from St.Helena Bay) come to load their barge, they will approach, without showing navigation lamps, from the north-west and hidden under cover of the westerly darkness in the pre-dawn, invisible to any vessel on the customary southerly and easterly approaches to the island and invisible to any observer in the lighthouse. They will load guano all day, then sleep until four or five o'clock in the morning, before departing the way they came, again under the blanket of the pre-dawn.

How did I find out about Mr Richardson's venture?

For more than a week following my arrival I tried to get Diamond and Isaiah to talk. I was mortified to discover, in the absence of being told, that Isaiah is deaf and dumb. Which goes to show that we should never make assumptions about people and the world. An assumption, like an old watchdog, is seemingly docile and benign, at least until you step on its tail and it turns and bites you on the calf.

Diamond was reluctant to talk to me, his demeanour suggesting that he was not ready to trust me, the young *umlungu*. After all, am I not one of 'them,' the oppressor class, the enemy?

After a lot of thought it occurred to me that, if I showed him some trust, he might just return some trust. Such an exchange would be like the laying down of spears, and I would go first. Would it be worth the gamble? To be sure, it would be a risk for me to trust first, but I was determined to sail round the rocks with Diamond, to find a passage to his mind.

And, as so often happens, a curious crossing of circumstances pushed forward the making of a decision, this decision for me to trust the black man.

I love walking about the island, wandering from bay to bay, often stopping to watch in awe as the Atlantic beats and thunders, like some angry god from Greek mythology, against nature's rocky battlements.

In my second week on the island, while taking another of my walks, this time along the western rim of the island, I came across a curious sight. There, digging away at a layer of guano, and recognisable even with scarves covering the lower half of their faces, were our labourers, Diamond and Isaiah. As it was my understanding that the guano-mining was performed by the concession-holders, not by the lightstation labourers, I was puzzled by what I saw. After all, since we were not trying to grow anything, why would we need guano?

While staying at a distance, and out of the line of sight of the diggers, I observe for a while, and as I watch I see a couple of coloured men – these men unknown to me – approach from the beach side with a hand cart, load the cart high with guano and leave the way they came.

I approach Diamond and Isaiah, with an aspect as casual as I can make it, as if I am just chancing upon their presence.

Isaiah saw me first, waved his hand in front of Diamond, pointed my way.

The grown man, the big Zulu, seems startled by my presence, stares hard at me for a moment, then remembers to greet me. '*Middag, baas.*'

'Hello, Diamond, how are you?'

The Zulu left my inquiry unanswered. Instead he asked, 'Do you have a job for me, *baas*?'

'No, not at all. I see you are busy enough with the guano digging?'

'*Yebo,*' he answers, 'Mr Richardson gives us this job.'

"This is not a lighthouse job, is it?' I ask the question already knowing the answer. What will the digger tell me now?

Avoiding the trap, Diamond says quite simply, 'Please ask Mr Richardson about that,' and, a little bitterly, he adds, 'I do what I'm told, *baas*. This is my life.'

I decide to nudge the labourer a little now. 'Do you think all white men are the same?'

'I suppose,' he says, shrugging his shoulders, uncertain what to say.

'Okay, okay. Let me ask you a different question. Do you think all Zulu men are good warriors?'

'No, not all,' he concedes.

'Do you think all white men have come to Africa to take away the land and the cattle of the Zulu?'

After a moment's thought Diamond replies, 'No, not all. I know a few who are different?'

'A few?'

'Yes, some Swedish people. They are good people.'

'Excellent! Just one more question for today. You already know that not all white people are the same. Knowing this, I ask you not to judge me with the other white people in this place. Is this fair?'

'*Yebo*,' says the big African.

'Now I'll go. I've interrupted your work for long enough. Maybe tomorrow we will talk again.'

I detect a slight nod from the listener, and I know that at least to some extent I have reached the man. Now I will make a point of talking to him regularly, getting the warrior to put down his spear and his shield, and encouraging him to tell me what *kak* is going on here on Dassen Island.

The next day I tell Diamond that, just by the way, I am not a completely white man myself because, in spite of my blue eyes and my light skin, my dear mother is a *baster* woman, all the way from the melting pot of Rehoboth. I want Diamond to take my disclosure as a signal that it will be safe to swap some secrets with me; as evidence that I am not 'one of them.'

Sure enough, two days later Diamond tells me exactly what is going on with the guano mining, He tells me about the barge from St, Helena Bay, about the secretive men and their coloured workers who operate the barge. Upon the honour of my father, John Palmer Fox, I have to swear never to tell anyone, least of all Mr Richardson, what he, Diamond, son of Siyanda, has disclosed to me. Both Diamond and I understand well enough that if the contents of our chats are ever disclosed, both our heads could roll.

At some point I must ask more questions. It will be easier now that the black fellow and I are, like the agents of some clandestine mission, comrades in conspiracy.

But first I will enjoy my week away from this shit-encrusted rock. There is still a world just over the horizon or, at least I hope there is – fingers crossed that it has not disappeared into the watery depths like some latter-day Atlantis.

As the *Lady Jane* sails away, my mood is light, and the day is smiling bright.

....

In the early afternoon we dock at the Alfred Basin and, not wasting any time, I stride quickly to Adderley Street, to Trafalgar Place, to the world of flowers, there to find Valerie - the prettiest flower of all!

She is there, busy with several customers and I approach unseen, concealing myself in the throng of pedestrians. Then, as I find myself close, within two or three paces, I clear my throat and ask in a bold voice, 'Excuse me, miss, please show me your best bouquet, I have a lady to impress...'

'James, you rascal! Look at you, Mr Lighthouse Man!' and promptly putting down the half-assembled bunch in her hands, she throws her arms around my neck and kisses me on the lips.

As happy as I am in that moment, I cannot help overhearing a middle-aged white woman comment to her husband, '*Sies!* Did you see that, Paul? What is this country coming to?'

In this life there are times to keep your mouth shut and times to speak out. This was my moment to speak out. 'Excuse me, madam,' I call to the women, 'I think you've forgotten something.'

'Forgotten?' she answered, looking puzzled.

'Yes, for sure. You have forgotten your manners, madam. You see, Valerie and I are getting married soon and you haven't congratulated us yet.'

'Come, Helen! Ignore the young upstart,' hastily orders madam's husband and, before I can say another word, they are gone.

Valerie is crying, pretending to be busy with the flowers, and she does not look at me. She asks me to meet her at Leeuwen Street in an hour.

Later, away from the flowers and the bustle of Adderley Street, unable to bear the fact that today Valerie has been crying, I ask her gently, 'I know I'm just a man and that there're many things I don't understand; please tell me why you were crying. I want to understand... was it what I said to those people?'

'No. James, it wasn't what you said. It is more about the necessity of having to say anything at all.'

'I don't understand.' What does she mean? Was she crying because of my saying something. Or because of what the woman said?

Then Valerie tells me. 'I'm not sure, James, whether I can explain this well but, of all the people I know, I believe you will do your best to understand.'

Valerie pauses, seemingly readying herself to tell me more. She is looking directly at me, intense but, behind the intensity, I think I detect a hint of sadness, of resignation.

'You see, James, I am a Malay, a woman of colour. But you know that, and you accept that...'

'You know I do,' I interrupt, reassuringly.

'What I'm trying to tell you is difficult to explain. Please, just let me talk until I'm finished.'

I nod and she continues, 'Your situation is unusual, James. Here you are, living and breathing the existence of a white man, something you've had all your life. Imprinted on your character, like some sort of stamp of approval, is your very whiteness. But, marked on me at birth, by virtue of the darker hue of my skin and the origin of my ancestors, is a totally different imprint, a mark of disapproval or rejection or inferiority or whatever we choose to call it. This mark, like the *fleur-de-lis* mark which was once used to label whores, holds me forever in a place of inferiority. I didn't choose it and I didn't make it so, yet, somehow, this is my reality.' Valerie pauses, then asks, 'I suppose all I've managed to do is to confuse you, dear James? Does any of this make sense?'

'Are you saying that somehow you feel inferior? Have I ever made you feel this way?'

'The problem is not you, James. You and your family embrace my mother and myself as equals and take us as we are, filthy dark skin and all. Whether this is so because your mother and your aunt are *kleurlinge,* I'm not sure, and in a way, it doesn't matter because we accept and understand each other ...'

'Accept and understand? Really, Valerie, when did love and longing get changed to accept and understand? I don't give two spadefuls of guano what people think. Surely, it's what we know, what we feel, that matters?'

'Of course, you're right, James, though it doesn't change the reality of the society we live in.'

Once, in a time before evangelists and Englishmen poisoned the minds and hearts of white people in Africa, intermarriage was common and seldom commented about. A long time ago there existed a convenient blending in the relationships of men and women but, today, people are fencing out the differences of races - creating separation, social distance, and despair.'

I ask her – I, the boy initiated into the rites of Christianity in the Holy Catholic Church – I ask Valerie, 'Does any of this matter to us? Doesn't the church tell us, above all else, to love our neighbour? Isn't this how we'll make a better world?'

'I don't know, James.'

'That's probably an unfair question. After all, I'm aware that many sections of the Christian church claim that dark-skinned people are inferior, that they bear the mark of Cain.'

"That's exactly what I'm telling you, James. Here I am, breathing the same air as you and filled with the same feelings, yet because of where I come from – you could say because of Cain – I am marked. Not because I'm a thief or a whore, but because my distant ancestor, Cain, was a murderer. If, because of this ancient transgression, I'm marked, and this is the teaching of Christianity, then I want nothing to do with such a religion.'

I feel her emotion, hear the tremor in her voice. 'Why James, tell me why am I condemned to be a lesser person? I've done nothing wrong.'

'Valerie, I can't change anything about the world, about the unfairness of it all. All I can do – the only thing - is to hold you close to me, and to honour you. And maybe here and there our lives will be an example to others.'

'Our lives?' she asks, poking a finger sharply into my shoulder. 'At the flower stalls you said to that woman something about us getting married. How do you work that out when you haven't even proposed to me?'

'Ha!' I answer, capturing her finger, 'I do apologise if you're planning to marry someone else! Was I foolish enough to think that between us some things are understood - just known and accepted – like the fact that water falls from the sky when it rains? Or that we will soon be married?'

'But, James, what if you have misread the stars? What if during the night the sun will snuff itself into darkness? What if I have been playing with your feelings like a naughty kitten playing with a ball of wool? Maybe I will tire of the game soon...'

I pull a face, gently pinch her lips together, and I shake my head vigorously in mock disapproval. 'You seduced me, didn't you?' Unable to speak with her lips pinched, she, the most beautiful of all women, naughtily nods her head in agreement. And, as I draw her close to me, our future is understood.

Chapter 10 – The Battle Spear

Holding his handiwork up to the feeble light of the winter sky, the big Zulu examines the spearhead. He checks it from every angle, runs his thumb lightly across the razor edges. Utters a grunt of approval.

He needed just the right piece of iron for the job, a ten-inch length of quarter-inch iron tent peg and from this plain peg he has laboured to craft a spearhead long enough and sharp enough to penetrate six inches or deeper into Pike's chest. All the way to his white heart.

Firstly, he has to flatten the iron rod into a blade. The process is slow, precise, and painstaking as the blade has to remain straight and strong but flattened enough, with the edges smooth and ready to be sharpened.

Over the course of several days, he hammers the rod on his makeshift anvil, which was once an anchor from a now long-departed vessel. The Zulu hammers and hammers and, when he is done hammering, he pours a little oil onto a flat slab of granite and, with single-minded attention to detail, he scrapes and rubs the iron blade on the oiled granite until the blade shines and it slices easily through a thick leather strap as if the strap is as soft as a ripe fig.

Finally, with a collar of tightly wound wire, he fastens the finely crafted blade into a slot he notched in a broom handle.

His battle spear is complete. He is ready.

. . . .

For years now Diamond has humoured the whites. Whatever they wanted him to do, no matter how dirty and dangerous, he always respectfully replied *'Yebo'* or *'Ja, baas'* with an agreeable nod of the head. He came to believe that this was his lot in life, that destiny had decreed that he should be a virtual slave, and that Europeans are both infinitely superior and untouchable.

But every man has a breaking point and he Diamond, son of Siyenda, has reached his breaking point. Like a wildebeest surrounded by a pride of lions, he is ready to make his last stand and, like a true Zulu warrior, he will fight to his last breath, stand erect and defiant until the last drop of blood leaves his body.

His appointment with destiny began a long time ago – around ten years ago – when he came here to Dassen Island. Now there is no turning back, no retreat. Only the final showdown.

He always expected to work hard, not to be sitting his days in a chair, but rather to toil with his strong body in the sun and the rain. Such hard work kept him close to *Nomkhubulwane,* the goddess of the fields and the rain.

But the *abelungu* had other ideas, other expectations of this man.

Van Staden was the first to abuse his authority when he ordered the *kaffir* to collect penguin eggs, eggs which Van Staden was selling, without the knowledge of the Lighthouse Service, for cash to a *boer* on the mainland. No matter the weather conditions or what other work needed to be done, *Baas* van Staden had to have his eggs and if the *kaffir* was not collecting the eggs fast enough to fill the quota, then Van Staden thought nothing of making the labourer work the entire day without a break - not even for lunch – and on other occasions into the twilight, past the time for supper.

Once the worker tried to object and Van Staden arranged for the *muntu* to have three shillings docked from his pay for being 'idle.' On another occasion when the kaffir tried to discuss how he could possibly get everything done, he forfeited four shillings and sixpence for 'questioning the authority of a superior.' No matter how hard the man worked, there was never any praise or recognition for him, just more work, and abuse of the sort that most men would hesitate to inflict on a mangy dog.

Before the Richardsons came, around '99 or 1900, the chief was Mr Bridgewater, a former keeper who, owing to the shortage of manpower during the Anglo-Boer War, voluntarily came out of his retirement to run the lightstation. Poor old Bridgewater, nearsighted as a mole, really had no idea what was going on, but he made up the numbers on the island and he unstintingly supported the ongoing profitably of the brandy industry through his unrelenting consumption of that fine product.

It was Bridgewater who allowed Isaiah to come to the island, falsified his age and informed the Lighthouse Service that the boy was on the payroll as a labourer when, in fact, he kept Isaiah's pay for himself to bolster his brandy fund and, on account of Isaiah being deaf and dumb, the boy was unlikely ever to say anything about his situation.

After the cessation of hostilities, Bridgewater retired again, and Richardson was appointed, on promotion from Cape Point, as the new chief lightkeeper. Richardson, formerly a lightkeeper at Flamborough Head in the East Riding of Yorkshire, was only a dozen years at the Cape at the time of his appointment to Dassen Island. And, coming along with him, was his considerable baggage, in the form of Mrs Richardson, a lady with a head full of notions and aspirations, a *faux* aristocrat.

Richardson himself, a man without scruples, a Yorkshireman of the worst kind, soon after his arrival on the island made an illegal agreement with some shady 'businessmen' to sell them boatloads of guano for his personal profit, while Mrs Richardson no doubt encouraged her husband in this venture as it was hugely expensive for her to keep up with the bone-china and sterling-silver set. Rowena, as she was known to Cape Town society, would spend weeks at a time away from Dassen Island parading her presence about the drawing rooms of Bishopscourt and Upper Claremont, the members' stand at Kenilworth

Racecourse and, according to rumour, the bedrooms of a number of influential men of the Colony. As for her husband, barring an occasional meeting with Mr O'Dwyer and the Lighthouse Service, he rarely leaves the island, preferring the company of penguins and seagulls and cormorants.

Periodically, when her excellency, Rowena Richardson, is on the island and taking a break from her frenetic round of social engagements, she often commandeers the hapless Diamond to be her unpaid attendant for a morning or an afternoon.

And Mr Richardson, ever unable and unwilling to say no to his wife, allows this arrangement, even though the hapless Diamond is already struggling to keep up with everything he is required to do and, although Isaiah is nominally also a labourer, the boy does not have the strength or the endurance of his powerful uncle and he takes three times as long to get anything done.

Rowena Richardson fancies herself as a painter of some talent and she has Diamond carry her easel and her large box of paints and brushes and her picnic hamper all over the island, has him pose on the rocks as a primitive fisherman, or as a black Neptune, trident in hand, controlling the roll of the breakers. She is a heartless bitch who will eat her picnic lunch, which is ever so carefully prepared by Mrs Andrews, in the presence of the hungry black man without offering him a morsel and, when she has eaten her fill of the picnic - which is invariably more than she wants - she will order Diamond to throw the leftovers into the sea as 'a snack for the starving fishies' which are darting about in the rock pools at the water's edge.

The other thing she does, something more wicked than denying Diamond the crumbs from her picnic, is to prod the male nature of the lackey. If the day is warm enough, she instructs the *kaffir* to be her lookout and she promptly strips off all her clothes and takes herself into the bracing Atlantic water. Then, after a time, she steps out of the water, like Aphrodite being born again from the sea foam, her wet body glistening with fine sand and shell grit, and she walks across the beach as naked as the day she was born, her thick hair matted by the salt water and her nipples raised and stiff from the frigid ocean. And while all this is going on, the man on the beach, the son of Siyanda, remains as impassive, as unmoved, as a child observing a lump of kelp being heaved this way and that by the ebb and flow of the waves.

Crossing the beach, the woman watches him carefully from the corner of her eye as she flaunts her nakedness, and the more he remains impassive, the more provocative she becomes, sometimes stretching like an awakening cat, sometimes raising her arms high above her head in tribute to the gods of the sky.

One day she walks right up to him and, stopping just half a dozen paces from the warrior, her naked chest still heaving from exertion, she demands to know; 'Tell me, *kaffir,* is there anything as beautiful as a naked European woman?'

The *kaffir* looks down and says nothing.

Again, she prods him, pokes viciously with her words, 'Don't be so fucking disrespectful, black boy, answer my question!'

'I am married, *nooi*. I am only allowed to say my wife is beautiful. This is the way of the Zulu, the way of my culture...'

'Culture!' she interrupts, 'did you say culture? You wouldn't know culture if it dropped on your head like a bucket of bird shit from the sky. Now give me my towel and look out for people like I told you to,' and, as an afterthought, she adds, 'Don't think I don't know that you have been staring at me. Well, stare away, because you'll never taste this sweet white peach.'

And, still impassive and seemingly intent on the performance of his duties, the Zulu sentinel stares out across the guano-encrusted wasteland. Stares out across his existence.

And he says nothing.

. . . .

Some men and women, those numbering among the host of 144,000 mentioned in the Book of Revelation, have a place reserved for them in Heaven on account of their flawless moral character and their immeasurable love for the Lord. But Alfred Pike is not one of these.

Because, you see, Mr Alfred Pike has a special place reserved for him in Hell.

When the orphan, Isaiah, came to Robben Island to be with his uncle, following the death of his parents from the bubonic plague which so severely ravaged Cape Town in the last year of the war, he was an undersized thirteen-year-old, malnourished and afflicted by the condition of being deaf and dumb. Because of his unfortunate circumstances, Isaiah's understanding of the world around him was on par with most children half his age, to the extent that, although he was theoretically a labourer in his own right, he was almost wholly reliant on Diamond, while Diamond himself was struggling to juggle all the responsibilities heaped on him by the *abelungu*.

One day Mr Pike approached Diamond and told him a story of how he, Alfred, had a younger brother, a boy just like Isaiah, afflicted and unfortunate. Pike told the Zulu how his brother had struggled to fit in anywhere, how he had been alternatively tormented and shunned by the other children in the community. Pike said though that, with careful guidance, he expected that Isaiah could learn, could over time develop into a self-sufficient man. On the other hand, without such careful tutelage, the boy had little hope, or none at all, of acquiring the needed skills to stand on his own two feet. And just what would happen to the boy should anything ever befall his guardian, his uncle-protector?

Pike said it would take time, said he had time on his hands, said that – as he had close experience of Isaiah's condition – he would try to teach the boy some skills, like how to count, to perform basic arithmetic, how to recognise everyday words including his own name, to recognise everyday images from pictures and sketches, and many other basic arts.

'I've never had the good fortune,' declares Mr Pike with a sad face, 'of being married and having children of my own. This is my greatest regret. So, then, if in some small way I can help your nephew in the long hours of my free time, it'll take the pain out of my regret and I'll find some purpose for my rather useless existence.'

The big kaffir looks dubiously at the white fellow and wonders to himself if Mr Pike has a heart after all? Could it be that the lightkeeper is just lonely and bitter and generally unable to show his better nature? Of course, he, Diamond, wants what is good for Isaiah. such is his duty and, yes, he is very much afraid that the boy will never learn to be self-reliant.

Pike senses the Zulu's reservations; he has been hard on this *muntu,* hasn't he?

The white man speaks again, 'I urge you to consider what is in the best interest of the boy. You are a grown man, and you understand hardship but, as for the boy, he is helpless and dependent and, if you deny him the chance to grow and to learn, then I fear for his future.'

'Aikona!' exclaims the warrior, rejecting Pike's proposal, 'I will teach him myself.'

'Now you are being stupid, kaffir! You have no knowledge of teaching a deaf-mute anything but, because of your pigheaded pride, you will deny Isaiah the chance to grow. I don't know what's going on in your primitive skull, and I don't really give a shit either.'

Diamond says nothing, but his eyes are smouldering. Can he trust the white snake?

'I'll tell you what, kaffir boy. Listen carefully!' Pike directs the Zulu, 'for Isaiah's sake, at least let me have a go at teaching him something. And then, if you find that he's learning nothing, then we'll forget the whole thing, hey? But I think you owe it to the boy at least to give him a chance.'

Diamond shakes his head, turns, kicks at a lump of driftwood sticking out of the sand, and walks away, his frame tense with anger and frustration.

But it does not take the black man long to come back though.

'Take the boy, *baas,* and teach him well.'

And that is how it happened that young Isaiah came under the influence of Mr Alfred Pike.

. . . .

Pike was visibly good to his word. He rigged up a homemade abacus and dozens of little clay figures to teach the boy how to count and to perform simple arithmetic; he acquired from somewhere a quantity of picture books to instruct the young fellow the fundamentals of reading by picture-to-word association and wooden blocks inscribed with the letters of the alphabet. Then, after supper, in the evenings when Alfred was not doing the night shift at the light, he would take the time to instruct his pupil in the mysteries of words and numbers.

Soon Isaiah could write his own name and the name of his uncle, the name of the island and several dozen other words such as penguin, sun, cloud, fish, bottle and spade. Show him the image, and he could faithfully scratch the name of the object on a writing slate or in the sand with a stick. Diamond was amazed to say the least. Clearly his nephew had a brain, but a brain previously shut off from the world by the profound silence of deafness.

Sometimes, on a fine day, the lad would spend hours with his slate, writing and drawing.

And Diamond would look on approvingly.

But one day Diamond came to question what the student was learning when he noticed some drawings which he did not expect to encounter in the classroom. There was Isaiah, sitting on a rock outside the *pondok*, the boy engrossed in constructing a detailed drawing, when the uncle noticed what he was drawing. The images were child-like but the subject of the sketch work was unmistakable – the boy was drawing a figure with an erect penis, this figure seemingly engaged in having sex with another figure. Now, the sexual act is hardly unnatural or unusual, but what was disconcerting was where the deaf-mute adolescent learnt about such a thing? And most puzzling of all, in an environment devoid of the usual sexual temptations and opportunities?

Diamond scratched his head. What to do? And for a while he did nothing; after all, what exactly could he say to Mr Pike?

Isaiah periodically made similar sketches, some images showing the erect *umthondo* clearly in the mouth of another person, other images of a pole-sized phallus being embraced by little sticklike characters. And Diamond noticed, too, that the boy was coming home groggy and red-eyed from his classes with Pike. No longer could these matters be ignored.

Via a mix of hand gesture and drawings, Diamond did what he could to work out where and how his nephew was getting his head filled with sexual notions. As for the grogginess, that he found out quite easily; he could smell the unmistakable heavy odour of *dagga* on the boy.

The guardian came to the conclusion that Pike had to be showing Isaiah pictures but, having no personal knowledge of sexually explicit pictures himself, he was somewhat at a loss how to have the have-to-have discussion with Alfred Pike. And was it Pike who was giving the boy *dagga*? And why? These things were a mystery to Diamond, a man for whom sex was a straightforward transaction between a man and a woman, a primal act of nature.

How could he speak to the white man about these things? And what precisely were 'these things' that needed to be talked about?

While the big Zulu was still turning over in his mind how he would approach the lightkeeper about his concerns, something happened. Something which drove Diamond into a murderous rage.

Late one evening Isaiah returned to the *pondok*. He was wailing, whimpering, obviously in pain. Diamond, by patient interrogation involving much gesturing and pointing, after a while discovered what it was that was troubling his nephew. The child showed his uncle where he was bleeding and demonstrated how Mr Alfred Pike caused the bleeding to happen by the repeated insertion of his swollen phallus.

And that was how the boy, too young to consent and senseless with *dagga*, allowed himself to be subjected to the desires of the *umlungu*.

And that was how the warrior, Diamond, came to the decision to make a battle spear, a cruel instrument to insert into the body of Alfred Pike, to make him bleed, to make him pay the full price with his blood for what he did to the child.

The spear is ready now.

Chapter 11 – The Girl Child

They say that seeing is believing, and on this miserable August day, from my position up the light, I spy something I never expected to see. A small figure running along the footpath, towards the big house.

What intrigues me most is that the little figure is wearing a dress, and it appears to be in a headlong hurry.

Where does she - I reasonably assume the figure is a girl - where does she come from?

A voice in my head tells me to descend from the light and find out what might be amiss. So, I come down as quickly as the treacherous iron stairway will allow and follow the figure in the direction of the house.

I call after the girl but she's too far ahead to hear me in the wind.

Reaching the kitchen door of the big house moments after the runner, I hear her in high-pitched conversation with Mrs Andrews.

'*Asseblief! Kom gou!* My pa is dead.' With her cries the child is gesticulating wildly, pointing back the way she has just come. She is small, somehow smaller than I expected, possibly not even twelve years old. She is an ever-so-pretty, olive-skinned doll, too small by several sizes for the pink and white dress which hangs loosely from her stick-like shoulders.

'Master James,' pleads Mrs Andrews, 'I'm too old and broken to run to see what the child wants. Would you mind going with her?'

So off we go, the child and I, heading northwards in the direction of Boom Point.

We are running too hard to have a proper conversation, but I do get to ask her name and, in the midst of tears and snot and gasps for breath, she answers. 'I'm Gina. Antonio is my father. But he is dead! *Gou maak nou, meneer!*'

We reach a rocky outcrop, a little to the east of Boom Point and following the directions of the shrill child, I discover a man lying there, seemingly wedged, way down between two mighty boulders. The man is wearing a diving helmet, a heavy brass thing, with the bonnet still bolted to the breastplate.

It is tricky to get to him but by careful manoeuvring I lower myself until I can grasp his shoulder. Shaking him quite vigorously, I yell at him to respond, but there is no response and I notice that there is no movement of his chest to suggest that he is still breathing. Now, with a fair degree of difficulty, I manage to loosen the helmet bolts and to lift the heavy bonnet from the man's head.

The helmet is full of blood and the diver is clearly dead.

I cover the head and torso with my coat, clamber up stiffly to the top of the rock, and take the howling child tightly in my arms.

. . . .

It turns out that Antonio, the salvage diver, came for a day of exploratory diving, looking for clues to the watery grave of the *Queen of Ava,* a wooden collier which was wrecked on the north side of Dassen Island in October of 1865. For years it was believed that she was only carrying coal but after the death of her master, Captain Petherick, in 1899, it came to light in a letter accompanying his will that the *Queen of Ava* was carrying a secret cargo of gold coinage, a consignment of funds secured in Europe and the British Isles by Grand Master Christoffel Brand for the construction of a new and opulent Masonic Hall in Cape Town.

This is how it came about that Antonio da Cunha, the best diver in the Colony, was employed by the new Grand Master, Mr Conrad Silberbauer, to look for that gold.

Early in the morning of that fateful August day in 1903 Antonio and his diving colleagues sailed down from Saldanha Bay and, it being school holidays, his daughter, Gina, came along for the adventure. Soon after landing the diving team discovered that the air pump for the diving helmet was damaged, so leaving Antonio and Gina on Dassen island, the diving crew hastened back to Saldanha to source a replacement pump and, while they were gone, Antonio was poking about between the big boulders and testing out the helmet, one he had not used previously. While this was going on, the child, Gina, like any lively and inquisitive little girl, was doing her own exploring.

Calling out for her father after not seeing him for a long while, the child became increasingly alarmed when her dad failed to answer her calls. After a lengthy search across and around the boulders, Gina eventually found her father, wedged and motionless and unresponsive. And that is when she ran for help.

The exact cause of Antonio's death – recorded on his death certificate as a 'diving accident' - was never ascertained but it was speculated that he fell and struck a rock while wearing the helmet and that the blow caused him to bleed from his head until he died.

Antonio da Cunha was just one of many men to die on Dassen Island. Since the early shipwrecks of the 15th and 16th centuries, scores of others have lost their lives on this grim and godforsaken isle.

As for little Gina, it is not until six or seven years later that I rediscover the skinny girl in the too-big dress. And, unknown to me, this little wretch is my cousin, the child of Christa.

Chapter 12 – A Step to Destiny

I come across Diamond on another of my walks. Today he has a box under his arm, so I stop to greet him and to satisfy my curiosity concerning the purpose of the box, a wooden container about a foot square and probably six inches deep.

What I do not realise is that it is not by chance that Diamond is where he is, on my path so to speak; he has placed himself where our ways will cross. I do not know it yet but he has something to ask me, something important.

'*Môre, baas!*' comes the greeting from the labourer.

'Hello, Diamond, how are you today?' goes my response. The fellow is behaving a little oddly, but I cannot quite work out why I think so. Does he have something on his mind? I make polite enquiry about the wooden box under his arm.

'*Baas,*' he informs me, 'this box is for the penguin eggs. I put them carefully in here with the cotton wool.' He tells me only as much as he needs to tell me. We both know that collecting the eggs is wrong.

Now, the *muntu* has to trust me since I am, after all, the only person on this island who might help him. He speaks again, after nervously clearing his throat, '*Nkosi,* soon I will be finished here.' Then he hesitates.

'Go on.'

'I'm not good with words, *baas*. I'll just say this the best way I can." He looks away from my gaze and goes on, 'I'm gone soon, and I need to send the boy to a safe place. A place among his own people. Can you help me, *baas?*'

'How?'

'I need to get Isaiah to Cape Town, to Ndabeni, to the house of my old friend Ephraim. Can you ask the captain of the supply boat if he will take the boy and ensure that he gets safely to Ndabeni?' Before I can answer Diamond, he qualifies his question; 'Of course, *meneer,* I will pay the captain's fee...'

'Why don't you go with him?'

'I have too much to do here. More than I can tell you right now.'

The Zulu man is intense, more intense than I have seen him, and I think of pressing him to explain himself. Why must the boy leave? Is Diamond planning to leave, too, but in a different direction, a way where he cannot take the boy? I cannot work it out, but I decide not to pry, not for now anyway. Keeping things simple, I ask, 'What else?'

'Please help me write a short letter to Ephraim.'

Gazing towards the horizon, now blackening menacingly with a wall of cloud, I take several minutes to answer. Clearly the *kaffir* is up to something, and he would not be asking for my help on some sort of silly whim; the man is serious and quite obviously he has nowhere else to turn for help. Never has he asked for anything before.

'Okay,' I consent to the request, 'what do you want to say in your letter?'

. . . .

Later, before supper time, we write the letter, with Diamond telling me what to say as I scribe the words onto a sheet of letter paper. The message is simple. Isaiah's uncle asks the man Ephraim to take care of the boy, to offer him the protection of his *ikhaya*. He says he is sending £42 5/9d, which is his entire life's savings, for Ephraim to use as he sees fit. And, finally, he offers the suggestion that Isaiah may find employment at Woltemade Cemetery as a gravedigger and that Ephraim should speak to a certain Jomo, a man who is already turning a shovel at the cemetery, in earlier times Diamond's shipmate on the *SS Quirimba*.

There is a curious finality about the letter but, again, I decide not to ask any questions. In time Isaiah's uncle may confide in me, or he may not. I sense that perhaps it is better that I do not know what is unravelling or I may be placed in a position where I may feel compelled to make a report of some sort to Mr Richardson. There is a time to ask questions and a time to mind one's own business. In the Fox household back at *Harrow* we were used to keeping secrets. Secrets such as the origins of my mother and her sister Maria.

Before Diamond leaves he does think fit to share with me that he believes Isaiah will be an excellent gravedigger because he cannot be tempted to stand around and chat with his pals nor to lean on his shovel and listen to the empty gossip of fellow shovelers.

With everything said and set, the Zulu farewells me, '*Uhambe kahle nkosi encane.*' I offer him my hand and the firm grip of our hands seals our transaction in the way agreement should be sealed among men of good heart.

Chapter 13 - The Last Stand

It is the night of the new moon in the third week of August when Diamond, the *kaffir* labourer, takes up his spear. For this one night he will become a warrior in the finest tradition of his ancestors; he will set aside his subservience to the colonial overlords, and he will seek out and kill the white snake.

He accepts that fate might condemn him to die this night; but what is death to a true warrior? Like a beaten cur, a man may pass his life from beginning to end in silent servility, or he may rise to strike out against evil and oppression. Diamond makes his choice.

The night is dark when the Zulu leaves his *pondok*. The boy, Isaiah, left the day before yesterday on the *SS Lady Jane* in the good care of Captain Jacobs, who refused any offer of money for the boy's passage. Only Assistant Lightkeeper Fox knows that Isaiah left never to return, and the signs are good that the young man will never say a word. He, Diamond, now unencumbered by his nephew, is ready to join his ancestors on the battlefield, ready to strike the enemy.

Heavy fog smothers the low island; the only sound is the roll of the surf and the intermittent thunder of a breaker on the rocks. The winter air wraps its bitter cold about the warrior's head, threatens to freeze his breath to his face but, as he strides purposefully along the well-worn track towards the lighthouse and the lightkeeper quarters, the man does not care about the weather. It will take more than a little fog and frost to stop him now.

He sees the light of the mighty lantern, watches the beam as it arcs mechanically through the foggy Cape night and how the finger of light seems to dissolve into the impenetrable soup of darkness. It is not a night to be at sea, not a night to challenge the perils of the deep.

Bang! Bang! Bang! The big Zulu pounds on the door of Pike's room. And the black man's voice booms, "Mr Pike!' from outside the door. There he goes again, thundering away.

In the next room James stirs. Is he dreaming? Is there a storm out there? No, it's a man's voice and there's door-banging. Something is wrong. Bang! Bang! Bang! 'Mr Piiiiiiiiike!'

James Fox rolls himself out of bed, reaches for his boots, and at the top of his voice responds to the noise with, 'Whaaat? Who's there?'

The noise stops as suddenly as it started. Assistant Lightkeeper Fox, now fully awake, decides to investigate. Something is going on out there. Has the light gone out? Pike is in the tower, and probably fast asleep and oblivious to everything. Is there a ship out there on the rocks? What dreadful thing could be happening in the menacing gloom of this winter's night?

James peers out from his doorway. Nobody there.

It is very cold and very quiet as James steps out of his room and scans the surroundings. The tower light is still on, arcing its way through the night. There is no lamp about across the land, no movement to be seen. Was that Diamond shouting at the door before? Is there a ship out there?

The young man will investigate. First, he must check on Pike and the condition of the light and, once up the tower, scan in every direction for distress signals or navigation lights or any other indication of something out of place. James decides he will not try to make his way to Diamond's *pondok*; if he attempts to cross the island tonight, he is likely to lose his way in the inky depths of darkness. No, he will make straight for the lighthouse.

The door is open to the base of the tower. Has anyone gone in there? Is Pike up in the tower?

James takes two steps into the gloom; listens for a moment. Hearing nothing, he feels his way towards the iron stairway. He regrets not taking a minute to light a storm lamp but, who knows, maybe the crisis is such that one minute will make the difference between life and death. Knowing his way about in the lighthouse, even in the tomb-like darkness, allows James to navigate his way within the structure.

His boots encounter the iron stairway, his hand the icy-cold rail, and with great care, rung by rung, he feels his way upwards. Whenever the rungs are damp or dirty, they are treacherous to the unwary user. Knowing this well, James hastens slowly.

Suddenly, from the top of the stairwell, there descends an almighty racket, shouts of anger, banging and clattering, monstrous consternation, and flashes of light from the tower room.

An object – lamp? – clatters down the stairs, strikes James on his shoulder, clatters to the floor below. And someone comes thundering down the stairwell, in the darkness collides with the ascending lightkeeper and both someone and the lightkeeper crash heavily to the base below.

The someone yells, '*Moer! Wie's jy daar?*'

Diamond! What is he doing? Has he gone stark raving mad?

Before James can utter a word, he knows he has hurt his leg. It hurts like hell! And his head aches.

And where is the big *kaffir* now?

. . . .

When James wakes, he is in a strange bed in a strange room. He struggles to focus on his surroundings, and he does not recognise this room. Where is he? And how did he get heare?

Grinding at his senses, the pain in his leg reminds him of his fall, his encounter with the *kaffir* on the stairwell. He remembers falling hard, then nothing.

His consciousness is still bobbing around like a lump of driftwood on the ocean swell, when he becomes aware of someone entering the room. It is Mr Richardson.

'Hello, lad. How you feeling?'

James has trouble forming a reply before Richardson continues, 'Aye, Master Fox, you took quite a fall. Broke your leg below the knee…'

'Broke?' mumbled James weakly.

'Aye, snapped the tibia bone. Must've hit something really hard. Maybe the fuel pump, or maybe the kaffir's head.'

'Where's Diamond?' asks the injured man.

'He bolted, but of course he's somewhere here on the island. We'll find him soon enough.'

James tries to wriggle his toes below the injured leg, tries to focus his mind on the matter at hand. Richardson is still talking, '…Mr Pike will be okay. 'Twas just a nasty flesh wound. The spear went right through his shoulder, front to back; didn't penetrate the lung, so he should be fine.'

'Pike? Why?'

'It seems the black bastard was planning to sabotage the light,' answers the older man, 'be sure that I'll get to the bottom of it all. Meanwhile I have two injured lightkeepers and a pair of fugitive labourers to worry about. You rest up, boy; I need you mended.'

James went right back to sleep.

His next visitor is the female rhinoceros, Mrs Bloxam.

'I've come to splint your leg, Master Fox,' announces the cook as she unpacks some bandages from an ancient Gladstone bag as scuffed and scarred as a blacksmith's boots.

James, feeling better now and more clear-headed, teases the cook. 'I don't believe you, madam. I'm very much afraid you're short of meat today and fancy a leg of man for your stew.'

'Be quiet, Mr Cocky! Or you may lose more than your leg. Now, be still while I splint your leg and ask you what the hell you think you were doing up the light without a lantern on the darkest night of the year?'

James recounts the events of the night; says he doesn't understand what happened or why. Was the *muntu* up the tower to extinguish the light as Mr

Richardson thinks, or was there another reason for his being at large in the middle of the night with a spear? Was he planning to murder Pike up there? Has the labourer for long concealed secret thoughts of insurrection? For the time being there are clearly more questions than answers.

As to his location, James finds he is for the moment in the main house, resting on a rather splendid four-poster bed with richly carved posts supporting a similarly carved tester. He wonders at the possible cost of such a fine article of furniture. The rooms at *Harrow,* the Fox family home, certainly never saw anything like it.

Later, Richardson returns. How much later James is unsure; he has been drifting in and out of sleep for what seems like a very long time. His leg is very painful now, and swollen, and he wonders whether Mrs Bloxam has overtightened the bandages holding the splint, whether she has stopped the flow of blood to his limb. He must tell Mr Richardson and ask if Mrs Bloxam can come back to check her handiwork.

Mr Richardson obviously has some news. What has happened since the midnight drama?

'I see you are awake, James,' begins the older man, 'Are you comfortable?'

James tells Richardson of the pain, and Richardson promises to recall Mrs Bloxam.

'But before I attend to that,' says the chief, 'I need to ask you if you have lately seen or heard anything out of the ordinary, particularly anything concerning the big *kaffir*?' The reference to 'big *kaffir*' and 'little *kaffir*' was commonly used to differentiate between Diamond and his nephew, particularly by those who could not be bothered remembering or using their names.

James wonders if Richardson knows anything or whether he is just fishing for any information. The man is still talking, '...and Rex tells me that you are quite friendly with the blackfellow... maybe he has told you something... given some clue.'

James says nothing. Just shakes his head. So, Diamond was up to something after all!

How glad is James now that he asked no questions, trusted his instincts, and minded his own business, and James convinces himself that the arrangement for Isaiah to leave the island permanently seems hardly relevant to the extreme actions – whatever they are precisely - of his guardian and uncle.

'We can only imagine that the big bastard nigger,' surmises Mr Richardson, 'has gone stark raving mad. Last night's events in the tower seem to support ...'

'No,' interrupts the man on the bed, 'I don't believe it, sir, that the kaffir is mad. I think there's more to these events, more than we know.'

'What are you saying?' demands the chief. 'What do you know of this?'

'Nothing, Mr Richardson, nothing. It's just that these actions seem totally out of character for the normally patient and forbearing kaffir.'

'By God,' growls the chief, 'I'll get to the bottom of this.' And in saying this, he turns abruptly from the patient and stamps from the bedroom.

Chapter 13 – The End of the Beginning

I cannot bear the pain. I have always thought of myself as stoic and strong. But this torture is reducing me to a snivelling coward! Never again, I promise myself, will I be dismissive when someone says they cannot bear their suffering any longer.

There is a knock at the door.

It is Mrs Richardson. She is wearing what looks like a floor-length dressing gown, a generous russet garment, possibly stitched from squirrel or *dassie* fur, and she is carrying a greenish medicine bottle and a teaspoon. But, notwithstanding the bottle and spoon, no one could look less like Florence Nightingale.

'Hello, James,' greets the lady of the house, 'I imagine you were looking forward to the care and company of Mrs Bloxam. Sorry to disappoint you.' Her irony shines at me across the room, and I half wonder why she is here, but my pain is so acute that, if she can take away the ache, to hell with her motives, and I will happily embrace her. She continues, 'The Bloxam is busy now, probably busy peeling potatoes, and my dear husband is running around the island looking for a feral kaffir, so now, Master Fox, I have you at my mercy.'

'Thank you, Mrs...'

'Call me Rowena,' she orders, 'but, mind you, not in the presence of others.'

Her statement should have set me thinking, set me pondering her motives, but I was too uncomfortable to think much about anything.

'Now, let's see your leg.'

I watch her face as she examines my leg and Mrs Bloxam's sorry attempt at applying a splint. Rowena is unflinching, as calm as an experienced doctor, as she applies herself to treating my fracture. She re-splints the leg, now applying a broad bandage from knee to ankle, and I marvel at her efficiency as she goes about the work. I think of asking her where she learnt to apply the splint so expertly, but the question remains unspoken as I marvel also at the easy feline way in which she moves. This woman is a lot older than me, probably old enough to be my mother but, unlike my mother, her skin is unmarked, her eyes are bright, and her hair is full and dark. As she hovers above my injured leg I simply cannot help noticing these things.

'There, James, that'll fix you until we can ship you back to Cape Town for a plaster cast. Here, take a little of this, Dr Love's laudanum; not only will it ease your pain, but it will send your mind on a journey of discovery.' Saying this, she goes ahead and doses me with the really bitter substance from the bottle and when she reaches over to my mouth with the second spoonful, her gown comes slightly apart at her chest, and I have a close view of her naked breast.

Rowena makes no immediate attempt to cover herself, and in a low voice she asks, 'Do you like what you see, James?' She reaches for my hand and, before I can fathom what she is doing, she lifts my hand from where it rests on the bedsheet, and she places it gently but firmly across her nakedness. 'This could be yours, James,' she whispers, and before I can say a word, she returns my hand to its rest, stands up, fastens her gown, and glides from the bedroom.

. . . .

Hours later, or what seems like hours later, Mr Richardson is back. When he enters the room, I am awake, but groggy, and thankfully the pain in my leg is a lot more bearable.

Mr Richardson seems pleased with himself. 'I have good news, James.' He pauses to check whether I am hearing him and, satisfied that I am lucid and paying attention, he continues triumphantly, 'By jingo, lad, we got the madman!' He pauses for effect, then pushes ahead with his report, 'Thankfully, the Lighthouse Service, in its never-ending wisdom, saw fit to equip us with a couple of Lee Metford rifles during the Anglo-Boer War; you know, just in case the enemy ever sprouted a notion to set foot on this island. And then, after the war, the rifles were simply left here, out of sight and out of mind. I tell you, I'm mighty thankful for this because today we benefited greatly by having these rifles here.'

He sees I am listening attentively, so he goes on, 'Van Staden and I circled the island and spied the big kaffir about halfway down the leeward side. He was sitting there on a rock, still as a statue. When he saw us, he rose to his feet, stood tall and faced us. Didn't say a word. We got within ten paces of the fucking heathen when, with the speed of a striking cobra, he picked up a spear from the ground and hurled it directly at me with all his force. By some miracle, praise the Lord, I ducked in time, just as Van Staden raised his Lee Metford and, with a single expert shot, blew the blackfellow's brains out of his head.'

I imagine I must look shocked by this account, for hastily Richardson adds, proffering me his cap, 'Look here, James, the spear went right through the visor. It missed my head by less than three inches. I tell you, I'm bloody lucky to be alive.'

It does not escape my notice that, if the spear were thrown horizontally from a distance of ten paces, it would have been impossible for the spear to penetrate the visor the way it did: it would have needed to be thrown from the ground up or hurled down from above the wearer.

But I say nothing. The pain is returning to my leg, and my mind is struggling to come to terms with Diamond's sudden and violent departure from the world of the living.

If the penguins, the feathered witnesses of the incident, could testify to what they saw that day, what would they say? How can I ever know the truth?

Chapter 14 – The Beginning of the End

At the urging of his good wife, Mr Richardson informs me that I will be evacuated for my convalescence - which Mrs Richardson expects will take several months – that I will need to attend Somerset Hospital for the application of a plaster cast to my leg and that, given my sorry condition, I will be escorted to the hospital and then to *Harrow* by Mrs Richardson herself.

What an unexpected turn of events! I do my best to decline the escort, insisting that I can make my own way on the trams but the chief will not hear of it, pointing out that I will likely be crushed and jostled on the tram and that my injury will not allow it. Unhappily I am left with no choice but to accept the offer.

Mindful of the Service's regulations on matters of ethnicity, and aware of the hardening of racial attitudes at the fairest Cape, I am filled with dread. What will Rowena Richardson find at *Harrow?* And, more importantly, *what* will she report?

. . . .

Today the passage to Table Bay is troublesome; the swells heft and heave the hull of the modest and long-suffering vessel, *SS Lady Jane,* as she beats her way southward along the western shoreline, past Melkbosstrand, and onwards through the gap between Bloubergstrand and Robben Island.

For most of the passage I huddle below the line of the deck, doing my best to shelter from the wind and spray, and I close my eyes to quell a surge of seasickness awakening in the pit of my stomach while the dull boom of breakers echoes across the water from Losperd's Bay and transports my consciousness back across a hundred years to a fearsome day in 1806 when General Janssens and his small Batavian force supported by a handful of mercenaries attempt to repel with cannon and musket shot two battalions of British invaders. For all the world the boom I hear as I huddle here now is the boom of Janssens' cannon from some mysterious parallel dimension in time.

We all know that it was at the Battle of Blaauwberg where the British stamped their authority over the Cape and eventually over the whole of southern Africa.

And we also know how they brought with them their peculiar notions of endless entitlement, and great moral and cultural superiority.

Notwithstanding the appalling weather the *SS Lady Jane* berths in good time in the Alfred Basin where Captain Jacobs promptly dispatches a runner to secure a covered carriage for Mrs Richardson and her patient for their trip to Somerset Hospital, just a short ride but an impossible distance to walk with a broken leg. I want to cry out in pain as the carriage bumps and rattles its way over the cobbled streets but, not wanting Rowena Richardson to witness my vulnerability, I clamp my teeth together so hard it is surprising I do not snap my jaw.

....

'That'll fix you, young man, 'announces the doctor as he steps back from my leg to wash the plaster residue from his hands, 'but, mind you, take extra care not to knock or flex the cast until it's fully hardened. Given that it was well splinted and therefore protected from movement, I expect that when we remove the plaster in six weeks' time, your leg will be nicely healed; then it could take another two to four weeks before you'll be ready to resume your duties.' I assume that the speaker is *Dr Ernest Moon – F.R.C.S. - F.R.C.Psych.* the name on the brass plate outside the surgery door; on that day I have no inkling that in years to come, in unforeseeable circumstances, our paths will cross again.

'Thank you, doctor,' I say. I cannot help noticing how the physician and his nurse are studying Rowena Richardson and myself. Are they assuming that she is my mother, or are they wondering something else?

We arrive at *Harrow* at the setting of the sun. Throughout our journey today Rowena has been unfailingly solicitous, several times asking me how I am feeling, do I have any pain, would I care for a tot of medicinal brandy, perhaps a roast beef sandwich, or a pork pie? As she speaks, she frequently reaches out to touch my hand, making a show of friendship or intimacy, and I'm not sure how to react to her newfound familiarity, so I do my best to remain totally impassive, unmoved as if she were one of my sisters ministering to me. At times on our travels this day, when she thinks I am looking elsewhere, I catch her studying me intently. What is she thinking I wonder?

And there comes to my mind Mrs Bloxam's warning. To beware of the tigress.

Rowena instructs the carriage to wait for her for her onward journey to the Mount Nelson Hotel and she escorts me to the front door of *Harrow*, to the care of my family.

Father answers the knock, opens the door and stares uncomprehendingly at me and Rowena. 'What have we here, James?' he remembers to ask as his eyes take in the pair before his eyes, 'have you fallen from a carriage or a horse?'

As soon as the explanations are made, Rowena excuses himself, 'Now I must go. Dear James, please take care of yourself,' and, saying this, she reaches up and kisses my cheek before turning back to the waiting carriage.

A little frown crosses father's face - now it is gone - and he has me firmly by the shoulder as he escorts me to the warmth of the kitchen.

When she sees me, mother's reaction takes me by surprise (not that her reactions are ever predictable, mind you). 'Oh James! James, my boy,' she exclaims in an uncharacteristically loud and demonstrative manner, 'I'm so glad you're safe. I was so worried about you! And of course, I had no quick way of communicating with the denizens of Dassen Island,' and she blankets me in an enormous embrace, a heartfelt maternal hug of a kind I have not had since my tenth birthday, and the heaving of her bosom and the slight scent of lavender coming from her person is both welcome and reassuring.

'What mother? What is it? Why should I be anything but safe and well?'

Mother's face is still wet with tears, but the flow of tears has ceased, and a glow of relief lights her eyes as she replies to my questions. 'I dreamt, James. I dreamt that you were falling, that you were crashing down a black void, and I woke with a start from this dream, and I felt both scared and frustrated. Frustrated that I didn't know what happened to you, and scared that something terrible had befallen you. And look, here you are standing beside me, safe and sound except, I notice, for a heavy cast on your leg.'

'Yes, I'm really here, Mother,' I satisfy her, 'and as for my leg, the doctor assures me it will heal, that it was well splinted and rested after my accident.' I proceed to explain how I came to break my leg but, not wanting to alarm my parents, I omit the involvement of the Zulu, and place all the blame on the poor lighting and treacherously slippery iron stairs in the lightstation.

After supper, a sumptuous feast of pork chops smothered in apple sauce and plated up with buttery mashed potato and green beans, father takes me outside on the pretext of bringing in some coal and kindling for the stove and as soon as the door is closed behind us, without any preliminaries, he speaks what is on his mind; 'Tell me, James, the woman who brought you here today, who is she? And what are you doing spooning with her when you're engaged to Valerie?'

Rather clumsily I struggle to explain how and why the chief lightkeeper's wife is being so affectionate with me and, though father wants to believe my explanation, there seems to be a nagging little doubt tugging at the coattails of his thoughts.

Father closes the matter, for now, by offering me a spoonful of his wisdom. 'Remember, my boy, running on both sides of the fence at the same time is likely to end in injury and severe pain. Therefore choose, and choose wisely, on which side you will run.'

I want to protest, but this urge is quickly suppressed by the knowledge that my father is merely doing what fathers do; trying to protect me from making a painful and costly mistake. Yet, I am unnerved that he will even entertain the thought that I am not telling him the whole truth about Mrs Rowena Richardson.

On another level I understand his suspicion. We - being men of the mortal kind - we understand intuitively the nature of temptation, the possibility of seduction, and the difficulty of resistance in the presence of a seasoned temptress like the chief lightkeeper's wife. This possibility has nothing at all to do with my love for Valerie or my good intentions towards her. rather it is honest acknowledgement of the base urges latent in me. And I suspect in all men.

I ask father, 'Where is Maria? Has she found a husband and moved out?'

My parent takes moment to answer, as if he is weighing his response before handing it over.

'Maria has indeed moved out,' he says, 'gone to the Malay Quarter, to the same address in Leeuwen Street... you know, where Aminah lives...'

'But how?' I interrupt. 'It's a small place and there's no room for another lodger.'

'I stand to be corrected, and you may wish to verify my understanding with your mother, but I'm under the impression that the three women are sharing a single bedroom, with the elder pair sharing a double bed.' He pauses, and involuntarily shakes his head before commenting, 'but I'll be damned if I know how that works.' Then father says no more and I get the distinct feeling that he has said more than he meant to say.

....

The next morning, I wake well before sunrise; and I hear father leaving for work, his heavy tread followed by the near silence of early morning. In an hour or so, carts and wagons will begin rumbling past along Main Road, going about their commerce, rushing to and from warehouses and wharves, railway sidings and depots, marketplaces, and factories. And then, from sunrise, the trams will start up for the day, transporting day travellers and commuting workers from the suburbs to the city and then back again to the suburbs.

My leg is hurting now. The comfort of Rowena's laudanum has left me entirely; left the door open for the pain to return.

I lie on my back staring into the gloom and struggling to focus my thoughts. I think of Diamond and his sudden end at the hand of a man with a Lee Metford. I picture the man spotting the defiant Zulu shaking his spear at the gods of the sky and I see the man deliberately engage the compact box magazine into the rifle and slide the bolt shut to lodge a cartridge into the chamber and then, seemingly from nowhere, I see Rowena Richardson intrude on the scene as she appears at the side of the warrior and commands the lightkeepers, 'Leave him alone! He is my kaffir!' And now Captain Jacobs is here alongside me, his firm hand grasping my shoulder as he instructs me in a low voice, 'Keep still, Master Fox, someone will die here today; don't let it be you.'

At sunrise I hobble to the kitchen where I stoke the stove and feed it a mouthful of coal from the scuttle and, as I am placing a kettle of water to boil, my mother appears. Like some wild creature of the Congo, her hair untamed and billowing intractably in the early morning, she fills the kitchen with her presence, her body encased in an ancient powder-pink quilted gown, a garment which may once have been worn by Naamah, wife of Noah, servant of the Lord and builder of the Ark.

When the tea is made and I have a man-sized marmaladed slice of bread before me, I ask my matriarch, 'Will it be possible, Mother, to get a message to Valerie. She doesn't know I'm home and that I must see her. There she is, selling her flowers, no doubt thinking I'm up a tower playing with a light...'

'I've foreseen your request, James, and I've instructed your father to have a railwayman deliver a message to Valerie this very morning. Now, as for your pain...'

'How do you know?' I interject.

'Even Toby would know...'

"Toby? Who's Toby?'

'Don't you know anything, my son?' she shot back, a playful glint in her eyes, 'we're talking about Toby, Sherlock Holmes' dog.'

'Mother!' I pleaded with the wild-haired one, 'what has a dog got to do with my pain?'

'Well, I'll spell it out for you then. The undeniable fact that you were moaning loudly in your sleep, combined with your out-of-character appearance in my kitchen at the awakening of the sunrise, is clear evidence of your discomfort, and even a detective's dog would know that to be so.'

I smile weakly. 'You make my head spin, Mother.'

Chapter 15 – Crushing the Flower

'Excuse me, miss, would your name be Valerie now?"

I look the man up and down. Maybe he has bought flowers here before, but how can he possibly know my name? I certainly do not recognise him, this middle-aged *witman,* but I recognise the uniform and, on his cap, the gold and green insignia of the Cape Government Railways.

As if reading my thoughts the railwayman continues politely, 'I beg your pardon, miss, for not introducing myself. I am Clarence Begg, a colleague of Mr John Fox of Rondebosch, and I have been asked to locate a young lady by the name of Valerie, and to pass her an important message...'

'Your search is over, *meneer,*' interrupts the flower seller. 'I am Valerie.'

The man tells me there has been an accident, an injury to 'Master James'; he tells me that I should make my way to Rondebosch as soon as possible.

'What injury, *meneer?*' I hear myself ask. 'Please tell me now or I will worry myself sick.'

'I have no details, nothing at all beyond what I've just told you. Farewell now, miss.' And as suddenly as he had appeared, just as suddenly Mr Begg was gone, blended back into the Adderley Street crowds.

. . . .

When Siti, my friend at the flower stall, sees me, immediately she knows, presumably by some sort of process of female intuition, that I desperately need to go, and without any fuss she merely says, 'Leave now, Valerie. I'll take care of everything.'

I am not inclined to argue with Siti, so I hand her my morning's takings of eighteen shillings, collect my warm-as-toast *kaross* (which *ouma* herself had lovingly made for me from a bundle of *dassie* pelts) and I go directly to Cape Town Station, as it is just a few minutes' walk from our flower stalls.

What has happened to James? It must be serious if he is home in Rondebosch? And why did I not hear from him soon after he docked as I usually do?

I pray that one day we will have a normal life, a little home somewhere, and regular working arrangements where James will come home each day, in time for dinner and, who knows, maybe in time to read the kids a bedtime story? I am not much good at reading myself; please do not judge me harshly for that. I know it, and sometimes I feel it keenly, but what I might lack in education I know I make up for in enthusiasm and hard work. After all, surely what matters is what we do with what we have, rather than being miserable about what will never be ours?

How did it happen that James and I found each other in the way we did? Are people not whispering that our connection is not meant to be, that there is something not quite right about a dark-skinned *maleier* girl being with a blue-eyed *engelsman?* Be that as it may, what I do know is that I have chosen this man and, if it is not right that I did so, then I shall account for it in the hereafter, rather than to the whisperers concealing themselves behind their lounge curtains, from where they watch the world and pass their small-minded judgments upon all who pass their way.

Woodstock, Salt River, Observatory – the train winds its way out of the city, counting off the stations as it goes, but I hardly notice, my mind being preoccupied with a hundred thoughts and reflections. And almost before I know it, I am in Rondebosch, with just a short walk ahead of me to Main Road.

As I approach within sight of *Harrow* with its unkempt hedge of hawthorn and wild privet, I hesitate. What if there is something seriously wrong? What if today of all days there is to be an almighty convergence of what ifs?

Silly woman! I shake my head vigorously to dislodge my girlish thoughts. Just a few more steps now – to *Harrow* and to my beloved James.

. . . .

Why was I worried so? Here I am with James now, my face generously covered with kisses, and my mind relieved to see that he is still the James I know, even with the addition of a heavy cast to his leg.

'I've been thinking Valerie,' he says, pausing a second to ensure my undivided attention. 'I think I misjudged what it would be like to be a lightkeeper. I haven't been in the job long enough... I have already seen two people die, as if by the hand of evil...'

'Ssshh, James,' I say soothingly. 'Your accident has been a shock to you. In a few weeks when your leg has mended, I'm confident you'll feel brighter about everything.'

'I suppose you're right,' James sighs. 'I think the pain is getting to me. Do you mind asking mother if she has some *muti* to dull this pain? It's driving me mad.'

'Is it there all the time?'

'Yes, I'd have expected it to go away now that the leg is in a cast, but not at all. I think the bone sliced a nerve or something. It's bloody intolerable.'

Mrs Fox (maybe I will also be Mrs Fox soon, then we will have to work out a way of telling us apart!) - anyway, the present Mrs Fox is unfussed by the request for a painkiller and she promptly removes from behind a tall and skinny blue bottle of castor oil, a little rectangular bottle labelled *Morphine Sulphate.*

'This is good stuff!' declares *Tannie* Eva (which is the name I call Mrs Eva Fox, this woman being probably a good ten years older than my mother.) 'Give James double the recommended dose,' she orders, 'to expel the pain quickly. It'll make him groggy, mind you, but groggy is better than agony.'

Tannie Eva seems experienced in the matter of pain relief, so I follow her directions and, sure enough, within minutes I detect the departure of strain from the patient's face. I kiss him gently on the forehead saying, 'Rest, dear James, we will talk later,' and I return to the kitchen to seek out the lady of the house.

Tannie Eva and I have been getting on really well. Not long ago she confessed to me that since her daughters - James's elder siblings, Emma and Louisa were now away for an extended time – Louisa as a live-in nurse trainee at Addington Hospital in Durban and Emma, also temporarily in Durban, working with the Women's Enfranchisement League - she misses them terribly, but now it gladdens her to have, from time to time, a young female presence about the house again. Although James's mother has not actually said it in words, I suspect, too, that she has a soft spot for me on account our shared *coloured* blood. Our roots grew from the same faraway fields, distant places of disfavour and disadvantage.

Since my mother and Maria now share the big bed in our Leeuwen Street room, I have found it convenient, and agreeable, whenever possible, to occupy Maria's empty bed at *Harrow*. And *Tannie* Eva is glad for the company, maybe because I instinctively know to leave her alone when she gets in one of what she calls her 'spiritual moods,' those times when she gets a faraway look in her eyes and removes herself from the kitchen, times she claims when she can communicate with the dead and the yet-to-be-born. I am the first to say that I do not understand any of this stuff even though my mother has told me stories from her childhood of a *toordokter,* a being who could supposedly levitate and disconnect his spirit from his sleeping body. I questioned *Tannie* Eva about the business of disconnecting the spirit from the body and she showed me a passage from the Bible (2 Corinthians 12) which she said proved it all, though I must admit it made very little sense to me.

I offer to take a week off from selling flowers, time to be close to dear James during his convalescence. *Tannie* Eva thinks this is a splendid idea and she slips me a gold half-sovereign, saying, 'Here, my girl, take this and don't stress yourself about not earning any money this week.'

I begin to protest about the generous gift but my mother-in-law-to-be cuts me short. 'What do you think I have some savings for? Surely not to pay myself a fancy coffin?' Well, that put out that discussion before I could light the kindling for it! So, I graciously accept the coin and make up my mind to start myself a little savings by setting aside half the value for the future.

The next morning there is a knock at the door.

Being up and about, I attend to the knock. And who is more surprised, the caller or the occupant? Standing before me, upright and confident and dressed in expensive-looking attire, is a lady of some presence.

'Good morning,' I say and, before I can think what to say next, the caller speaks. 'Please inform Mr Fox that Mrs Richardson is here and ask him if it is convenient if I step inside to ask him about his health.'

I am used to bossy *witmense,* yet this white woman's superiority is something to behold. But I have learnt how to play the role of the agreeable little being, the humble and obedient servant. I let the woman in and ask her to wait.

I tap on James's door and there is no response. Glimpsing inside and noting that he is fast asleep, I retreat and inform the caller that he is resting. 'Do not disturb him then,' she orders, 'I shall leave him a small gift at his bedside, then I'll be gone from here,' and without invitation, her majesty walks right past me and glides into James's room.

I watch her from a discreet position in the passage as she removes from her richly beaded reticule a small book which she places at the bedside. Then she reaches across the sleeping James and brushes his cheek with a kiss. Quickly I shift from her view and, like a respectful maidservant, I wait for her to reappear in the passage.

'Be sure to tell him that Mrs Richardson called and tell him that I expect to be back in a day or two,' she orders as she brushes past me on her way to the front door. 'I'll let myself out' and even before I can say, 'nice to meet you, too,' she is gone.

What do I make of the visit? And the attractive but mannerless visitor? I try to repress any feeling of jealousy by telling myself that the lady is merely showing care and concern for my James, that there cannot be any more to it. Clearly her majesty is simply wanting to know, firsthand as they say, the condition of her injured subject? I tell myself off for being so small-minded and I promise myself not to allow my mind to run off on wild imaginings.

A while later I check on James. He is still fast asleep, breathing heavily. There's an empty teacup beside his bed which I reach to take away, when I notice the book, the volume left for James by his lady caller.

There is a note protruding slightly from the book. Well, I do not suppose it will matter if I just glance at the note, will it now? I admit it, curiosity is winning. I want to know who this woman is, and I want to know what she is saying to my James. If this offends you, I apologise.

It is a small book, well-worn, grubby, and it appears that at some point its spine has been repaired, somewhat sloppily, with glue and cloth, the cloth quite roughly trimmed to fit. The title, *The Lustful Turk,* is faded but legible, and the author, *Anonymous.* Not a writer I know.

Opening up the book at a random place in the story, the following passages catch my eye; *I got between her thighs, and laying myself on her, entreated her to say she loved me,* and, further down the page; *...I had stripped her entirely naked, having nothing but a loose robe on myself. In this state I directed her* *to lean on the couch with her face downwards...* and, even more; *The ecstasy seized me, I discharged myself into her...*

Never did I know that such things could be written in a book! Who would read such a thing and who would give another person such a thing to read? I feel hot and cold just thinking about it. Who exactly is this Mrs Richardson and what business does she have with James? What intimate thoughts do they share that she can hand him such a book?

And then there is the note, propped carefully into the book. The neatly written words burn into my already overcooked mind:

> *Dear James*
>
> *I am waiting with some expectancy for you to be better.*
>
> *Meanwhile, do read with care the words within these pages and find some account to raise your manly spirit.*
>
> *Till later*
>
> *R.*

I glance at James. He is still asleep, so, without any thought or consideration for what I am doing, I take the book and the note and I hurry from the room.

What will I do now? I race to my bed and, hurriedly, I stuff the offensive objects under the mattress coir. I have no idea what I might end up doing with them but, by instinct, I know that I want to separate them from James. I do not know what to think beyond this moment or where the situation will drive me next, although, in some small way, the action of removing the items from his room makes me feel as if I have taken a decisive step.

What dark secrets are there between James and that woman? For how long have they been so intimate? And, while things are happening on that island, am I being treated like a toy doll, a thing to be caressed for a moment on a whim and then discarded in a corner like an old slipper? Bitterly I think, *Am I just his Cape Town flower, a throwaway thing blowing in the wind?*

....

I cannot bring myself to say anything to James. Not yet. I guess I am hoping, unrealistically but hopefully, that James will speak to me about Mrs Richardson, about his conduct on that island. Maybe there is, somehow, some explanation to be offered? I am just a *meisie,* a little thing, but I believe I have a big heart and that I deserve some happiness. How is it then that this man can trick me so? Does he sit around on that island with his lightkeeper pals and entertain them with tales of his ever-willing flower seller? And what, just what, does he tell that woman, the amazing Mrs Richardson, about me? Does he describe in detail, like that horrible little book, how I bend and twist my body to satisfy his desires? It is all too much to endure, and I remove myself from the house and take a long walk along Main Road for several miles to Mowbray and beyond. I want to cry; I want to scream; but the tears will not come, and the scream is strangled in my throat.

I tell James that Mrs Richardson called. He seems mildly surprised, and then I think slightly alarmed when I inform him that she intends to call again soon. Now why would he be alarmed? Does he have something to hide from me? My mind is still unsettled, and I am not entirely sure why I have returned to *Harrow* after my long walk. What exactly is it that I, Valerie the Flower Seller, am hoping for? And I ask you, is a hopeful heart not a common problem with young women everywhere?

Mrs Richardson does come back, conveyed to the address by private carriage, and she appears on the threshold of *Harrow* in considerable splendour, a modern diva. Standing there in her generously feathered hat, snow white bodice and elegant black skirts, she looks for all the world like Miss Sarah Bernhardt, just arrived at the theatre.

Again, I let her in, but today I neglect to greet her, and I reply with a simple 'Yes' when she asks if 'Mr Fox' is awake and ready to receive a visitor. Her majesty glances at me disapprovingly, then she sails past the little cockroach at the door and makes her way directly to James's room.

Again, I position myself to spy on the interaction between James and the caller, and I no longer feel any guilt about what I am doing. The man in that room is supposed to be my future husband; I have a right to know what is going on. The possibility that, when presented with a multi-dish menu, James the *engelsman,* seemingly so devoted to me, will choose a serving of white meat before all others, fills my mind with fury at the unfairness of my existence. How, I ask you, can I fight against the right that comes with whiteness?

'Hello, James,' I hear the visitor say, 'I had to see how my patient is doing. No, don't move now.' And, saying this, she grasps his hands in hers, leans forward and kisses him on the lips. 'You need me to nurse you,' she whispers, 'I'll have you standing upright like a sentry in no time at all...'

'Quiet, Rowena!' the patient protests, 'now do be careful what you say...'

'Why?' she cuts him short, 'are you embarrassed to have a real woman in your bedroom? Really, James, here I am thinking you are a real man, a man who knows what a woman wants.' James does not answer. Rowena relents a little, kisses the injured man again, and observes quietly, 'You'll be better soon enough and then we'll talk again. Meanwhile, do tell me - and share your inmost impressions with me of the content, James - of the little gift I left for you?'

'Gift? What gift would that be?'

'You know, the little book, filled as it is with wonderful surprises. Have you read any of it?'

'There's no book here,' replies James, sweeping his arm about the room. I think you must be mistaken...'

'No! Not at all,' interjects Rowena Richardson, 'I left it right here on the bedside stand, and there was a note in it.'

'Note?'

'Yes, you heard me, James. A note. Now, what have you done with it? I hope your mother hasn't cleared it away? Or the servant girl stolen it?' The visitor's voice is rising now, her agitation beginning to show.

'There's no servant girl here...'

Rowena cuts him short. 'You know perfectly well, James, that I'm speaking of the girl who is lurking about in this house. Call her here and ask here about the book! Do it now!'

Then, as James does not respond promptly to the woman's orders, she turns from the bed to the door and I am barely quick enough to melt down the passage before the diva is filling the doorway of the bedroom and calling; 'Girl! Come here now! Just you step inside this room.'

Surprised, and momentarily stunned by the caller's imperious tone, I approach, and I meekly step inside the bedroom, like an obedient child. For that moment I decide to comply and to see what comes of this situation.

'Tell me girl, did you see a slim book here at the bedside?'

'Yes, madam,' I reply, playing along with her perception of me as a servant, 'I saw it.'

'Well, girl,' continues Mrs Richardson with considerable impatience, 'kindly tell me where the book is now.'

'That's not so easy,' I respond, pretending to fumble with my thoughts, 'in fact, I'm not entirely sure...'

'Not sure! Not sure! What the fuck do you mean not sure?'

'Well, madam,' I hesitatingly begin while I make a show of vigorously rubbing my forehead, 'I believe that when I finished reading the book that I may've used the pages to light the stove or, come to think of it, I may've donated it to the Salvation Army collector who called here yesterday...'

'Valerie!' James attempts to stop me, 'Valerie, what has got into you?'

'It's pretty clear to me what's got into the little wench, James, and it's more than just a little insolence I can tell you...'

'Rowena, shut up!

'Did you read that book?' Rowena demands to know from me, 'tell me now!'

'Why yes, madam, of course I did, cover to cover, and I found it very instructive. The book informed me in no uncertain way what been happening between you and Mr James Fox.'

'Wait, Valerie, for God's sake, wait...'

'Wait for what, dear sweet James, when it's perfectly clear to me what you and this *ouvrou,* this sad old whore, have been doing behind my back?'

I am near to falling to pieces, and fighting back tears of anger and humiliation, as I turn from this room, from this house, and from the pain of this connection.

....

Stupid, stupid me! I should have known better than to give my heart away so easily and so freely.

Chapter 16 – The Edge of Despair

'What happened, James?' The voice belongs to Bayes. Or I think it does.

Am I dreaming or is he here?

The morphine sulphate works wonders for the pain but it alters my perception to a point where I am unsure whether I am sitting on a cloud or just dreaming about it. By turn I hear voices, and I hear the deep well of silence, the curious silence which waits for the stone to drop far below into the water. As for my body, the bundle of skin and bones and muscles, it does not know properly whether it is hot or cold, whether it wants to thunder like a wave against the breakwater, whether it wants to ping like a horsefly against a pane of glass, or whether it wants to drift aimlessly like a lump of flotsam on the surface of my consciousness.

'James!' It is Bayes, and he is not going away. 'Wake up, James! It's your favourite brother here.' By God, it is Bayes; only he would give me that 'favourite brother' line.

Although I hate him at times, I guess he has to be my favourite male sibling because, if the story be told, Bayes is the only brother I really know. My other brothers, Charles and Albert, left home when I was just nine or ten years old to scratch for gold in Pilgrim's Rest and they have not been home since. Several times they have written to father, at first to plead for a few pounds for essential provisions, but in more recent times to tell father of their success. Charles and Albert turned up too late in Pilgrim's Rest to find much gold, but what they did find was an opportunity for the cartage of machinery, equipment and provisions for the growing town and that is how the firm of Fox & Fox, Cartage Contractors, became well known throughout the Eastern Transvaal, the Lowveld and beyond, to Portuguese East Africa and to the port of Delagoa Bay.

Now my brain has connected with my mind and Bayes has my attention, and he repeats his question, 'What happened, James?'

'Depends what you're talking about, Bayes. If you're talking about my leg, I fell down the stairwell at the lightstation. On the other hand, if you're referring to an argument which happened here between Valerie and Mrs Richardson, I have no bloody idea what that was all about...'

'This Mrs Richardson,' interrupts Bayes, 'have you been pleasuring her behind Valerie's back? Tell me the truth now.'

I shake my head and pull a face at Bayes. 'She's nearly mother's age.'

'Jesus, James, what's wrong with you? Opportunity comes to us in all shapes and sizes and at the most unexpected times. One day you'll be sitting in your rocking chair, and you'll think back to this time, shake your white-haired head and wonder why you let this fish go.'

'Bayes! Shut up, will you!' He is being typical Bayes, talking shit, lighting the fuse. 'I'll tell you the whole truth, Bayes, if only you'll listen for a minute. And the price for the truth is a huge favour, the sort of deed I may only expect from my favourite brother.'

'Speak, James! You have a deal. Now, I'll probably regret doing business with you but, hey, what are brothers for?'

I tell him all I know, and I conclude the brief history of James and Rowena with this remark; 'You see, Bayes, nothing happened. Not yet and maybe never.'

Bayes says nothing, seems to be processing the information and to be weighing whether I have revealed the whole naked truth.

'Now, Bayes, let's talk about the favour. Being a man of your word, I have no doubt that you'll do precisely what I ask...'

'Do get on, James! Let me have the pain of it.' My brother pretends to stumble under the weight of the cross I am placing on his back. 'Speak,' he urges me.

'I need you to go to Adderley Street and to Trafalgar Place, and possibly also to an address in Leeuwen Street and make some enquiry concerning the whereabouts of Valerie. When you find her – which you must – tell her I have to speak to her, that there appears to be some great misunderstanding. Tell her, too, if you will, that I love her...'

'Enough,' says Bayes, 'I'll do what you ask, but I'll leave the love bit for you to tell her yourself.'

. . . .

Am I imaging it or had Rowena and Valerie been standing in my bedroom arguing about a book? A book I never even saw. And if they were quarrelling, whatever was so important about a mere book to ignite an argument? One moment they were there, and the next minute both women were gone. I am still young, and you may say inexperienced in the ways of the lioness of the human species, and I am damned if I can say what took place before my eyes. What happened here, in this very room?

Mother has no explanation, and she says she was out when Mrs Richardson called. Mother being as insightful as she is, does think that one or both women may have misunderstood the situation of the other. I ask mother to explain what she means by 'situation.'

'It's like this, James,' begins Mother. 'Consider these questions. Firstly, does Mrs Richardson know that Valerie is your fiancée? Secondly, is Valerie aware that Mrs Richardson is the wife of the chief lightkeeper and that, in consideration of the seriousness of your injury, she was asked by her husband to accompany you here?'

I acknowledge that mother's view is probably correct, but it still does not explain how a mere book could cause such an almighty stir.

Now my head hurts and my leg hurts! And I ask my nurse-mother for another dose of morphine sulphate and nurse-mother complies but she looks at me keenly before saying what is on her mind. 'I'm afraid, James, very much afraid, that you're becoming addicted to this painkiller. Sleep now, my boy, but from tomorrow I'm giving you no more of this stuff. There's no value acquiring...'

Somewhat annoyed by Mother's seemingly sudden and harsh decision to discontinue the painkiller, I interject irritably, 'Yes, Mother, now please give me my dose that I may sleep.'

Chapter 17 – A Hesitant Spring

The only good news I have is that the pain in my leg is subsiding; it must be mending now.

For four or five days, my body and mind protested at the withdrawal from the sweet comfort of my painkiller. I suffered variously from aches and pains, sweats and chills, blurred vision and loss of appetite. I was unsettled and unhappy in the extreme; unsure if it was day or night, uncertain whether I wanted to live or die.

Adding to my malaise are Bayes's reports that, try as he might, he has no news of Valerie. She is no longer selling flowers and she is no longer living at Leeuwen Street, and she did not even tell Aminah where she was going. She disappeared, along with her clothes and a bead purse containing her savings. Seemingly no one knows where she went. Or no one is willing to say.

Aminah and Maria come to *Harrow*, come to look for some clues concerning Valerie's sudden and out of character departure. I endure Aminah's wailing, but I cannot help the woman. I feel like wailing myself, like breaking something - or someone - to relieve the tension in my mind, but I control myself and sublimate my urge to destroy by writing a rambling journal, by hurling and flinging words onto paper, by purging the consternation of my brain with ink and nibbed pen.

I am restless. Restless to be rid of this damned plaster cast and restless to look for Valerie. Confound Rowena Richardson! What did that siren do when I was incapable of looking?

....

It is mother (who else?) who finds the evidence to solve the mystery of Valerie's disappearance and Rowena Richardson's hasty departure.

When it became clear to my mother that Valerie was no longer going to be using her bedroom at *Harrow*, she ventured into the room to pack up a few trinkets belonging to my fiancée. Once in the room, she knew – let us say intuitively – that there was something concealed there, so she checked in the wardrobe and the tallboy, going as far as removing the drawers of the tallboy to check behind and under. Finding nothing, she stripped the bed and shifted the mattress, and that is when she discovered Rowena's grimy little book. *The Lustful Turk* looked at my mother and she looked right back at it and it took her all of two minutes to deduce that it was the lustful volume which was the cause of so much trouble.

'Well, James, there you have it,' says mother in conclusion of her explanation. 'My I ask, what now? Where do you think Valerie may be, and what can be done about that Richardson woman?'

I take a minute or two before I answer, then I hear myself saying helplessly, 'I don't know. I really don't know. It seems to me that maybe I have no control about how my troubles can be solved. Once I'm up and about and walking, no doubt I'll feel stronger and more resolved, but, right now, I feel about as useful as half an umbrella in a thunderstorm.'

What I do not know, but soon find out, is that the storm clouds are building, and moving closer.

Now I make the effort to walk, with the help of a crutch which father has improvised for me. First, I walk up and down the hallway; six times, twelve times, twenty times. Then I venture out along Main Road; 100 yards, 400 yards. A little further every day.

One afternoon I return from my walk to find a horse hitched at the gate and the rider at our front door. He is very official looking, a member of the Cape Mounted Police, a bear of a man who looks ready to erupt from the constriction of his tunic.

The upholder of the law turns to me. 'Do you live here, sir? There's no answer at the door."

'I am James Fox, a resident here...'

'Well now,' the policeman cuts me short, 'just the man I want to see. May I come in?'

Mother is nowhere to be seen within as I lead the bear into the kitchen, and I beckon him to take a seat, father's seat, near the stove.

Without further formality, the policeman comes straight to the point. 'I am Lt.Guilfoyle, sir, and I'm here on the orders of the Colonial Secretary to inquire into the sudden and violent death of a kaffir labourer named Diamond, a former employee of the Harbour Board.'

The man pauses to scan my face as he announces his business and I say nothing, so he continues; 'Mr Fox, I understand you knew the deceased and that you spoke to him on a number of occasions? And I understand that this labourer was planning to kill Mr Alfred Pike, a lightkeeper, and to sabotage the Dassen Island lightstation...'

'What!' I exclaim involuntarily, 'I think you have been given the wrong information.'

'How so?'

'This man Diamond was a hard worker, and although he was certainly a big and strong Zulu, I don't believe he ever hurt a fly. I believe I knew the fellow well, well enough to know that he was a loyal and honest worker.'

The policeman regards me strangely, almost distastefully. 'Do I detect Mr Fox that you are being defensive about the actions of a kaffir? Perhaps Mr

Richardson is right when he says that he believes that you were encouraging, perhaps even aiding and abetting, the actions of the deceased?'

'What the devil! Why would he make such an outrageous accusation?'

'I don't rightly know, Mr Fox,' says the lieutenant while extracting his notebook. 'I suppose that is why I'm here today, to hear your side of the story. Please tell me everything you know, from the very first day you encountered the deceased.'

I pour myself a cup of water and offer the policeman a cup, which he accepts. And I recount to my guest everything I know of Diamond and his actions. Which really is not much at all.

'You say that the kaffir was a peaceful man,' asks my inquisitor, 'then how do you explain his possession of an *assegaai* and his movements in the dead of night while clutching the weapon?'

'I cannot explain that,' I reply simply, 'I never saw a violent side to Diamond's character.'

'Do you think it was the man's intention to spear Mr Alfred Pike?'

'The circumstance of the kaffir seeking Mr Pike at his quarters in the middle of the night suggests to me that he had serious business with the lightkeeper, but what his business was I can't say, although I suspect it wasn't to share a few drams of *vaaljapie*.'

'Do you think Mr Richardson or Mr Van Staden were in any sort of danger in the moment Mr Van Staden shot the Zulu dead? Why would armed men have anything to fear from a single man brandishing a spear?'

'I have myself wondered about the shooting, but I was laid up with a broken leg and unconscious in bed when this happened; I don't know the answers to your questions, sir.'

The policeman lifts his bearlike frame from the kitchen chair, pockets his notebook and he leaves me with the following observation: 'You have been most cooperative, Mr Fox, and I think candid, too. As there were no witnesses to the shooting other than Richardson and Van Staden themselves, I guess that leaves me with just their unverified testimony and no further avenue of inquiry.'

'Where does that leave me, sir?' I ask dubiously, not fully comprehending what the investigator has just said to me.

'Well, Mr Fox, I'll recommend the matter be closed as I have no evidence of wrongdoing and, as I said, nowhere left to make any further inquiry. Expect to hear nothing further about this. Thank you, sir, and good day.'

Now, if Richardson thinks I was helping Diamond to commit a murderous and subversive act, where does that leave me? How can I possibly hope to return to my duties on the island? And how is it, I wonder, that Mr Richardson seems to have turned against me?

Which leaves me with the thousand-pound question; what has Rowena been saying?

. . . .

My cast is off! I am a free man again and my leg is well healed. The muscles are wasted by lack of use but, after being thoroughly bored by weeks of inactivity, I am pushing to regain my strength and endurance and, to do this, I am now taking longer walks, each day walking further and faster, almost to the point of wearing a new track into Rondebosch Common.

There is, of course, a second reason for rushing to recover my fitness. I am planning to go searching for Valerie and, to be sure, this may be a long and arduous task. She could be anywhere.

In my long hours of enforced immobility my mind has often turned to the problem of where to find Valerie. Bayes says – and I have no reason to disbelieve him – that she is no longer selling flowers in Adderley Street. Maybe she has friends or acquaintances outside the city? Maybe even far away, in Calvinia, or Laingsburg, or Swellendam? I suppose the logical place to start my search is in the flower-growing areas near Cape Town, such as the farmlands between Constantia and Steenberg, the Parow valley and out towards Klapmuts and Mamre. There is a dreadful lot of ground to cover!

What, I wonder, is the likelihood of Valerie contacting her mother before long? Given their closeness, a high probability I should think, but will Aminah bring herself to tell me? Although I believe I have had a good rapport with her, as you know, so often in these matters blood is thicker than water and, if Aminah believes she is acting to protect her little flower from the treacherous *witman*, then she will do nothing for me.

My ponderings about finding Valerie are still pacing around my mind when they are brought to a brick-wall halt by the arrival of a registered letter. From the Harbour Board.

A letter which will change everything.

Chapter 18 – The Hoerkind

Yesterday, I was eating my bread and minding my own business when Velna, one of the big girls at Mrs Oosthuizen's school, came to sit next to me on the log bench and came right out and said to me, *'My ma sê jou ma is 'n tweesjieling hoer. Wat sê jy nou,* Gina?'

I did not know the meaning of what a two-bob whore might be, but I know enough to know that calling someone a *hoer* is a nasty thing to do; it is like saying someone is a *domkop* or a *kakkerlak.*

I knew better than to answer Velna, so I just looked down at the ground and kept chewing my bread. No one messes with fifteen-year-old Velna; she's big and nasty and ready to torment anyone younger and smaller than herself.

So, I kept my mouth shut and, in the evening, while shoveling fish stew into my gob, I asked Ma to tell me the meaning of *tweesjieling hoer.* Her response was very quick and very to the point; the back of her open hand hit me smartly across my eleven-year-old face as she screamed, 'How dare you use such words in this house! Never, ever, let me hear you speak like that again!' And the next moment my mother was holding her head between her hands and sobbing loudly.

Timidly, my face still stinging from the slap, I placed my hand on her shoulder. She shuddered, briefly stopped her wailing, gasped for breath, and whispered hoarsely, 'I'm so sorry, Gina. My life has been very hard since your father died.'

I waited, and after a minute she continued; 'I am so afraid for you, Gina. Afraid that you'll end up like me, like...' Her voice dribbled away, and she was sobbing again. Long, terrible sobs.

. . . .

My name is Rainha Daisy da Cunha and for now I am eleven years old; at least for a few more weeks, until 13th February, when I turn twelve.

Six months ago my father, Antonio, died on Dassen Island while testing a new diving helmet and I miss him very much and sometimes, when I wake up in the quiet of the night, I cry for him until my pillow is soaked. He was a good man, always kind to everyone, even to the *boemelaars* and the *bedelaars.*

Antonio da Cunha, my father, was a salvage diver and his connection with the sea is a family tradition which goes back to the year 1506, when our ancestor, Tristão da Cunha, a famous Portuguese navigator, discovered the islands of Tristan da Cunha, way out in the mid-Atlantic Ocean. The story goes that the weather was too rough for Tristão to land, but, whether he did or not, that does not alter the fact that he was the first man to see the islands.

My name, Rainha, means 'Queen' in Portuguese. As you may expect, Rainha got shortened to 'Inha', but 'Inha' was often mistaken as 'Gina' to the extent that almost everyone now calls me Gina. My mother wanted to call me Daisy, after the colourful and delicate Namaqualand daisy, a happy flower which always smiles when facing the sun. In the end I got both names, with the royal 'Rainha' in first place. But, unlike most children of a Roman Catholic family, I missed out on getting a baptismal name like Maria or Magdalena, for the simple reason that my parents never got around to getting me baptised.

My mother, Christa, rarely speaks about her past. From the few bits and pieces of information I have pasted together, I think she comes from up north, and that she has two sisters, but she does not know where they are. As for Christa, she was taken away (or ran away?) from a place where there was a mission church.

I think a mission church is a special kind of church where heathens get turned into Christians, but I am not sure how it works or why anyone would want to make the change. No one has explained this to me. Ma did not learn much at the mission church and she does not want anyone to know that she cannot read or write. Ma said her name Christa means 'servant of Christ' and when I asked her what that means, she said, with a wry look on her face, it means that a woman should give to man, the living embodiment of Christ, whatever he wants. I did not understand her explanation, and I soon lost interest in the subject.

....

I wonder about the two-bob whore business though. Now, I am not a little kid, and I do know that a whore is a woman who shares her bedroom with men who pay her to be there. What exactly happens in the bedroom I am not really sure but, one day, when my friends Huibrie and Sarie and I are walking down the road looking for adventure, we come across a pair of dogs mating furiously or, at least, the male is pounding his arched body furiously into the submissive female, and Sarie says to me that this is what men and women do in bedrooms when they close the door. I ask Sarie how she knows this, and she says that one Sunday afternoon when her parents must have thought she was out playing, they carelessly neglected to shut the bedroom door, and Sarie looked on mesmerised, and in dry-mouthed amazement, at the rise and fall of her father's body as he thrust himself upon her mother.

I ask Sarie why some men will pay money to a woman to thrust her body, and she says she believes the man gets a big thrill from this activity, that it excites him, possibly in the same way as riding a bicycle as fast as possible down a steep hill. Then I ask Sarie if the woman gets a thrill, but Sarie says she does not know and that she is not about to ask her mother.

After this question-and-answer session, some things are beginning to make sense to me.

Men have been coming to our house at odd times and, when Ma opens the door, there is a whispered conversation and then Ma and the man go to her bedroom and close the door.

Sometimes I hear noises from the room, sometimes not, and mostly the men leave after half an hour. A few times Ma has reappeared after one of these episodes with marks on her face and tears in her eyes, but she says nothing to me. I have been told though that when we have 'visitors' (as my mother calls the men at the door) that I am to disappear and to be totally quiet until the visitor has gone.

It is understood between mother and me that I should ask no questions about what is going on. What happens in grown up bedrooms is clearly not a subject for discussion with children.

As for the two-bob price for a woman's body, well, I cannot say if that is right or whether the price should be higher or lower. For me two shillings is a lot of money; sixpence is the most I have ever had myself.

We live in a whitewashed stone house, on the track to the Jacobsbaai farm, on the outskirts of Saldanha town. It is an old place with two tiny bedrooms leading off the dining room, the roof leaks in places, and the sash window in my room is stuck in the closed position. When it is windy, which is often, the seagulls come further inland, and it is possible to hear the boom of breakers somewhere in the distance. It is here on this saltbush wasteland where my father first took me to try our hand at flying a kite, a colourful box contraption which he fashioned with a sturdy bamboo frame and fabric panels, small remnants of cloth which he sourced from heaven-knows-where. We shared many hours out here with Cachorro, our woolly-haired dog, with the wind in our faces and the kite weaving and bobbing high above our heads.

The nearest neighbour is the Steenkamp couple, their place being just where the track curves downwards towards the village. Mr Steenkamp works at the harbour where he is some sort of official who wears a dark uniform with gold braid on the sleeves, but Mrs Steenkamp rarely leaves her house as she is crippled in one leg, Ma said Mrs Steenkamp had polio which shrank the muscles in her leg, and now a widow, Mrs Gouws, a very old woman of more than fifty years old, lives with the Steenkamps and helps Johanna Steenkamp with the housekeeping in exchange for a room. But things are about to change for the Steenkamps. And for me.

. . . .

I know something is in the air when Ma tells me to have a good wash, to pay particular attention to my ears, and to change into my Sunday dress.

'Are we going somewhere, Ma?'

'No, Rainha, we're staying right here.' For a moment Ma keeps me guessing before satisfying my curiosity. 'No, we are staying here at home, but we're expecting guests.' It does not sound like more of the usual guests, so I stare at Ma, waiting for another morsel of information, like a puppy waiting for a piece of gristle. 'You see,' says my mother, the Steenkamps are coming over. They say they have something really important to talk to us about.'

Late afternoon the Steenkamps turn up, Mrs Steenkamp riding aboard a small Cape cart drawn by a bored looking little donkey, with Mr Steenkamp leading the donkey. I wonder why Ma and I did not simply walk the half mile down the track to the Steenkamp house, but I say nothing. As we know, it is not for children to question their elders.

Johanna Steenkamp is a frail birdlike woman, and her husband lifts her easily from the Cape cart. Her eyes are sharp and bright like the eyes of a crow, and her raven-like image is accentuated by the black crocheted shawl across her shoulders and the coal-black of her hair and eyebrows. I get the distinct impression that this woman is all-seeing and all-knowing and that it would be impossible to conceal anything from her. In contrast to his wife, Willem Steenkamp is a slender man, well groomed, and ever-so-dapper in his braided uniform. There is something odd and curious about the couple, but I am not experienced enough in these matters to say what exactly is odd other than to notice the curious, catlike way in which Mr Steenkamp walks and moves his hands. I have never seen anything like it.

'*Middag, mevrou*,' Steenkamp greets my mother as he approaches while supporting the hobbling Mrs Steenkamp. 'I dare say, it's *fris* outdoors today.'

The raven is more to the point, and she looks directly at me. 'So, *mevrou*, this is the girl?'

'Yes,' replies Ma, 'this is Rainha. Most people call her Gina. It's easier to say. Do come in please, out of this chilly breeze.'

I may only be a child, but from this brief exchange between the women, I get the clear impression that that have spoken before. That is to say, about me.

Soon the adults are settled around the kitchen table, each with a tumbler of brandy 'to warm them from the inside'. Ma has beckoned me to sit at the table with the adults.

'Well, now,' begins Mr Steenkamp, speaking in a serious and measured tone like a schoolteacher, 'we – that is Mrs Steenkamp and myself – we have a proposition for the two of you, and I urge you to give our proposition very serious consideration. We are not in the habit of acting hastily or without forethought ...'

'For God's sake, Willem!' interrupts his wife, 'get to the point.'

'Why, yes, Johanna, of course. Our proposal is that Gina here comes to live with us…'

'No!' I protest, 'I want to stay with Ma. No! No! No!' and I move to rise from my chair but, deftly, Ma blocks me with her arm and orders me to stay.

'*Wag 'n bietjie*, Rainha, and listen to the man. Mr Steenkamp is a kind man and he'll not hurt you.'

Again, I get the distinct feeling that my mother has already discussed the matter at hand with the visitors, and that, whatever this is about, now they are ready to enlighten me, rather than to ask me.

Willem Steenkamp clears his throat, and continues, now looking directly at me, 'Gina, we would like you to live with us. And it is fair to ask why, so I'll inform you and then I will answer your questions.' I am not at all reassured by the man's statement, but what can I do? I am just a child.

'As I was saying,' continues Mr Steenkamp, delicately brushing back the hair on his forehead with his fingers, 'we would like you to come and live with us. I've a new position on Robben Island and soon we'll be leaving Saldanha. We're offering you a job as Mrs Steenkamp's helper, and we'll teach you all manner of household skills, and treat you like our own daughter. We have no children, you see, and having you around will give us the opportunity to raise you like our own child. I believe it is God's will that we should do this…'

'But,' I interject (not something I will normally do when speaking with adults), 'tell me why I can't just stay here with Ma?'

'Allow me to answer that question, *meneer*,' offers Ma. 'I believe I can explain it best for Rainha.'

And, so, my mother says to me that she cannot cope now that father has gone; she simply does not have enough money to keep the house and to provide for both of us. Also, she says, now that I can read and write, there is nothing useful left for me to learn at Mrs Oosthuizen's school, and that learning domestic duties will be very useful skills to have in years to come and such skills will no doubt also improve my marriage prospects when I am grown up. She adds that the Steenkamps will pay me eight shillings a month, half of which will be saved for me until I turn eighteen.

Tell me, how would Ma know all this detail if it had not already been settled with the Steenkamps? My mind is filled with horror and with a choking foreboding of what is to come. Is this really happening to me? And how did God get involved in all of this?

I try to protest, I really do, but what chance do I have against three determined adults? They do not seem to care that I will lose my friends, Sarie and Huibrie.

But if I do not see that bully, Velna, again, I do not mind at all, but I do mind, very much, that I cannot bring the woolly, wet-nosed Cachorro with me to Robben Island. And I ask you, where is Robben Island? It sounds so far away. As for Ma, she is shaking and looking ready to die and her eyes are filled with tears, but somehow, she does not actually cry, and all the while Mr and Mrs Steenkamp look on impassively, patiently waiting for my protestations to ebb away.

Chapter 19 – An Unexpected Visitor

I am leaving here, with the Steenkamps, on 14th February in the year 1904, this day being the day after my birthday.

I have come to accept that I have to go, but I do not know how I will fare on a strange island with strange people. Because I am a girl, I am allowed to say that I am scared. So, here you go. I am scared. Very scared.

. . . .

It is not unusual for there to be a knock at the door in the evening, for another man to be calling, but tonight is different.

I hear voices, my mother's voice and a female voice, and they are not whispering but speaking normally. Most of the time adult conversations are boring, you know; all that talk about the weather, the price of *snoek* and *kabeljou* and petticoats, and about the news from Cape Town. Normally it all just makes me sleepy but, like I said, tonight is different.

Tonight, there is something afoot, something even I should know about, so I creep closer to the door in order to hear what is being said.

Mother is saying, 'Do come in and sit down, *mevrou*. I'm sorry, you'll need to sit in the kitchen as I've recently had to sell the lounge furniture to pay some expenses.'

'*Dankie*,' says the voice of the caller. 'Please allow me to introduce myself properly. I'm Gloudina Gouws, from down the track. You know, Mrs Steenkamp's housekeeper. Thank you for seeing me at this hour; I'm afraid I couldn't come earlier. I have to be available at the house...'

'No need to explain,' says Ma. 'Please make yourself comfortable.'

Ma offers the caller some tea and not much is said while she fusses around with the kettle and cups and searches unsuccessfully for the tin of *beskuit* because now there is only the tin, and no *beskuit.*

When the women are settled, my mother asks the older woman politely, 'What brings you here tonight? How can I help you?'

Then Mrs Gouws is talking. 'Maybe I can help you, Mrs Da Cunha. You are wondering why I've come here tonight. I'm not good with words so I'll just say what I have to say the way it comes out of my mouth.'

From my position in the darkness of the doorway I cannot see my mother's face and I have only a side view of Mrs Gouws where she sits at the table. She looks very old. Her hair, where it shows from under a scarf, is completely grey, and her posture is stooped as if her muscles are too weak now to hold her head up and her back straight.

'Please tell me what's troubling you, *mevrou*.' It is my mother speaking.

Mrs Gouws talks now. 'I will come straight out and say it to you that I'm dreadfully worried about your little girl.' Then Mrs Gouws loses her courage, or her words, or both, and she is silent.

'Come now,' encourages my mother, 'let's not have any secrets here. If it makes you feel better I won't tell anyone that you've called.'

'That's a relief. Okay, then, let me speak without interruption or I may forget where I'm at.' There is a little pause before the caller talks again.

'Right,' begins Mrs Gouws, 'I think all my thoughts are in the *kraal* now, so I'll close the gate, and go back to the beginning, back to 1897. I was living in Port Elizabeth, and I remember the year well as we endured the severest flooding in a generation that year and Hennie, my husband, died of sepsis in June, the month after the flood. Now Hennie had been well acquainted with a certain Mr Uppleby, a wealthy and influential merchant and, with the help of a good word from that worthy gentleman combined with a little nursing experience from my younger days, I was lucky enough to secure a position as a carer for Mrs Steenkamp.'

This is starting to sound to me like one of those long, boring adult conversations. You know, the talk about past times and dead people and places which are no longer there, and I am tempted just to glide into my bed, when I detect a change in Mrs Gouws's tone and the phrase, '...bad people, evil to the core...'

My young ears are suddenly interested to hear about the bad people. It is the same fascination as wanting to hear stories of monsters and ghosts and the *tokoloshe*.

Mrs Gouws is saying, '...afraid for the moral safety of your little girl.'

'But why?' asks my mother, 'what's the matter with these people? What troubles you so?'

'Have you heard of an hour house, Mrs Da Cunha?'

'Sadly, yes. But please continue.' I cannot see Ma from my position, and I have to rely only on her words to tell me what she is saying.

The visitor is talking again. 'The Steenkamps lived in a lovely old double storey house, an imposing sandstone place, just a couple of hundred yards from the harbour, and Willem Steenkamp oversaw the bond store and was a very familiar face on the waterfront.

The Steenkamps, being the sort of people they are, saw a business opportunity by virtue of the good fortune of having the big house and by virtue of Willem's employment at the harbour, so they set up their residence as a classy hour house, if ever such a place can be called classy. They catered particularly for people who were willing to pay a little more for privacy and comfort in preference to conducting their lechery in alleys and alcoves. And it turned out to be part of my job, one of many parts I can tell you, to maintain the hour rooms, to ensure a supply of fresh sheets and towels and to replenish the bonbons and brandy decanters and the lamp oil in the rooms. The clients paid the whores and, in turn, the whores paid the Steenkamps for each hour of the use of a room.'

My mother interjects at this point and there is a bitter edge to her voice, 'I know, Mrs Gouws, I know exactly how it works. But please continue, *mevrou*, and when you're done I might just tell you a thing or two myself.'

'Okay then Mrs Cunha...'

'No, please, call me Christa. I'm a lot younger than you, *mevrou*.'

'As I was saying Christa, they set up the hour house and they were doing very well out of it, sometimes taking in several guineas a day, the equivalent of a month's pay for me. But let me tell you, their depravity didn't end there – no, not at all.'

I need to hear about this thing called depravity. I do not know what depravity means but it sounds like it could be interesting, like fire-breathing creatures with three eyes, so I keep my ears pinned to Mrs Gouws's words, and she is saying, '...they set up the hour rooms on either side of an unoccupied room and from the unoccupied room Mr Steenkamp put in place cleverly hidden viewing holes. Both he and Mrs Steenkamp entertained their senses via these viewing holes and, I suppose, this was a sort of sick outlet for their repression...'

Ma's voice cuts in, 'Repression? *Wat sê jy, mevrou*? Didn't they have each other?'

'Oh no, not at all. Allow me to take a step back and explain.' Mrs Gouws pauses, takes a drink of tea, and continues, 'Johanna Steenkamp, as you'll have noticed, is quite deformed by the polio, and let's not be unkind and simply say that she's a singularly unattractive and charmless woman. On the other hand, her brother, Willem...'

'Brother?' interrupts Ma, 'did you say brother?'

'Yes, Christa. I did.'

'*Mevrou*,' I hear my mother say, 'before you continue, I need to pour myself a brandy. Would you care for some yourself?'

The brandy poured, Mrs Gouws picks up her story. 'I dare say, Christa, no man would willingly step forward to marry Johanna and, as for her brother, poor Willem is afflicted by an unnatural attraction to men. Back in the 1880s the Gouws family lived in Hermanus and, back then, Willem wanted to be a *dominee*. But, from what I understood at the time, someone whispered in the ears of the hierarchy of the *Nederlandse Hervormde Kerk* that Willem was a little queer, and potentially a future embarrassment to the NHK. So, rejected by the *Kerk,* Willem resolved to leave Hermanus and start a new life in another place, and that is when he and his sister came up with the idea of pretending that they were a married couple. It was quite easy because, after all, they already had the same surname. Pretending to be married would give them a veneer of respectability and at the same time conceal from general observation Willem's lust for males.'

Now my ears are burning! Never have I heard of such strange carryings-on, and this strengthens my view that most adults are either boring or disgusting. I am not sure I know what Mrs Gouws is saying but if I listen a little longer it may all become clear to me.

The visitor is still talking, now deep into her story, '...and I found myself an employee in that wicked place. But please, Christa, don't judge me for staying there. I had to keep a roof over my head and feed myself – what's that English expression about beggars can't be choosers? I worked hard for every penny and at night before going to sleep I'd pray to the Lord to give me strength and to shield me from the evil around me.'

'You did no wrong, *mevrou,'* says my mother reassuringly. 'Let's have another brandy, shall we, and then you can tell me how you and the Steenkamps washed up here in Saldanha Bay?'

I am feeling dreadfully tired now. Why do grown-ups have to be so longwinded, I ask you? But I will hear this out, or I know I will wonder forever what happened next.

Mrs Gouws is speaking again. 'As you know, Christa, during the war there was a lot of troop movement through our ports, including Port Elizabeth, and demand for rooms at the hour house was huge. All the officer types who didn't fancy competing on the streets or in grubby bars with enlisted men for the attentions of a *hoer* were discreetly invited to the Steenkamp place. Both husband and wife, or brother and sister if you prefer, were not only getting rich but gaining immense satisfaction from their voyeuristic activities. Willem got quite carried away at times, and I heard him telling Johanna, after a few ports, how he loved to watch the men's athleticism in the bedchamber, and how he longed to reach out and touch those pale English bodies.'

Here, listening to this account, my mind wanders a little and I wonder if the English bodies

are like spooks and whether they glow in the night-time? I am not sure that I would like to touch a spook; what if my hand goes right through to the other side? I keep myself listening for more detail.

'Then, one day in February of 1901, just a few weeks after the last breath of Queen Victoria, the Steenkamp world crumbled. The detail is sketchy, but seemingly Willem propositioned, with the offer of a case of finest cognac, a young lieutenant whom he had spied in an hour room on several occasions. The young officer apparently agreed to the transaction but when he found out the full extent of what he was expected to do to satisfy his thirst for cognac, he changed his mind a few minutes into the hour. Willem was enraged, and nothing could stop him as he subdued and savagely raped his pale-faced victim right there next to the bonbons and the brandy decanter, after which he forcibly ejected the half-naked man into the street.

Not until one of the pleasure girls, a witness to the throwing out of the young victim, informed Willem Steenkamp, he didn't have an inkling that the colt he'd so viciously brutalised was no lesser a person than the nephew of General Sir Geoffrey Barton, one of the most powerful men in the British army.

Through his actions Willem had just signed his permanent exit pass from Port Elizabeth, and in the forenoon of the very next day he was arrested, shackled, and taken away by a small contingent of the Cape Mounted Police assisted by a couple of military policemen.

It turned out that he was summarily charged with being a Boer conspirator, and, as you'd expect, some evidence was quickly found, and the hapless Willem was shipped to the colony of Ceylon to serve out the duration of the war at the notorious Ragama prisoner of war camp, and we didn't see him again until he was repatriated several months after the Treaty of Vereeniging.

Mrs Steenkamp was also arrested and charged with living off the proceeds of prostitution. The magistrate spared her from going to prison on account of her deformity, but she was ordered to pay a fine of £100 and barred for ten years from living in the municipality of Port Elizabeth.

One month later, the house having been put up for sale with a local agent, Johanna Steenkamp left to return to Hermanus, at least for the time being.

And I went with her, Christa, mainly because I had nowhere else to go.'

. . . .

That was almost the full extent of Mrs Gouws's account other than for her to add that after his return from Ceylon, Willem returned to Hermanus, reclaimed his sister-bride, and found himself a job in Saldanha Bay, on account of his prior experience, as the West Coast customs officer.

In the immediate aftermath of the war, with experienced and able-bodied men being in short supply across most areas of the colonial administration, the Public Service Board clearly neglected to look too closely at Willem Steenkamp's past.

Chapter 20 – Christa's Story

Now I am ready to jump into my bed and leave the adults to ramble on over another glass of brandy but, as I am about to move away, my attention is hooked again by my mother's voice. What is she telling Mrs Gouws now?

'...in Port Nolloth. Suleiman had a plan for me. Rather than rent out my young body to every unwashed sailor, he devised a scheme to fill his pockets in a single transaction and to be rid of the responsibility of looking after me.'

What is Ma saying? I have never heard this story before.

'Now that I was fifteen, a well-trained filly or, as Suleiman told his brother, *broken in but not broken down*, Suleiman's plan was to sell me to the highest bidder, and he was confident that a fine young thing like me, with perfect teeth and smooth-as-silk skin, would command a premium price. They loaded me on a coastal cutter bound for Walvis Bay and started putting out the word in the right places that they were holding an auction of rare and exotic merchandise at the end of the month.

After the customary auction of ivory, zebra skins, a very rare quagga skin, and assorted *kaffir* curios, selected bidders were invited to stay back and bid for the most exotic item of all: a beautiful *baster* girl.'

'Didn't anyone alert the police?' asks Mrs Gouws. "Hasn't slavery been illegal for many years now?'

'*Ja, sekerlik,*' answers Ma. 'Illegal, yes, but it's like everything else, *mevrou.* Pay the right people and you can do what you want, and this is why no one interfered in Suleiman's auction.'

There is a pause and I see the visitor take a sizable slug from her brandy glass. Am I dreaming it or is my mother saying that she was up for sale to the highest bidder? How did this happen?

As if reading my thoughts, my mother picks up her story again. 'With no authority there to intervene, I was put up for sale, in a closed sale attended by seven or eight men, mostly older men with big bellies, and in ten minutes it was all over, and Suleiman was £41 richer and rid of me.'

'That's a lot of money!' exclaims Mrs Gouws.

'I was no ordinary girl, *mevrou.* I was a fine chocolate princess, and I was well trained in the art of pleasing men. But *mevrou*, let me not keep you here with lurid details. Let me get this story out while I'm still in the mood to talk.

I was bought by the only young and presentable man in the room. This man was Antonio da Cunha, a salvage diver, and unmarried. I felt curiously unafraid in his presence as he firmly took my hand and led me away from that place. This man was kind to me, bought me some decent clothes and took me along with him to his salvage jobs. Without being asked I prepared his meals and washed his clothes. He demanded nothing more of me, so, after a few weeks of this new life I gathered enough courage to ask Antonio why he bought me and why he paid so much.'

This story is the strangest dream I have ever had; I mean, just imagine dreaming that your mother was sold as a lot in an auction, just another lot like a zebra skin or an elephant tusk.

The story moves on. 'Antonio didn't answer me then but a long time later he told me how his sister had been coerced into marrying a rich merchant, a man thirty years older than herself, to promote the influence of the Da Cunha family. And Antonio told me how he'd sworn to himself that one day he'd make right the wrong which had been visited on his sister and, to do this, he, Antonio José da Cunha, would personally set a woman free from her captivity. Now his promise was fulfilled, he said. As a scared teenager, I didn't really understand what he was talking about but, as each year passed, I understood a little more of the soul of this complex man. He told me, too, that although he had paid for me, the payment was not to possess me, like a horse or a cow, but to secure my freedom, and then he said the strangest thing of all; he said I was free to leave anytime I wanted. I ask you, have you ever heard such a thing in all your life?

And now, *mevrou*, I will answer the question which you're too shy to ask, namely, did

Antonio force himself on me?'

'*Nee! Nee!*' protested Mrs Gouws, 'I wasn't...'

'Don't protest so loudly, *mevrou*. If we're to be friends, there's no point being dishonest with me.'

There is no answer from Mrs Gouws, and I cannot see the expression on her face. How is she reacting to my mother's directness?

Ma continues, 'In answer to your unasked question, no, Antonio made no demand on me, but he didn't need to, because after being with him for two weeks, I offered myself to him. And for the next thirteen years, we were man and wife, and we were blessed with our only child, Rainha.'

For a full minute there is complete silence, not a word passing between the adults, then follows a long sniff from Ma. 'I'm sorry, *mevrou*,' she says, 'I don't know how I'm going to deal with losing both my husband and my daughter within eight months of each other; it's all too much.'

I see Mrs Gouws rise from her chair, presumably to comfort my mother. And again I hear the sobbing sounds until, after a while, Ma clears her throat and speaks again. 'You came here tonight, *mevrou*, to warn me about the Steenkamps and now, look at me, I've kept you up late telling you about myself.'

Mrs Gouws mumbles something I cannot hear and Ma answers, 'As much as it breaks my heart, I have no choice but to allow Rainha to go with the Steenkamps to Robben Island. I can't afford any longer to pay Mrs Oosthuizen's school fees, and truth be told I can't even feed the child properly. Then, *mevrou*, there's the moral dilemma…'

'*Wat sê jy nou, Christa?*' interrupts the visitor. 'What is this, what do you call it, moral dilemma?'

'You may or you may not know, *mevrou*, that I have no savings at all and that I survive by being a common *hoer*.' And bitterly she adds, 'I am illiterate and unskilled and the wrong skin colour, and the only things I know how to do well are to make fish stew and to open my legs for a few shillings.'

'*Genade,* Christa! It can't be true what you're telling me?'

'Why would I lie to you, *mevrou*? You may spit on me if you like and you may choose to avoid me like a leper, but what I've told you is God's whole truth. Now maybe you'll understand why I can't raise my daughter myself and expose her the depravity of her mother as she grows into a woman. If I do that, I deserve to go straight to Hell.'

There is another silence and just when I am beginning to think that no one is ever going to speak again, mother asks her guest in a calm voice, 'Tell me, mevrou, now that we've exposed all my dirty washing, tell me what you're going to do, because clearly you're not going to Robben Island with the Steenkamps?'

'*Nee,* Christa,' replies Mrs Gouws, 'you're dead right. In the last five years I've had enough of the Steenkamps. They have put my very soul in peril and it's time for me to take a different path. I have a sister living in Gansbaai who was widowed about a year ago and she has asked me to come and live with her. She's very lonely and not in the best of health, but she inherited a modest house and a couple of morgen of land suitable for growing vegetables and for keeping chickens and pigs. We'll be penniless but we'll have enough to eat, Christa, and so we'll live out our days as humble servants of our Lord.'

. . . .

I went to bed and, even though I did not really know how, I tried to pray, to seek divine protection for my mother and for myself. Then I slept.

Chapter 21 – The Harbour Board

'James Fox!'

I look up at the sallow young man calling my name, a well-oiled youth. You know the type, with pomaded hair perfectly parted down the middle of his pointy skull. My mood is dark, and I am expecting the worst.

Doing my best to calm the foreboding, which is pacing backwards and forwards through my mind, I answer, 'I am James Fox.'

'The Board is ready, Mr Fox. Please step inside.' The pointy-skulled fellow opens a heavy oak door and waves us (Bayes and myself) through and I wonder, somewhat uncharitably, why such a creature was not smothered at birth.

It is Wednesday, 17th February 1904, and I am here for my appointment with destiny, to answer, as they so elegantly worded it in their registered letter, 'allegations of misconduct' and 'allegations of dereliction of duty.'

I should already be back on Dassen Island, lighting the lamp by night and polishing it by day, but I have been directed not to return to duty for the time being, not until the conclusion of my hearing before the Board.

As for this hearing, Bayes, predictably, advises me that the best defence is attack. If you are going to fall, says Bayes, you may as well fall like a comet, in a blaze of glory, rather than be kicked out the door like a whimpering cur. I have brought Bayes along with me as my spokesman, in line with the Harbour Board's generous offer of allowing me representation at the hearing, and I pray that Bayes will not be embarrassing me here today.

Father's advice is predictable, too. He says just to tell the truth, the entire unvarnished truth, and to trust in God Almighty for right and justice. I have no intention of telling anything other than the truth, but today is the day when the truth may need a little help.

Contrary, however, to my expectation, Mother refuses to be drawn, and declines to offer any advice of her own. I wonder why, and I can only assume that she can see what the outcome will be and, therefore, that it is futile trying to alter the course of destiny. I do not understand the concept of fatalism; if everything is ordained then, I wonder, what is the point of having a choice? Is my parent in her curious way sparing me from the revelation of some sinister foreknowledge?

Instead of giving advice, Mother chooses to tell me about a recent dream.

In this dream she met a black man, a seer and holy man named Makana, or Makan, and this man told her that a great red tide was coming, the biggest tide in the history of the world.

And he said the tide would be caused by a great eruption beneath the sea far away across the oceans, and the unstoppable tide would wash away the land and the cattle of all the tribes and drown all those who could not swim or find a boat in time to save themselves. He said people would run away in terror, that the only way to escape the tide was to hide in the high mountains of the hinterland or in faraway waterless plains. But, for those who did escape the tide, he said their children would die of hunger for there would be no food for them to eat, not even grasshoppers and flying ants. When she asked the holy man what she should do, he looked away from her gaze and reminded her that, for five or six generations, the tide would be unstoppable, and he advised her to hold her children close to her and to wait in hope for the tide to ebb from the lands of the world.

Mother claims that she does not know how to interpret this dream, and I certainly do not begin to understand the reference to a mighty red tide which will wash over the earth for many decades. Even at my age I have been exposed to the power of the sea, to the unpredictable and formidable force of tides and waves. I have learnt to respect their power, to be cautious. Is there a message for me? Can it be to walk my way with caution in the presence of danger?

Bayes and I step into the hearing room, and we are acknowledged by a woman behind an *escritoire,* and she instructs us to sit down on a small, padded bench to her right and she tells us in a kind of stage whisper that the gentlemen of the Board will be with us shortly.

Despite the electric light installed on the ceiling, the room is dark and heavy, and the entire space is dominated by a massive and highly polished oval table which is encircled by padded chairs; a *laager* of correctness, standing firm against the onslaught of modernism and anarchy.

. . . .

There are three of them. And one witness, Mr Richardson.

They are introduced by the pasty-faced lackey. There is Mr O'Donnell, secretary of the Board; Capt.Nuttall, the assistant harbourmaster, and Mr Strangeway, from the Colonial Office. My heart sinks. I was hoping that Mr O'Dwyer, whom I believe to be a gentleman and a fair-minded administrator, would be here today. Looking at the dour trio before me at the table, I feel like a convicted man, a felon awaiting my sentence to be hanged by the neck.

The woman is not introduced, but I deduce that she is the stenographer, just an anonymous female in a club of privileged men.

Firstly, we have the formalities.

'You are James William Fox?'

'Your date of birth is 11th December in the year 1884?'

'You live at Harrow, Main Road, Rondebosch?'

'Did you, Mr Fox, receive a registered letter dated the 5th ultimo, from the Harbour Board?'

'When you were employed last year as an Assistant Lighthouse Keeper, were you provided with a booklet containing the regulations of the Lighthouse Service and were you instructed to read and memorise the regulations contained within the said booklet?'

Wryly, I wonder, when do we get to the part where they place a hood over my head and a noose around my neck?

I hear Mr O'Donnell, his voice somehow distant and disembodied, like the voice of a teacher when you pass a busy classroom, but he is speaking to me. 'Mr Fox, I refer you to the section of the Regulations headed, "Professional and Familial Relationships," which states: "In order to maintain and to promote the highest moral standards within the Cape Lighthouse Service, lightkeepers are forbidden from consorting or cohabiting with kaffir women, or dark-skinned women of mixed race or any other race of women of dark complexion." Now, Mr Fox, is there any part of this regulation which is unclear or ambiguous?'

'No, sir.'

'I have a sworn statement here from Mrs Rowena Richardson, that when she you called at your home in Rondebosch to inquire about your welfare following your fall at the Dassen Island Lightstation, that she discovered by question and observation that the house is occupied by persons of various races. Is this correct?'

'Yes, sir.'

'Furthermore, it was discovered that a female person, of dark complexion and believed to be a Cape Malay, was present in the house and that this person is said to be betrothed to you.'

'Yes, sir. But the person in question has since run away.'

'Really? Did she come to her senses and realise the wrong thing she was doing by seeking to marry above her station?' asks my inquisitor with raised eyebrows.

'Actually, no!' Bayes jumps into the fray, 'Valerie, my brother's betrothed, came to the conclusion, the mistaken conclusion may I say, that Mrs Richardson and my brother were fucking each other...'

'Mr Fox!' O'Donnell, his reptilian face twisted with rage, screams at Bayes, 'Withdraw that statement, sir! Mrs Richardson's husband is present in this room, and I'll thank you to be respectful and to modulate your language.'

'Yes, sir, of course. Please allow me to rephrase my reply.'

'Go ahead then.'

I can hear Bayes's voice, but I cannot believe what he - he who cannot even recite a Hail Mary without stumbling over the words - is saying; 'The Holy Bible says there is neither Jew nor Greek, there is neither slave nor free man, there is neither male nor female; for you are all one in Christ Jesus. Similarly, sir, the Cape Malay and the European and the Chinaman and the negro are all one, all equal.'

'Really, sir!' protests Mr Strangeway from his hibernation. 'What are you saying? We know these people came down from the trees not very long ago and that their thin veneer of civilisation barely conceals their primitive nature.'

And O'Donnell rejoins the fray, 'We are here for the serious business, Mr Fox, of conducting a hearing. Please keep the Sunday school lesson for another time and place. Did your brother have an intimate relationship with the Malay servant girl?'

'The "girl" you speak of so disdainfully has a name and an identity. Her name is Valerie, and she is an honest woman, a person of the highest moral character, dare I say the equal of every person in this room, so I'll thank you gentlemen to refer to her respectfully...'

'What the blazes!' roars Capt.Nuttall, his jowls vibrating with consternation. 'Answer the question, you young upstart.'

'Was he sleeping with Valerie? Well now, the way I see it, that's really none of your business since the act of sleeping is a private arrangement which has nothing whatever to do with James's ability to perform his duties. And, since no relevance can be drawn between his mating habits and his attention to his lightkeeping duties, there's really nothing more to be said, is there?'

Nuttall turns to Strangeway and makes the observation, 'You find them everywhere, you know. That's what happens when you spare the rod, when you spoil the child...'

'Gentleman!' It is O'Donnell again, trying to keep order at his increasing chaotic hearing. 'For the moment let's put aside the matter of the Malay girl and let's proceed with the second matter at hand, namely, the matter of failing to go to the aid of a fellow lightkeeper.' And he allows his statement several moments to circulate the room before he asks; 'Mr Fox, I have here a statement from the Chief Lightkeeper, Mr Richardson, a statement which alleges that when the labourer, armed with a spear, went to attack Mr Pike in the lightstation, you did not arm yourself or even equip yourself with a lamp; that you followed the assailant seemingly to support his misdeed and that, when the *kaffir* bolted down the tower, you failed to apprehend the attacker.' O'Donnell looked me straight in the eyes as he said this. Clearly, he was trying to gauge my reaction.

I said nothing; just looked straight back at my accuser.

'Well, what do you say, Mr Fox?' O'Donnell struggled to hide his irritation.

Bayes doesn't know the finer detail of what happened that night, so I take a deep breath and I answer in my own defence. 'It seems, sir, that the only reason that Diamond, the labourer, failed in his mission to spear Mr Pike, that's to say, if that really were his intention, was that Pike, contrary to regulations, had likely bolted the entry to the lantern room to avoid being found asleep. The night was devilishly dark, and I did not actually see in which direction Diamond went. But, having heard the load banging on the door of Mr Pike's room, I knew something was afoot, something serious.'

'If, as you say, you didn't see which way the *kaffir* went, how did you know to go the lighthouse?'

'Well, sir, I didn't know it at all, but it did seem logical in the first instance to check on Mr Pike and the functioning of the light and, in the second instance, to check from the height of the tower if there might be a ship in distress. I judged that there could be great urgency and for that reason I made the snap decision not to bother with lighting a lamp; rather I'd head straight to the illumination of the tower.' Now, I think I made sense of that explanation.

For the next while I followed my father's advice and told the three wizards the truth, the entire truth, and not once did I deviate from the truth.

O'Donnell had only two more questions. Two large-calibre questions pointed straight at Mr Richardson. 'Tell me, Mr Fox, is it the practice on Dassen Island for the hatch to the lantern room to be bolted at night? And tell me, how often does the chief lightkeeper check on the light and the lightkeeper at night?'

'Only a certain lightkeeper bolts the hatch...'

'Come now, Mr Fox!' interjects O'Donnell, 'don't be coy. Answer the question, if you please.'

'Alfred Pike bolts the hatch.'

'Thank you. Now, be so kind as to answer my second question.'

'Well, sir, bearing in mind that I have only been in the service for a short time...'

I am cut short again. 'Dammit, Mr Fox! Will you answer the bloody question?' O'Donnell's eyes flash with annoyance now. Clearly, he is a man who is used to getting his way, and used to getting it promptly. 'For your benefit I'll ask the question again, Mr Fox. Was Mr Richardson, the chief lightkeeper, in the habit of performing checks at night?'

'No, Mr O'Donnell, sir. I never saw him out after dark.'

Richardson, about to explode, rises from his chair, 'He is a lying little bastard, sir! Not only does Fox...'

'Mr Richardson! Shut up and sit down!' commands O'Donnell. 'Clearly there are a number of irregularities occurring on Dassen Island, and these will all be dealt with in due course.'

Now the inquisitor turns his attention back to me. 'Mr Fox, I'm about to close this hearing. Do you have anything further to say before I do so?'

. . . .

I say nothing more, and that is that, and I am told I will be given a written decision within one month.

Chapter 22 – Changing Direction

Bayes and I leave behind the halls of administration, the turned and polished wood, the chequer-tiled floors, and we walk out into the February brightness.

The sky is blue, but I neither notice nor care; 'never felt the witchery of the soft blue sky!' And the outlines of our shadows are boldly trimmed as if they are recently sketched with a newly sharpened pencil yet, in the midst of all this clarity, I feel removed from the reality of the clamour and clatter in the street, from the bustle and colour of the passersby, and I feel strangely disengaged and above the drama, like someone calmly inspecting a diorama.

'That's it, James, you know it's all over, don't you?'

Reluctantly, and no doubt looking blank, I turn to Bayes. What is he doing disturbing this moment of reflection?

'There's no way except out, dear brother. We'd best be talking about where to from here.'

'What?' It is all I can say.

'The good thing, James, is that you're just nineteen years old. A mere boy. You've learnt some valuable lessons this past year. You've discovered that not everyone has good intentions and that even fewer follow through with good actions. The world is an unfair place, and this Cape of ours is perhaps the unfairest place of all...'

'You're rambling, Bayes,' I interject irritability. 'Now, what's the point you're trying to make?' And, in saying this, I kick a beer bottle hard into the gutter; a bottle which had the audacity to be in the way of my boot.

'I'll spell it out, James. How shall we say, brother to brother?'

'If you must.'

'If you're found guilty of the charges levelled at you by the Harbour Board, you'll be sacked. Bang, gone, and goodbye. As for demotion, it isn't an option as you're still on the lowest rung of the service and stationed at one of the most God-forgotten lights in the Cape Colony.' Bayes pauses, looks hard at me to check whether I am listening. 'On the other hand,' he continues, 'O'Donnell and his prehistoric pals may decide after all that the charges cannot be sustained. That, in fact, you're not guilty of doing anything wrong.'

'You know damned well I did nothing wrong'. Annoyance rasps at my tone; Bayes has his special way of grating on my good nature.

'Consider your situation, dear boy. Either you get booted out of the Service, or you end up going back to that nest of vipers. And, sooner or later, one of those vipers will sink its fangs into you. As for reinstatement, it won't save you; it'll only serve to agitate the bastards.'

I say nothing. It would, of course, never occur to me to interrupt my brother

'You must resign, James, and you have to do it smartly. This way you can leave with a clean record and a hopeful heart to restart and make something of your life.'

'No doubt you're right, Bayes, but before I make a decision, I'd like to talk this over with father and mother. I'm too drained to decide today.'

We take the train to Rondebosch and, all the way, past the grimy factories and warehouses of Salt River, past the humble terraced homes of Observatory, I stare fixedly out of the window, avoiding further conversation and wondering silently where I might find myself in the months and years ahead. Bitterly I reflect how, just a few months ago, my future seemed so clear and certain; so set for a lifelong partnership with Valerie and for a fifty-year career with the Lighthouse Service.

. . . .

At first Father objects to the notion of resigning. If you knew him like I know him, it would be clear why he does not like the idea of my departing from the Lighthouse Service in such a way and under such cloudy circumstances. My father is an honest man, you see, the type of citizen who will walk a mile to return a sixpence to its rightful owner, and part of his outlook on life is that the truth will always prevail and that people will mostly do their best in their dealings with each other. In a way I envy this simplicity, this trust. The sort of childlike trust which Jesus Christ spoke about to his disciples.

Eventually though, Father comes to accept Bayes's line of argument, with the result that after supper I sit myself down at the kitchen table and write out my resignation. In the morning I will hand deliver it to the Harbour Board, and it will all be over.

Am I making a mistake to resign? To be frank, I am unsure but, for better or worse, my mind is made up.

As for mother, she seems to have no firm opinion one way or another, which I find a little odd as she is usually the one in our family who has the greatest insight. Later, when Bayes and our father have left the kitchen, I question my female parent.

'Mother, surely you have a view about the situation we've been talking about. Do you think it's right for me to walk away?'

Mother's attention is seemingly immersed in applying stitches to a sock which she has stretched tightly over a darning mushroom and she does not look up as she answers.

'Eventually, James, every road comes to a fork. Your life has come to a fork and there's no use pretending that it hasn't. You must choose, and you have. There's really nothing more to be done.' Now she glances at me sharply and adds, 'You're a man now, James, and you make your own decisions. We all live by our decisions and, one day, when we least expect it, and irrespective of the decisions we make along the way, our chosen road will end at the grave for each of us.'

Neither cheered nor enlightened, I do not know what to make of my mother's words.

. . . .

A couple of days later Father has more to say; call it a proposition or an idea. Clearly, in his calm and reflective way, he has been thinking. Thinking about my future, and his.

'Now, lad,' he introduces his thoughts, 'You're aware that next month I'm retiring. Not only because I'll be sixty-five but also because I find that my eyesight is playing up, which I suppose is the price I have to pay for having forty years' worth of soot and grit in my eyes from the locomotives passing at the crossing. Time to pack it in and to have the grandchildren around to pull at the shiny buttons on my coat and to plead with me for a few pennies to buy a bag of apples or a handful of barley sugars.'

I am listening to Mr John Palmer Fox, known to me as my father, and he keeps talking.

"Well, you see now, James, I could have a word with the powers that be in the CGR to see if there might be a position for a robust and educated man like yourself; I mean, for a start they are going to be needing to replace one Fox, that half-blind old fossil who mans the crossing at Kenilworth...'

'Father!' I protest, 'I'll thank you not to be so disrespectful about my parent. The elder Fox of whom you speak so disparagingly has all his life worked diligently and without complaint to provide for his family. I say, let us salute him!'

Father pulls an amused face; 'Aye, my boy, you have a way with words, don't you now? Now, if you'll stop interrupting, I'll get to the point I want to make.'

'Yes, father,' I answer smilingly and with an undertone of mock humility.

'I have discussed this with your dear mother, and we'd like to propose that you return to live with us here at *Harrow* and so much the better if we can secure you employment with the CGR. I may as well tell you that our reasons are not entirely unselfish as your mother and I will look to you for support in our twilight years. What do you think, James?'

I agree (why would I not?) and I feel some relief knowing that I am not going to end up a *bergie,* wandering homeless and hungry around the environs of Table

Mountain. Maybe this change really is for the better; in time the lonely life of a lightkeeper would probably have dragged my mind down into the sewer of insanity.

True to his word, Father speaks to the hierarchy at the Cape Government Railways, both to settle arrangements for his retirement and to inquire about a possible position for me and, as it turns out, that august organisation is unwilling to place me in a gatekeeping position, unwilling on account of, as they put it, 'my above-average education.' They think I am better suited to start out as a trainee ticket examiner, a job which they say requires a little administrative skill.

I will have preferred to commence in a month or so, after father's last working day, and this interval will have given me time to exert myself on my mended leg, to wander about in search of Valerie. But it is not to be, and my commencement date is set for Monday, 29 February 1904.

The disappearance of Valerie is eating at me, keeping me awake at night. I absolutely need to explain to her about Rowena; I need to hold Valerie and to tell her I love her.

Right now, I feel I am drifting, drifting away, and I am in desperate need of an anchor to stabilise my existence.

Chapter 23 – A Change of Heart

Adderley Street and Trafalgar Place are the obvious places to start looking, so mid-morning the train takes me to the city.

Today Table Mountain is covered with a heavy tablecloth, and if you were an early seafarer and you did not know there is a massive mountain here, you may just have dismissed the tablecloth as a colossal and insubstantial cloud bank. This morning, energetically spreading the tablecloth, the Southeaster is blowing 'seven devils,' as Father so colourfully describes the relentless buffeting of the trade wind. No one ever gets used to it; one just learns to tolerate it and wait for it to disappear in the autumn.

Questioning the flower sellers is difficult. I get a succession of looks which I can only interpret as, 'what do you want with Valerie?' to 'why is this *witman* asking about one of us?' Nobody owns up to knowing where Valerie is or where Valerie may be or where Valerie is sometime likely to be in the future, so I wander about quite aimlessly, through parts of the Malay Quarter, Oranjezicht, Vredehoek and back, down the oak-lined walk of the government gardens, into the top end of Adderley Street, and back to the station.

Memories of sunny days, leisurely walks, picnic lunches and long embraces invade my mind as I go but, rather than these recollections lifting my spirits, I begin to feel more and more dejected. Is it all over, I wonder, and am I on a fool's errand to nowhere?

Today's wanderings are far and away the farthest since my accident; my leg is aching and I am spent.

. . . .

On the first Sunday afternoon after my fruitless visit to the city, Bayes turns up at *Harrow* with James Middleton, my brother-in-law, husband of Harriet. James is known everywhereas Jim and, although a stonemason by trade, today he works as a groundskeeper at the Newlands Rugby Ground. Jim is a knockabout sort of fellow, a living stereotype of manhood, a hard-talking character who can recite the names of every cricketer and rugby player of our era and revels in the backslapping bonhomie of clubrooms and public bars.

On the other hand, my sister, Harriet Susan Middleton, is more like my aunt than my sister. Having married Jim Middleton in 1893 (apparently two months after the birth of their first daughter, Mabel) Harriet left home when I was just eight years old. As a child I remember her as a pale and sensitive being who was known to burst into tears at the smallest provocation, like the day when cheeky little Emma hid one of Harriet's slippers on the high shelf in the pantry.

Although Jim and Harriet lived not far from us in a cottage behind the Newlands ground, we seldom saw them, I guess on account of the challenge of visiting us with half a dozen very young and mostly shoeless children in tow.

Why am I telling you about the Middletons, you may wonder?

The year 1904 is only in its second month and already I have changed occupations and moved back home, my fiancée has disappeared, and my confidence is in tatters. Little do I know it yet, but the presence of the Middletons, particularly the Middleton children, will be the steadying influence, the anchor, which I need to balance my unsteady existence and to give me new purpose.

It turns out that it is not by chance that Jim Middleton is at *Harrow* today, as I soon discover.

By way of conversation, I tell Bayes (and Jim, because he is here with us) about my search for Valerie and about how challenging it is likely to be. A Malay woman could, after all, be anywhere in the vastness of the Cape Colony, any place from Salt River to Mamre, Swellendam to Beaufort West, De Aar to Mafeking or even beyond the colony to Walvis Bay or Lourenço Marques or anywhere else.

'The magnitude of the task may crush me.' I hear myself saying despondently to Bayes and Jim. 'And the open suspicion of the Malay people when I talk to them is unsettling me no end. I ask you, just what have I done to offend them?'

'Why don't you just let her go?' asks Jim as casually as asking if I would like to take a walk across Rondebosch Common sometime.

'There's been a terrible misunderstanding, that's why...'

And, cruelly, Bayes contributes his view of the situation; 'Think about it for a minute, James. If this girl really loves you as much as you think she does, then surely when she has cooled down, she'll bring herself back and attempt to work things out with you.'

'It's not that simple.'

'It never is where women are concerned,' remarks Jim. "They need to understand that it is men who make the decisions, that it's not their place to examine the actions of men nor to demand explanations. That's inviting trouble if you ask me...'

'I didn't actually ask you anything, Jim Middleton, not a fucking thing...'

'Down, boys, down!' commands Bayes, before he turns his gaze to Middleton and says soothingly to our brother-in-law, 'James has been through a lot lately, Jim. Let's keep things civil now.' And, now, turning his attention to me, Bayes adds, 'I acknowledge that Valerie is as pretty as a ripe peach, and no doubt just as sweet, but soon you'll realise that it was – how shall I say it delicately – it was what the poets call first love, the totally reckless first flight of the fledgling, the falling from the nest. It's a sweet memory, James, that first flight, but I'm telling you it's hardly the real thing.'

'You know this how?'

'Eventually, the pigeons want to fly with pigeons, and the chickens with the chickens...'

'You're talking bull, Bayes, chickens don't fly. What's your point?'

'What I'm delicately trying to say, dear boy, is that sooner or later you'll have tired of Valerie.'

Jim has been dying to add a little more fuel to the fire, and he does. 'We're men and I hope we can speak plainly. The honest thing to admit here is, firstly, that coloured girls are delightful demons in the bedroom, unconstrained by prudish notions, but they're totally untrustworthy outside the bedroom. There're not like us you know...'

'.. not like us ...not like us ...not like us.' The phrase clangs about in my head.

And, unbelievably, I admit, 'Maybe not.'

Bayes got to me I think when he said that if she loves me, she will come back to me by herself. He is right, is he not? Does Father Kelly, our parish priest at St.Michael's, not love to quote St.Paul's epistle to the Ephesians; 'Be kind to one another, tender-hearted, forgiving one another...'

By staying away, by not returning with a tender heart, is Valerie not making a choice? After all, she knows exactly where to find me, does she not? If I continue on my fool's mission to find her, I may be looking for the rest of my life and, even if I do find her sometime, is there not a good chance that she will refuse to listen to me? As much as I hate to admit it, I think Bayes may be right. As for Middleton, he is just an idiot, but he probably means well. For Harriet's benefit, I will tolerate him.

The topic of my search for Valerie rests now and I boldly ask Jim Middleton what brings him here today. He seldom comes this way, always having better things to do, like hitting a cricket ball about or swapping tall stories over a pint of ale.

'Since we're brothers bonded by marriage,' Jim answers, 'I'll confess my purpose but, mind you, it's not for discussion outside the family.' He seems ready to embrace Bayes and myself, ready to drop his usual chest-thumping demeanour, so I listen without interruption as he opens his mind to us. 'I've come here today, cap in hand, to speak to Mr Palmer and Miss Eva (he always refers to my parents in this way) to ask if they will have Mabel and Evie at *Harrow,* if the girls might share a room and help their grandmother about the house. With the approaching birth of our ninth child, of which number two have sadly returned to Heaven, we simply have no room in our two-roomed cottage for everyone, nor enough food to feed so many...' Jim falters here, clenches his jaw and looks fixedly past his brothers-in law, as if regretting that he has told us so much.

Bayes, in typical Bayes fashion, makes light of the situation by saying, 'I think, old boy, that Pope Pius and, for that matter, the Lord himself, are well satisfied by the efforts of yourself and Harriet to populate the world. It might be time to practise some well-timed withdrawal, or interruptus, as I'm told it's called now.'

We laugh out loud, Jim's mood lifts, and he resumes what he began to tell us. 'We think Mabel, who is now ten years old and as wise as an owl, and Evie, just shy of five years old, should be the chosen ones to live with their grandparents. That still leaves us with two girls, Alice and Annie, both old enough now to help Harriet around the house, along with James junior, now a man of eight, and little brother, John, almost three and as cheeky as a chipmunk. The full account has two more refunded to Heaven, and one replacement arriving from Heaven soon.

This is how it comes about that *Harrow* acquires three new residents: Miss Mabel Middleton, aged ten; Miss Mary Evelina Middleton, know to all as Evie, aged four; and yours truly, James William Fox, a trainee ticket examiner, aged nineteen.

....

My thoughts remain conflicted about Valerie's disappearance. Some days, I tell myself, I must go looking for her; after all, she can hardly be blamed for the damage inflicted by Rowena's wiles. But, at other times, I remember what Bayes said about her returning if she really cares.

Why does the situation have to be so damned complicated?

The thought has crossed my mind, too, that I was lucky to escape from Rowena's clutches, that right now, like the sweetly scented but deadly Pitcher plant, she is likely drawing some other hapless bastard into her trap.

Chapter 24 – Staying on the Rails

Cape Town to Wellington. Wellington to Cape Town. This is my new life.

Already I can recite the name of every station, every road crossing, each ticket category, the type and number of every locomotive on this line. In contrast to lightkeeping, being a ticket examiner places me squarely in the midst of the hustle of humanity. Some days the swell of humankind is oppressive, days when I long for the isolation of Dassen Island, for the wind and the waves and the calls of the seabirds.

As for humanity, it is a lucky dip. I am seeing every imaginable type and variant of *homo sapiens*; from the pock-faced adolescents riding to school, to elderly gentlemen, their jackets soiled with cigar ash and their hats stained with years of sweat; from matrons tightly wrapped in their drab shawls, to labourers in their well-trodden boots and paint-stained overalls; from the perfumed *mademoiselles* in their stylishly feathered hats, coquettishly cocking their heads behind their brightly-patterned fans, to dapper businessmen with neatly clipped moustaches, tie studs and brightly polished shoes.

The work itself is straightforward.

Tickets please! *Kaartjies asseblief!*

Check the tickets. Valid for today? No, you can't use yesterday's ticket. The right line? No, sorry, Claremont is on the Wynberg line, please change trains at Salt River. Clip the ticket. What, no ticket? Are you able to buy a ticket? No money? In that case, get off at the next stop. Sorry, sir, I lost my ticket. You'll need to buy a replacement. No money? Get off at the next station. Please, sir, I'll bring the money tomorrow. Sorry, you'll need to get off this train. What if I give you a kiss? Sorry, miss, just wave goodbye at the next stop. *Asseblief, meneer*, just give me a chance. You'll have your chance to get off at Bellville, our next stop. And so it goes; different days, the same routine.

At the end of each working day, I conscientiously hand over my written report, which is a brief reconciliation of tickets checked, tickets sold, and money collected. For two weeks I work with my trainer, Mr Aggenbach, an examiner with fifteen years' experience and a lifetime of unbendable attitude. There is nothing on God's green earth which Aggenbach has not encountered on these rails and he happily shares his stories with me, stories such as: the account of the farmer who brought his full-grown pig on the train after a wheel fell off his cart on the way to the abattoir and how he was required to buy a ticket for the hog; the story of the little miscreant who was unceremoniously suspended by his ankles from a carriage window for daring to spit on Mr Aggenbach (a big mistake!), and the tale of another teenager who covered himself in red ink and tried to get a free ride by claiming that he been attacked and robbed by a gang of *tsotsis*. The *tsotsi* story, like a good fishing story, grew bigger with each telling;

eventually three thugs became six thugs, and six thugs multiplied to become a dozen thugs.

In June, the fourth month of my new employment, in the worst flood in Cape Town's recorded history, the railway lines within Cape Town Station and down the line in the vicinity of Woodstock are covered with up to a foot of water and the line itself is dislodged and displaced as the ground turns to sludge, and for nearly a fortnight the rail service is suspended between Cape Town and Salt River.

. . . .

These days, when I get home to Rondebosch after a long day on my feet, I am happy to sit a while, my boots at the door, and this leads me to an unexpected discovery.

More and more I find that I am drawn to the company of my nieces, Mabel and Evie. The way they demand to be hugged and to be sat on my knee enchants me. There is nothing complicated or hidden about what they want; they just come right out and claim it.

I discover that there is no money to send Mabel to school and when little Evie is of age for school she will be in the same predicament. It is hard enough, the Lord knows, just to clothe and feed them and their four (soon to be five) siblings and to keep all their little faces clean.

These two sisters are amazingly bright and inquisitive, natural learners, their minds like deep barrels demanding to be filled but, here they are, threadbare little 'poor whites,' shut out from school by their family circumstances, and it dawns on me that, rather than allow my mind to rust through boredom and routine, and rather than dwell on some of my recent misfortunes, I can make it my goal to teach these children, to pass on the blessing of my own fortunate education. So, before long, as soon as the plates are cleared away from the kitchen table, the routine is established that the area is transformed into 'Uncle James's school.'

Out come the slates and out come the readers and out comes the folding world map which their uncle James has acquired somewhere, and school is on.

With Mabel's help we create an alphabet poster for our class, and we allow Evie to colour the letters as best as she can with the three half-used crayons at our disposal. At 'Uncle James's school,' it is all about working together in a team, about making mistakes today and about making more but different mistakes tomorrow. The girls love the interaction, take great pride in sounding out their letters, in practising their penmanship on their slates, and learning the basics of arithmetic, such as solving the mystery of taking two apples from a basket of ten apples and discovering, by careful calculation, that there are only eight apples left. When the formal lesson is done, I make a fuss of checking the time, make a show of tut-tutting that it is very late, but agree - with pretended reluctance – that there is only time for 'just a little' bedtime story if they hurry to change into their nightdresses.

This is how it happens that we read everything I can find suitable for little girls and, to support our reading habit, I befriend a bookseller in Mowbray to ensure myself a regular supply of tales both old and new to amuse and entertain my pupils.

In quick succession we devour the book supply: books about dragons such as *The Reluctant Dragon* and Nesbit's, *The Book of Dragons;* Rudyard Kipling's, *The Jungle Book,* with its larger-than-life characters like Shere Khan and Baloo, and Kaa, the snake; and the children's favourite book of all, George McDonald's, *The Princess and the Goblin.*

Here I am, my father's son, immersed in the fantasies of children and hereby released from the concerns of grown-ups. Now I have purpose and pleasure together, and I look forward every day to my time with Mabel and Evie.

. . . .

It is October now, the days warmer, the skies blue. On my days off I have been out and about with Mabel and Evie, to Camps Bay, Muizenberg, even to Cape Point. The Cape Point lightstation stirs in me recollections of my brief but dramatic time on Dassen Island; much can be said about that time but even more ought to be shut away within the file of things past.

Our favourite place for excursions is King Edward Park in Wynberg. What a magical place to play hide-and-seek! And we play tag around the memorial fountain until we all collapse on the grass with parched throats and partake of a bottle or two of Nickoles lemonade (which I am always particular about buying beforehand at the station cafeteria).

From bits of rope and wooden pegs which I find here and there, I make us a game of quoits, a game to amuse us when we are tired of running about the park, and it is not unusual to have other children join in our game. Being the adult, it falls to me to calculate the appropriate handicap (the distance from the peg) for each child, according to age.

I am clearly not old enough to be the girls' father and likely too old to be their brother, so I have adult users of the park look at me strangely, speculatively, trying to calculate the relationship. Some of the bolder and more inquisitive grown-ups find a reason to stop and chat and to offer some carefully worded observations in an attempt to uncover something tangible to satisfy their curiosity.

'What energetic little people you have, sir!' or 'If I may say so, a beautiful afternoon to be spending here with your girls.' I smile to myself and make a little game of giving nothing away, sometimes to the point of frustrating the inquisitors so much that they cannot help themselves from asking directly; 'Are these your daughters then?' And, in such a situation, I often respond with a question of my own; 'Do you think the girls look like me?' or, cheekily. 'Well, now, I can hardly be their grandfather, can I?'

With the help of the undeniable charm of my little princesses I can make some friends on our outings, but I choose to hold myself back from friendship; I am still emotionally unready for new connections. For now, my work, my family and my princesses are enough.

Early in November we hear that Paul Kruger is coming home. Well, not exactly *Oom Paul* himself, but his exhumed body, which is being returned from Switzerland for burial in his own country by kind permission of the British authorities; incidentally, the same 'authorities' who stole *Oom Paul's* nation.

Many among the good citizens of Cape Town are quite blissfully unaware of exactly what did happen in Southern Africa in the years 1899 to 1902, unaware of how the mighty British Empire methodically starved to death many thousands of Afrikaner women, children and elderly folk, as well as tens of thousands of black people who were so easily disposable that their deaths were never even officially tallied.

But we, the Fox family, we know a bit about the sordid truth. And how so, you may ask??

My dear sister, Emma, always the agitator in the family, has for several years been corresponding with the British aristocrat, Emily Hobhouse, who campaigned fearlessly for improved conditions for Afrikaner women in British prison camps, as well as with Annie Kenney, an activist for women's suffrage, who involves herself in many public and provocative actions in the British Isles.

But Emily Hobhouse, known unaffectionately by the English ruling class as 'that bloody woman,' is the one person who most influences my sister's view of the world, a view which Emma in turn is keen to share with her family and everyone she meets.

After the unloading of the coffin, there is to be a procession through the city for the late president of the *Zuid-Afrikaansche Republiek,* and King Edward has magnanimously approved for the firing of a twenty-one-gun salute from Signal Hill (somehow deemed fair compensation for the destruction of the Boer nations).

On the occasion of the procession in a few weeks' time, my dear sibling has taken it upon herself to emulate her influential friends in Britain - to act, and so to proclaim the misdeeds of the Empire for all to know.

....

Mother stays home with Mabel and Evie on the day of the procession while Father, Bayes, Jim Middleton and I, all under the influence of Emma's persuasiveness, make our way to the environs of Adderley Street to view the proceedings. Emma and some of her more radical friends station themselves at the intersection of Adderley and Strand where, in homage to the late Paul Kruger, they intend to make their anti-imperial protest.

Emma has hundreds of pamphlets for distribution quoting the text of Miss Hobhouse's 1901 submission to the British government entitled *Report of a Visit to the Camps of Women and Children in the Cape and Orange River Colonies*, and in addition she and her helpers have prepared pamphlets and posters of their own with messages like, 'Oom Paul - We Salute You,' 'Farewell to a Man of the People,' and 'Vale, Kruger – Victim of Imperial Aggression,' and a massive poster with a telling satire picturing a cowering bulldog being chased from the gates of Heaven by St.Peter brandishing a staff and yelling, *Voetsek!*

It is not long before a large crowd gathers around the protesters. Here and there are a few hecklers but for the most part the crowd appears to be supportive, or at least curious. Emma is addressing the gathering throng in a strong, clear voice and I marvel at her spirit; could my sister one day be the first female prime minister of the Cape Colony? And I answer myself that probably she will not; she is too idealistic and too brazenly honest, and more than that she despises the self-proclaimed superiority of the British culture, and the irony of her part Cornish heritage matters nothing at all to her.

We are standing elbow to elbow, Jim directly in front of me, when suddenly a wild-eyed man steps towards Emma, snatches a wad of pamphlets from her hands, scatters the papers furiously and proceeds to push Emma to the ground. And before I can even think of reacting from my boxed-in position, my brother-in-law, Jim Ask-Questions-Later Middleton, launches himself like a bolt from a crossbow at Emma's assailant and, in an instant, we find ourselves in the middle of a free-for-all. I push forward having in mind to save Jim, but Jim needs no saving from me as he clearly has got the better of the wild-eyed one. Then, as quickly as it started, it is all over when half a dozen constables intervene and frog march three or four people, including Emma and Jim, from the scene.

The upshot of Emma's protest is that she is fined £10 for causing a public disturbance; her helpers are each fined ten shillings, while our hero, Jim Middleton, is fined £2 for public affray. Father, being a pensioner, cannot contribute even sixpence towards paying the fines and, as for Middleton, even on a good day Jim never has more than a half-crown in his pocket. That is how Bayes and I end up paying the fines for both Emma and Jim.

What I do not know yet is that the disturbance is witnessed by a young woman in the crowd, someone who takes great interest in the proceedings but who keeps herself well enough aside not to be noticed by those who know her.

Chapter 25 - My New Home

Where is *Pa* now? And tell me, what is the real reason *Ma* has given me away when she says she loves me very much, as much as the moon and stars all together?

In the eyes of adults I may still be a child, but I have seen enough and heard enough to understand some things, like why *Ma* has to take money from strange men, and the adults would be surprised to know that I know (or I think I know, which, to my young mind, is the same as actually knowing) what happens when *Ma* closes her bedroom door.

I am not cross with my mother for handing me over to the Steenkamps, but my heart is sore. I know, too, that *Ma* wants what is best for me, her only child, but still my heart aches with a dull and never-ending emptiness. Why could my mother not take over *Pa's* equipment and become a diver like he was? After all, she must know quite a lot about it, about helmets and hoses and pumps, and about the danger of the bends. Then, surely, we could have stayed together, neither needing to worry about money and food, nor requiring to concern ourselves about the generosity of strange men?

Here I am now, with the Steenkamps on Robben Island, living in a stone cottage, just three or four buildings away from the big white church, which I think is the tallest building on the island, not counting the lighthouse and I think there is only the one boat, *Tiger*, a wheezy beast covered in coal dust and tar, steaming to and from the mainland.

Meneer Steenkamp is a warder here and I understand it is his job to watch the lunatics.

I have never met a lunatic and *Nooi* Steenkamp seems to take pleasure in telling me that lunatics are dangerous and unpredictable, that they talk to themselves, to donkeys and to cabbages, and that they especially like to catch and cook young girls. Of course, I am not silly and do not believe the bit about cooking young girls. It is nonsense and I know it. And I ask you, what is wrong with talking to donkeys? I think they are cute, certainly cuter than humans.

Nooi tells me that, besides the lunatics, there are lepers on this island and criminals, too - dangerous black criminals. I think dangerous because black people are a lot harder to see in the dark, so you do not always know where they are lurking. Anyway, I would rather not think about black criminals because I have other things on my mind.

Within a few weeks of arriving here, I was doing the cleaning and the cooking; washing the clothes; churning butter from the milk we get from the Wheedles (who have six cows and a bull) and just to be sure I have no time to be idle, I am also *Nooi's* personal nursemaid, the one who fetches and carries, washes her feet and brushes her hair. I do not mind the work as I have come to accept that to succeed as a wife and mother when I grow up, I need to know how to do all manner of household tasks, and to do them with a good heart. The alternatives are to marry a wealthy man (no chance of that!) or rent my body to men (no chance of that either!). I understand my place in the world but, in spite of this understanding, I do think the Steenkamps have done well to have me, such a willing *meidjie*, in their home.

There is a change happening in the mood between *Nooi* and myself and it seems somehow to be linked to changes happening inside my body. The monthly thing has started and it is causing me to cramp and curl up in agony, but *Nooi* will permit no let-up in my duties; if anything, she seems to add to my workload when I dare to say anything about pain or discomfort, and she says things like; 'Give me your young and well-portioned body, Gina, and I will never complain about such a trivial thing as a little bleeding. If only you could live in my body, even for a day...' And so it goes.

A nastiness has come over my employer, or maybe it has always been there but only now showing its ugly face. She seems to view me as a slave rather than as an employee. I work tirelessly for the Steenkamps but I am not allowed any room to express myself or even to be friendly with our neighbours or with occasional callers at the house. One day the Crowley boy from across the road knocked on the door and asked if his mother might borrow a bucket of coal. *Nooi* heard us in conversation, and she jumped to the conclusion that we were making arrangements to meet in secret. My punishment was blindingly painful: I had to remove my linen dress and stand directly in front of *Nooi* while she slowly and deliberately pinched my nipples so hard that I screamed and wet myself.

I am scared and trapped and alone here. More and more often, in the silence of my bed, situated here in the *buitekamer* of the Steenkamp residence, I cry myself to sleep. Sometimes I try to pray, but I do not really know how and, anyway, I find it difficult to have a conversation with a spirit who never answers me. I often think about running away, but how do I run away from an island? And, even if I could run away, where would I go? My mother does not want me and my father rests forever in his grave. I believe I have some aunties somewhere, but I have no idea where somewhere might be or whether they would want to know me.

As for *Baas* Steenkamp, he rarely speaks to me; he just allows his wife total control over my life and instinctively I know that there is no point appealing to him for help. He requires me to polish his boots and to iron his clothes very precisely as he is very particular about how he looks when he leaves the house. He has a few male friends who come and go very quietly, sometimes at most unexpected times very late at night but, beyond these night callers, few people ever knock on the door.

The only place I am permitted to go is to the church on Sundays, where I sit at the back with the dark-skinned people, while the Steenkamps join the other *witmense* where they are seated closer to the pulpit and, I suppose, closer to God. Occasionally, late at night after my employer has turned in, without her approval I take myself for a short walk; pause to listen to the barking of dogs, to look at the finger of light from the lighthouse, to shiver a little in the sea breeze. Because of the risk of meeting a black criminal or a gibbering lunatic out there in the darkness, I never go far though, but I will stop a while to savour the forbidden freedom of being outdoors at night.

It is at times like these when I spy the late-night callers who tap lightly at the cottage door.

In the evenings, after I have washed up and tidied the kitchen, I am expected to sit at the kitchen table, ready to see to *Nooi's* needs until such time as she is undressed and installed in bed. In this way I may be lingering, ready to be summoned like a genie from a bottle, for an hour or longer in the half-darkness of the kitchen.

Rather than sit still indeterminately waiting to be turned into a shadow, I sometimes tiptoe close to the door of the sitting room and listen in to the conversations of my employers but, maybe, I should rather block my ears than discover their evil schemes by eavesdropping as I do.

I hear them making plans. Plans to use me better.

Chapter 26 – A Meeting with Valerie

She comes alone to *Harrow*, on a Saturday, one day early in 1905, while I am at work, I think just a few weeks after the new year and a couple of months after Paul Kruger's funeral procession. She speaks briefly to Mother and asks my parent to tell me that she will be out the front of Stuttafords in Adderley Street on the next afternoon, Sunday, if I would like to see her.

I do not know what intelligence was exchanged between my mother and Valerie; what I do know is that my flower seller is nowhere to be seen in the vicinity of Stuttaford's on Sunday afternoon.

It is a blue-sky day with a thin tablecloth spilling over the edge of the mountain, and seemingly half the inhabitants of the city have turned out to walk here and there in company with the sunshine.

I wait for two hours until I cannot escape the conclusion that she is not going to show up. Has she thought better of meeting me? Or has her courage failed her? A thousand thoughts go through my mind as I alternately pace and loiter. With Stuttafords being right across from the flower stalls, I keep a keen eye on the activity at the stalls, just in case Valerie is there somewhere, her head and face possibly well covered with a shawl.

. . . .

'*Meneer?*'

I am roused from my reflections by a voice at my shoulder.

The speaker is a round woman, perhaps fortyish, Malay in appearance. Now that she has my attention she asks in a raspy voice, '*Ekskuus, meneer*, Are you *Meneer* Fox?' I suppose I nod to the question, so the person continues, 'Valerie sent me and asked me to give you this note.'

I almost snatch the note from the woman's hand, and I unfold it without waiting for the messenger to go.

In childlike writing, the penciled note says:

> *Dear Jems*
>
> *I am very sorrie. Next Sunday I will come to your howse – Valerie*

Well, I ask you, what do I make of that? Part of me is irritated by the note and about being enticed to the city on a wild goose chase, but a larger part is excited by the prospect of seeing my Valerie again. There are those walls of misunderstanding which must be broken down and cleared away from my life.

I give the round woman, who is lingering expectantly, a shilling, and thank her for delivering the note, and I take myself home.

After one of the longest weeks of my life, next Sunday comes, right after Saturday as you would expect. I take my princesses, Mabel and Evie, to the early mass; today I will be home when Valerie comes.

A hundred times I roleplay in my mind what I will say and do when I see her. Do I hold back and respond to whatever she wants to say, or do I pre-empt her concerns and come straight out with my explanations? And, whatever I say, will Valerie believe me? This is the make-or-break question which torments me every waking hour.

....

From a long way off I see her coming down Main Road. a little figure, smaller and more doll-like than ever. She is carrying a little wicker basket and a small bouquet of oriental lilies.

She stops when she sees me, and waits, so I take myself towards her.

When I reach her, I move to hug her but, adroitly. she avoids the embrace and offers me her cheek saying, 'I'm sorry about last Sunday, James, I lost my courage, and I lost the words I wanted to say. I'm very sorry...'

'Never mind,' I interject. 'You are here now. I have some things I need to say.'

'My turn first!' declares Valerie, showing a hint of the cheekiness I love so much. 'You'll be quiet, James, while I say what I have to say or I'm afraid I'll never get it out, or I'll make a complete mess of it.'

'Ladies first.' I try to answer in the best playful tone I can muster.

For several minutes she is quiet, presumably lining up her words. Then she speaks, pointing to the lilies in her basket, 'Let's walk while we talk, but first I need to drop these flowers for your mother as we pass the house.'

We proceed in silence for another minute to leave the flowers, then we walk on, in the direction of the Common, and Valerie begins 'You'd think that after all this time I'd know exactly what to say and exactly how to say it, James. But I suppose my mind doesn't work like that. Some days I've wanted to tell you off, other days I've been tempted to say none of what happened matters and then, on the dark days, I've wanted to walk away and say to myself: 'To hell with it, Valerie. It was never meant to be." But, somehow, I feel the need to finish what I started, you could say to tuck in the loose threads of my actions.'

'Your actions?'

'Yes, James, my actions. It was my decision to take you to my bed and it was also my decision to hold onto you and to build up a romantic sandcastle where we could live happily ever after. And you know what happens to sandcastles when the waves wash over them...'

'Did you say waves?'

'Shhh! I'm talking.'

I smile. Smile weakly, even though I am a little unsettled by Valerie's unexpected reference to waves.

'Now, I dare say, that without my encouragement, nothing would have happened for us. Both of us would soon have forgotten our brief encounter on that day at the flower stalls, the day the white knight came to my rescue.'

She pauses, scans my face, then continues, 'The business about that horrible little book, so thoughtfully left for you by Rowena Richardson, has bothered me no end. At first, I thought it was absolute proof that you were cheating on me on that island, but the longer I've thought about it, the more I'm not so sure. It's occurred to me that the woman is a temptress and a troublemaker. By itself that horrible book isn't proof of anything, is it?'

'Permission to reply to your question please? The truth must be told, or I will die.'

Pulling a face, Valerie sighs heavily and pretends to be exasperated. 'If you must but, mind you, it'll be your fault if I forget what I came here to tell you.'

Ignoring her show of exasperation, I say what I have been wanting to say for months. 'I did nothing with that woman, Valerie, nothing at all.'

'Really?'

'Yes, really. After breaking my leg from the fall in the lightstation, and the cook proving to be a useless nurse, Rowena Richardson appointed herself to the role of my carer. Prior to my accident she had ignored me but, once she and I were in close physical proximity, she seemed to develop a sudden interest, a flirtatious interest, in me. It was like she wanted to seduce me, not that I have much experience in such matters, just instinct. Anyway, this shameless interest persisted to the point where the fine lady left that dreadful little book at my bedside, along with the suggestive note. I had no knowledge of the book or the note while I was lying there on my back. No, not until Mother found it a long time later.'

'That's all that happened?' Valerie asks, her expression thoughtful.

'That's all that did happen, but...'

'But what? Is there something else?' Valerie wants to know, a hint of surprise creeping into her voice.

'Nothing else happened, nothing at all. But when I think about what was going on and, if I am completely honest with both of us, given a little more time, something may have happened.'

'Something?'

'Rowena Richardson is, I think, an accomplished and experienced temptress; in the end she may have succeeded. And how so, you may ask, when I have sworn to love and cherish you. Am I, after all, just a cheap liar? This is another good question which is desperately looking for an answer.'

'I don't understand…'

'Human nature is a curious thing, Valerie, and the nature of the human male is even curiouser. Here I am saying I love you and here I am saying, too, that maybe I would've slept with the Richardson woman. The design of nature is for the male to hunt, to seek to mate, to mate wherever and whenever he finds the opportunity. On the other hand, he often pledges his love to one special person and even he believes that his promise is sincere. Swearing to love just one person is against our instinct, that is if we are completely honest. I think it's likely quite unnatural, like walking backwards.'

'I think I understand. No, better still, I do understand,' says the slight woman walking here with me. 'Thank you for being honest, James, and the reason why I'm thanking you is that you've just made it easier for me to tell you what I must tell you. To tell you what I've been too afraid to say.'

'Afraid?' I ask. 'Surely you've never been afraid of me…'

'No,' Valerie interjects, 'not afraid of you. Afraid to face the truth, that's what.' Now she lapses into silence, looks straight ahead, and walks on as if she is going somewhere.

I keep pace with her and respect the silence.

Then, without introduction, Valerie declares, 'I'm leaving you, James. That's what I've been needing to tell you.'

'What? I don't understand. I've told you the whole truth, and more. I've thought about you every day we've been apart and missed you terribly, and I'll marry you tomorrow morning if that'll prove, once and for all, my intentions towards you. Why this talk of leaving me?'

Valerie stops and turns to face me. 'Dear James, I don't doubt that you love me or even that you'd marry me in the morning. But it's too late for that.'

'Too late? How on earth can it be too late? Tell me this is all a stupid dream.' And I shake my head hard as if attempting to push aside my dream, to raise my level of consciousness enough to grasp what is going on.

I see the tears in her eyes, the tears which she is struggling to hold back. 'Please, James, don't make this harder than it has to be. Just listen and try to understand what I'm saying.'

Solemnly I nod.

'The day I discovered that little book next to your bed, that day when I left feeling enraged and cheated and ready to die, I made my way to Steenberg to the home of my friend, Siti, where, seeing my obvious distress, her family agreed for me to stay there with them on condition I helped them on their smallholding with the endless chores of collecting eggs, plucking chickens and tending the vegetable beds.

I was happy to do this. I was also happy to have the time to think, both about my life and about life in general. Happy to have a complete break from my old surroundings.

I am not saying anything at all, but I must be looking puzzled as Valerie rolls out her story further; 'You know, James, how you were being tempted by Rowena? '

I nod.

'Well, something similar happened to me, except... except I let him...that's Hennie... I let him have me. And I suppose it shames me to say that I didn't even resist his advances.'

Now the tears are coming, drawing wet tracks down her cheeks, and her voice is hoarse with emotion. 'My heart was empty, James, and I let Hennie – that's Siti's brother – I let Hennie talk me into sleeping with him and the next month I knew I was going to have his baby. And Hennie did the right thing and married me two weeks later.'

'Jesus! Are you saying... are you seriously telling me that you have fucked with this fellow Hennie after knowing him for five minutes, that you've made a baby with him and now you're...'

'James! James! Please don't be so angry; he didn't make me do it. I made a choice, maybe a bad choice, maybe a good choice, and now I 'll accept whatever happens to me. But I thought it important to tell you myself what I've done. Now you're free, James, free to walk away and to forget about me. Believe me, James, it's better that it ends this way'

Chapter 27 – A Backward Glance

Telling James was the hardest thing I have ever done.

I feel hugely relieved, unburdened that I found the courage to tell him about Hennie, about my pregnancy and my marriage. At the same time, I am torn apart by guilt and unease by the heartless way I have treated James.

James does not deserve this outcome; he is the fairest, kindest man I have ever met and I have no doubt at all that he loves me very much, maybe too much for his own good. Things may have been less complicated, less painful, if we had - surrendering to the mating call - just had sex to satisfy the heat of the moment, pulled our clothes back on and walked off in different directions.

As I walk away from my first love, James Fox, I need to answer the obvious question. Why have I chosen this path? Since, even though I have gone and married Hennie, a man caring and hardworking enough but devoid of romantic instincts, I have to acknowledge that I still love James.

It is a fair question to ask whether I have lost my senses.

When I went to live in Steenberg with Siti's family, a curious thing happened to me. Yes, I was shattered by James's perceived treachery (which turned out to be nothing of the sort), but I also felt a deep connection with the families in Steenberg. These are my people, Cape Malays, people with two hundred years of tradition at the Cape of Good Hope, and it dawned on me then that I do not belong in the world of *witmense, and,* even when the *witmense* are kind and accepting like the Foxes, they are still not my people.

Hennie's persistence to have me, to take me at my weakest, was, as James so clearly described it, the hunting instinct of the male, and I understand that. I did not have to say yes. But I did say yes, and I said yes because my instinct tells me that I belong with one of my own kind. Not with the *witmense* of Rondebosch.

Once, when the Cape was lightly populated, mixed marriage was quite a commonplace thing and quietly accepted, and it occurred mostly out of necessity as there were simply not enough white women in the colony, but now the situation has changed and there is increasing pressure from people of influence and power that the races and religions should be kept separate from each other.

I am afraid that the time has come for us coloureds to live on the other side of the white man's fence.

Where we belong.

Chapter 28 – The In-Between Years, 1905 to 1908

Following my father's example over many years, I settle myself into an unchanging routine of commitment to my work and my family.

For six days a week I examine tickets and on the sabbath I examine my soul at St.Michael's, our regular place of worship, where I take my nieces in their freshly laundered frocks to mass, and for them to marvel at the creaminess of Our Lady's plaster features. Is it not curious that Mary is always depicted looking like a Nordic virgin when in real life she was likely olive-skinned and dark-haired, fully Arabian in appearance; what we would call 'coloured' here at the Cape?

Mother, who has always been lukewarm about worship, stays away from St. Michael's, while with the passing of each month my father finds it an increasing struggle to walk the distance from *Harrow* to Rouwkoop Road on account of arthritis in his legs and knees. Reluctantly, Father stays home, and he is frustrated by his failing eyesight which, even with the aid of eyeglasses, limits his ability to read the Holy Bible.

Most evenings I spend schooling Mabel and Evie; reading stories together; assembling jigsaw puzzles and playing card games, such as *Snap*. Evie will sometimes fall asleep at the kitchen table, sometimes in the middle of an activity, and Uncle James will lift the sleeping princess to her bed, where big sister Mabel will help her into her nightdress.

On Sunday afternoons I walk the girls to Newlands to visit their parents and their siblings and there I will spend an hour or two chatting to Harriet and Jim about nothing in particular.

Poor Harriet! She looks so old and so beaten by life. Her new baby, Leonard, is a sickly child who seems to wail unremittingly all day and night. She is haunted by the death of baby William John who died in 1898 at the tender age of twenty-five days and his replacement, William (without 'John') who, in 1902, returned to Heaven after just two months in this world. Now, with every passing hour, she fears that baby Leonard is also going to die.

Harriet and I have never been close, I suppose on account of the age difference, and I think she still sees me as just a boy with mud on his face and scrapes on his knees.

Despite his wife's obvious distress, Jim Middleton does not believe that caring for children is a man's responsibility. He spends his days tending the fields at the Newlands Rugby Ground where he gets to talk to the sportsmen and to swap legends over pints of beer. All this, while back home, there's not enough food for the next meal nor enough coal to warm the house in winter.

From time to time, taking care not to make it obvious that I am dispensing charity, I will take my sister a *snoek* or a sack of potatoes or a bag of mealie meal, and say things like, 'I bought too much of this,' or, 'the *smous* needed a quick sale and offered it cheap,'

Jim does not know what to make of me, barely grown up but so responsible, so ready to spend my spare hours in the company of two little nieces. Jim tried to interest me in rugby, then in cricket but, you know, I see no appeal in standing for hours in the sun and the wind waiting for a cricket ball to come my way and crack me on the head.

Through his contacts at the club Jim manages to secure me a ticket for the fourth test between the English touring team and South Africa at Newlands in March (1906), but, to his surprise and incomprehension, I forget the ticket in a drawer and fail to turn up to the game, and I fail to see Blythe take six wickets for the English team, in an historic game where England wins by four wickets.

As for my employment, these days I am a qualified ticket examiner, no longer under the day-to-day supervision of Aggenbach or anyone else. My confidence has grown as I have learnt how to deal with fare evaders, hard-luck Harrys and other chancers. The Cape Government Railways expect their regulations to be applied, strictly and without exception, at all times: 'No ticket, no ride' – 'Do not spit' – 'No standing in doorways' – etc.

I am experienced now, in control, and not easily intimidated by anyone.

There is pressure on the CGR to segregate the carriages, with whites apart from the darks; whites on one side and the *hotnots* and *kaffirs* on the other side. To demonstrate its compliance with the racist sentiments of the pro-British, pro-imperialist government of Mr Leander Starr Jamieson (the same fellow who tried to overthrow Kruger's Transvaal government in the ill-conceived Jamieson Raid), the Railways introduces a system of first-class and second-class carriages, the plan being that the cheaper second-class travel option will end up being used by the poorer dark-skinned people. To outward appearances it will seem to be a rational and reasonable system of economic separation, based solely on the travellers' ability to pay, when the reality of the arrangement is something a lot more sinister.

In view of the new arrangements, I am directed to 'encourage' the coloureds and the blacks to travel second-class until, predictably, the separation will be incorporated into the CGR Regulations.

While this shift is taking place, I remember some of my discussions at various times with Valerie and with Bayes; how year by year we can see the changes in our society; how we can see the little fires of racial tension taking hold all around us.

....

From week to week, month to month, for several years, I live by my rigid routine, rarely allowing myself the indulgence of doing something new. Father's decision about what gift he and Mother should bestow on me for my twenty-first birthday (on December 11th, 1905) is easily made, and unsurprising, on account of my love of regularity. They present me with father's treasured Waltham pocket watch, duly serviced and oiled for the occasion, that very timepiece which served my father so well for decades.

Emma, whom the family are now sometimes calling 'Emmeline' after Emmeline Pankhurst, by reason of her anti-establishment views, tries hard to do a little matchmaking for her brother, a young man mentioned in whispers as an eligible bachelor with regular employment. She drags various of her bohemian friends, many of them activists like herself, to *Harrow* for what is made to look like a chance introduction, but it is not hard to fathom what she is up to, and I know she means well, but I am unready to disrupt my existence. I am not made of stone though and I quite enjoy examining the prizes which Emma places before me. I even indulge in a little measured flirtation with some of them. With others, particularly those with strong political views, I relish a robust exchange of opinion. But, always, there is an invisible line which I will not cross in my dealings with these fair damsels. for example, I will always have a reason not to go to dances or to musical evenings or to the Kenilworth races.

In 1907 Emma has a proposal for me. She has been keenly following little Mabel's progress as I have schooled her diligently in the finer points of the English language, handwriting, arithmetic, history, geography, and the biological sciences. Emma says we should consider sending Mabel to high school; she believes Mabel has a good mind which will be wasted in early marriage and the annual production of a new baby.

I have to agree that Mabel has a fine mind; she can hold an informed discussion about many subjects: from the tribes of the African hinterland to the curious life cycle of the butterfly, from the significance of the Battle of Hastings to Mr Charles Darwin's outrageous theory of evolution. Mabel loves to comment, in her fourteen-year-old way, that, 'even a child can see that Mr Darwin was deluded. I mean, just imagine a fish turning into a bird. It's *Alice in Wonderland* stuff, isn't it, Uncle James?'

Now, when Emma says, 'we should consider,' she really means that I should consider, because, you see, my dear sister does not have ten bob to her name. Fortunately, because of my sober and frugal habits, I do have some savings and I will not think twice about spending it on my niece, Miss Mabel Fox, whom I love as much as if she were my own child.

Little Mabel looks a lot like her *Ouma* Eva must have looked as a child. She has coal-black hair which tends to frizziness, acorn-brown eyes and caramel skin. Unlike her parents, she doesn't look white. She's not pretty in any classical way, but clearly beautiful and caring by nature, a little girl with a big heart and a big smile, and always protective of her little sister, Evie.

With my full support guaranteed, Emma makes enquiries about a suitable high school and she soon discovers that high schools for girls are few and far between in Cape Town and only one, Springfield Convent School in Wynberg, offers a Catholic education. The school is run by the Dominican sisters; apparently it has a fine reputation of academic excellence, and is the first school in the Cape to offer young ladies the opportunity for matriculation.

Harriet declines to visit the school with me, I suspect because she is afraid that her own lack of education will be put on display, and Jim declines as well, in his case because I think he may be embarrassed that he cannot pay or even offer to contribute towards the school fees.

So it happens that one fine day early in the summer of 1907, Emma, Mabel, and I ride the train to Wynberg and we make our way to the Springfield Convent School. In a satchel I bring numerous samples of Mabel's school work, albeit the tasks she has completed with me in the evenings at *Harrow*. We have examples of composition, arithmetic, tracings of maps, samples of penmanship and much more, hopefully enough to impress the people at Springfield. But, if Mabel's work samples are not enough for the Dominican Sisters, I have something extra in my satchel, no less than a letter of introduction from our parish priest, Father Kelly, who has known little Mabel since the day of her baptism back in 1893.

The Springfield Convent School, a group of low stone buildings, is located on vast grounds in the rural part of Wynberg, and it invites us to enter and to take in the serenity of the place.

After some polite inquiry we are ushered into the school office and invited to seat ourselves on a stinkwood bench to await the appearance of the headmistress herself. Sister Immaculata, the headmistress, is nothing like I had imagined her to be. She has a round and friendly face with the pinkest cheeks I have ever seen; she certainly does not look like someone who spends all her days on her knees in the silent shadows reciting her rosary. No, not at all, this person bubbles and pops with life and energy; she almost seems to have to check herself from embracing all of us like long-lost family.

We are offered cups of tea which we gladly accept, then it is down to business, that is to say, if the term 'business' can be used to apply to the education of a young lady.

I cannot fail to notice that the good sister, while scrutinising the documents I have brought, is frequently looking up to inspect Mabel who is sitting ever so primly and quietly while the adults are speaking.

The inspection of the documents complete, along with the utterance of 'Aah' at the viewing of Father Kelly's letter of introduction, the holy woman, now quite solemn, asks Mabel to step outside in order that she might address the adults in private.

'Sir and madam,' she begins, 'clearly young Mabel is a capable student and more than ready for high school, but...'

'But what?' Emma, dear Emma, she cannot help herself.

'Allow to explain please,' continues the headmistress not unkindly. 'By outward appearance your niece, Miss Mabel Middleton, does not appear to be white, that is to say, not of exclusive European descent.' She pauses, raises her hand to indicate that she is not inviting any interruption. 'Please, please, do not be offended by my observation. Things have changed in our country and we, that is Springfield Convent School, we have had to bend to the winds of change.

Two years ago, the Cape School Board, at the behest of the Cape government, instructed all schools in the colony to choose to be open for whites only or open only for people of colour. No longer would any school, even Catholic schools like ours, be allowed to have a mixture of races in our classrooms.' Sister Immaculata still has her hand raised, indicating that she has yet more to say. 'As we are now a whites-only school, we are required by law to make inquiry into the racial background of every child presented here for enrollment.'

Emma cannot contain herself in spite of the raised hand. 'Are you saying that because Mabel has a naturally dark complexion that she'll not be allowed to attend this school?'

The headmistress lowers her voice, probably hoping to calm Emma's rising agitation. 'Madam, it is not the child's complexion in itself which matters here. What does matter is what race the child's parents and grandparents may be, and that must be determined by examination of birth certificates. Any failure on my part to examine the birth certificates may result in the school being fined or even being shut down.' The holy sister pauses for a moment as she looks directly into our eyes. 'I'm so sorry, sir and madam, my hands are completely tied.'

. . . .

This is how it happens - by an accident of ancestry - that Mabel Middleton never goes to high school.

Chapter 29 – The Tightening of the Screw

Meneer Steenkamp has a new friend. This man is the new lightkeeper, a replacement for the dead one who, one particularly stormy night, fell fifty feet from the lightstation balcony to the stony ground below.

The Steenkamps call the new lightkeeper Alf, which I think is short for Alfred, and his surname is Pike, and I know this because I have been told to call him *Meneer* Pike.

This man Pike spends most of his off-duty time here. He has various arrangements with the Steenkamps, one of which is to have his meals here. I am supposed to be given three shillings a week by *Baas* Pike for preparing the extra meals, but *Nooi* Steenkamp takes the coins for herself. After all, you may ask, what need does a *meidjie* like myself have for money? Do I not have food and a dry bed and at Christmas time a colourful dress or a pair of sandals; what more can I possibly want?

As for Pike's other arrangements with the Steenkamps, I find them odd. I had better try to explain or you will call me stupid, and I hate being called stupid. I get more than enough of that from *Nooi*.

Mr Steenkamp is bringing boys and young men, all of them lunatics, from the asylum where he is a warder, to this cottage. After my mistress goes to bed, he brings one at a time here, and he places the person in the spare room. I am not supposed to know because I am supposed to be in bed myself but my natural curiosity and my ability to fade into the shadows allow me to discover the after-dark movements in the home.

Some nights *Baas* Steenkamp will spend an hour in the room with the male guest and on other nights *Meneer* Pyke will appear and similarly spend an hour in the spare room. I am determined to find out what goes on in that room. I just need to wait for the right opportunity.

There are some clues. Often an empty brandy bottle in the morning. Sometimes moaning or shouting at night; occasionally crying, even screaming. I do not know what to make of it all, but my instinct tells me that evil things are going on. Sometimes the noises sound like the noises I used to hear when a strange man would come to our place in Saldanha Bay, those times when mother would shut her bedroom door and allow the man to possess her body. But this is different. Here there is no woman to give her body, just men and boys, and some of the boys are very young, maybe even less than ten years old.

When I myself do not understand what is going on, how do I explain this to you, so it makes sense? All I can tell you is what I see and hear in the lateness of the night.

As for *Nooi* Steenkamp, she has a secret business, a business which she says will make her rich and me famous. That is if we do everything the right way, part of which is not telling anyone what we are doing, says *Nooi,* or others are bound to steal her idea and line their pockets with gold sovereigns which are rightfully hers.

But promise me now not to say a word and not to try this idea yourself and I will tell you about the secret business if you come a little closer. *Nooi* must never know I am telling you or she will skin me like a freshly killed rabbit.

It is three or four years I have been here with the Steenkamps. In the early days after our arrival the Steenkamps mostly kept to themselves and my days, long and dreary days, were filled entirely with my servant-girl duties. As time went by the Steenkamps did make a few friends here and there; warders and their wives, some orderlies, and nurses, and *Meneer* Martin Vickery. I think Vickery is some sort of assistant or advisor to the island superintendent and I overheard someone whisper to *Nooi* that he was once upon a time a minister in the Church of England but that he had been caught with his 'pants down,' whatever that expression means.

As for me, Gina da Cunha, I am not allowed to have friends for fear they will distract me from my duties. Or, possibly, for fear that I will tell them about some of the things which go on here.

It would have been a year to eighteen months ago when the Steenkamps befriended Vickery. This man has a lean and hungry look about him, a bit like a vulture, and a curious habit of licking his lips before he speaks, as if to moisten his words before he allows them to leave his mouth. This Vickery has a special hobby of taking and developing photographs, an activity which he likes to refer to as 'the expression of divine innocence.' In the attic of the Steenkamp cottage Vickery has a 'darkroom,' a particular place filled with trays and chemicals and tanks, where he develops his photographic plates into what he enthusiastically calls his 'immaculate masterpieces.' The former churchman is full of such odd expressions. Until *Mevrou* Steenkamp and I get involved, the subjects of the photos have apparently always been young boys, in various poses, and invariably as naked as the day they were born. Mind you, the photographs have never actually been shown to me but they are periodically left lying about where I will come across them in the course of my housework. I could say that I come across them entirely by chance but, since I am telling your all my secrets, I will be honest with you and admit that I occasionally have a little snoop around to satisfy my girlish curiosity.

Apparently in Cape Town *Meneer* Vickery has a circle of admirers, a group which he calls, 'Mr Wilde's fine-feathered friends,' (who is this Mr Wilde, I wonder?). My mistress, herself an admirer of Vickery's photographic skill, realises soon enough that the scope of Vickery's fine works can be widened to having nude images of a suitably beautiful female subject. Perhaps someone like the sixteen-year-old servant girl in the Steenkamp household who, apparently by any measure, is a well sculpted example of young womanhood. A single skillfully mastered image of this dusky virgin is worth £5 in the hands of the right buyer. And the result? A clear profit of £4 for Mrs Steenkamp, after paying Martin Vickery the sum of £1 for his services.

No doubt you are wondering how I am required to present my nakedness for some 'immaculate masterpieces' of the feminine variety? Vickery particularly fancies what he calls 'the voyeur poses' which I understand to mean poses which are borrowed from everyday existence which have the appearance of the subject being unknowingly observed, as through a keyhole. For such poses I find myself being photographed, always butt naked, doing everyday things like soaping my body at the washstand or standing on a chair to reach a high shelf, or polishing the floor with a coconut brush.

At first, I feel awkward and self-conscious having this Vickery fellow see my nakedness, but I soon discover that he has nothing beyond a professional interest in me, as if he were merely photographing a colourful butterfly among the daisies. He keeps his distance, and his hands to himself, so soon I relax, and I hardly notice that he is there with his lamps and his Kodak camera contraption.

Nooi though is not entirely satisfied with Vickery's artistry; she wants something more erotic, more risque – in truth, something more saleable. Something for which a man will willingly part with no less than five gleaming sovereigns. The images she wants are not for the eyes of tramps and labourers; she wants a product for the well-to-do gentlemen of the Colony, for men of distinction and power. Men with the means to pay for what they want.

This is how it happens that the rather innocent bare-bottom pictures are put aside in favour of somewhat more tantalising images, for example, there is an image - favoured by my mistress - of a puppy licking my nipple (which was made by applying a drop of fish oil to that part).

There are the other images, too; one showcasing my body arching upwards on a zebra skin with my puckered lips encircling a banana; another featuring a fearsome Doberman standing over my bareness, and yet another picturing me fingering the beads of a rosary between the mounds of my breasts. The images are close to the lens-eye of the Kodak, almost near enough for the beholder to touch. And, I think, close enough to stir a dead man from his grave.

I am an uncomplaining subject for the photographer, even though I often wonder how long it will be before I become famous. As for *Nooi,* she seems well pleased with her part of the deal; I suspect that soon the Royal Mint will have to increase its production of sovereigns just to keep pace with her appetite for profit.

If you happen to know my mistress like I do, you will know that enough is never enough.

....

Ma has visited me just once, about two years ago, I think it was the week before Christmas of 1906. She looked tired and her front teeth were missing which changed the shape of her mouth. It is not a nice thing to say about my own mother but the truth is that she looked old, well-used by several hard years and weighed down by the constant struggle of existence.

Ma, with her coffee-coloured skin (which seems to be getting browner as she gets older?) is quite obviously a *hotnot* which means that the Steenkamps did not want her in the cottage anywhere beyond the kitchen, so for the two nights she spent on Robben Island, she slept with me on the ancient coir mattress in the *buitekamer.*

After all, it really would not do to have a woman such as Ma staying in your house. Whatever would your friends and neighbours think of such a thing?

When *Mevrou* Steenkamp was not looking, Ma gave me a gold ring with the advice to keep it for a 'rainy day' and to hold it sometimes close to my heart and try to remember the happy times when Pa was still alive, when we were together and had lots to eat.

This ring is far too big for my fingers; likely it was given to Ma in payment by one of her gentlemen clients, but why should that matter now? I will keep it close to me and out of sight of *Nooi* – for she would surely find some excuse to take it away from me.

Chapter 30 – The Year 1909:
Changing Course

'There's no future for you, James, as a ticket examiner.' Coming from my father, this is a somewhat unexpected point of view. Did he not spend almost his entire life working for the railways?

'It's a steady job, Father, and guaranteed, unless I'm foolish enough to pilfer some ticket money or throw some dignitary off the train.'

Now Bayes jumps in, adding his two bobs' worth to the discussion, 'Don't be dim, James, a young man with your education is wasted going about demanding tickets on the trains...'

Father interrupts him, 'That's the point. An honest job is a thing of value and I've never looked down my nose at any person performing an honest job, but here we have a situation where the employee is suited to better things. Bayes is right. With your matriculation you can go far, James, much further than being a ticket examiner on the Wellington line.'

'My father-in-law to be,' Bayes reminds us, 'Captain Nelson of the 1st Police District, is looking for recruits; he wants some fine young men for the Cape Mounted Police and he wants them right now. Training starts on 28th June.'

'There you go, James, my boy,' instructs my father. 'Strike the iron while it's hot and one day, that is if I live long enough, I'll get to see you as the Inspector of Police, your chest full of medals, and enough gold braid to outshine the Prince of Wales.'

They are right, of course. I am comfortable as a ticket examiner and the pay turns up every month without fail, but there is no challenge, nothing new. I am twenty-four years old, young enough to change course, and old enough to offer some experience of life. This fork in my path has appeared at the right time for me, a time when I am ready to turn off the old road.

Just two weeks later, here I am, just done with being interviewed and with the verbal assurance of being accepted for police training.

Captain Nelson was there, along with two other officers whose names I cannot recall, and straight away Nelson figured out that I am Bayes's brother, even though we look nothing alike, Bayes being the ugly duckling of the family - and myself the modern Adonis!

The captain is suitably impressed that I survived the rigours of Dassen Island, the terrible cold and the isolation of that place, and he is equally awed with my experience as a ticket examiner and the grounding it has provided me in dealing with chancers and other elements of society's underbelly. And, finally, the fact that I am tall, with the physique of an athlete, is the deciding factor for the good officers.

I had been concerned that my inability to ride a horse (along with my near inability to tell a horse from a donkey) and my lack of knowledge concerning the firing of a rifle or a pistol would be an impediment to my recruitment but I am promptly assured that those skills will be provided in abundance in my training. No, they tell me, there is nothing to worry about. Just do your best young man, they say.

'By the right, quick march!' 'Company, present arms!' 'Eyes left!' 'Attention!' 'About turn!'

The training takes over my thinking, fills my head with commands, informs me that I am 'lower than a snake's belly' and 'the property of the Colony.'

I learn, too, that I am now in a most intimate relationship with my rifle, that I must never let 'her' out of sight; at all costs I cannot allow any other man to touch 'her'. I am commanded to clasp 'her' butt into my shoulder, to finger lightly at the sensitivity of 'her' trigger and daily to plunge 'her' barrel with a rod and oily patch. She and I are to be inseparable. This is the way. Welcome to the Cape Mounted Police.

The Calvary Camp in Maitland is our training ground; a flat and sandy tract of *fynbos* smattered with patches of large and small Cape rushes and clumps of brightly flowering *vygies*. Part of the site, farthest north and closest to the sea, is where horses are corralled before and after being transported by sea. The south side adjacent to the railway line is the location of the cemetery and in the middle, immediately north of the train track, is the police camp, a place set aside 'to break boys and remake them into men.'

I find that I have trouble getting the cooperation of horses. It is as if the beggars know that I do not know a stirrup from a bridle, and they seem keen to take full advantage of my ignorance. I can swear that these beasts are laughing at me, challenging my patience, and waiting for an opportunity to bite off my fingers.

But I am determined to succeed and to pass every aspect of the training. To this end, I convince a fellow trainee, Baksteen du Plessis - with the inducement of two bottles of Van Ryn's best brandy - into giving me extra riding lessons at his family's smallholding in Klapmuts. This is how it comes about, after several misadventures and bruises, that I sort out the horses' hoofs from the hindquarters; how I even get to like horses as I get to understand them better.

Father and Bayes are well pleased with my progress, Louisa and Harriet are indifferent and submerged in their own concerns; Jim Middleton is too busy telling cricket and rugby stories to care; but Emma, dear Emma, is furious with me. She claims that I am 'sleeping with the enemy', that I have sold my soul to King Edward, 'that philandering old cock.' Her annoyance unsettles me, not because I cannot take the criticism, but because I have come to value my relationship with my sister, come to appreciate her support with the care of Mabel and Evie. After all, what do I know about the inclinations and needs of little girls?

Emma's attitude to my new career does make me think though. Why, I ask myself, do I want to play policeman? Is a colonial policeman, as Emma is quick to point out to me, not merely an instrument of the ruling classes, a baton to bludgeon the seldom-washed masses into submission? Maybe she is right; maybe I have been nudged down this path by Father and by Bayes. No doubt they are well intentioned, but do they realise the full extent of what they want for me? And what is it that I, James William Fox, 'my father's son,' what is it that I want?

I ask Mother for her insight. I can always rely on her to see a matter from a different perspective.

'The wave, James,' she tells me, 'which, if you were listening, I told you about a long time ago, is still building. Soon - next year I think - it will break, and not long before there is going to be a great light in the sky, an omen if you like. You must be very careful, James.'

'But I don't understand...'

'Nor do I, James, nor do I. Sometimes I see things and the meaning is obvious. But much of the time there's a degree of haze which distorts my view. If you like, it's like surveying a room through a glass, where at times the image you see is quite clear and reliable and at other times the image is just a distortion, a jumble of arms and legs in a pickle jar.'

I cannot help noticing the worried look on her face. She is clearly not telling me everything.

'Let's return to the question, Mother. Should I be riding with the Cape Mounted Police or am I, as Emma is saying, riding with the enemy?'

'It really makes no difference, James. Do what you will and always try to do what is right. Doing right can be done anywhere you find yourself but a possible advantage of joining up with the forces of justice is that you can influence from within, rather than pushing from without. In other words, do your best where you can, And while you can...' She looks away, and it may only be my imagination, but I suspect that she can no longer hide the fear and misgiving within her mind. What is this vision, this terrible vision which troubles her so?

To calm Emma and to keep her close to me I decide that my best course of action is to provide her with certain assurances, specifically that, as a policeman, I will do what is just and, if that contradicts what is expected of me, then to hell with the job.

I will not put a price on my soul. That is what I decide, but I will not share my decision in these terms with Bayes because, Bayes being Bayes, he will call me an idealistic idiot for harbouring notions of right and wrong in a such a flawed society.

Emma is a little suspicious when I tell her what I have decided, but she knows me well, which means that she knows that I will do my best to do exactly what I say. With a wicked twinkle in her eye, she instructs me to be looking the other way the day she and her comrades decide to blow up the grand new Anglo-Boer War Memorial opposite the Drill Hall. 'That thing,' declares Emma, 'is a fucking disgrace. Imagine commemorating the infliction of death and suffering on innocent people as if it were something honourable to do.'

. . . .

The training goes on for a full five months. Drill. Weaponry. Regulations. More regulations. Target practice, More target practice. Formations and escorts. Briefs and warrants. Vagrancy, loitering and stock theft. Horsemanship and dressage. Summons and bail. Plaintiff and Respondent. Handcuffs and leg-irons. This administration of justice business is an arcane affair, a business requiring privileged admission into hushed halls, concealed corridors, imposing chambers of polished wood and stone, brass plates, oaken shelves filled with legal tomes, damp underground cells, iron gates and oversized locks.

Our squad graduates on Saturday, 27th November. Families are invited and, after the passing out parade, with all its pomp and ceremony, the big day is to be celebrated with a *braai* and beer which is to be provided by the great generosity of the Cape government.

Father says he is not feeling up to it – actually he is nearly blind now and would not see a thing - but he will rather say that he has a pain in his foot, and Mother, well, as you know, my female parent prefers to shun the darkening rays of the sun. But Emma is here, doing her best to be inconspicuous in 'the enemy camp' as she calls it, and Bayes has turned up, and the whole Middleton family, too, to benefit from the opportunity of free food. Along with the free beer for Jim, who always has a great thirst, not matter how humble or how grand the occasion.

Inspector Robert Crawford, resplendent as a peacock in his dress uniform, is here today for the presentation, along with the Prime Minister, Mr John X.Merriman - whom Emma insists on calling 'somebody's Uncle Xavier' – and the Governor, Sir Walter Hely-Hutchinson, temporarily descended from his vice-regal throne for this auspicious occasion.

Sir Walter takes the time (is it an hour?) to remind the assembly of the majesty of our monarch, King Edward VII, and the magnificence of the British Empire, an empire which has brought great enlightenment, progress and economic development, blah-blah, and blah-blah, to every corner of the globe.

When all is done, Emma, noticing that I am the only graduate without a female admirer on his arm, sidles up close, kisses me on the cheek and offers me her arm. And here we are, mingling with the crowd, arm in arm, as sweetly as

Sunday afternoon lovers on the Green Point Common. I remind myself to keep my promise to her, to do what is right and fair, and never to allow myself to be corrupted by self-interest or by the self-interest of others.

Bayes is enjoying the day, glowing in the reflected importance of Captain Nelson, his future father-in-law, and Jim, well Jim is doing what Jim knows best, which is weaving fantastic stories about the gentlemen's game of cricket. Jim tells the story, a story I have heard him tell before, of how a certain batsman named Bowler (believe it or not!) scored forty-two runs in an over. Even an elementary school boy knows that the maximum number of runs possible in an over is thirty-six and not a single run more. Now, assuming that you are uninitiated into the game of cricket, please hear the explanation of how it happened, according to Jim, that forty-two runs were scored by a man named Bowler.

In the game of cricket there is a man with a bat, called the batsman, who tries his best to hit the ball which is bowled to him by a player called the bowler. The bowler bowls six balls in a bowling turn which is called an over. The batsman can score a maximum number of points, called 'runs', of six per ball. Arithmetic informs us that six balls multiplied by six points ('runs') comes to a maximum score of thirty-six runs per over.

Of course, everyone is quick to laugh a Jim's incredible story and to point out the arithmetical impossibility of scoring forty-two runs in an over. Then, with a straight face, Jim tells his audience how, on the occasion in question, a memorable summer's day at Newlands, back in '96, the bowler's attention drifted from the task at hand and he ended up bowling seven balls in one over, and the batsman, Mr Bowler, who was in remarkable form that day, scored six from every ball bowled to him. And that, chaps, is how it happened that forty-two runs were scored in one over.

Harriet, carrying a large basket, is content to find herself a quiet corner from which to direct her children to attend, as many times as possible, the trestle tables where the food is set out, for helpings of sausages, chops, buttered bread and sweet cakes, which items she is quick to conceal under a shawl which she has draped over the basket. The children love the buzz and bustle of the occasion and when they are not running for more helpings of food, they are gaping at the beautifully groomed police horses and hiding between the parked wagons, carts and carriages which have transported everyone and everything to this place.

And here I am, strutting about, a newly graduated constable in the Cape Mounted Rifles; who would ever have thought to see my father's son here today?

....

It is the first week of December and already I have my registered letter informing me of my posting, a month sooner than expected. I admit that I am taken aback to learn that my first posting will be on Robben Island, a place so near and yet so far from Cape Town, a place seldom mentioned in polite conversation.

Why Robben Island? Is this the way it is going to be for me, I ask myself, to spend half my life on a succession of islands?

Chapter 31 – Family Matters

My imminent departure, unexpectedly to Robben Island, changes everything. If I were merely being posted to Mowbray or Salt River or Simonstown, I could probably, with some adjustments, continue living at *Harrow;* but Robben Island; well, that is something else.

Mother seems the most distressed. How will they manage with father's near-blindness and her increasing frailty? And what will happen to Mabel and Evie?

Something must be done, and it is Bayes who takes the initiative, who calls a family meeting for Saturday 12th, the day before I sail. Clearly Bayes has something in mind since it is not like Bayes not to have calculated his position.

Bayes expects to be married in the new year to Miss Evelyn Nelson, youngest daughter of Captain Nelson, the second in charge officer of District 1, Cape Mounted Police. In spite of Evelyn's fine pedigree, she's an unpretentious little creature, eminently suited to being overshadowed by her husband-to-be, prepared to allow him to make every decision about everything, even down to what time she will clean her teeth and how they will decorate their living room. Why she is marrying Bayes has mystified me for some time; the only possible explanation which has occurred to me is that maybe she sees something of her father in him - a man who likes giving orders and derives his joy from controlling others.

The current arrangement for Bayes is that he is paying a mortgage for his modest cottage in Mowbray, a cottage which he shares with our sister, Louisa (who is in great danger of becoming a lifelong spinster). As the manager of the Marsh & Sons tea importing business in Berg Street, Bayes's financial position is secure; secure enough to pay all the household expenses at Mowbray and to indulge himself in a little wagering on the races at Kenilworth, and lately also at the new Milnerton track, while Louisa keeps house for them and attends church for both of them (on account of Bayes's soul being at some risk of being forfeited to Old Nick).

Emma, my free-spirited sibling, wanders between homes. Sometimes she stays a while at *Harrow,* sometimes at Mowbray with Bayes and Louisa, sometimes at the homes of her kindred spirits; there is no pinning her down to any permanent arrangement. Similarly, she will not serve any man; she will always come and go as she pleases. In a way I envy her, so brave and free, so ready to go wherever the wind may take her.

Jim and Harriet decline to attend the family meeting, Harriet tearfully informing Bayes that they have nothing to contribute, that they can focus only on making it to the end of another day, like prisoners of fate, doomed to breaking a quota of rocks before being allowed another meal.

. . . .

Father, our patriarch, wants to speak first but Bayes convinces him first to hear the proposal which he, Bayes, has formulated. Clearly Bayes has a plan, as I suspected.

"I have a suggestion,' begins Bayes from where he is standing in our midst, 'a suggestion to which I have given much thought this past week since we have discovered that James is to be posted to Robben Island.'

Bayes has everyone's attention. 'Maintaining separate households no longer makes sense.'

He pauses briefly to let his statement register, then he pushes on, 'Father and Mother, our selfless parents who have spent all their lives feeding, clothing and educating us, now need us to look after them. I believe you'll agree with me that this is the way it should be.'

Detecting no dissent, Bayes pushes his barrow further down the road, 'There is a house for sale in Claremont, in size equal to the two small homes in which we now find ourselves. I should like to propose that Father and I sell our humble dwellings, that we combine the funds and use the money to buy the bigger place in Claremont. The house in question has four bedrooms and I think that, with a little careful sectioning, it may be possible to expand it to five or even six bedrooms. Enough room for all of us and for Evelyn, too.'

Now, Emma, wise to Bayes's ways, is compelled to ask, 'Tell us Bayes, whose name will be on the title, should we agree to your buying the Claremont house?'

And, Bayes being Bayes, now exposed, lies and answers, 'If Father and I buy it together, then naturally we should be the joint owners. This is fair, don't you think?'

Now Father speaks. He clearly has his own view on what is fair. 'Your mother and I will contribute a sum equal to Bayes's investment. No more, no less. If there is still money owing, then Bayes must pay the mortgage. In return for our investment, we - that is your mother and I – will live at this new address, without any cost to us, for our remaining years. When we depart, our share of the property will go to Bayes. Which means that in the future he will not be required to sell in order to settle our estate. Whatever cash and savings we have when we leave this world will be shared equally between our other children. This is the way it has to be and, to make this official, the detail will be set out in our last will and testament.'

Bayes is clearly not entirely happy that he will not have everything his way, but he knows better than to disagree with our father, a man who, when he has set his mind, is as unshakeable as a bulldog on a burglar's leg.

Now it is my turn to ask a question. 'Tell me, Bayes, will there be room for our nieces, Mabel and Evie, in this new house?'

I sense that the nieces were not part of his plan but, now that they have been mentioned, he is pushed to respond. He answers, 'The truth be told, James, I will struggle to feed so many mouths...'

I cut him short (any shorter and I will have scalped him), 'Don't you worry about it, Bayes. I will pay for them, for their food and for every need. No need at all to trouble yourself at on their account.' In saying this I notice that Emma is looking at me approvingly and, when I catch her eye, she flashes me a cheeky wink.

This is how the wheels are set in motion for a family move to Claremont, a move which is accomplished early in 1910, just a few weeks before the wedding day of Bayes and Evelyn.

Chapter 32 – Welcome to Robben Island

Tiger is waiting for me at Dock Basin.

It is a blustery morning in Table Bay on this early summer's day, and there is enough gritty smoke from the ferry's boiler to fill the basin in every direction.

I half expect to see Captain Jacobs here but, of course, he is not. This is not his run nor his boat. This sooty-faced little tramp, *Tiger,* is another man's girl.

I find the *Tiger's* skipper, a fellow with a cap so besmirched that it looks like it was reclaimed from a fish market floor, and he shrugs carelessly and does not bother with returning my introduction, and clearly he does not seem to care whether I - just another *fokken diener* - am aboard or not, as he supervises the loading of several casks, and a couple of lepers under the supervision of a crumpled little man in a khaki uniform.

What am I to expect on Robben Island? I have heard, of course, that there are lunatics there, and lepers, and a lighthouse but, beyond these small snippets of general knowledge, the place may as well be in the Caribbean or in the Straits of Malacca. I try to engage the crumpled man - his features and his uniform being equally crumpled by hard wear – in some conversation, but like the skipper, he is reluctant to talk beyond telling me that he is escorting a couple of 'filthy lepers' to the 'lazar house' (which I later discover is a term for a leper hospital).

The dark green waters of the Atlantic brood below my eyes as *Tiger* chugs on her way towards the dark smudge on the horizon while I am left alone with my thoughts for the rest of the one-hour voyage, and I cannot help wondering what the future holds. Will I fit with the job and will it fit with me? How is it that I am posted to this place and not to some remote backwater like Beaufort West or Sutherland or De Aar?

These thoughts and others are still churning through my head when *Tiger* docks at the Faure jetty, a narrow trestle structure protruding like a finger into the surf. Here, standing on the jetty, I see a solitary and motionless figure, a man with his arms folded and his face expressionless. As it turns out, the figure is waiting for me. And as it turns out, this figure is Sgt.John Boyce himself.

He is not a big man and not immediately recognisable as a policeman as he is wearing a floppy fisherman's hat and non-regulation boots. The sergeant has an erect and watchful presence, a presence which pops the word 'sentinel' into my mind as I clamber onto the pier dragging a bag of belongings with me.

The figure waits for me to reach him, then his face splits in two with a remarkable smile as he reaches forward to shake my hand, 'Welcome James!'

'Thank you!' I say a little more enthusiastically than I feel. 'Reporting for duty, sir.'

'Our first duty today, James, is to settle you into your quarters. I've arranged for them to be swept and scrubbed and sanitised and I'm hopeful that my instructions have been followed or we may have to arrest someone for taking money under false pretences, won't we?'

I am unsure what Boyce is talking about – who is the mysterious 'someone' who is taking money? Maybe it is best that I just keep my mouth shut in order not to reveal my ignorance and wait and see where the day - and my mentor - lead me?

John Boyce leads the way from the jetty, following what he calls the 'tram' track, but which is really just a rail line for a modest donkey-powered wagon train designed to convey provisions from the jetty to the store.

Boyce seems friendly enough, but he is not a particularly talkative man; he seems happy to be socialising with his own thoughts as we trudge silently through the village, past rows of stone cottages, past a school and a white church, which is the tallest building in a mostly depressed landscape. There are a few people shuffling about, downcast souls dressed in odd and ill-fitting garments. These shufflers appear, to my unaccustomed eye, to lack purpose or a place to go.

I remember Father's advice, given long ago, about asking questions in order to show interest, so I decide to ask a few here and there without imposing too much on the sergeant's silent nature. 'Tell me, sir, do we have horses to get about the island?'

'No, lad, not here, Here, on Robben Island, we are known as the Cape Dismounted Police as the inspector figures that, as the island measures just one mile wide by two miles long, we should walk our beat and not drain his budget for horseflesh and hay.'

'And tell me, sir, who are these sorry looking people staring at us from the edge of the road?'

'These are mostly lunatics, James; the harmless ones who are allowed to walk about. Here and there we'll come across lepers, too, and, across the island, *kaffir* prisoners, mostly minor chiefs and agitators who have been exiled here.' Boyce relapses into silence and I feel that I have used up my morning's quota of questions.

Table Mountain, only seven miles distant, is ever present in this flat landscape; then beyond the rows of stone cottages and the grim largeness of the asylum buildings, the place is near barren heath and criss-crossed with sandy tracks.

We are making our way northwards towards Murray's Bay, to the police post and police quarters, in the area where the *kaffir* prisoners have their tents and *pondoks*. Without notice, Boyce speaks again; 'I recommend you join our angling club, constable. It's the best way to get to know the locals. The locals are strange, James, and a secretive lot, who hold themselves apart from regular citizens of the colony; I think on account of the stain of working with the damned and the outcasts of society.'

I tell the sergeant that I have some experience of line-fishing from my time on Dassen Island, and I promise to look at joining the angling group. Even if I catch myself no humans, I shall have the pleasure of regular meals of fresh fish, which is no small reward for casting a line.

. . . .

Comprising several low whitewashed buildings, the police block is marked by the Cape Colonial flag flapping vigorously in the brightness of this summer's day, and the seagull perched precariously on the flagpole pretends not to notice our approach.

A man and a woman appear from one of the buildings and they wait there in the brightness for us to reach them.

The man, dressed in a dun-coloured, double-fronted jacket and a cloth cap, and much older than the woman, speaks first, *'Ons is klaar, sersant.'*

'Dankie, Steenkamp,' replies the sergeant, and reaching into the breast pocket of his tunic, he extracts a half-sovereign which he hands to Willem Steenkamp. 'Be sure to buy Gina a pretty scarf or a bangle for her trouble.'

Steenkamp pockets the money without acknowledgement of the instruction, tips his cap in greeting and leads the young woman, Gina, away, without giving her a chance to say anything.

I cannot help noticing how Gina kept her mouth shut and her eyes downcast throughout the transaction and it all seems rather odd. She is clearly not a child, yet this man, Steenkamp, seems to be in total control of her. I am troubled enough by my observation to ask Boyce, 'Who are these people?'

Boyce thinks a moment, seems to be unsure how to verbalise his response. He looks at me with a wry smile, 'These people, James, are two of the odd local inhabitants, I could even say the local oddities, I mentioned earlier. The fellow, Steenkamp, is the chief warder at the asylum while the young woman, Gina, is his adopted daughter. She never goes anywhere unless escorted by him. Today they were here to clean the police quarters – Gina to clean and Steenkamp to supervise and take the payment.'

'Adopted daughter?' My question is reflexive. But some time ago, somewhere beyond my immediate recollection, I did hear the name Gina before.

Boyce is saying, 'Yes, adopted, I understand. Mrs Steenkamp is a cripple who apparently couldn't bear children, so the Steenkamps adopted Gina, maybe six or seven years ago, I think from somewhere up the west coast – might've been Saldanha Bay.'

My memory is unready to reveal the connection yet. Gina? Gina who? Gina where? It troubles me because I know I ought to know.

Chapter 33 – The Unholy Plan

I see we have a new constable, a big fellow. I noticed he was looking me up and down, sort of thoughtfully, and I wish I knew what he was thinking. I did not get to talk to him, of course, so I will never know.

Every day I wonder how I can escape from here; there must be a way! Maybe the new constable can help me? I tried to talk to *Sersant* Boyce one day a year or so ago, on a day when he came to the house to inquire about an accident at the asylum which caused an injury to a lunatic boy, but I had hardly opened my mouth before *Baas* appeared on the threshold and shooed me away. I do not think it is right that I am kept in the house and made to work from sunrise until the moon has risen in the sky, but what am I to do? I have never been allowed to have friends, never been allowed to go anywhere by myself.

I have thought of poisoning the food with strychnine (which *Baas* keeps in the coal shed to poison rats) but, when I am arrested for murdering the Steenkamps, I will probably be hanged or, worse still, certified as insane and kept for all the years of my life right here in the Robben Island asylum with gibbering idiots who will eat the living flesh from my limbs and suck the blood from my veins. Some nights I wake in fright and take hold of the extra-sharp kitchen knife which I keep hidden under my pillow. I may be a girl, but I will not surrender without a fight.

There has to be a way out of my enslavement and the hope of the right opportunity is all that keeps me going.

Apparently *Nooi* is doing well from the photo business, selling images of my bare-bosomed brazenness to *witmense*. I have a feeling though that no one knows who I am, that the promise of my becoming famous was a lie, a hook to get me to expose myself willingly for Martin Vickery's lens. In a way I do not care though. A chattel of the Steenkamps, I do not own myself, so I ask you, what difference does it make whether I am famous or not?

Now my duties have been expanded to include cleaning for money, yet another way for the Steenkamps to profit from my existence. Occasionally I clean the police compound; other times, at the request of the Medical Superintendent, I clean the guesthouse in preparation for important visitors to the island, and regularly I scrub for Dr Moon and Dr Black (the doctor who tends to the lepers). The quality of my work is unquestionably good – I have been well trained, have I not? – and the employers pay my owners well for my services. But I am always chaperoned by *Baas* Steenkamp wherever I go, even to the doctors' cottages, not only to ensure that I say nothing to discredit my employers but also to ensure that no man ever gets close to me.

Pike the lightkeeper still visits at night, lunatic boys and young men are still brought here after dark, and *Meneer* Steenkamp is back and forth in the shadows. By day he is tired and grumpy and now that he has been promoted to Chief Warder, he frequently slips away from the asylum during working time and takes an hour's nap to refresh himself.

I still eavesdrop on the conversations of the Steenkamps; it is the only way I get to know what is going on in this place and, in this way, I learn that Dr Moon has been asking questions about injuries to lunatic boys and that Warder Hendrina Barber from the female asylum has, on more than one occasion, been seen in serious discussion with Sgt,Boyce, and *Meneer* Steenkamp is increasingly concerned that 'people are not minding their own fucking business,' that they are 'poking around,' and, 'looking for trouble.'

Mevrou Steenkamp suggests – I am not sure if she is serious – that Warder Barber may perish 'accidentally' at the hands of a crazed inmate. And Dr Moon – well, we must think about a nice ending for old man Moon; something delightfully painful, hey?

I listen regularly to the chatter of the brother and sister and that is how I discover their newest plan for me. A plan to make a princely sum of money in a single transaction. Bear with me as I try to explain the scheme.

As you have learnt so far about me, Gina da Cunha, I have led a sheltered life, or you might go so far as to say that I have been a prisoner these past six years, which happens to coincide with the transition period from girlhood to womanhood. The result of my containment is that I am still a virgin, as immaculate as Mary herself, and according to *Mevrou* Steenkamp, 'as pretty as a picture,' pretty enough to drive a man mad with desire. And pretty enough for a man to empty his cashbox for the pleasure of satisfying the lust which lights the fire in his loins.

The unholy plan, so carefully constructed by my employers, is for my virginity to be sold by tender to the highest bidder, and the natural choice to promote the scheme discreetly among the well-to-do men of the colony is, of course, Martin Vickery, a man with established access to the necessary offices and boardrooms where the rich buyer of my body may be found. Vickery's photos of my nakedness are sure to quicken the blood of the tenderers and to promote my virgin price way beyond the financial ability of ordinary men and, finally, to arrive at the offer of a king's ransom for the right to desecrate my hymen.

Finally, to heighten the expectation and the interest of the tenderers, the process will run for one entire year, that is until December of 1910.

Of course, the Steenkamps have no idea that I know of their scheme. No doubt they believe that on the appointed day I will be quietly handed over to the buyer like lamb on a rope.

But this lamb knows what is coming. And she will rather die than submit herself to the slaughter.

Chapter 34 – Robben Island

Robben Island is – how do I describe it? – like an author's concept of a nether world, a distasteful place, sometimes grimy and menacing, sometimes restless, sometimes moody, like Dickens's slums of London, a place where life is short and brutal, where the dead are quickly forgotten. Where, for all the difference they will ever make, the living may as well be dead also.

It is a place where misfortune and misery cling to each other, each desperately seeking company and solace, each trembling in fear of the approaching darkness.

Here, in 1909, there is a multitude of people banished to this almost featureless lump of land; a shelf of sandstone, granite, shell grit and bird shit which sits only seven miles from Table Bay but which may as well be a thousand miles away. Escape from this place is nearly impossible. Henry Hooper's seven-hour swim to the mainland this year is the first fully authenticated crossing to the mainland by a swimmer in four hundred years. Here, where the Atlantic broods and incubates the cold Benguela current, the sea is freezing, treacherous, and home to forests of kelp and to man-eating sharks.

The natural plant life is stunted and sparse and it has taken much effort to establish some groves of drought-tolerant wattles and gums from Australia. An acute shortage of water, too little to waste any on the growing of gardens or the irrigation of crops, adds to the general discomfort of this place.

What Robben Island lacks in flora, it makes up for, by the tens of thousands, in sea birds: penguins, cormorants, oystercatchers and terns, and it is not uncommon for the raucous cries of flocks of these birds to drown out the boom of breakers down on the rocks.

You may be wondering though, who are the unfortunate souls who are banished to this place? Sgt.Boyce tells me that confined here, give or take a dozen or two, are around fifteen hundred involuntary inhabitants and several hundred colonial employees (who are, of course, free to come and go). The 'involuntaries' are the sorry souls who have been herded here, by various Acts of Parliament, out of the sight of genteel society, to live out their miserable existence on a diet of mealie meal, rabbit, *dassie* and indifference.

Boyce cautions me not to look too closely at the squalor and the misery for fear it might affect my state of mind. We are here, he says, to uphold the law as it is written; and he adds his considered opinion that benevolence is best left in the hands of God and His henchman.

For my part, I am unsure what to think of Boyce's views. I will keep an open mind and allow time to tell me whether Boyce is right.

Chapter 35 – Christmas and Emma

Boyce allows me to go home for Christmas, saying that my family are doubtlessly missing me and surely endlessly curious about my new occupation.

I am glad to go. Excited by the prospect of Christmas with Mabel and Evie - how I have missed my princesses!

. . . .

Still gasping with the effort of the crossing, *Tiger* docks at half past three in the Alfred Basin and, without even wishing me good health and a merry Christmas, she allows me to depart.

In a cloth bag and out of sight I have treats and surprises: penguin eggs for Mother and Father, fresh *snoek* for all (including the ever-hungry Middletons) and some wonderful carvings which I purchased at the Robben Island bazaar from Kronkelvoet, one of the few lunatics trusted enough to have access to knives and chisels. For Mabel, I have a small camphorwood treasure box with a concealed pin to release the lid, and for Evie, a carving of a little bonnet-wearing figure with moveable arms and legs.

It feels strange not to be returning to *Harrow*, my childhood home, but to the new place, a much larger residence at the corner of Vineyard Road and Dreyer Street in Claremont. I will miss the old place with its sun-bleached whalebones in the front garden and its ancient grapevines framing the stable door at the rear, but do not misunderstand, I am happy to be here, back with the Foxes.

Mabel and Evie almost bowl me over in their enthusiasm to hug their Uncle James and in equal keenness to peer into my cloth bag, but with mock severity I shoo them away and tell them that 'all good things come to those who wait.'

Early on Christmas morning, with Mabel and Evie in tow, I walk to Newlands, to the Middletons, to deliver their share of fresh *snoek* before it will spoil, and to ensure that they have a hearty meal today. As usual, Harriet is overcome, and tearful; the children boisterous and in need of a bath and delousing, and Jim... well, Jim is still asleep, claiming to be unwell with 'asthma,' but more likely suffering the aftershock of too much beer.

Father has a thousand questions about my new life as a constable. Have I arrested anyone yet? What sort of crime is prevalent of Robben Island? Affray and disorderly conduct? Really?

Louisa has a suitor now, Darrell Fields, and he is joining us for Christmas lunch. Poor Darrell, he is a little slow upstairs, but perfectly agreeable and I think well-suited to the placid nature of my least demonstrative sibling.

Mother is even more withdrawn than usual, seemingly too busy communing with the inhabitants of the astral plane to spare much time for those who are still earthbound and breathing. Certainly, I will speak with her, only just as soon as she can take a break from her communing.

Emma is behaving a little oddly. Dare I say even more oddly than usual? One moment she is playful and laughing, happy to be the star of the show, and then... then she seems worried, even afraid. Is Mother's mood affecting her, or is she disconsolate to be without a suitor now that Louisa is being wooed by Darrell Fields? The latter possibility seems unlikely as Emma has never needed to lean on a man to display her singular character to the world. Emma is Emma, independent and strong-willed, but now unaccountably troubled by something.

Emma and I have become close in recent years. I know she will tell me what is on her mind; we just need a quiet moment together away from the hustle and bustle of Christmas day. Sure enough, when all bellies have been filled to bursting with Christmas fare, when the dishes are washed and stacked away, late afternoon discovers a suitable break for brother and sister to talk. I invite Emma to take a walk with me down Vineyard Road 'to take some sunlight and fresh air.'

I know that with Emma I can dispense with the niceties of polite conversation; I can get straight to the point. We walk a few hundred yards in silence, then I come right out with the question, "Tell me now, Emma – or tell me never – what is troubling you? Don't even try to say nothing, because I won't believe you and I'll be grumpy until the day after tomorrow. Then I'll sail back to Robben Island and shut you right out of my mind.'

Emma pulls a face, and for a moment I see the well-known cheeky glint in her eyes. 'It's that obvious, is it?'

'Yes, like an elephant in a room. You don't have to be a highly trained elephant-spotter to notice...'

'Okay, James, shut up and listen. And for Christ's sake please stop comparing your prettiest sister to an elephant.' A veil of seriousness now falls across her face. I wait, say nothing, give her a moment to compose what she needs to say. 'I'm pregnant, James,' she announces, 'pregnant as a cow in a bullpen. There, my secret is out!'

She is crying now, each moment louder and more uncontrollably. 'I'm fucking pregnant, James,' she bawls. 'Can you believe it? Me, Emma, pregnant!'

I have no immediate response ready, so I hold my sister in my arms and allow her to wet my shirt with her tears and snot. I ask you, what does a brother do in such a situation?

Eventually, when there is a break in the tide of tears, she continues. 'No doubt, James, you want to know who, and why, and how, I'm not going to tell you everything, not because I don't want to, but because I don't have many of the answers, Now, don't interrupt! I'm talking and I'm going to keep talking until I'm done talking. So, listen, will you?'

Before I have time to nod, or even to blink, she rushes on. 'I was at a party in Sea Point and there would've been at least twenty of us there, at Clementine's place. We were fooling around, having a drink, maybe even smoking a little opium, making rude speeches about King Edward, creating *tableaux vivants* – bold poses, a little cheeky and a little saucy - that sort of thing. Then, at a certain time in the night I felt very, very tired, so I found myself a bedroom and I promptly fell asleep. And, just in case you're wondering, I was alone.

'Go on.'

'Hours later - at least I think it was hours later - I was awakened by a great weight on my body and for a moment I thought it was a nightmare, one of those nightmares where you feel as if you're being crushed. But this was no dream, it was a wide-awake nightmare. Some fellow was on top of me, pinning me down with his weight, driving his body between my splayed legs.' Emma pauses, looks at me hard. 'There was nothing I could do, James. I was fucked, both literally and figuratively. And then he was gone.'

'But you saw him, didn't you? You know who he is?'

'No, James. It was very dark in that room. He was heavy and he smelt of wine and he took me without saying a word. That's all I know.'

It is a warm day, almost windless, with very few people out and about as we walk on, a long way, along Main Road and Campground Road, to Keurboom Road, all the way to the Keurboom Estate.

Eventually I ask her what has to be asked. 'What now, Emma?'

'I don't know. It's not as if I can take a bath and wash away the thing which is growing inside me...'

'Are you sure you're pregnant?'

'Am I sure? What kind of question is that? Sure, I'm sure. At first, I wanted to deny the possibility. I've missed two cycles now and my breasts are swelling. I can sense and feel the changes in my body and there's no denying it any longer, James. I'm not mistaken, nor half pregnant. I'm going to be a mother for God's sake!'

'And how do you feel about that?'

"Predictably,' Emma replies, stopping for a moment to look directly at my face, 'I wanted to purge the scum from within me. I couldn't bear the thought of that uninvited seed germinating in my body, feeding on my flesh and blood like some sort of ... of parasite...'

She's crying again, and I let her cry and after several minutes she pulls herself together enough to speak again. 'As the seedling grew, and my body adapted, my mind also adapted, and I've gradually came to accept the new life within my belly. I've now come to the point where I want to keep the child... '

"But the father...'

'Damn the father! Whoever he is, he donated his seed. I no longer want to know who the father is, and I certainly don't want him to be part of my life. Can you, James, even for a moment contemplate the possibility of my marrying or cohabiting with a man who violated me? As it is, I've never intended to marry anyone.'

"Why not?' I quickly edge that question into the discussion.

'You know me well, James, perhaps better than anyone else. Do I look like the marrying type?'

'I suppose not. Not that I've ever given it much thought.'

'No man' adds Emma, 'will tolerate me for long and, equally, I'd poison a husband within three months, so, no, James, marriage is not an option for me - even if I could persuade some clown to have me.'

'If we exclude marriage as a possibility,' I reason, 'then what are you to do?'

'We're judged in our society, often unfairly, for things – like this pregnancy, for example - over which we have no control. It's wrong in every way, not unlike being looked down upon for having a dark skin. But the judgment is here and ever present,' she continues bitterly, shaking her head to emphasise her incomprehension, 'I'll be damned, James, if I will allow my child to be labelled as illegitimate, as a bastard, and I ask you, how will the child deserve such judgment?' It's the same flawed judgment as blaming us for the sins of Adam and Eve. I say it's nothing short of sheer undiluted lunacy.' Emma is working herself up, allowing her fighting spirit to ignite her emotion.

'I hear you, dear sister,' I respond in a measured way, 'but let's return to the question of what you will do?'

'I have an idea, James, an idea which is both immoral and illegal...'

'Maybe I can deal with immoral but, now that I'm a constable, a sworn upholder of the law...'

'Except,' Emma interjects, 'when the law is an ass and blocks well-intentioned citizens from doing what's in the best interest of themselves and their children.'

'You've lost me now, Emma. Can we please take one step backwards so you can explain to your dim-witted brother what you're trying to say. This stuff about immoral and illegal makes no sense to me.'

'Okay.' A minute's silence drops between us, and I can almost hear her thinking.

'It's like this, James, and hold off on the Mr Policeman stuff while you hear me out. What I need is the name of a man on the child's birth certificate, and this man must appear to be my husband. In this way, the birth will be legitimate. And society will have nothing to say.'

'But how?'

'I'm asking to use your name, James William Fox, on the birth certificate, to make it seem that you are my husband. After all, we've already crossed the first hurdle by having the same surname. If any question arises about your whereabouts, I will tell them that you, Constable Fox, the husband I miss so much, is presently stationed for a spell on Robben Island and unavailable to attend the registration of the birth, And, when they hear that you are a member of the Cape Mounted Police, a protector of our colony, they will gladly register the birth and offer their congratulations on the birth of our child.'

'What a devious plan! You know, I believe it may succeed. But my question to you is, will I do it?'

'Yes, you will,' replies Emma with absolute certainty.

This is how the matter is settled between us. I do have misgivings, of course, but there comes a time when misgivings have to be thrown overboard and allowed to sink.

Chapter 36 – Currents and Undercurrents

It is 27th December, and I am back on Robben Island.

Sergeant Boyce will be away from tomorrow until after the new year to visit his wife, Elizabeth, and the little Boyces, at the family home in Plumstead. Despite his drawn-out separations from his family, the upholder of the law seems content with his existence on Robben Island - content in this curious world in two square miles of stuck-together grimness.

Over the years successive governments have enlarged the scope of the island in order to decant the insane, the incurable, the leprous and the subversive elements of society into a common pool of misery. Most of the unfortunates, involuntary residents scratching out the months and years on the slates of their lives, come here wailing and leave the world with nothing more than a hastily muttered prayer at the graveside. You may ask, as an observer of the actions of men, why it should be any other way? Why contaminate our pious and polished community with those who are mental and physical cripples, with those of evil intent, with those who would defile our society with their cursed disease? Look at strong clans and nations, look even into the dens of lions, and you will find that the weak are purged, that the strong and clear-minded are allowed to thrive. Is this not the law of nature?

Whatever you may think, the reality is that the damned of humankind are being held here and here is where they will mark out their existence. They came from everywhere, from Hemel-en-Aarde, from the old Somerset Hospital, from the Breakwater Prison. They came, scores of them, eventually hundreds of them, from all over the Cape of Good Hope.

The Leprosy Suppression Act of 1882 ensures that, for lepers (all races, men, and women) the door of possible return to clean society will remain firmly shut. Theirs is the journey of the damned, a one-way trip to the pit of Gehenna.

....

'Now, mind you, constable,' instructs the sergeant as he is about to leave for his tryst with *Tiger,* 'note any complaints or incidents in the running log and be sure to record the names as accurately as possible. I doubt whether anything will require immediate attention but, if I'm wrong about that, I'm confident you'll deal with it. If anyone is drunk and disorderly, clearly a possibility in this festive season, lock them in the cell until they sober up and give them nothing more than bread and water.'

'Leave it to me, sir, and have a good break, sir.'

I am feeling powerful now, filled with the authority of the law. Let us just hope that the wheels stay on the wagon until Boyce gets back.

It is that quiet time between Christmas and New Year, that time when the earth briefly stops revolving on its axis, when honest citizens are home with their families, Except for the few, like myself, who keep a watchful eye on the horizon; just in case.

With time on my hands, I decide to look about the island. Boyce says, and I have no reason to doubt his wisdom, that local knowledge is vitally important to the job of effective policing. We of the constabulary, he says, should know 'the ways of the place in the dark,' so, to this end I set out on my first solo patrol.

I discover the *pondoks,* a group of haphazard dwellings, home of the island's prisoners, almost all detained here for political reasons, many having been judged to be subversive, usually for the crime of protecting their lands and cattle from dispossession by the *abelungu.* Of course, the white man's words described 'the problem' in different terms; in terms of 'belligerent *kaffirs'* for becoming protective of their property and 'thieving bastards' for having the confounded audacity of taking something in return for their land and cattle.

A group of prisoners are sitting in a ring around a steaming *kaffir pot.* They are singing, chanting and clapping in beautiful unison, the songs of their forefathers, songs of the old country, of former glory. I approach a little closer to the group, then I stop and listen to the strange and stirring words. The group has seen me but refuses to look in my direction.

A fellow with a distinctive conical hat - like an old-time whaler's hat – rises lazily from the group, walks over to the pot and gives the contents a stir. Then he fiddles a little with the fire before he resumes his position in the circle. 'Nothing to see here' is the unspoken message I receive from this little assembly so, without saying a word, I continue on my way.

At Murrays Bay, a place where John Murray conducted a whaling station a hundred years ago, there is little to see other than some ancient lumps of driftwood close to the highwater mark, lumps which may once have been part of the structure of the whaling station or equally may be from the shell of a long-dead sailing vessel.

I turn northward; I am keen to see as much as I can, but I hardly cover a quarter mile before I am accosted by a sharp-tongued female sentinel and questioned about my purpose for venturing close to the female leper camp. I am tempted to arrest the woman for obstructing a constable in the line of duty, but I think better of it, and settle for introducing myself as 'the new man, recently arrived from seven miles 'across the water,' here to uphold the law for all.

'If you care about what is right,' the sharp-tongued one says, waving a yellowed finger under my nose, 'then, *konstabel,* you will see to it that the lepers be allowed to return to the mainland. We have committed no offence, we have done nothing to deserve being locked away like common criminals, but here we are, shut away on this cursed island. Yes, we have sinned grievously by cursing God Himself, but that is a matter between us and God, isn't it?'

Who is this creature? She does not have the voice of an old person, but the skin of her hands is wizened, her fingers gnarled. Is this the sign of leprosy? Her face is veiled by a threadbare scarf which obscures both her expression and her appearance. Is she as angry as she sounds, or is it a plea of misery which is begging me to listen?

I clear my throat and find a few words, 'What is your name?'

'I am Queen Victoria. Welcome to my estate, but mind not to step in the shit...'

Playing along with the veiled sentinel, I bow and reply, 'I am Constable Fox, ma'am, your humble and obedient servant. To think that since 1901 I've believed - quite wrongly, of course - that your eldest son, Albert Edward, has been our new monarch...'

I break off my response at this point as I spy a man approaching from behind the Royal One, a stocky fellow wearing a bowler hat and striding along with purpose. Could this be Prince Albert I wonder? Albert, Prince Consort, about the island, looking for his good woman, his *Gutes Weibchen?*

He is carrying a gladstone bag, a weighty looking piece of luggage, and the image of a person of his appearance lugging a heavy bag in this landscape strikes me as a little odd. Odder still, he is heading directly for me, as if we have an appointment on this spot.

'Good afternoon, constable!' greets the bowler hat, 'I see that you've met Victoria, Queen of England and Empress of India and Robben Island.' This being an observation rather than a question, I make no immediate reply and allow the speaker to continue. "Allow me to introduce myself. I am Dr Black, the physician charged with the care of the unfortunates who have been diagnosed with Hansen's Disease. It's a rather depressing occupation, if I may say so, on account of the fact that this disease is incurable.'

'Hansen's Disease?'

'A disease previously known since ancient times as leprosy, but now called Hansen's Disease in medical circles. In acknowledgement, of course, of Gerhard Hansen's discovery that this affliction is caused by a specific bacterium.'

'I am Constable Fox,' I say, 'young and vastly inexperienced both in policing and medical matters, but here to learn...'

'I dare say, sir, you'll learn a lot here, and quickly.' And with a half-concealed smile he adds, 'I see you've already been having some instruction from Victoria. Come to the male leprosarium any time you like, constable, and I'll be glad to show you around.'

I excuse myself from the presence of the queen and the good doctor, and I continue on my way, past the quarry which is today taking a rest, and I am careful to avoid that area, farther west, around the Bath of Bethesda (a salt pool reserved for the use of female lepers), an area where no men, no matter what their purpose, are welcome.,

The flatness of the isle, with its scant bush, has little appeal for the eye. Yet for several hundred years this unappealing lump of land which stubbornly resists the onslaught of the Atlantic Ocean has been useful both to navigators and successive administrations; a convenient place to banish the unwanted and at the same time useful as a place to harvest food: penguins, penguin eggs, shellfish, *dassies* and rabbits – always very welcome victuals for starving mariners and banished souls.

The mix of unfamiliar sights and sounds and fresh air has made me hungry; I cut short my patrol and head back across the island to the station. After all, justifying my decision, a member of the constabulary needs to be available should anything need to be reported. In my notebook I write myself a little reminder to ask Dr Black when I see him next to tell me more about the exile of lepers to this place. Is this going to be a situation for me where the law and what is right are not on the same path? What does Boyce think? And what will Emma think, she who has accepted from me my word that I will do what is right?

Chapter 37 – The Mysterious Visitor

'Everything's changed, James, everything!'

Waiting to discover the nature of 'everything' I look keenly at Emma in search of a clue. She is waiting for me to say something but, a little mischievously, I am in no hurry.

'Damn it, James, do you want to know, or don't you care?'

'I care, I care,' I answer in mock exasperation, 'but unlike our dear mother I'm not a mind-reader. Talk to me Emma, and tell me what you're going to tell me anyway…'

'You don't need to be the father…'

'What! Have you found the real father then? And persuaded him to make an honest woman out of you?'

'No, James, there's no longer any need for a father. I've lost the baby…'

'What?'

'Don't be dim, dear brother. I have miscarried. The baby is gone. Gone - tightly wrapped and forever nameless - to the municipal tip.'

She is crying now, her fingers shoved disconsolately through her mass of hair.

'I'm sorry.'

She cries a little longer and then, in a few snot-filled moments, she pulls herself together. "Thank you, James, for agreeing to be the father, for being here for me. Now I can get on with my life and indulge myself without any thought for another.'

'So, I'm free to marry someone else?'

'Yes, James, you're free to go. To find yourself a dutiful wench…'

We have a good laugh and Emma's mood brightens visibly before she composes herself and lowers her voice, 'Before we drop this subject forever, I need to share my recent thoughts with you. These thoughts, were they come to be known in Heaven, would ensure my one-way passage to Hell.'

She pauses, looks fearsomely into my eyes. "You will never tell any person alive what I'm about to tell now.' I nod solemnly, agreeing to her instruction. And, satisfied by my response, she continues. 'Before I miscarried, I stopped to think about my future. Quite out of character, isn't it, James? But that's what I was doing and I entertained the thought of taking the idea of your paternity of my unborn child a big step further. To get straight to the point, James, I was going to propose that we move away from Cape Town, that we set up house together, that... that we live as man and wife...'

'Jesus, Emma! I love you, but you're my sister!'

'Judge me not, James. I'm not much drawn to men. I would've done my best to be a good wife. But, mind, I wouldn't have promised to obey you.'

. . . .

It is February now, 1910, a time of long twilit evenings, of long walks, of late suppers.

I am having a few days at home, my monthly break from policing and from the wretched beings who dwell on the island.

I love being home with 'my' Evie and 'my' Mabel. I love being home with Father and Mother and Emma and Louisa. Mabel reads to her grandfather, sometimes for an hour or more; Emma reads to Evie and encourages her to write little stories of her own. As for Louisa, when she is not out and about with her beau, Darrell, she likes to sit in a corner of the kitchen with crochet hook and cotton making intricate doilies and table runners which she dutifully adds to the dozens of such items already in her bottom drawer. To be sure, when the time comes, the contents of that drawer will be enough to set up two households.

At last, I get to talk to Mother. The troubled look she has had since Christmas is still there. Or is that a look of fear? And, if so, fear of what?

'James, this is the year,' she is saying, 'the time when we'll be filled with fear and misgiving, when the sky will be lit at night, when the... '

'Please, Mother, please stop! Is no good ever going to happen? How is it,' I plead, 'that there is no good news? Does your vision refuse to see anything of beauty and hope?'

'My vision, James, is a curse. All my life I have gained nothing, neither for myself nor for others, by my ability to see the unseeable. I tell you, it's a curse and I'd be rid of it if only I knew how to expel it, to return it to its owner...'

'Owner?' I hear myself ask.

'Yes, this ability belongs to Satan himself, and here and there he empowers some people, such as myself, with the ability to use this power. Read Ezekiel 13:23 where it talks of God's people being delivered out of the hand of the diviner, and it becomes clear that divination is a message from the Darkness. I can no sooner block this message than I can stop my breathing, James. The message infests my mind, and it gives me nothing but pain.'

I am trying to understand what my mother is telling me. Is she saying that she has been a tortured soul all these years? That we have always misunderstood her moods and visions?

'Last year was a quiet year, James, the calm before the storm. One event which you'll no doubt recall was the disappearance of the steamship *SS Waratah* somewhere off the coast of the Eastern Cape. The disappearance was only a mystery insofar as no one witnessed her quick and total disappearance.'

'I'm listening, Mother.'

'Well, on the day of the disappearance the weather was particularly foul, gale force winds combined with huge swells. It was 26th July, and the powerful steamer was seemingly not greatly disturbed by the weather. What the investigators don't know is that, through a million to one freak of nature, a once-in-one-thousand-year event occurred when numerous swells combined into a high wall of water, and this fast-moving wall of water rolled the giant steamer like a toy, in an instant snatching away with its tremendous power at least half of the 211 crew and passengers. The steel plates of the mighty ship sheered apart at the weakest point along the bilges to expose all eight of the watertight compartments and, within five minutes, the five-hundred-foot monster lay dead in the deep of the Indian Ocean. They will search endlessly for this vessel, James, and they will speculate wildly about how such a ship could simply disappear, but it will take a hundred years before they locate her grave on the seabed.'

'You tell the story like an eyewitness, Mother…'

'You could say that I was an eyewitness, James, but let's put that aside and talk about this. year. Some people we know well will be leaving us this year. Edward VII exits this world; some will wish him well and some will say good riddance. Then, barely two months from now, a great comet will appear in the sky, a light known as Halley's Comet. This light loops through the universe and reappears about every seventy-five years; it was last seen here in 1835.'

'What is the problem, Mother, with the comet reappearing? Isn't it just an interesting phenomenon, like an eclipse?'

'The comet itself is no problem and nobody, not one single person, will be harmed by it. The problem is the doomsayers, some of them scientists, some of them ministers of the church, who are telling a fearful population that this comet will smother our planet in toxic gas…'

'Isn't that a real problem then?' As usual Mother is ahead of me. How is toxic gas not a problem?

'No, James, the toxic gas won't reach us, but first we'll have to endure widespread panic and hysteria, a worldwide gnashing of teeth, at least in the countries where people are hearing the doomsayers.'

'You know this, Mother?'

'Yes, I know. But I have one more thing, just one thing I want to tell you about…' Mother hesitates, studies my face, then unrolls her scroll of revelation a little further, 'This thing is unusually vague, and I have no explanation for it. Maybe

I have no point of reference for it; I don't know. Anyhow, I'll just tell it the way I see it.'

Mothers sips her tea, gathers her thoughts, and I take the opportunity to refill my cup.

When I am sat down, she continues, 'There's a *kaffir* woman looking for you James. She is asking questions everywhere concerning your whereabouts. She seems desperate to find you...'

'Why?'

'I have no idea why, James. I can't even speculate why she's seeking you.'

'I don't know any *kaffir* woman. Are you sure the person is a woman? Could it be a man? Perhaps a man in some sort of traditional dress?'

'It is a woman, James. That part is certain and all I know. Maybe this revelation wasn't intended for me; how do I know?'

I shake my head. This time her vision has surely let her down.

Next month it will be Mabel's seventeenth birthday. She spends most of her days caring for her grandparents and doing much of the housekeeping. But, more than anything else, she loves reading and she will read anything, from Mary Shelley's *Frankenstein to* Von Goethe's *The Sorrows of Young Werther.* She refuses to be channelled by genre or style; there is simply too much to explore to set such silly limitations on oneself.

Under the pretext of 'a day out with the girls.' I take Emma, Mabel and Evie by train to the city. We plan to buy cakes and *mebos* and flowers and, seemingly by chance, we will find ourselves browsing in Brigl's Booksellers in Long Street. My devious plan involves having Mabel select several interesting books 'for me to read' when what I am really doing is gauging what appeals to her. The plan works well, and the mission is accomplished with the purchase of Percy FitzPatrick's *Jock of the Bushveld* and Defoe's *Moll Flanders.*

Considering the nature of the protagonist's exploits in *Moll Flanders,* I express to Emma some misgivings about this volume but, Emma being Emma, she tells me in no uncertain terms, right there in front of Erwin Brigl, that Mabel is 'almost grown up' and she questions my right to be Emma's 'moral guardian.'

I give her a murderous look, but a minute later I acknowledge - at least to myself — that she is right.

. . . .

When I next return, Emma and I are taking the girls to Camps Bay, to the rotunda, to celebrate Mabel's birthday and to surprise her with her book selection from Brigl's.

It is a little unusual to make a fuss of a seventeenth birthday and, when I stop to think about it, I have no explanation. Why not wait for her eighteenth birthday, or, better still, her twenty-first?

Could it be that that time is talking to me, telling me not to wait, urging me to do it now.

Chapter 38 – Dr Moon and the Asylum

Sergeant Boyce says that policing is an odd occupation. Why, he asks, would a man voluntarily enforce the rules which are imposed on society by the political class? On the other hand, he says, when you agree to do this job, you are often agreeing to do exactly that which offends you. He says it is a paradox, and that not all men can deal with such a contradiction. Some will succumb to the temptation of corruption and self-interest: others will harden their hearts and not blink an eye at the misery of the weak and the defenceless. Some will even participate in the brutalisation of the most vulnerable.

Boyce goes on to advise me that policing is like navigating a craft near the rocks; that there is no room for inattention or for being unready. If, urges the good sergeant, the counteracting forces of policing are beyond your endurance, then be kind to yourself and leave. Become a stonemason or a clerk or a schoolmaster or a clown, he advises, and stay well clear of the moral dilemma.

In a way his homely wisdom reminds me of my father, but that is where the comparison ends. Boyce is a man of the world, ambitious and eloquent, my father a simple man with humble appetites.

As far as the lepers are concerned, my senior says he does not know what to make of them. They are an angry group, a group which believes it is being unjustly punished for the 'sin of being sick.'

The damned bacterium which causes this disease seems to lurk like a scorpion under a rock, harmless unless roused to strike, but the horror of this affliction is twofold: it seems to strike at random and the journey to extinction is always a long and horrifying descent into the pit.

The law is clear though. Without exception all lepers are to remain on Robben Island, to serve out their lives in this place. Held without recourse, the lepers - and mind you, only the male lepers - have at least the opportunity to pray to the Almighty for their salvation at the Church of the Good Shepherd. This good church is closed to the female lepers; they are left to pray from their straw mattresses to whichever god they can find.

So, you may ask, what value is a woman's soul? And I will answer that, by the measure of the Cape Colony, nothing at all.

. . . .

I visit the asylum, a grey and foreboding place resembling a prison. This is unsurprising because, for many of the lunatics held here, it is a place of confinement, just a prison by another name, and only those lunatics who are deemed to be harmless and relatively *compos mentis* are allowed to wander about the island to perform menial work or to collect food.

Two warders, dour looking individuals, are on sentry duty at the mighty oaken entry doors and wordlessly they allow Boyce and me to pass into the sanctum beyond where a third warder occupies a glassed-in office. The place is stark except, high on the wall, halfway between the dado rail and the cornice, hang a pair of oversized portraits in gilt frames. The occupant of the first frame is our familiar near-bald monarch, King Edward (according to Mother soon to be the late King Edward) while the second frame is inhabited by Dr William Dodds, a heavy-jowled man with a fearsome set of whiskers.

The man in the glass office, a little fellow in a tightly buttoned tunic, greets us without enthusiasm or niceties, 'I suppose you two fellows are here to see Dr Moon?'

'Your supposition is correct,' I hear Boyce reply with complete equanimity.

The tunic man snaps his fingers and, as if by some miracle of illusion, a boy appears, seemingly from behind the glass box. 'Fetch Dr Moon now and make it snappy,' orders the tunic man scowlingly before returning his attention to some order or manifest on his desk.

'Who is that Dr William Dodds, King Edward's companion on the wall?' I ask Boyce, to pass the time while we wait.

'No idea, constable, best ask Dr Moon.'

'And tell me, sergeant, what sort of man is Moon?'

. . . .

Twenty minutes pass before Dr Moon, an ageing but surprisingly spritely man, the medical superintendent of the largest psychiatric institution in southern Africa, appears before us. Boyce's description of him was accurate enough but even his description did not prepare me for the fresh-faced and well-nourished look of the doctor, a living and walking recommendation for his profession

'Aah!' exclaims Moon, 'I see you're well mended, James Fox. If I may say so, I did a splendid job on your leg, didn't I? And greetings to you, too, Sergeant Boyce.'

I am astounded. This is Dr Ernest Moon, the doctor who splinted my leg at Somerset Hospital half a dozen years ago. What a remarkable memory! He may be burdened with the responsibility of a thousand patients, but it has not blunted the razor-like edge of his mind.

'I apologise, doctor,' begins Boyce, 'for taking up your valuable time. I came here today to introduce you to Constable Fox, but it seems you have already met, albeit under different circumstances...'

'And my message,' interjects Dr Moon, 'no doubt you came in response to my message?'

'No, I've had no message from you.' Turning to me, the sergeant asks, 'Did you take a message for me, constable?'

I shake my head.

'Damn that Steenkamp!' curses Moon, 'I'll wager that bastard never sent my message. But, of course, he'll say he did and blame some pathetic lunatic for failing to do his bidding. But, no matter, you're here now. Come, gentlemen, let us speak privately in my surgery.'

When we are settled in the surgery, with notebook in hand (and hinting that I should follow his example), Sergeant Boyce invites the doctor to speak.

'When dealing with the mentally disturbed,' Moon offers by way of a preamble to his report, 'it's often difficult to determine who is doing what and to whom. These people are often devious and frequently lacking in the moral constraints we find in normal society. What I'm saying is that there's often a pathological absence of judgment in the actions of these people and, to add to the confusion, the reports by the lunatics concerning a particular event may be totally incomprehensible. How does one tease out the truth from the tangle of mental disconnection? I venture to say, with great difficulty.'

'I hear your words, doctor,' replies my superior, looking a little perplexed, 'can you illustrate your point with an example. This may be helpful for my understanding...'

'Certainly. Let's say that lunatic Jack is inclined to engage in a sexual act with lunatic John. John doesn't seem to care what Jack wants to do and like a child John allows himself to be used by Jack. Jack happens to hurt John, but John accepts that the pain is just part of the game he is playing with Jack. John's injury could be quite serious but, when John is asked what happened, even if he is able to express himself, he'll likely say that he and Jack were just playing a game and that he wanted to be part of it. In other words, John has trouble working out the reality of his situation and misreports the assault as a game, perhaps even a game he was keen to play,'

'It's clear to me Dr Moon,' offers Boyce, 'that your example lies not far from an actual occurrence...'

'Yes,' confirms the doctor, 'there's no prize for working that out, and now that I've flagged the difficulty surrounding what I'm about to tell you, allow me make my report.'

Dr Moon goes on to tell us that some of the lunatic boys, notably several who are functionally dumb, have been referred to him for medical treatment for bleeding and bruising beyond the normal level at which such injury may be expected to occur. 'In summary,' concludes the physician, 'these boys are being systematically brutalised or, if I may speak plainly here among men, they are being regularly sodomised.'

'How old are these boys?' inquires the sergeant.

'They range in age from eight to fourteen. Both as children and as committed lunatics, they have no capacity to consent ...'

'Besides,' interjects Boyce, 'buggery is a crime by the laws of both God and the Cape Colony.'

'My role, gentlemen, is to protect and to treat these children, and your role I respectfully suggest is to enforce the law of the land; that's why I'm making this report.'

Dr Moon shows us out to the entrance hall as far as the portraits of King Edward and the fearsomely whiskered Dr Dodds, and I remember to ask the doctor about the monarch's companion.

'Aah, constable, an important man! Dr Dodds is a personal appointee of the Colonial Secretary, his title no less than the Inspector of Asylums - dare I say a role for a man of unquestioned sanity. On a more serious note, he's done much to reform the treatment of lunatics, even to setting up the secure and specialised Valkenberg Asylum for the most troubled patients. Before Dr Dodds's appointment, all lunatics, from the mildly touched to the violently malevolent, were all held here on Robben Island, in those days a place just one step removed from Hell itself.'

. . . .

'You may wonder, James, where do we begin with this investigation? Under normal circumstances, that is when dealing with sane people, it's logical to start by interviewing the victims. But these are neither normal circumstances, nor normal people.'

I look hard at the sergeant, and I wait.

'Fortunately, we have an informant, constable. Miss Hendrina Barber, a warder at the female asylum. has spoken to me about her suspicions concerning the assault of lunatic boys. It'd seem from her information that the assailants may not be other boys, rather adult men, and possibly adult men in positions of trust.'

'Positions of trust?'

'Warders, James, and possibly other colonial employees, friends of warders.'

Didn't you say, sir, that this Hendrina Barber works in the female asylum? How'd she have knowledge of assaults on boys?'

'Aah! A great question. Firstly, she's not an eyewitness as her information is hearsay and, to some extent, speculation. The standing arrangement is for young boys to live with the women; it's safer for them there. Older boys, from the age of twelve, are required to live in the male asylum. Hendrina's brother, who also happens to be one of my regular fishing companions, works as a warder at the male asylum but, although he almost certainly knows something about what's going on and shares some of his concerns with his sister, he's too scared to say anything to me.'

'Scared of what?'

'Scared of the Chief Warder, Willem Steenkamp; a man who has everyone on a short rein.' Boyce lets his statement sink in before he continues, 'What we need James is evidence, a witness, who can link the offender or offenders with the victims. Right now, we are stumbling about in the dark, just speculating who the perpetrators may be. The only thing we know with certainty is that the boys are being subjected to ungodly acts; this has been verified by Dr Moon.'

Chapter 39 – Mabel's Birthday

Camps Bay Tramways Company Ltd.

The legend emblazoned on the open-sided electric tram beckons us closer.

And invites us aboard.

Today is Thursday, 31ˢᵗ March 1910. Mabel's seventeenth birthday.

Mabel, Evie, Emma, and I are on our way to Camps Bay for the day, to celebrate this great day in the history of the world, to frolic by the sea, and to partake of tea and crumpets, lemonade and ice cream.

My female companions, all three dolled up in snow-white summer dresses and wide-brimmed sunbonnets, look like a carefree trio of well-to-do young ladies unacquainted with the working classes of the colony, and I am determined to treat them all, to make this a day for us to remember.

It is a splendid day painted over with a large blue sky, with not a wisp of cloud on the mountain. It is autumn, the best season in Cape Town, a time when the days are still long, and unbothered by wind or cold, The tram rattles its way along Kloof Road though Sea Point, clattering loudly along the slope around the seaward side of Lion's Head, and we allow our attention to drift as we absorb the views of the mountainside, of the opulent homes encased in the landscape, and of the sky mirrored in the Atlantic waters. What a fine day!

On our approach into Camps Bay, on the final section where the tramline runs parallel to the sea, Evie is as a lively as a barefoot child on a hot rail and, as the rotunda and the pavilion come into view, she squeezes my hand and whispers into my ear, 'Thank you, Uncle James, this is so special.' I ask you, who am to contradict my smart little niece?

We decide to walk about a little, to stretch our legs and to take in the sights and sounds, before having our refreshments. We stop to watch the magical fountains thrusting their watery fingers high above our heads, and to listen to the laughter and squeals of little children splashing each other in the paddling pool, their high-pitched voices ringing merrily across the environs of the rotunda, and we stare in awe at this unusual circular structure which boldly proclaims itself as the *Beach Pagoda,* as if it were some exotic construction from Japan or China.

'Well,' I say teasingly to Mabel, 'next year you'll be all grown up and I suppose some handsome young fellow will be escorting you some place nice on your birthday?'

'Not likely, I'd say,' she answers, 'not unless he's half blind...'

'Nonsense!' I interrupt, 'get Emma to show you how to flutter your eyelashes and soon enough you'll catch yourself a prince.'

"

'Bad example of seductiveness, dear James,' adds Emma, 'the only thing I could charm is a starving seagull and I'd need a handful of breadcrumbs even to do that.'

So, we banter away the time, with Evie periodically darting away to hide or to wet her hot feet 'one more time' in the paddling pool.

After an hour or so of meandering, we find our way up the steps of the railed-in pavilion which surrounds the *Beach Pagoda*. It is time for refreshments!

My father's son (who also happens to be my sister's brother) orders crumpets – piles of them – and tea and fizzy lemonade. Our appetites are sharp, and our tongues as parched as boot leather after our exertions in the sun. Bring the refreshments if you please!

To a point it is busy here on the pavilion and, although people seem to be waiting, possibly for as long as twenty minutes, the orders are being served and no one seems fussed by the slight delay. After all, where could you be hurrying on a splendid day like this?

When, however, the Waltham instructs me that we have been waiting for at least forty minutes, I begin to suspect that something is wrong. I also happen to notice that there seems to be a conference of whispering in our vicinity and a build-up of odd and furtive looks. Is there something going on here, something I have failed to notice before, something happening which has ducked past my inattentiveness?

Emma notices my unease, my looking about, and before I decide what to do, she has risen from her chair. 'Keep chatting to the girls, James,' she orders, 'I'm just going to see what's happened to our order.'

I think nothing more of the delay as I turn my attention back to Mabel and Evie. 'Tell me now, Birthday Girl and Princess, how would you like sometime soon to sail...'

Loud shouting cuts short my words.

'Get away from me! What the hell do you mean you won't serve us? Who do you think you are?'

It is Emma and she is screaming at a big balding fellow. What the blazes is going on?

In a dozen quick bounds, I am next to Emma. Mabel is right behind me. And the big fellow (who might be the manager), his jowls quivering, is saying, '... she's a coloured, that's obvious, and some of our patrons are offended that this creature has the audacity to step up onto the pavilion...'

'This creature...this creature,' screams Emma, visibly quivering under her white frock, 'this is my niece! You can take your fucking crumpets and stuff them down your fat gullet!'

Bigfellow makes the mistake of reaching forward to take hold of Emma's arm and in that instant, I step between Bigfellow and Emma. 'Now look here, sir,' I growl as I push my police badge under the fellow's nose, 'keep your hands to yourself or I'll be obliged to charge you with common assault. Shame on you, sir, for threatening a lady and for creating a public disturbance,' and I turn to Emma and Mabel. 'Come with me, ladies, if you please. No one will lay a hand on you.' Emma wants to protest but, for once, perhaps to spare Mabel from further embarrassment, she thinks better of it. Mabel, a picture of misery, is crying silently.

We leave, collect Evie on our way out from the table where she has been waiting for us. The little princess, not comprehending what has just taken place, declares quite innocently, 'I'm so hungry and thirsty, Uncle James. How much longer...'

I take her hand firmly but gently. 'We'll talk about it later, Evie. We must go now.' And being the clever little girl she is, she falls in silently beside us as we return to the tram terminal.

Chapter 40 – The Woman at the Door

Despite the widespread gnashing of teeth at the prospect of the arrival of Halley's Comet, it came and went in April and the general observation was offered, 'what was all the fuss about?' Which proved my mother to be correct; not that I ever entertained the thought that she might be incorrect about such a thing.

I am settling into the routine of policing on the island. By and large it is petty crime we are dealing with here; stock theft, affray, trespass. The involuntary inhabitants of this isle are often 'not of sound mind' which means that the usual processes of law frequently need to be suspended or adjusted, quite simply because the judicial process is beyond their comprehension, akin to conducting a trial in a Russian court using the Xhosa language.

In this place punishment often needs to be more immediate, more consequential, not unlike the correction which may be applied to children. Affray? Well, now, fellows, you need to say sorry and shake hands and promise never ever to do it again. Theft? Give it back, right now. Trespass? If you get chased away with a *kierie,* or the owner's dog chases you and bites you on the leg, well, that is all you can expect.

A stern word here and a stern word there is usually enough; occasionally the offender may need to go to 'prison' for a few hours, possibly even for a whole day.

As for the voluntary residents, mostly warders, they predominantly get themselves into trouble for poaching - but they are damnably hard to catch! The persistent and widespread poaching of highly desirable *kreef* and penguin eggs, is depleting the natural fauna to such an extent that possibly within a few decades several species may no longer exist here. There are regulations, of course, but as is often the case with regulations put in place by the ruling class, there are simply not enough resources – in the case of Robben Island, just two policemen – to ensure compliance. And, make no mistake, the poachers are a crafty lot, expert at distracting our attention in one place to commit their wrongdoing in another place.

There are other more serious crimes being committed by the voluntary inhabitants. But a combination of an attitude of white-man's privilege (a birthright sitting above the unpalatable laws and regulations which apply to lesser dark-skinned mortals) and the solidarity of needing to 'stand together' against the forces of madness and leprosy and treason, conceals all manner of wrongdoing behind locked doors, in silent outbuildings and within darkened rooms. The fear of being cast out of society holds even the relatively honest citizens back from speaking out to denounce one of their own, even when 'their own' are doing the Devil's work.

There are rare exceptions to this rule; Hendrina Barber is one of those exceptions. No doubt she has her reasons for daring to speak, reasons which we have yet to discover.

As for my superior and mentor, Sergeant Boyce, I am amazed by his ability to remember every detail, seemingly about everything. He knows the names, the faces, the regulation sections, and sub-sections - everything. He fills notebooks as regularly as other men have breakfast. He is physically not a large man, but his mind is a vast archive; I imagine that under more favourable circumstances he may have been a judge or even a privy councillor. Not that becoming a privy councillor can ever happen now, mind you, as we find ourselves in the final week of the existence of the Cape Colony. Just days from now, on 31st May, the Cape Colony will cease to exist as a separate entity as it becomes incorporated into the new Union of South Africa, a confederation of the Transvaal, the Orange River Colony, Natal, and the Cape; together under the motto, 'Unity is Strength,' and designed forever to remain a faithful and obedient servant of the British Empire.

Unsurprisingly (at least to me), King Edward VII left this world, left his wife, Queen Alexandra, and left his mistress, Alice, all at the same time, on 6th May, on an otherwise uneventful day, and for an entire week the newspapers were filled with the expurgated details of his life, without a single mention of his devoted bedmate, Mrs Alice Keppel.

Again, Mother was right.

My mind turns to her other, and unusually vague, prediction regarding the appearance of a black woman, from nobody knows where, or why. For once, maybe she is mistaken or maybe there is mischief in the ether messing with the messages; you know, like static on a telegraph line.

....

It is June now. Not cold yet, but the days are short, and the blue of the sky faded like paint exposed to many summers.

....

'Where is Mabel?' I want to know, but Evie does not answer straight away as she twists her puckered lips in childlike fashion. 'Evie! Do pay attention. Where is your sister?'

'Working.' There she goes, twisting her lips again.

'Right, princess. Here, take these, some lemon drops to sweeten you up.' The child seems uncharacteristically moody, and I decide to ask my questions elsewhere.

But she has not dismissed me yet. 'Uncle James, can you come back to live with us? Please!'

'Why, Evie, why do you ask that now?'

The girl is crying now, a little silent cry, and I draw her close to me and hold her tight. She's so small, as lost and frail as a motherless stick insect. What troubles someone so young?

'I miss you, Uncle James, it's so lonely here.'

'Lonely?'

'Yes. Mabel is working all day. Grandma is talking to people she cannot see and grandpa cannot see anything and talks less and less every day.' I wait, leaving room for her to continue, while I study her sad and intense face. 'Say, Uncle James, can I come with you to Robben Island? Maybe I can help you catch some *skollies?* I'd even wash your clothes, even though it's my least favourite chore in the world. Please, Uncle James!'

I do my best to console my little insect and I promise to discuss her situation further before I return to the island. I need time to think. What am I, a single man working in a strange and inhospitable place, to do? And where the hell is Emma? I thought we had an understanding about the care of Evie. To be sure, there are a lot of questions lining up for answers.

Father cannot tell me anything and it is with some alarm that I realise that every time I see him his conversation is becoming progressively more incomprehensible. Where is the ordered mind of my father which I knew so well as a boy growing up at *Harrow*? Now he is rambling, speaking repetitively of 'the old days.'

I notice, too, the presence of the empty brandy bottle next to his armchair. Perhaps the golden liquid is softening his departure from reality, but it makes me want to cry to see him like this, addled, and nearly blind.

When Mother is done for the day with her talkative spirit friends, I make her a cup of tea and seek an audience at the kitchen table.

'Before you say anything, James, and before I forget, I need to tell you that you've had a caller. An elegant lady...'

'Rowena Richardson?' I demand.

'Don't be silly, James! Why would that vampire bother with you again after all this time?'

'Enough, Mother! If it wasn't her, and presumably it wasn't the Tsarina of Russia, then who would bother calling here for me?' I make as if I am most exasperated by this conversation which is going nowhere.

'Here,' she replies, 'here is her calling card.' From its safe place in my mother's worn ostrich-skin purse, she removes and hands me the card, adding, 'the caller will return in two days, and you need to be here.'

I examine the unpretentious card in my hand. All it says, in small print in three lines, is:

Fröken Zenzele.Persson

Kulturella attache

Konungariket Sverige

'Who is this person named Persson? What language is this?'

'Ask her when you see her, James. She's very polite and agreeable, but nonetheless she's adamant that she'll speak only to you concerning the purpose of her visit. For this reason, you must be here when she returns...'

'What else did she say?' I feel a great need to know more.

'Well, now, my boy, she did remark that the weather is wonderfully fine for the winter season, much milder than where she comes from.'

'Which is where?'

'Sorry, James, I forgot to ask. But do make a note to ask her yourself if you must know.'

Sensing that my parent is not about to tell me anything worthwhile, with a big sigh I shake my head in bewilderment. Who is this person? One of mother's spirit friends?

'One more thing, James,' offers Mother, 'it probably makes no difference to anything, but I think you'd like to know that the woman caller is... a little bit black. African black.'

Chapter 41 – The Proposal

'But why?' I plead.

Mabel looks at me and looks right through me before she answers, 'Because,,,'

'Because what?'

'Because I look and feel like a *hotnot*. I'll never be accepted by white society, and I have to live with that. You can protect me all you want, James, but you can't alter the unalterable. So, since there's no place for me in white society, I have to work as a maidservant...'

'No!' I can hear myself protesting, 'no, damn it, no! You are well educated and...'

'It's no use protesting,' Mabel cuts me short, 'no one will stop long enough to look past the colour of my skin. My destiny is in my pigmentation, in my frizzy hair - my destiny is to be a second-class citizen in my own country, and to make things more difficult, in case you haven't noticed, I'm a mere woman,' and she adds bitterly, 'perfectly suited to cleaning houses.'

'We'll see about that,' I mutter irritably. 'Now, tell me, where is Emma? Why is Evie alone at home with her grandparents?'

'I don't know. She doesn't tell me where and when she is going, she just appears and reappears without notice, and answers to no one.'

....

I am like a caged leopard; pacing, turning, pacing, turning. Who is the black Persson? And where on God's green earth is Emma?

Mabel is working as a house servant in the home of a Jewish family in Green Point. Each week she has a day off on Saturday which coincides with the Jewish sabbath. Mrs Kaplan, the lady of the house, believes that Mabel is undernourished and insists on provisioning her with *gefilte* fish and all sorts of traditional delicacies which she is happy to bring home to Claremont to share with Evie and her grandparents.

....

One day, two days... Nothing! Is this all some kind of weird prank? A dream? An unlikely plot in a penny novel?

On the morning of the third day, my last day home before returning to Robben Island, I am having my favourite breakfast of haddock and poached eggs in the kitchen when Evie rushes into the kitchen, exclaiming, 'Come quickly, Uncle James! There's a fancy carriage out the front and people at the gate.'

'What?' Really?' The breakfast forgotten in the moment, I am down the passage and at the door where a light knock is calling for my attendance.

I stop myself, just in time from throwing open the door and, taking a couple of deep breaths, I count silently to twenty before I reach for the handle. Steady now.

'Good morning!' says a deep female voice, 'you are James Fox?'

'Yes'

'I am Zenzele Persson and I am pleased, very pleased, to meet you.' And for longer than politeness will allow I stare stupidly at Z.Persson, a tall and elegant woman dressed in some sort of bright orange traditional African garment. Her bearing is regal, and she may well be the Tsarina of Russia except for the small matter of her skin colour. You see, Zenzele Persson is 'African black,' like a Zulu.

In spite of Mother's tip concerning the caller's ethnicity, my surprise is great, and the caller must think I am a mannerless oaf just to stand here and gape at her.

She laughs, a deep and resonant laugh, 'Aah, James Fox, of course you have no idea who I really am or why I'm here invading your doorstep. May I come in and explain?'

'I'm... I'm so terribly sorry,' I stutter, 'please forgive me for forgetting my manners. Yes, please, do come in.'

Instructing her companions to remain with the carriage, the caller steps into the hallway. And immediately I have a dilemma at my throat in that mother is occupying the sitting room, where she is no doubt communing with her spirit friends. What am I to do with Madam Persson?'

Sensing my discomfort, the observant caller puts me at ease, 'Your mother and I chatted in the kitchen, Mr Fox, and I'm perfectly comfortable to chat there again.' Will this person, Persson, continue to surprise? What business can she possibly have with me?

Evie offers to make us cups of tea and, when we are settled at the table on opposite sides of the sugar bowl and Evie has left us alone, I invite the caller to state the purpose her of visit.

'You're a remarkable man, Mr Fox...'

'James. Please call me James.'

'I was saying, Mr James, that you're a remarkable man and after so many years it's a privilege for me to be here today, to thank you in person...'

'Thank me?' My interruption is reflexive. What in the world is she talking about? I do not remember doing anything for which I need to be thanked.

....

She is saying, '...the people at the Harbour Board were less than cooperative. No doubt they were perplexed concerning the jumped-up *kaffir* woman inquiring about one of their former employees. But I am persistent, Mr James, and with the help of the Cape Mounted Police, not only did I find you but I also discovered your new occupation and your address.' She pauses to scan my face, then remarks, 'Clearly you still can't connect me to past events, so I'll give you two names to point you in the right direction. Diamond and Isaiah.'

'How?...'

'My brother and my nephew, no less. Now I must take us back many years, back to Zululand, and all will become clear.' She takes a sip of her tea, declines the rusk which I offer her, and tells her story.

'Diamond and our mother found their way to Durban to look for jobs when our employers, the Perssons, a Swedish family who lived near Weenen, made the decision to return to Sweden after unsuccessfully trying to assimilate into the European community in Zululand. The Perssons offered to adopt me and to take me with them to Sweden, and my mother. Ayize, agreed to this believing that I'd have a better future with this kind and loving family. To cut a very long story very short, the Perssons did adopt me and changed my surname to match theirs; they took me to Sweden and for the next dozen years they bestowed on me unending love and kindness; treated me as the equal of their biological children and provided me with an education to match the most privileged children in the kingdom. I completed my education at Uppsala University, majoring in sociology and anthropology, and I was the university's first ever African graduate. Although I didn't view it as remarkable, my graduation was widely reported as something amazing and unprecedented and this is how I came to the attention of the late King Oscar.' Zenzele pauses, takes a sip of tea, and checks with me, 'Am I making sense, Mr James?'

I nod, and she picks up her story, 'The king requested that I attend an audience with him at the *Kungliga slottet* - that's the royal palace in Stockholm. The meeting went well, in fact, so well, that three weeks after our first meeting, I was summoned again.'

"You must have made a good impression?' I remark, encouraging her to continue.

'I suppose I did. In any event, I attended the second audience and that is when King Oscar offered me the opportunity to be his cultural attaché in southern Africa. What a surprise and privilege! Of course, I accepted his offer with both hands. But at this point you may be wondering where I'm taking you with this story. After all, what has any of this to do with you, and I daresay, it'd be a fair question to ask.'

'Please continue, madam, I'm sure there's a purpose to your story. Another tea?''

'No, thanks. Allow me to continue if I may. When I did get back to South Africa, now in my role as the Swedish cultural attaché, I discovered two things; one, that you saved my nephew from the fangs of a predator and, two, that you did your best to advise and to guide my brother, Diamond, in his dealings with his European superiors in the Lighthouse Service. Tragically, Diamond could not be saved, but the defenceless Isaiah was rescued, thanks entirely to you. This is why I have personally come here, Mr James, to have the privilege to meet you face to face and to thank you as much as any human being can ever thank another.'

'Please, it was no more than the decent thing to do...'

'No! I disagree,' she interjects, 'you were jeopardising your position by standing up for a couple of *kaffirs* to whom you owed nothing. No, Mr James, you did a remarkable thing.'

I look away from her gaze. Well, what can I say to that?

'Wisely you're not contradicting me, sir, because you know I'm right. Now I have an offer to make...'

'I cannot...'

'Hear me out, Mr James. I'm not here to embarrass you.' Here is a woman who knows precisely what she wants and who has no hesitation saying it clearly. She continues, 'King Oscar, and his successor, King Gustav, have authorised me to recommend twenty educational scholarships a year for deserving children from southern Africa. Now, in my recent conversation with Mrs Fox, your mother, I've discovered that your nieces, Mabel and Evelina, have no educational prospects here in the Cape Province or, for that matter, anywhere in South Africa. Mrs Fox has told me, too, how Mabel, a capable student, was refused access to matriculation studies for no other reason than her dark-skinned appearance. Well, Mr James, that's plainly cruel and unnatural, while in Sweden people are seldom judged by the colour of skin and for this reason your nieces would have the opportunity to access all the education they want. I am prepared to recommend both the girls...'

'Wait!' I interject, 'your recommendation would be a great honour, a great privilege, but there's one impediment.' A deep frown crosses the woman's face; she must be thinking what silly objection is he about to make? But my words soldier on in the face of her obvious consternation; 'Miss Persson, although I provide for my nieces, I'm not their legal guardian. Whether or not they will be allowed to travel to Sweden is not my decision but the decision of their father.'

'Where is he?' she demands, 'surely, he'll have no objection, but understandably I'll need to put his mind at rest concerning their welfare and safety. And do tell me, where is their mother?'

'According to the custom in our society, it is the father who makes the important decisions for the family, and my sister is not the type to go against custom. Their father will have the last word.'

. . . .

We agree that I will be the one to crack open the subject of scholarships with the Middletons, then arrange a follow-up meeting to include Zenzele where details of accommodation, travel and expenses can be discussed.

Chapter 42 – Information

'There's talk, constable,' explains Boyce, 'talk that Steenkamp and his wife are selling photos, but apparently no one has actually seen the photos.'

'Photos?' I ask him, puzzled why the sale of photos may be important.

'Obscene photos, reportedly of the most shocking kind. Rumour has it that the photos are of the pretty dark-skinned girl who works for the Steenkamps.'

'Gina? Isn't that her name?'

'Yes, but as yet we have no evidence that these photos even exist and even less evidence that Gina is the subject. Yet the rumours are persistent. But, constable, that's not the only rumour circulating here in paradise.' The sergeant pauses, stabs a little circle of dots onto his blotter, and lets his statement register in my brain before he continues, 'There's a second and even more wicked rumour doing the rounds that the Steenkamps are running a clandestine auction to sell the girl's flower to the highest bidder.'

'How do you know these things?' I ask incredulously.

'Robben Island is a small and closed community, James, and like small communities everywhere, there's a lot of whispering over fences and over cups of tea. People like to watch the comings and goings, who is talking to whom, all that sort of thing, For example, there's a fellow, reputedly connected to the superintendent, no less, who arrived here on the ferry with a cartload of fancy photographic equipment and this fellow has been seen frequenting the Steenkamp cottage. Now, what might he be up to? After all, Johanna Steenkamp is as ugly as Dracula's sister and Steenkamp himself isn't exactly a latter-day Adonis or a Prince Charming. Clearly the fellow with the photographic equipment is snapping pictures of something interesting. That's a fair assumption, don't you think?'

'Has there been a complaint, sergeant?'

'No, and therein lies half the problem. The wrongdoing of which we speak is, right now, just rumour and innuendo, hardly the stuff of proper policing. But, constable, that's not to say that we block our ears, rather that we should keep gathering our sardines until we have enough for our pot...'

'Said like a true fisherman, Mr Boyce,' I reply with a cheeky smile, 'we'll be patient, sir, and keep our nets in the water.'

Boyce laughs. And when he is done laughing, he asks, 'Let's imagine, Mr Fox, that you are in charge of this operation. Where'd you focus your attention? What might be your next step?'

'Well... let's see...' And I literally scratch my head. Being in charge changes the perspective, like moving from behind a desk to the firing line.

'If the girl, Gina, is the possible object of wrongdoing, then surely, sergeant, we should make it our business to speak with her? This way we may gain some insight into the validity of the rumours.'

'That would be useful, constable. But we have a couple of problems staring us down. What do you think they might be?'

'Maybe she doesn't want to talk...' I begin. A little lamely, I think.

'That's possible, I agree, but the bigger problem is that we may alert the wrongdoers that we are on their *spoor*. Wherever the girl goes, which is hardly anywhere, she is chaperoned by Mr Steenkamp. Certainly, we can insist on speaking with her, but not without the chaperone knowing about it. Such is the problem...'

'What if,' I interrupt, 'what if, sergeant, we can distract Steenkamp; you know, create some pretext, some situation to lure him away from Gina?'

'Now you're thinking, constable! Who knows, there may be a bright future for you in the Cape Dismounted.' He chuckles at his own joke and, pointing his index finger like a pistol, he takes aim at the imaginary offender before he adds, 'And by God, James, we'll get the bastard.'

....

In the weeks which follow more clues step into our field of vision.

Firstly, Boyce considers making some pointed inquiries through usually reliable contacts at Headquarters concerning the background of the photographer but, without a name to attach to the man, he rests this idea for the moment and decides to use a spy to follow the nameless one to see where he goes in Cape Town and to try to uncover his identity.

Without needing to twist her arm, Boyce persuades his informant, Hendrina Barber, to be that spy and to stalk the cameraman, to take her chances with *Tiger* on the next occasion the nameless man leaves for Cape Town. It is often an inconvenience having just the single ferry to and from the mainland, but in the present situation it works in favour of the investigation and, just in case the photographer is on his guard, a female, thinks Boyce, will be a less obvious stalker.

Secondly, and unexpectedly, another piece of the puzzle locks itself in with this case. Boyce will often say that fortune favours the diligent investigator, and he is not wrong.

Boyce is out doing whatever Boyce is doing when a man turns up at the police station wanting to 'make a report.' I am struck by the man's appearance as there is no doubt that he is an employee of the Cape Lighthouse Service; as you know, an organisation so familiar to me.

He asks for Sgt,Boyce and when I tell him that Boyce is out, he seems disappointed and he turns to leave, but I hear myself call out, 'Excuse me, sir,

I'll be sure to take down every detail of your report. Is there something amiss at Minto Hill which we need to know about?'

'Oh, how do you know I'm from the lighthouse?' His well-weathered face seems impressed by my recognition of his occupation and the location of his employment.

'It's my business to know, sir,' I respond in my friendliest tone. I am not about to tell him that I once worked for his employer.

The caller seems to have gained some confidence in the young constable, my father's son, who is ready to take his report.

'I am Jacob O'Hare, sir, a lightkeeper, one of three not counting the chief, stationed, as you already seem to know, at the Robben Island Lighthouse on Minto Hill. My colleagues and I are charged with tending the light every night of the year and with ensuring the perfect functioning of that light. But that's not why I'm here.'

O'Hare pauses, frowns thoughtfully and seems uncertain how to continue.

'Maybe,' he continues after a full minute of silence, 'maybe what I'm about to tell you is better directed to the Lighthouse Service, but, on the other hand, my instinct tells me that something illegal is going on. Which is why I'm here, constable.'

'Please continue with your report, Mr O'Hare, and allow Sgt.Boyce to decide whether this is a police matter. Sometimes the smallest clue is the one which reveals all.'

'Very well. The subject of this report is my colleague, Mr Pike. Mr Alfred Pike.'

Involuntarily I start at hearing that name in this place. What the blazes!

'Is this man known to you, constable? You seem surprised to hear his name.'

'It's that obvious, is it? Well, sir, I won't lie to you; I've made the acquaintance of Mr Pike in the past but, so as not to prejudice your report, I'd rather not reveal the time and circumstance of our acquaintance. Sgt.Boyce always says to judge each report on its own facts and not to be influenced by hearsay or reputation. Please continue, Mr O'Hare.'

This is how it happens that O'Hare reports that his fellow lightkeeper, Mr Alfred Pike, has a habit of 'disappearing' after dark, at times even when he is supposed to be tending the light. Pike is gone for hours, sleeps at the oddest times, displays the appearance of a man who parties too hard. The question troubling O'Hare is where does Pike go under cover of darkness? Where does he wander when the upstanding inhabitants of this isle are safely tucked into their cottages or suffering the misfortune of performing the nightshift at the asylum? O'Hare has often contemplated reporting Pike to the Lighthouse Service, but he knows that Pike will be fired for dereliction of duty, and he cannot bring himself to do it, to be the cause of the man's dismissal. Notwithstanding these considerations, O'Hare's instincts tell him that Pike is engaged in wrongdoing, and he believes that this wrongdoing needs to be exposed. O'Hare is clearly conflicted in this matter; on the one hand wanting to protect Pike from himself and, on the other hand, wanting to expose Pike, perhaps to protect heaven-knows-who from the nocturnal wanderings of this fellow.

What, I wonder, will Boyce make of it all? And, I wonder, too, are Pike's activities related or unrelated to the matters raised by Hendrina Barber

Chapter 43 – On the Edge

I am scared. Scared as a rat in a nest of cobras.

I live in dread of December. In dread of the Steenkamps. In dread of my own tortured mind.

Who will buy the privilege of spoiling that which is untouched, immaculate, and unstained? Will it be a balding aristocrat with yellowed teeth like dried mealies and whiskers smelling of stale tobacco? Or an overfed businessman with a hairy gut restrained by leather corsets? My mind is unable to control the torments of the grossest imaginings; the threat of penises as large as axe-handles threatening to split me in half like a log; the grip of strong fingers snuffing the last flicker of resistance from my unwilling body; the crush of a man's oxlike massiveness on my girlish frame. *Ek is bang!*

I know, right now, that my own mind is my worst enemy. I cannot think straight. My instinct behaves like a fly in a jar. For a time I will crash fitfully against the glass walls of my prison then, for a while, I will lie, seemingly expired, at the base of the jar. I ask you, what will become of me? Is there any escape?

Escape. Of course, the thought of escape has crossed my mind a thousand times. But how? There is just one way in and one way out of this place. I know this and the Steenkamps know this, too. If I were to disguise myself, I know I cannot pass as a male, not with my silky skin and girly voice, and an unchaperoned young female passenger will be certain to attract comment and attention.

Besides, I have not been near the ferry since the day of my arrival, and I cannot begin to imagine the procedure for registering as a passenger. Do I have to pay? And how will I answer if I am questioned about where I am going?

Over the years hundreds of hopefuls among the unwilling inhabitants have dreamt of quitting this isle, of regaining their lives among their kinsfolk and in their ancestral lands. But in the face of the obstacles placed here both by man and nature, their dreams, like their mortal bodies, eventually crumbled to dust in this place; their short and brutish lives occasionally commemorated by a silent wooden cross.

There is another possibility for escape, a way to remove myself from this place and to release myself from the approaching horror. But this possibility makes my blood run cold because it involves ending my short life; ending it even before I have tasted it properly. It may be my only way out of this jar but, *Here Jesus,* how will I find the courage to see it through? But, looking at my situation another way, how can I fail to do what I know I have to do? I have heard the expression, 'between the Devil and the deep blue sea,' and now I really know the fullness of its meaning.

Probably the most fearful aspect of ending my life is that I may fail, and what is more soul destroying than failing at failure? Even success is failure in this business I am contemplating, for the Lord will surely not look kindly on me for surrendering the breath which he has bestowed on me. I beg you, what am I to do?

If I do not cut deeply enough and in the right place, I may just disfigure myself. Or, if the rope is too weak or the noose improperly tied, I may just end up crumpled in the dust with a broken neck. How can my purpose be done without pain and with a guaranteed result?

The new terror is Mr Steenkamp.

While Mrs Johanna Steenkamp has always had a heart of ice, probably from the day she was born, Steenkamp himself, once distant but tolerant, has lately shown a violent side, and has demonstrated the ferocity of a speared bull.

The turning point came the night he surprised me. I was out, according to my habit, for some fresh air, to study the stars and the flickering lamplight in the nearby cottages.

The moon was up when I saw Mr Pike leave our cottage and glide away among the shadows. But what I failed to see, as I closely observed Pike, was that Steenkamp followed barely a minute later. I failed to see him or hear him until his left hand was clamped into my hair and his open right hand was beating viciously me across my face.

'*Fokken hotnot!*' he screamed, '*wat maak jy hier?*'

I tried to protest but my protests seemed to fuel his anger and he beat me until blood poured unstoppably from my nose and my ears and my beaten face. Then he dragged my near unconscious body to my room where he stood over me like Frankenstein's monster. And, as I lay there like a broken doll, his rabid words bit into my mind; 'You, Gina, you're an ungrateful little *hoerkind*! In return for eating our food and enjoying the comforts of our home, here you are creeping around in the night, spying on us and communing with the Devil and his familiars. Now, be warned! I'm tiring of you. I'm seriously thinking of handing you over for some sport to some of the energetic lunatics in my care.' In saying this, he smiled an evil smile, spat on the floor, turned away and strode from my room.

The next day a bolt was fixed to the outside of my door. And, from then on, Steenkamp unfailingly bolted my door at night, and now I am a prisoner, both in mind and body, enslaved by the very people who once promised to set me free.

. . . .

For a long time, I have thought about making a complaint to the police. But tell me, how is this possible when Steenkamp does not let me out of his sight when we leave the cottage? I have even considered finding my way to the police station at night, rousing the *sersant,* and pleading with him to protect me. The difficulty is I do not know how to find the police station but, even if I were lucky enough to find my way in the dark and to speak to the *sersant,* who knows whether this white man will help me or march me straight back to Willem Steenkamp's loving embrace?

Now the door is bolted shut; I am not going anywhere at night.

Least of all to the police station.

Chapter 44 – Disappointment

'No! Never! Have you lost your fucking mind, James?' Jim Middleton is frothing at the mouth, 'How can you come here advocating that I allow two of my daughters to go to Sweden, a country totally devoid of morals, with a *kaffir* woman? You can't be bloody serious...'

'Hold your horses, Jim!' I cut in, 'these girls are Harriet's as much as they are yours. What, I ask you, does she want for them?

'She thinks, James, whatever I tell her to think. After all, I'm her husband and that's my right.' And with a vicious look he adds for good measure, 'If I'd known Harriet wasn't altogether white, I'd never have married her. But, by the time I found out, the nuptials were done and Mabel was on her way, and there was nothing that could be done for it to be undone.'

'Harriet has been a good wife to you, Jim...'

'Leave Harriet out of this; I make the decisions for my family, and I say that my daughters are not going to Sweden. If they are inclined to be whores they can learn it here, they don't need to go to anywhere else for that.'

I ask you, have you ever tried to argue with an idiot? But I must try, for the girls' sake.

'Jim,' I begin, with my voice lowered, 'I didn't come here today to antagonise you. This opportunity is being offered to your daughters by no lesser a personage than the King of Sweden; Zenzele Persson just happens to be his representative in this part of the world. For God's sake, Jim, the offer is for an expensive European education, something they can never have here in their own country...'

'What for?' demands Jim, 'why'd these girls need a fancy education? You listen to me, James, and I'll spell it out for you. I'll tell you just the way it is here in the real world, not on some *kaffir*-loving planet where you want to take me.' Jim reaches for another beer, and overlooks to offer me one. 'You see, dear brother-in-law, it's like this. But, first, let me ask you a question.'

I nod. What now?

'How many women do you know, James, who are members of parliament? Or surgeons? Or King's Counsels?'

I shake my head.

'This proves the point I'm about to make, James; the point being that educating women is a waste of time. We all know that women are irrational and emotional creatures, placed on this earth to serve men and children. You're a religious sort of fellow, James, and you know that the Good Book instructs women to obey their husbands. This, dear boy, is the divine plan and what makes you think we should mess with this plan?

I notice the challenging glint in his eye, daring me to contradict him.

'Women,' he declares, after detecting no argument from me, 'women are good only for three things and, in case you're in doubt what these things are, I'll list them for you. Number one: women are useful for menial and domestic work; work which would bore a man and lower his estimation in the eyes of his friends. Number two: women are admirably serviceable for the care of little children – look no further than the fact that, unlike us, they have tits filled with rich milk. Number three; women are constructed to serve the needs of men and it makes little difference whether the men are paying customers or their husbands. In both cases the need to be satisfied is the same need. Consider this, James. A husband feeds and clothes a woman, he might even buy her some baubles, and in return she opens her legs for him when he needs her legs to be opened and if the wife is a religious person, after she has received her husband – but especially on a Sunday – she will make the sign of the cross in gratitude for her opportunity to satisfy her spouse...'

'Jim! Jim!' Now I'm yelling.

'What?'

'Is this the way you see your mother, your sisters, your daughters?' I demand to know.

'Sometimes we may pretend otherwise, but when we fan away all the chaff from our relationships, women are women. Useful in their rightful place. And nowhere else.'

'What am I to tell Zenzele Persson then?'

'Tell her, James, to put aside her European pretensions, to return to her *kraal* and to take up her proper role in *kaffir* society.

And tell her to keep her filthy black hands off my girls.'

. . . .

Emma has returned. From a three-month spell in Pretoria Central Prison!

This clears up the matter of her 'disappearance.' According to Emma (always the agitator), she and an unspecified number of conspirators and fellow travellers, journeyed to Pretoria to protest against various measures being contemplated by the first Union government of Mr Louis Botha. The measure which most choked fair-minded people was the proposed Land Act which would strip away the right of black people to own land in their own country.

The protests were loud and violent. Botha sent in mounted police with *sjamboks* to disperse the *kaffirboeties.* Being a military man himself the prime minister had little understanding or sympathy for human rights. As for the protesters who dared to return ('those treasonous bastards'), they were promptly arrested and dragged before a magistrate on a charge of 'inciting civil unrest.' Emma, never one to back down from confrontation, was one of those arrested and, needless to say, the magistrate was unimpressed by her defence of acting 'to uphold common decency in a morally bankrupt society,' and he sentenced my dear sister to a stay in 'the Factory,' the government laundry attached to Pretoria Central Prison.

············

I tell Emma about Jim Middleton's extreme reaction to Zenzele's offer, but Emma appears not to be surprised. 'We all know what Middleton is like, James' she explains as she twirls her tight black curls, 'he's a bigoted, beer-swilling thug who'd happily have his wife go begging and his kids go without shoes while he entertains his pals at the clubhouse. He's a special kind of bastard...'

'Own up, Emma...' I interrupt. 'What has he done to upset you so?'

'Shit, James! It's that obvious? At times it's damned disconcerting the way you read me.' I look expectantly for her to continue, and she does. 'He tried, James, to grope me with his boozy hands one afternoon when Harriet was at the doctor's with little Leonard and I was minding the other kids. He even offered me three shillings to comply as if I were one of those poxed whores soliciting on the Dock Road. Again, she pauses, 'He was persistent even in the face of my clear refusal and I could see he was planning to force my cooperation by brute strength – so I stabbed him in his leg with a kitchen fork and you should've seen the disbelief on his face. Disbelief and shock at having a woman reject him so.'

'Jesus, Emma! Remind me not to upset you; not if I value my life.'

'I've heard your account, James, of Middleton's refusal to allow Evie and Mabel the opportunity of a lifetime. He played the racist reason with you for saying no, but I know that there's more to his denial than he'll ever tell you.' Emma sees I am listening intently, so she continues, 'Because I've been helping Harriet out from time to time – the poor thing can hardly cope with her little zoo and a useless husband – I've come to know a few things.' Emma pauses again; almost seems to have nothing more to say.

'I'm not a violent man, Emma,' I growl at her, 'but, by God, if you're going to tease me so, I may just grab hold of a notion to stab my sister in the leg. And I'll tell the judge that I acted in self-defence...'

'Woo, big boy! I'm trembling in my culottes. But rather than risk grievous injury, I'll tell you all. On one condition, mind you.'

'Condition?'

'The condition is simple and binding. When you hear what I'm about to tell you, you're not to go to Newlands to confront Middleton or, worse still, knock his block off. Promise me this for Harriet's sake and for the sake of the Middleton kids.'

I look at her dubiously. And promise.

. . . .

'You know how Mabel is working now for those Jewish folks,' begins Emma by way of a statement rather than a question, 'well, our dear brother-in-law, Mr Middleton, is requiring Mabel to hand over three-quarters of her pay to him towards household expenses even though she lives with us here in Claremont.' Emma senses my rising anger and cautions me, 'You promised, James. Sit down, dammit!' Then she continues, 'But that's only the half of it for, you see, Bayes is giving Evie five shillings a week for helping out around the house. And Father, bless his soul, is giving his granddaughter another five shillings. And, you've guessed it, Evie's father is taking seven shillings and sixpence a week from this child, for the same reasons he takes money from Mabel.'

'He takes money from a child? Surely...'

'Yes, James, as surely as the sun will set tonight. Now you know the real reason why he doesn't want his daughters going to Sweden.'

I stare at Emma, stupidly I imagine. I think she is done but she has one more log for the fire, 'As you know, James, Middleton is an uneducated clot, a fellow who has probably not read an entire book in his whole life. How do you think he will react if his children turn out smarter than him? Worse still if the daughters – mere females – outshine their father in the mental department? No, James, that cannot be allowed to happen.'

Chapter 45 – Setting the Traps

'Everything in policing,' instructs Boyce, 'relies on evidence. We, as investigators, may think that because a gem is pink or blue that it cannot be a diamond, but then one day we discover that pink and blue diamonds do exist and all along we have been mistaken. Mistaken, because we lacked some key information. For this reason, we must constantly ask ourselves, is it really so?'

We are discussing the curious matters which have come to light in recent times. We (or I should say Boyce) wonder whether there are connections to be made or whether a number of quite unrelated things are taking place at the same time?

Boyce, as much to clarify his own thoughts as to enlighten me, sets out to list the matters which are staring at us.

'There's the business of Alfred Pike the lightkeeper wandering about at night, sometimes to the dereliction of his duty. What could he be doing abroad at night which he can't transact by day?'

'His wandering is suggestive of clandestine activity,' I volunteer, 'but evidence of nothing.'

Boyce nods approvingly. 'You're getting the picture, James. Now, secondly, we have information via an asylum employee, Hendrina Barber, whom I think may be a mostly reliable informant, that obscene photographs of a young female, who may or may not be a willing subject for the camera, are being offered for sale. And I have a further suspicion that the subject may a young, coloured girl who lives in the home of Chief Warder Willem Steenkamp. As yet we have no evidence, not even a single photograph. While you were last over in Claremont, our informant returned with good news after travelling to Cape Town on the same day as the photographer. She spun a story, baited with sweetness, about looking for the best photographer in the city and, in no time at all, she discovered not only the identity of our man of interest but also useful snippets of information about him which may turn out to be useful to us.'

'Snippets?' I ask, my curiosity aroused.

'This man, Mr Martin Vickery, called "Reverend," apparently on account of the fact that he was once associated with the church and, I'm told, at a certain time excommunicated by that organisation for actions which cannot be spoken about in polite society, this man is what is called a society photographer, the man to see when you want the finest snaps which money can buy. He moves in high circles, among high-ranking government officials, wealthy businessmen and the Cape aristocracy. He is a member of the City Club and a frequent attendee at the De Beers marquee at the Kenilworth races. In summary, our man Vickery is a fellow with connections, and it wouldn't even surprise me, constable, if he wines and dines with the leadership of the Cape Mounted Police...'

'You're pulling my leg, sergeant!' I chuckle, 'next you'll be telling me that Vickery is the cousin of George, Duke of York, our next king.'

Laughingly Boyce answers, 'I'm glad to see, Mr Fox, that you're able see discern the line between information and humbug. I think there's a future for you in this occupation.'

'The third matter before us, constable, is the rumour that the young woman, possibly still legally a child, the same female said to be in the photographs, is being put to tender...how shall we say? ... her virginity is to be sold to the highest bidder. True or false? Who knows? But if it's true then I'm of the view that this is a particularly heinous crime, an offence on par with slavery.'

'But, sir,' I inquire, puzzled, 'how can such a venture be promoted without posters, or handbills or newspaper advertisements? Surely, it's doomed to fail?'

'In the absence of any evidence, I theorise that our new friend, Mr Martin Vickery, is promoting the venture by word of mouth among our monied inhabitants. And, doubtlessly, there's a handsome commission in it for him. It's my view, constable – mind you, just my considered view and not a fact – that the dirty pictures and the virgin price are closely related. The common factor? The girl. The one who lives with the Steenkamps.'

'And, sergeant,' I surmise, 'I guess there're no prizes for guessing who might be behind this evil...'

'No, James, not even a sixpenny reward.' Boyce stretches, takes a minute to twist his torso, and to flex his arms and his neck before he reels in the last yards of his analysis. 'The fourth matter before us is Dr Moon's report. We appear to have a situation where a number of lunatic boys, defenceless and inarticulate children, are being regularly sodomised. This is a tricky situation, partly because of the type of victims we are dealing with and partly because we just don't know if the perpetrator or perpetrators are fellow lunatics or whether the assaults are being committed by perverted wardens. The legal challenge for us is that the victim lunatics aren't competent to make a police report, even if they were able to say what has been happening to them. Equally their testimony will be thrown out by a court; the word of the insane cannot be relied upon as evidence of anything at all. Therefore, without meaning to be disrespectful to the deficient ones in our midst, Master James, putting the lunatics before a court would be like putting a troop of baboons in charge of King George's approaching coronation. So, since the victims cannot be relied upon, what we need is third party evidence. There's simply no other way.'

．．．．．．．．．．．．

'Since we cannot alert our suspects to the fact that we're wise to what's going on, we must approach from downwind like a pride of lions closing in on grazing zebra.'

'Zebra on Robben Island?'

'Shut up, constable!' orders my superior, pretending to scowl. 'Pay attention, will you?' I can read the seriousness in his voice; I nod quickly to show my agreement with his instruction. 'I was saying, constable, that we have to be crafty, like the lions if we want to catch ourselves some crooks. Here's what I propose.'

Boyce goes in some detail how we will proceed. 'We must speak to the girl, Gina, without alarming Steenkamp. An opportunity is coming our way, in fact on Monday, 17th October, when Captain Nelson, Crawford's second-in-command, will be coming here for an official inspection of our station. I will ask Steenkamp to have Gina here on Sunday 16th to clean the place from top to bottom, to make everything shipshape for Nelson's inspection. According to the usual arrangement, Steenkamp will chaperone the girl and remain here all the time while she cleans. With the help of Dr Moon and Warder Barber, a situation must be set up at the asylum to require the urgent and immediate attendance of Steenkamp at the institution. He'll likely want Gina to leave with him, but I will insist, absolutely insist, that she stays to finish her cleaning given the importance of Nelson's imminent visit; naturally, however, we'll undertake to safeguard the girl until he returns. In this way we'll create the opportunity to speak privately to the girl. And Steenkamp will be none the wiser. Any questions so far?'

'No, sir.'

'Good! Now, part two of the plan involves volunteering you, constable, for some evening shifts.' At this point I must be looking perplexed for the sergeant repeats himself. 'Some evening shifts, for the express purpose of tracking Pike, the lightkeeper. We must discover where he goes in the hours of darkness, and this seems to be only one way to do it.'

I cannot argue with the boss's logic. This is the way it will be done.

But I have a little surprise for Boyce. 'I understand the plan, sergeant and, although it has nothing to do with our investigation, you may be interested to know that my brother, Bayes, is engaged to Captain Nelson's daughter. Why am I mentioning this when I should be focussed on the investigation? Well, you see, my brother, bless his soul, is a man of limitless ambition and he knows that it can be most helpful to his future to have connections in high places. To set fate up to fall his way, Bayes does his utmost to fly in high circles - you could say, to soar with the eagles. Well, Bayes, unlike anyone else in the Fox family, attends the Kenilworth races, corresponds with politicians and attends society events such as the mayor's charity ball. I'm thinking, sergeant, that maybe my brother can make some very discreet inquiries in those high circles. Inquiries about titillating photographs, and more.'

Boyce looks thoughtful. Then he smiles a wicked smile, 'Yes, constable, a great idea! Who knows what he may turn up? And, you know, he may be just the sort of man we need with us in the force.'

Chapter 46 – Gina's Orders

'*Kom!*' orders Steenkamp, 'we have work to do.'

It is Sunday and we are barely back from the church service and here is *meneer* ordering me to work even before I have changed out of my Sunday frock.

'Where're we going in such a hurry?'

'We have a big job, Gina,' an important job, for Sgt.Boyce. He says it cannot wait...'

'Please, *meneer,* let me change into my work clothes.'

'You have five minutes,' he agrees grumpily.

....

Sersant, hands on hips, is waiting for us outside the front of the police station.

'What took you so long Steenkamp? he sternly demands to know from my chaperone.

'Sorry, we were at church...'

'Never mind!' growls the policeman, 'just get on with it. Every inch has to be scrubbed and polished and it has to be finished today or this'll be the last job you get from me.'

Meneer Steenkamp looks peeved at being chided - usually he's the one doing the chiding - but he is wise enough to keep his mouth shut.

The young constable is at the door now and I take another good hard look at him. 'Wait!' I think, 'it's coming back to me. Different uniform, different island, same man, the lightkeeper? But how can it be? How can he be a *konstabel* now? But it is him, I am sure it is.'

Just half an hour into the clean-up, a boy, maybe thirteen or fourteen years old, probably one of the trusted lunatics, comes running up to the police station. He looks ready to collapse from exhaustion, he has clearly been running hard, and he struggles to squeeze the words from his mouth. '*Meneer* Steenkamp! *Meneer* Steenkamp! Come quickly!'

'What is it, boy? For heaven's sake, take a deep breath and give me your message.'

'There's a fire in the locked ward, *meneer!* And Gerrit is yelling something about bringing Hell...'

'Shut up, idiot! You'll be going to Hell soon enough, you and Gerrit and all your *befok* kind.'

Mr Steenkamp turns to Boyce. 'We have to go…'

And the sergeant cuts in with his severest tone, 'You will leave the girl here…'

'But…'

'But nothing. She's safer here with us, *meneer*, than in a convent. Now piss off and attend to your fire while Gina gets this place smelling sweet and nice.'

. . . .

Meneer has hardly gone a hundred yards, he is still in sight, when *sersant,* totally unexpectedly, turns to me and without introduction asks, 'Gina, will you help us please? We desperately need your help. Will you talk to us if we promise not to tell Mr Steenkamp?'

Is this man serious and am I really hearing what I'm hearing? For months I've been wondering how to get to speak to the police and here, now, the police are asking to speak to me!

I guess I am looking stupidly at the sergeant. He is gentle now, not like when he was speaking to my escort, 'It's okay, Gina, you don't have to say anything, and nobody is going to force you to say anything. But if you do speak to us, I promise I'll tell nobody, not even Mr Steenkamp.'

I have an idea, and I point to the *konstabel,* 'I trust this man and I will talk to you if he can hear what I say. Please, *sersant.*'

'You know this man?'

'Yes, from a long time ago. He's a good man.'

Boyce gives the younger man the queerest look and hastily the *konstabel* tries to reassure his boss, 'I will explain..'

'Yes, you will! But at this moment we have limited time. We must speak with Gina.'

. . . .

I answer all the policeman's questions and he seems really pleased with my answers. The younger man is not saying anything, but he makes me a cup of tea with lots of sugar while the older man is talking.

I ask you to imagine that; a white man, making me, Gina, the servant, a nice cup of tea. The world really is a strange place at times.

When we are done with the questions, the sergeant says with an air of urgency, 'Listen very carefully, Gina. Any moment now Steenkamp could be back here, so I have only one chance to give you my instructions. Are you ready?'

I nod. What now? How complicated is this going to be?

'Firstly,' says the sergeant, 'I must impress upon you to be careful. In my opinion, we are dealing with dangerous people. But, for us to catch them, we need proof, and for this we need your help. Clear so far?'

'*Ja, sersant.*'

'I want you to look for two things. Number one: I need one or two of those photographs which Mr Vickery takes of you. Number two: I need a letter or a diary or any other document which talks about you getting sold in December. You can read can't you, Gina?'

I nod vigorously. 'I can read whole books, and the Bible.'

'Excellent!' The policeman replies approvingly.

'Number three: I need descriptions, as detailed as possible, of the young boys, the ones Mr Steenkamp brings to the house after dark. Because somehow you need to see without being seen, this is the hardest request I'm making of you.'

Sersant has stopped talking; he is looking at me appraisingly, no doubt wondering if I am capable of fulfilling his requests.

He seems satisfied and voices his final instruction, 'In about two weeks a female warder, Miss Barber, will call at your house when Mr Steenkamp is at work, and when you answer the door, she will ask if she can borrow a cup of sugar and a tablespoon of yeast. When you hear this request, you'll know for certain that it's Miss Barber. If you have any photographs or documents or descriptions which you have written down of the asylum boys, have them ready and hand them over to the caller – making sure, of course, that Mrs Steenkamp doesn't see the transaction. If you have nothing to give the caller, she'll return after a further two weeks – this time to return the sugar and the yeast – and this'll give you a second chance to hand over the items I need.'

My head is spinning but, really, the instructions are clear enough.

I hear myself say, with more confidence that I feel, 'I will do it, *sersant*. Everything you ask.'

Chapter 47 – Clouds at Claremont

'She's completely withdrawn, James, and I'm buggered if I know what to do about it…'

'How long…'

'Jesus, I don't know,' answers Emma, seemingly exasperated that I should be concerned about how long our mother has been acting strangely; that is to say, even more strangely than usual.

'You say she's not eating, refusing to move from her bed, muttering Lord-knows-what incantations. What do you think is wrong?'

'Like I said, buggered if I know.' She shakes her head; seems to forget to stop.

'I'll talk to her.'

. . . .

For perhaps the first time in my life my mother refuses to answer me, acts as if I am invisible, will not even look in my direction. I am used to her strangeness, but now she has lifted strangeness to another level. I approach and bend over her, and I kiss her gently on the forehead. 'It's James here, my mother's son.' But there is not a flicker of recognition.

I try to talk to father but I am disappointed to find that most of his communication is with the Van Ryn's brandy bottle which winks warmly at him in the lamplight. So it goes, he and Van Ryn, he and Van Ryn, and his family are fading not only from his vision but also from his consciousness.

But tell me, what can I do?

At least Evie is happy to chat. I am entertained by every detail of her days: how she discovered a dead squirrel in the shed, how big sister Mabel helped her to bury God's little creature next to the white rose (which Mabel explained represented innocence). Evie informs me how the neighbour's kid yelled his head off when he was stung by a nest of wasps. How Mrs Van der Spuy fell asleep in church two Sundays ago and drowned out the sermon with her snoring until Mrs Cooper gave her a smart poke in the ribs, How the mastiff dog from down the street made himself stuck to a little fox terrier bitch and how it took two buckets of water and lots of shouting to cool them down enough to get themselves unstuck. How Mr Duckworth saw Jannie Fourie stealing apricots and how Mr Duckworth quietly opened the gate to the orchard and for a full hour allowed his ridgeback to circle the tree containing the terrified Johnny.

Mabel is talkative, too, but seems a little subdued. I ask if anything is troubling her and, with a wry smile, she replies, 'I don't think so.' She seems to have come to terms with her fate, to be resigned to being someone's house servant. Because I know she has the ability to be a doctor or a natural scientist or a high-placed administrator or anything else she sets her mind to be, I find that I am feeling annoyed and frustrated on her behalf. There is something deeply flawed with our society, a supposedly civilised society, which promotes the suppression of a good mind.

But, tell me, what can I do?

It seems that Emma, Mabel and Evie are conspiring; trying to work out a way they can live with me, or I with them. As much as I try to explain that my quarters on Robben Island, comprising a single bedroom with an iron bed, are inadequate for sharing with three young ladies, the more they object and insist, against all logic, that 'there must be a way' if only I will look for it. So, to keep the peace, I promise to raise the matter of accommodation with Sgt.Boyce - sometimes the impossible has to be attempted for no better reason than to support our relationships with those who matter the most to us.

I am now approaching a year on the island, and a year with the 'Dismounted', and I wonder when I might reasonably ask for a transfer to the mainland; something else to ask the boss. There is the risk, of course, that I will get to the mainland and find that I am posted to the *gramadoelas;* some place like Victoria West or Leeu-Gamka. For this reason, asking for a transfer can be a risky business.

Remembering my offer to Boyce to speak to Bayes about whether he can keep his ear to the ground concerning erotic photographs and other matters, I invite Bayes to 'walk the Common' the way we used to do before I took up policing.

It is already the first week of November, but the air is still chilly and, up towards Table Mountain, curls of cloud, like brushstrokes on a canvas, lie motionless against the backdrop of the brooding monolith. Today is the perfect day for a brisk walk.

Bayes being Bayes, he shows no surprise when I raise the matter of the photographs. In fact, he responds quite matter-of-factly, as if we were discussing the merits of stallions versus mares as racehorses, 'Why, James, of course I know about these cheeky snaps. In fact, I've seen one, but I had to pay no less than ten shillings just to look at it. To have it to keep would have set me back five guineas, a lot more money than I'm willing to part with for a paper girl. Whoever she is, she's bloody beautiful, enough to blow the lid off a man's kettle...'

'Bloody hell, Bayes, control yourself! 'I playfully reprimand my sibling, 'you said it yourself, she's just a paper girl.'

'What does she look like?'

'She's clearly lacquered, possibly Portuguese or Arabic or Malay, black hair, formed like a perfect breeder, with large breasts, wide hips and a narrow waist. Ready to breed...'

'I get the picture. But tell me, Bayes, where can I get the photograph?'

Bayes thinks for a moment before he answers. 'Leave my name out of this constable, and I will tell you, but, if I'm ever asked about it, I'll say that you're a bloody liar and that I never told you a thing. Do we understand each other?'

'Yes, yes, and three bags full.'

'One of our better known turf accountants, Mr Colin R.Owen, is offering them for sale to 'the right people,' I think on behalf of a well-known photographer.'

'Being?' I urge him.

'I think the fellow known as Reverend, one of Satan's agents here in Cape Town. He was defrocked you know…'

'What about the virgin auction business, do you know about that, too?' Often, talking to Bayes is a rotten idea, but today is different. Today, he seems to have something worthwhile to say, something in his mind worth knowing. What more will he tell me?

'Aah, James,' exclaims my brother, I think surprised by my question, 'this virgin business, christened by Reverend as, 'The Offer of the Immaculate Hymen,' is whispered about in worshipful tones behind closed doors all around our fair city. The event has already become part of our modern folklore, the story of how the most desirable maiden in Cape Town, possibly the most delectable specimen of unspoilt womanhood in the entire world, is to be handed over to the highest bidder.'

'Have you put in a bid, Bayes?' I cannot help myself. I have to ask.

'No, dear brother, I haven't. As much as I'm a great admirer of the best of womankind, I'm not about to bankrupt myself. After all, until I taste it, how do I know the fruit is sweet?'

'Enough about you and fruit-tasting, Bayes. Tell me more about the offer process.'

'You cannot afford to be part of it, James, not on a constable's wage. But, since you're so interested in the process, according to my understanding it works like this.' Bayes pauses, presumably to gather his words and to fill his lungs with clean air. We have walked the best part of two miles but neither of us seems conscious of the time or distance.

Now my brother produces that little fake cough of his, a sign that he is about to say something of importance. 'It's a wicked scheme, James, and the promoter stands to make a great deal of money. You see, besides the sum of the winning bid, which I assume will be substantial, every prospective bidder has to register his interest in bidding by paying a non-refundable entry fee of ten guineas. Ten guineas! It's robbery, James, and as an agent of the law, James, I say you should do something about it.'

'Watch closely, Bayes, that's exactly my intention.'

. . . .

It is time to take my leave of Claremont, to return to Robben Island for my next block of duty.

My father and Van Ryn are still communing at the kitchen table, and it is with a heavy heart that I farewell the man I knew, the family man who worked so diligently for decades to support us all, and Van Ryn's friend, a man I hardly know. Maybe a man I hardly care to know.

I must at least try to talk to Mother. What can be ailing her? I cannot make any sense of it; then again, there is nothing particularly unusual about that.

I approach her bed. 'Mother,' I call out, 'I need to go. Back to the island.' Her head remains motionless on her pillow, but I notice, with some satisfaction, that her eyes are following me.

'Goodbye, mother. Please take care of yourself...'

'I will, my boy,' she answers hoarsely, haltingly, 'I will. And, James, when we meet again and I ask you who you are, you will say, "I am my mother's son." If the response is, "I am James," I will know it is not you. It's important, so remember this instruction.' Hoarseness aside, her words are clear.

'I've no idea what you're talking about Mother...'

'You will. Now go away and let me rest awhile.'

Chapter 48 – Gina's Trouble

Finding one of *Meneer* Vickery's photographs was easy. I waited for the right moment when Steenkamp was at work and *mevrou* was occupied writing letters (which she does regularly), then I slid silently into the darkroom where Vickery develops his film and, right there where he pegs the photographs to dry, I discovered not one but two pictures, left there I think because they were imperfect.

I concealed both in the folds of my house dress and left as silently as I came.

Finding documents or letters which may help the police is a lot more difficult. Sifting through papers without leaving any trace of disorder is tricky and reading the documents is time consuming. Have you ever noticed how much writers preen and fluff their words before getting to the point? The result of my document search to date is exactly zero; *sersant* will be disappointed, I think.

Even trickier than trying to find the right documents is the task of recording the description of the boys who are brought here after dark. Firstly, the darkness in itself is a problem, unless you happen to be an owl, and, secondly, I am now locked into my room when *Nooi* goes to bed, and before the boys come to the house. So, I ask you, what can I do? From some place in the past when I was a twiggy little kid, a little saying comes to mind which Ma liked to quote, *'die boer maak 'n plan, maar die hotnot het een.'* This little saying brings an involuntary smile to my face. Doubt me not, I will show these *witmense* that I have a plan – just as soon as I can work out what it is!

....

Warder Barber comes to the house at the appointed time, asks to borrow some sugar and yeast, and I hand her the photographs which I have carefully placed between some sheets of newsprint.

Miss Barber looks at me strangely and declares, rather than asks, 'So you are the girl the men are whispering about.' I do not know how to respond, so I look down from the caller's gaze and say nothing.

'I must say,' continues the warder, 'for a *hotnot* you are very pretty, too damn pretty for your own good.'

Now, I ask you, is that a compliment or a criticism?

....

Some days later, in the mid-afternoon, *Meneer* Vickery returns, and when I see his face at the door, my blood runs cold with fear. Will he notice that two of his photographs have disappeared? Or has he forgotten they were there?

But I hardly have time to worry properly before two more faces appear at the door – Sgt.Boyce and Constable Fox – looking official and stony-faced.

Without familiarity, as if we have never met before, *sersant* instructs me, 'If you please, *meisie,* ask Mr Vickery to step outside.'

Vickery is promptly arrested. His protestations are loud and long; he threatens to lodge a complaint with the island superintendent for 'false and unfounded imprisonment' by the 'low incompetents' of Robben Island. Do they (the incompetents) know that he is Mr Martin Vickery, the foremost photographer in Cape Town, if not in all of Southern Africa?

But his protestations are useless, and he is led away like a sheep on a rope.

When *Baas* Steenkamp gets home and demands to know where Vickery has gone, he is possessed with indignation (and fear?) when I tell him of the arrest, and immediately he storms off, I think in the direction of the police station.

You understand, if Vickery is cowed into talking, there could be big trouble. Now, is Steenkamp rushing to Vickery's aid? Or rushing to threaten Vickery to keep his mouth shut?

. . . .

The matter of the plan to sight the boys has been tormenting me night and day; I think I have it figured out, but it is a scheme not without huge risk. If Steenkamp catches me, I am likely to be crucified on Minto Hill or thrown to the lunatics for breakfast.

When *Meneer* locks my door at night, I have noticed that he just glances into my room by the light of his lantern, says nothing, and secures the door. If I am already in bed, he does not come close to check on me; seemingly the shape under the blanket satisfies him of my presence.

This is the plan. You might say it is a stupid *hotnot* plan, but it least it is a plan. When *Mevrou* goes to bed I will quickly hide somewhere outside the room, maybe in the coal shed, after ensuring that I have created a lump resembling a sleeping person under the blanket on my bed. Hopefully Steenkamp will stick to his routine of taking a quick glance into the room before locking the door. And there I will be, outside that room and free in the night, free to wonder at the stars and free to watch the comings and goings of human traffic from a hiding place where I can get the best view of any activity.

When Steenkamp unlocks my room in the morning he never checks inside; all I will need to do is to melt back into the house when I am sure no one is watching.

It is a simple plan. And I have to make it work. And I have to work it quickly before Warder Barber comes back to 'return' the sugar and yeast.

Since there is no point waiting a single night longer, I gather up a spare blanket, a *kaross,* and some mealie meal bags to make my 'sleeping person,' and I hide some notepaper and a pencil (which I have pinched from *Mevrou's* writing desk) in order to make notes of what I see. I am ready.

As soon as Mrs Steenkamp dismisses me, I scurry silently out of the house through the kitchen door (which is always unlocked) and conceal myself in the coal shed. I am unsure where Steenkamp is; possibly still in the *voorkamer* with the *Cape Times*. It is not long though before I see from my hiding place Steenkamp and his lantern moving about, following their nightly routine. And, sure enough, before long the chief warder departs with his lantern towards the asylum, still following his routine.

I move my position to be closer to the path, to a spot concealed by a couple of empty barrels and a dense clump of cannas. They will pass just a few yards in front of me if they return by the path as I expect.

. . . .

My expectation is correct – here they come! Steenkamp and two boys. I cannot see them well; the moon is not up while Steenkamp and his lantern are walking a couple of paces behind the boys with the result that the boys' faces are just smudges in the night.

I shift my position and crane my neck; I need a better view, but in that moment, there is a loud and alien cry to my side, 'Steenkamp! Steenkamp! Look here!'

Standing there, his approach a total surprise and his presence a materialisation from the dark, is Mr Pike. Pike! Of course! Steenkamp's frequent nocturnal visitor. Pike, completely overlooked in my calculations.

Steenkamp makes for me, but he is stiff and slow, while Pike, being a younger and more athletic man, rushes at me like a rugby flanker and grabs hold of my arm before I can move two steps. I try to twist away, I try to kick, I try to gouge his eyes with my free hand. But it is hopeless; the fellow hangs onto me like a rottweiler.

Steenkamp is surprisingly calm, icily unmoved, and this frightens me even more than when he swears and stomps about the house. Now I am in trouble, I tell you. Very serious trouble.

'Aah, Gina, out for a walk I see,' he oozes sarcasm, 'such a pleasant evening and what a surprise that we should bump into each other at this hour...'

'What?' exclaims Pike, not registering the Chief Warder's sarcastic tone, 'this little bitch...'

Steenkamp continues as if he has not heard a syllable of Pike's protest. 'Now, Gina, my favourite little *hotnot* in all the world, there's so little here on the island to occupy your inquiring mind and only recently I've realised that you've never had a holiday since you came to share our little home. Mrs Steenkamp is so terribly reliant on your good care, that I'm ashamed to say that we've quite forgotten to thank you...'

Again, Pike butts in, now quite agitated, 'Steenkamp! What the fuck are you talking about?'

And, ever so calmly, *Meneer* turns to the lightkeeper, 'What I'm talking about, Alf, is sending little Gina for a holiday, and you'll ask, where to? And I'll happily share the good news that Gina is going to spend two weeks in Cape Town. Now, Cape Town is a big place with many fine destinations but I'm sending my little *hotnot* to the finest destination of all – to Valkenburg Asylum, that fine establishment on the Liesbeeck River, a place of diverse entertainment and endless possibilities. Gina will make new friends and see new horizons she didn't even know to see in her sheltered little life.'

The light goes on in Pike's face and he picks up the tone. 'You are such a generous man, Steenkamp, generosity being a trait of yours not always appreciated by those who are close to you.'

And, gritting my teeth, I hiss viciously, 'You can both go to hell! Just you wait until I tell Sgt, Boyce...'

Damn, that slipped out! Too late; I know I will pay dearly for mentioning the *sersant.*

. . . .

Welcome to Valkenburg! 'You are here, as per Dr Moon's request...'

'I never saw Dr Moon...'

'I was saying,' says the cow-shaped woman referred to as matron, 'we have a request here from Dr Moon that you undergo a two-week assessment and that's what we intend to do.' She pauses and glares at me as if defying me to contradict her, or to protest. I say nothing.

'Mr Steenkamp says that you've been displaying increasing episodes of hysteria in recent times. Rest assured that we'll look very closely at the problem and take all necessary steps to cure you, Da Cunha, but I must caution you that we have methods of dealing with wilful behaviour. That is all I have to say,'

I am dismissed as promptly as I was introduced.

I am escorted to the 'sanitation block,' told to strip naked and ordered to sponge my hair with paraffin, to follow with a soak in a deep tub of Condy's solution. Apparently, and contrary to the normal instruction – per Mr Steenkamp's express request - my hair is not to be cut off.

Throughout this cleansing rigmarole I am attended by a couple of warders who whisper constantly between themselves, I think commenting on my appearance and proportions, as I notice a fair amount of pointing towards myself – pointing which to my overcooked mind seems to be loaded with dark meaning and indefinable threat.

My clothes are taken away, 'to be boiled,' and I am provided with a coarse gown to wear, a laundered-to-death garment which is supposed to tie at the back; except one of the ties is missing, which makes it necessary for me to have one hand constantly behind my back to hold the gown together. Welcome to Valkenburg!

. . . .

It does not take long for the indefinable threat to show itself. The warder known as 'Potdeksel' - I think on account of her curiously flat head, like the lid of a pot - beckons me and in a low voice says to me, 'Things can get pretty rough around here for a young girl like you. It's a really good idea to have a protector.'

'How do you mean protector?' I suspect I know what she means, but I need to play for time.

'Well, it's like this. Some of these dribbling lunatics may take a fancy to you, may refuse to leave you alone, may insist on touching you. That sort of thing. If you have a protector though, then the pests will find someone else to pester.'

'Why'd anyone want to protect me?' I ask, 'I'm just a *hotnot* and, as Mr Steenkamp is quick to remind me, a whore child, a thing rejected by her own mother.'

'Now, Gina,' says Potdeksel, checking that no one is overhearing the conversation, 'it's hardly your fault if your mother is a *hoer*. I know the church says we must pay for the sins of our fathers and mothers but, let's face it, girl, the church is full of shit. You don't deserve to be here and for this reason I'm willing to be your protector. It's simple and it works like this; I look after you and you look after me, and we'll both be happy.'

I feel like crying, like screaming, like curling up in a ball. I feel like slitting the bitch's throat and, if that doesn't work, I'll just say to hell with this life and slit my own throat.

But, instead of doing any of these things, I simply nod my head and hear myself asking the flat-headed one, 'Please, miss, can I think about it for a while?'

'Yes, Gina, think carefully about what I've said. Tomorrow we can speak again.'

. . . .

It does not take long for word to spread that there is a new arrival, an 'Assessment Case,' meaning a patient not yet certified, not yet condemned to living out her days in an asylum.

They come to inspect me; the wild-eyed, the dead-eyed, the mumblers and the dribblers. Who's the new girl? Is she here to poison us? Is it true that she's from Robben Island? But not from the island asylum? Isn't that proof that she is a spy? And tell me now, why didn't they cut her hair?

These people! They get right into my face, some spitting, some dribbling. I want to yell at them to get the hell out of my space but for a time I resist this urge. Surely, they will get used to seeing me in their midst and leave me alone? I reason that if I yell and create a spectacle, then I will be seen as cheap entertainment, which will draw more of these creatures to me, the way a candle draws moths to its light.

Can I somehow find the strength to endure the next two weeks?

I am feeling almost in control of my situation. With open eyes and a clearly functioning mind, I think I can do it, hold back the gibberers and the screamers. I am, after all, Gina da Cunha, the daughter of a fearless deep sea diver.

My positive thoughts keep me going – I can do this! I urge myself to cling fast to the deck rail and soon enough the storm will pass.

But everything changes from the moment I meet 'Fishfinger.'

Fishfinger is a lunatic, an unsanitary sow, a creature obsessed with body openings. She introduces herself by holding the middle finger of her right hand against my nostrils and immediately I retch as the smell of her digit invades my nose. The finger is at the same time brown and slimy and smells of shit and the old-fish odour of unwashed underparts. Oh God!

Involuntarily I push the fat sow from me with all my strength and she goes crashing to the floor. Did I do that? The thing grunts and rises; the thing charges at me but she is so heavy and awkward that I manage to sidestep her charge, manage to put ten paces between her and myself.

And now I know I am in trouble! When Fishfinger catches me and traps me in her grasp, I will be in real trouble. More trouble than I can handle.

I have to survive, so, the next day, I make a deal with Potdeksel.

Judge me not, you are not in my shoes. There are times I want to die, but there are still more times I want to survive. For this reason, I do what Potdeksel wants.

On the morning of the fifteenth day, which happens to be Wednesday, 16th November (not that the date matters to me), *Meneer* Steenkamp is here. To take me home.

Chapter 49 – The Hunters and the Hunted

The photos supplied by Gina, via Hendrina, along with the intelligence given to me by Bayes, Boyce now considers sufficient evidence to arrest Vickery. To this end Boyce enlists an informant at the jetty to let us know when *Tiger* regurgitates Martin Vickery on Robben Island.

Just two days later he turns up and, amid loud and terrible howls of protest, we arrest the photographer, and frogmarch him back to the station. Vickery curses us, threatens us, snarls at us like a cornered hyena – but tells us nothing, admits nothing. Instead, in keeping with his ecclesiastical style, he promises us damnation in a pit of eternal fire and brimstone.

The very next day we bundle our prisoner into *Tiger's* belly and, on the strength of Sgt.Boyce's carefully worded remand warrant, Vickery is taking a one way trip to a secure cell in Roeland Street. Boyce intends that our friend Vickery will feel the full impact of the scales of justice when they come crashing down on his head.

....

'I'm telling you sergeant,' complains Hendrina, 'something's wrong. Very, very wrong. Gina has disappeared and, in her place, as Mrs Steenkamp's carer, is Sophie, a trusted lunatic. Sophie tells me that Gina has gone on a holiday…'

'Holiday!' interjects Boyce, 'that'll be the day!'

'That's what Sophie told me and that's all I know.' Hendrina looks at Boyce and me despairingly. '*Wat maak ek nou?* What if Steenkamp comes after me?'

'Gina won't say anything,' Sgt.Boyce reassures the panicky warder, 'after all, she'll be throwing herself in the fire with you if she utters a word to the chief warder.'

'You know, James,' says Boyce after Hendrina has gone, his eyes flashing, 'if that bastard Steenkamp has harmed that girl, I'll personally feed the swine to the sharks in Table Bay and damn the consequences. There's a limit to being nice, James, and I'm past that limit.' I have never seen the normally calm and analytical Boyce this agitated; he is looking positively dangerous. 'We'll find that girl, James, and we'll chop off the all the heads in the snakes' nest, be sure about that.'

How can I add to his outrage? All I can do is nod in total agreement with the sergeant.

....

Three times I follow Alfred Pike in the dark of the night. The first time he loses me in the shadows but on the second and third occasion I manage to keep him in sight, to follow him all the way to the Steenkamp house. I report my finding to Boyce and, not unexpectedly, my superior replies, 'Well, that's curious, James, that this fellow will risk his employment to visit Steenkamp after dark but, on the other hand, visiting someone after dark is not an offence.'

'No,' I answer, 'even on Robben Island that's no offence. So, sergeant, what now?'

'What, nothing, James! We need reasonable cause to arrest Mr Pike, and reasonable cause is what we don't have,' declares Boyce, pulling a face.

'As for turning up and banging at the door of the Steenkamp place, and in the process possibly needing to arrest several people, clearly the two of us can't do the job alone; we have no idea what we might encounter, and for that reason we need some extra constables.' I cannot fault my superior's logic; with him everything is controlled, detailed and planned; is that not why he is the sergeant? He continues, 'What I'll do, James, is to put forward the case notes, as well as the details of the statements of Dr Moon and Gina and Hendrina, to headquarters for their advice and, hopefully, for their support. We simply cannot risk Steenkamp and Pike slipping off our hook by reeling them in too early. Now, while my report is doing what reports do - that is taking a long time to get a response – I want you to ask some questions at the jetty and from *Tiger's* skipper concerning the transportation of Gina to the mainland. Someone will have seen her; someone will know something.'

....

My task proves to be easier than expected. A young, coloured woman being a somewhat unusual passenger, several people recall seeing Gina on the jetty or on the ferry. The other unusual aspect about her presence on the ferry, as recalled by several witnesses, even *Tiger's* skipper, was that she was being closely chaperoned by no lesser a personage than *Meneer* Steenkamp himself.

But no one seems to know where Steenkamp and the girl went after their disembarkation in Table Bay.

To my complete surprise – and Boyce's disbelief when I inform him – I learn that Gina has now returned from the mainland. Again, she was escorted by Steenkamp, who had her head covered with a shawl and ensured that she never spoke to anyone throughout the voyage.

The news of Gina's return fills Boyce and me with the relief and joy of parents who have just had their wandering toddler returned to them. Thank God the girl is safe! Where did Steenkamp take her for a two-week 'holiday' and tell me, why was she so shielded from conversation with the other voyagers?

Boyce says that he will get Hendrina back onto the case, to call at the Steenkamp place, ostensibly to return the sugar and yeast which she borrowed a while ago.

'We'll hasten slowly, James,' declares the sergeant, 'and eventually the tortoises will catch the hares.'

. . . .

On Wednesday, 23rd November, in the early afternoon, the shadows of two callers fall across the doorstep of the Robben Island Police Station.

Who are the callers belonging to the shadows? Well, no one has seen them before and, in all probability, no one has seen them since.

There are two men. A tall man in a suit, this gentleman as sour and dour as an undertaker who has just swallowed a lemon, and a young fellow with a protruding bottom lip, a surly creature with the appearance of having been bludgeoned and abandoned at birth.

Without introduction the lemon-man demands to speak to Boyce who is at his desk doing whatever a sergeant does at his desk, and to my surprise, I am ordered by lemon-man to step outside.

I consider protesting but, before I can say a word, my sergeant nods slightly to indicate that I should comply and leave.

They are in there a long, long time, so, with folded arms, I stand here idly on the *stoep,* surveying the movement of some *kaffir* prisoners in the distance where they appear to be fossicking for something. *Vygies?* Bird eggs? Not sure. Standing here, I wonder, what in the world can they possibly be talking about in there that I should be excluded? Could it be that they are making a report about me? But try as I might, I cannot think of any transgression for which I might need to be reported. So, I shake my head in silent incomprehension and continue to stare unseeingly at the figures in the bright afternoon landscape.

After a while I am feeling curiously light-headed, so I sit down to wait on the *riempie* bench which serves as our outdoor 'waiting room.' It being already mid-afternoon and not having had anything for breakfast or lunch, I figure that my body is probably telling me that I need to eat something.

Then, without even acknowledging my presence on the *stoep,* the callers leave as suddenly as they came. I know I am only a constable, but I would say that I am hardly an invisible presence.

John Boyce calls me in, orders me to sit down. I look closely at the man but he is expressionless, and he avoids looking directly at me, so, pretending not to notice the sergeant's uninviting aspect, I ask lightly, 'What's up, boss? What did those charming fellows want?'

Boyce grimaces visibly and for several minutes fusses unnecessarily with some files, then he slams them down hard on his desk.

'It's fucked, James! Totally and utterly fucked,' growls the sergeant. "Never would I've thought it possible...'

'What, sir? What are you talking about?'

'Don't ask me to explain it, constable, because I don't understand it myself. I'll tell you what I've been told because I think you need to know but, by God, I don't understand a word of it.'

I say nothing, and Sergeant Boyce proceeds to unfold for me the purpose of the callers; 'These men were from the Cape Provincial Prosecutor's Office. The older man is the deputy prosecutor, a very important man, and the younger man is the deputy prosecutor's secretary.' I imagine I am staring hard at the speaker and, apparently satisfied that he has my full attention, he continues, 'They came here today to tell me that Martin Vickery has been released from custody; they came here today to tell me that my remand warrant has been revoked because the evidence I have detailed is, to use their words, "mere speculation" and that my witnesses are "persons of unsound character." And they came here today, James, to tell me that my actions amount to nothing less than sloppy policing, unworthy of a non-commissioned officer of the Cape Mounted Police. In short, James, they are telling me that this is the end of the Vickery case.'

'You can't be serious, sir...'

'Look at my face, James, and tell me again I'm not serious. How I wish it were so! But, since I am serious, I'm letting you know that I'm closing up the station and going fishing.'

'Are you all right, sir?'

'No, I'm not, constable. Not at all. But that is my problem. Before I go, there's just one more thing.'

'Sir?'

'When the men from the prosecutor's office came across on *Tiger* today, there came along with them and under their generous protection - presumably for the purpose of visiting his friend Chief Warder Steenkamp - Mr Martin Vickery. Our Martin Vickery, photographer and man of influence.'

. . . .

What now, I ask you?

As we grow older there comes a day when we discover that things are not always what they seem, a day we discover that justice and right do not always prevail. It is like looking at the ocean from a boat. Here is the surface, visible and known; here is also the realm below the surface where we cannot see, a realm inhabited by cross-currents and fearsome fish. One day, the day the boat capsizes, that is the day when we discover what is lurking beneath.

Today is such a day.

It is not really surprising then that I am feeling sick in my stomach.

Chapter 50 – I am my Mother's Son

Sometime during the night of 23rd to 24th November 1910, Gina hanged herself in the coal shed of Chief Warder Steenkamp's house on Robben Island.

This happened six months after the formation of the Union of South Africa and just one week after Gina's release from Valkenberg Asylum.

Although Dr Moon had no hesitation recording 'Death by Suicide' on the death certificate, Sergeant Boyce had reservations about the true cause of the girl's death. After all, he knew of a number of people who may have wanted the girl dead.

The policeman was keen to investigate the death, but on the day after the discovery of the body, his offsider, Constable Fox, was feeling very ill – so ill, in fact, that he took himself across to the asylum to seek some treatment from Dr Moon.

The good doctor had seen James's symptoms a hundred times before and his diagnosis was immediate and certain; the young man was suffering from enteric fever, more commonly known as typhoid. Dr Moon did his best to appear positive and calm in the sight of his patient, but he knew there was little he could do for the young constable other than to treat his symptoms and to make him comfortable, as comfortable as it was possible to be in the noisy and crowded asylum hospital.

The doctor urged James to rest and to drink as much clean water as he could take but, by the first week of December, James Fox's condition was in sharp decline. On Thursday, 8th December, to his dismay Moon diagnosed pneumonia in his patient, pneumonia being a well known complication of advancing typhoid. By the following Monday it was clear to the physician that his patient was suffering from double pneumonia, being pneumonia of both lungs, and it was also clear that his patient was in terminal decline.

Sergeant Boyce was summoned and instructed by Moon to send word to James's parents that their son was in a critical condition and that he was not expected to live beyond another week.

. . . .

There was a fire at the Steenkamp house that December.

The fire was the result, in Sergeant Boyce's assessment, of an act of arson, for there was no indication of the usual source of accidental ignition, such as from a lamp or a candle or embers from the stove or the fireplace. The policeman's hunch was that the fire was lighted by Hendrina Barber and that her motive may have been frustration that the evildoers within that house were seemingly beyond the grasp of the law.

Sergeant Boyce had no evidence, merely his experience, to support this speculation and, as there is no record that Boyce tried to prove his hunch by investigation, it is not unlikely that he shared Hendrina's frustration with the situation and found himself other things to do.

As a result of the fire the chief warder's house was temporarily uninhabitable; Mr and Mrs Steenkamp relocated temporarily to Salt River. Just weeks later, Steenkamp resigned.

He and his sister-wife were never seen again on Robben Island.

Sometimes, as in the case of the house fire, when justice seems an impossibility, a person may act alone in a quest for justice; at other times, destiny itself seems to take over, to grasp the helm so to speak. The situation which comes to mind, is what happened to Mr Alfred Pike, one of Satan's emissaries at the Cape of Good Hope.

One particularly dark night in October or early November of 1910, an hour before the rising of the moon, the liner *Edinburgh Castle*, a fine vessel launched just six months earlier by the Union-Castle Line, was on her approach to Table Bay when her short life almost came to an abrupt and watery end. She was steaming in the vicinity of Robben Island when, fortunately, the alert officer of the watch noticed a patch of white breakers to the south-east, breakers on an otherwise black ocean. He ordered an immediate change of course to the west and, as a precaution, ordered all hands on deck to man the lifeboats.

The liner passed within a hundred yards of the treacherous Whale Rock, thanks to the Lord and the alert officer, and she steamed safely on her way.

That night there was no light visible from the Robben Island lighthouse.

Captain Oswald Davies, master of the *Edinburgh Castle,* filed a damning report with the Table Bay harbourmaster, and an immediate enquiry was ordered. The investigation did not take long to determine that the light was out, that the lightstation was unmanned, that the lightkeeper assigned to the night shift was Mr Alfred Pike, and that the chief lightkeeper, Mr Younghusband, did not conduct a check of the lightstation after sunset.

Alfred Pike was summarily dismissed from the Lighthouse service, without any reference and without any pension entitlements.

His superior, Mr Younghusband, was demoted and posted to Dassen Island.

. . . .

Mrs Eva Fox, James's mother, and Miss Emma Fox, James's sister, attended the asylum hospital on 15th December to visit the gravely ill man, while Mr John Fox, James's father, was reported to be indisposed and unable to walk.

Dr Ernest Moon took the two ladies aside and told them, as gently as he knew how, that James was going to die, that now they could visit him but that it would most likely be the last time they would see him alive. He cautioned them that, other than for a moment here and a moment there, James was mostly incoherent and quite confused.

Eva approached her son where he lay on the iron hospital bed and she spoke to him gently, close to his ear, 'It is I, James, your mother. Speak to me, my boy.'

For a minute it seemed that James would not respond, then, quite unexpectedly, he rasped and tried to say something.

His mother bent closer, urged him again to speak, 'Talk to me, James.'

And James rasped again, both Eva and Emma hearing his last words, 'I...I am...I am my mother's son.'

And Emma, being Emma, responded, 'That doesn't make any sense at all.'

POSTSCRIPT

Presented below is some information about actual historical characters who walk through and across this novel. The situations and events described in the text are almost entirely fictitious.

James William Fox

Birth	11th December 1884, Rondebosch, Cape of Good Hope
Father	John Palmer Fox
Mother	Eva Fox (née Christoffel)
Baptised	4th January 1885, at St.Paul, Wynberg & Rondebosch
Occupation	Constable, Cape Mounted Police
Race	Documented as "European," even though his mother was a person of mixed race
Death	16th December 1910 at the Robben Island Asylum Hospital
Cause of Death	On the death certificate issued by Dr Moon, the cause of death is noted as, 'Enteric Fever and Double Pneumonia,' which had endured for 22 days.

James is buried in the Robben Island general cemetery. Below is his actual gravestone inscription:

In Loving Memory of

JAMES FOX,

Beloved Son of

J.P. & E.Fox,

Who Died on the 16th Dec.1910

In His 26th Year.

Lord All Pitying, Jesu Blest,

Grant Him Thine Eternal Rest.

***John* Palmer Fox,** James's father, was born in Hingham, Norfolk, England, in 1838, and passed away at Vineyard Road, Claremont, on 26th September 1913. He is buried at Maitland Cemetery. His occupations were recorded as 'railway porter' and 'gate keeper.'

He married Eva on 23rd May 1867 at St.John's Church, Wynberg.

John arrived in South Africa in the 1860s on a posting with Her Majesty's 9th Regiment of Foot (in 1881 renamed the Cornwall Regiment).

Eva Fox - James's mother, Eva Christoffel or Christofell, is several times documented as a person of 'mixed race.' The origin of the Christoffel (or Christofell) ancestors has not been established and it is the author's view that 'Christofell' may simply be a spelling variation of 'Christoffel.' This variation may have been the result of a transcription error, or it may have been a subterfuge to hide her less-than-white ethnicity. Eva's marriage certificate states that she was married in 1867, aged nineteen, but her death certificate states that Eva was aged just fifty-six at the time of her death in 1918. The death record is clearly wrong about her age. The 1867 marriage certificate is a curious document where Eva's maiden name is recorded as 'Christoffel' but her sister's name (she was a witness) is shown as Emily 'Christofell.' Her sister, Emily, married John Mackana, a man of mixed race, in 1868.

The archival evidence supported by modern DNA evidence obtained from some of her descendants suggests that there may have been an 'Indian' component to Eva's racial profile.

Eva passed away on 13th or 15th October 1918 (records vary), a victim of the Spanish flu pandemic.

Emma Jane Fox, six years older than her brother, James, was twice married, and she passed away at her home in Quiet Street, Claremont, on 9th February 1939. She lived just a block away from her brother, George Bayes Fox.

George Bayes Fox, two years older than his sibling, James, 'Bayes' married Constance Carelse at St.Paul's Anglican Church, Rondebosch, on 18th November 1903. Bayes left this world in 1931. His death notice states that he was of 'mixed race.'

The usage of 'Bayes' as George's preferred name is a matter of authorial choice. Also, he was never engaged to a Miss Nelson.

Louisa Maud Fox married Darrell Magson Fields on 26th February 1917, and they lived at St. Andrew's Road, Rondebosch, After the death of Darryl Fields in 1930, Louisa married Charles Robert Henkins.

She died in Groote Schuur Hospital on 29th January 1964.

James Middleton, for many years caretaker at the Newlands Rugby Ground and the husband of James's sister, Harriet, died on 23rd December 1913, aged just forty-eight years.

Harriet Middleton (née Fox), James's sister and wife of James Middleton, bore nine children but two were lost in infancy. High infant mortality was a common problem in the early 20th century.

Harriet passed away on 14th September 1935.

Mabel Middleton, James's niece, died aged twenty-eight, on 8th October 1918, in the Spanish flu pandemic. At the time of her death, she was employed as a 'domestic servant' in the home of Mr Charles Wagner of Abbey Road, Wynberg.

The death certificate shows that the first notation next to the 'Race' category on the death certificate was deleted and amended to read 'European.'

Mary Evelina 'Evie' Middleton, born 1899, was James's niece and Mabel's younger sibling. She seems to have adopted the name, 'Evelyn,' in preference to Evelina.

Mary married Sidney James Tredree on 31st May 1920 at St.Saviour's Church in Claremont. She died in 1991, outliving her sister, Mabel, by seventy-three years.

The pet name, 'Evie,' is a creation of the author.

Dr Ernest Moon, doctor at the Robben Island Asylum from 1904 to 1920, outlived most of his contemporaries and passed away on 27th April 1955, aged eighty-five. Ernest Moon was born in Northern Ireland and worked at the Derby Borough Asylum before moving to South Africa.

John Henry Boyce, former sergeant in the Cape Mounted Police (and later in the South African Police), died on 4th December 1931, aged sixty. He worked as a night watchman after retiring from the police service.

John married Elizabeth Hamilton Schäfer, aged eighteen, in March 1902. They had ten children, the last born in 1920. Elizabeth passed away on 26th September 1967.

The author has seen a photograph of John Boyce with a group of fishing companions where Boyce is described as a 'warder'. This description is incorrect.

GLOSSARY

Afr. = Afrikaans

aap (Afr.)	- *ape*
abelungu (Zulu)	- *white people*
aikona (Nguni)	- *definitely not*
amaZulu (Zulu)	- *Zulu people*
asseblief (Afr.)	- *please*
assegaai (Arabic & Portuguese)	- *a short fighting spear*
baas (Afr.)	- *boss, master, male employer*
baie (Afr.)	- *very, many*
baster (Afr.)	- *historically, a mixed-race person from Namibia*
bayete! (Zulu)	- *hail!*
bedelaar (Afr.)	- *beggar*
befok (Afr.vulgar)	- *screwed up -*
bergie (Afr.)	- *a vagrant living on or near Table Mountain*
beskuit (Afr.)	- *rusk*
biltong (Dutch)	- *dried, cured meat*
blerrie (South African)	- *bloody*
blink klippies (Afr.)	- *diamonds (literally 'shiny little stones')*
bob (English, old slang)	- *shilling*
boemelaar (Afr.)	- *vagrant*
boer (Afr.)	- *farmer*
boet (Afr.),	- *brother -*
bokkems (Dutch)	- *salted, dried fish*
bonita (Portuguese)	- *pretty*
braai (Dutch)	- *meat which is grilled outdoors*
bredie (Afr.)	- *stew*

buitekamer (Afr.)	- sleep-out or a room with only outdoor access
by jingo! (archaic)	- by Jesus!
CGR (abbreviation)	- Cape Government Railways
clairvoyante (French)	- a female clairvoyant
coloured (South Africa)	- a person of mixed race
compos mentis (Latin)	- sound of mind
Condy's solution	- a solution of potassium permanganate
daai skeeloog (Afr.)	- that cross-eyed person
dagga (Khoikhoi)	- cannabis
dankie (Afr.)	- thank you
dassie (Afr.)	- rock hyrax
die boer maak 'n plan, maar die hotnot het een (Afr.)	- the white man makes a plan, but the coloured person already has a plan
die mond (Afr.)	- the mouth
die munt (Afr. & Zulu, offensive)	- the black person
dominee (Afr.)	- reverend
domkop (Afr.)	- idiot
ek is bang (Afr.)	- I am scared
ekskuus (Afr.)	- I beg you pardon
engelsman (Afr.)	- Englishman
escritoire (French)	- small writing desk
faux (French)	- fake
flagrante delicto (Latin)	- in the act of wrongdoing
fleur de lis (French)	- lily flower
flower (archaic)	- virginity
fok (Afr.vulgar)	- fuck
fok jou (Afr.vulgar)	- fuck you

fokken hotnot (Afr.vulgar)	- *fucking Cape coloured*
fokken moerskont (Afr.vulgar))	- *fucking twat*
fokken skaap (Afr., vulgar)	- *fucking dimwit (literally 'sheep')*
fris (Afr.,)	- *fresh*
Fröken (Swedish)	- *unmarried woman*
fynbos (Afr.)	- *heathland characteristic of the Western Cape*
gefilte (Yiddish)	- *finely chopped, deboned (fish)*
genade (Afr.)	- *mercy*
gou maak nou (Afr.)	- *hurry up now*
gramadoelas (South African)	- *wild, remote country*
Gutes Weibchen (German)	- *good little woman*
haai meidjie! (Afr.)	- *hi, little maid!*
handelshuis (Afr.)	- *trading store*
Here meisie! (Afr.)	- *Lord, girl!*
hier kom die dieners (Afr.)	- *here come the coppers*
hoenderhoer (Afr.vulgar)	- *chicken whore*
hoerkind (Afr.vulgar)	- *whore's child*
homo sapiens (Latin)	- *human being*
hotnot (Afr. offensive)	- *a mixed race person, particularly from the Cape*
ikhaya (Zulu)	- *home*
impis (Zulu)	- *battalions*
in situ (Latin)	- *in position*
insizwa (Zulu)	- *a young man approaching manhood*
isibunu (Zulu)	- *vagina*
isiZulu (Zulu)	- *the Zulu language*
ja (Afr.)	- *yes*

jammer (Afr.)	*- sorry*
kaartjies (Afr.)	*- tickets*
kabeljou (Afr.)	*- kob fish*
kaffir (Arabic, offensive)	*- a black African*
kaffirboetjie (Afr.offensive))	*- a white person who loves black Africans*
kaffir pot (South African, offensive)	*- a three-legged iron pot for outdoor cooking*
kak (Afr.vulgar)	*- shit*
kakkerlak (Afr.)	*- cockroach*
kaross (Khoikhoi)	*- animal-skin blanket or rug*
kerk (Afr.)	*- church*
Khoi (Khoikhoi)	*- indigenous nomads of southern Africa*
kierie (Khoikhoi)	*- walking stick or club*
kleurling (Afr.)	*- a person of mixed race*
knobkerrie (South African)	*- a stick with a knob at the top, used as a weapon*
koekemakranka (Koina)	*- Gethyllis fruit*
kom (Afr.)	*- come*
kom baas, ons moet gaan (Afr.)	*- come boss, we must leave*
konstabel (Afr.)	*- constable*
Konungariket (Swedish)	*- kingdom*
kraal (Afr.)	*- traditional Africa village*
kreef (Afr.)	*- lobster*
Kulturella (Swedish)	*- cultural*
Kungliga slottet (Swedish)	*- the royal palace of Sweden*
laager (Dutch)	*- a secure encampment*
laatlammetjie (Afr.)	*- a child born many years after its siblings*
ma (Afr.)	*- mother*
mademoiselles (French)	*- young unmarried women*

maleier (Afr.)	- *a Malay person*
mebos (Japanese)	- *apricot preserved, dried and rolled into a sheet*
meid (Dutch)	- *maidservant*
meidjie (Dutch)	- *little maidservant*
meisie (Afr.)	- *girl*
meneer (Afr.)	- *mister, sir, Mr*
mevrou (Afr.)	- *mistress, madam, Mrs*
middag (Afr.)	- *afternoon*
moer / jou moer (Afr.vulgar)	- *stuff you*
moerskont (Afr.vulgar)	- *twat*
môre (Afr.)	- *morning, tomorrow*
morphine sulphate	- *an addictive narcotic painkiller*
muntu (Zulu, offensive)	- *a black person*
muti (South African)	- *traditional African medicine*
my ma sê jou ma is 'n tweesjieling hoer (Afr.)	- *my mom says your mom is a two-bob whore*
Nederlandse Hervormde Kerk (NHK)	- *Dutch Reformed Church*
nooi (Malay)	- *female employer*
ons is klaar sersant (Afr.)	- *we are done sergeant*
Oom Paul	- *President Paul Kruger (literally 'Uncle Paul')*
ouma (Afr.)	- *grandma*
ouvrou (Afr.)	- *old woman*
pa (Afr.)	- *father*
pap (Afr.)	- *porridge*
perlemoen (South African)	- *abalone*
peter (archaic)	- *penis*
poes (Afr.,vulgar)	- *twat*

pondok (South African)	- shanty dwelling
potjie (South African)	- stew, traditionally cooked in a 'kaffir pot'
rainha (Portuguese)	- queen
riempie (Afr.)	- rawhide webbing (for chair and bench seats)
riemstrop (Afr.)	- leather strap
sawubona (Zulu)	- Zulu greeting ('I see you')
sebenza (Zulu)	- work
sekerlik (Afr.)	- certainly
sersant (Afr.)	- sergeant
shiboka (Zulu)	- traditional Zulu greeting
sies! (Afr.)	- yuck!
sjambok (South African)	- a hide whip
skaap (Afr.)	- idiot (literally 'sheep')
skelm (Dutch)	- scoundrel
skollies (Afr.)	- rascals
skeeloog (Afr.)	- cross-eyed
slottet (Swedish)	- palace
smous (Yiddish)	- hawker
snoek (South African)	- barracouta
spooning (archaic)	- kissing and cuddling
spoor (Dutch)	- track
stoep (South African)	- veranda
Sverige (Swedish)	- Sweden
tableaux vivants (French)	- living sculptures or dioramas
tameletjie (Dutch)	- a type of toffee containing almond and pine nuts
tannie (South African)	- aunt, term of respect for an older woman
tokoloshe (Zulu)	- a mischievous spirit

toordokter (Afr.) — witchdoctor
'twas (archaic) — it was
tsotsis (Sesotho & Tswana) — black street thugs
tweesjieling hoer (Afr.) — a two-bob whore

uKhahlamba (Zulu) — the Drakensberg
ultimo (archaic) — last month
umfaan (Zulu) — boy
umlungu (Zulu) — white person
umthondo (Zulu) — penis

Vale! (Latin) — Goodbye!
veld (Afr.) — open grassland
vetkoek (Afr.) — deep fried dough ball
vinho (Portuguese) — wine
voetsek (Afr.vulgar) — piss off
voorkamer (Afr.) — front sitting room in a house
vygies (Afr.) — mesembryanthemums

wag 'n bietjie (Afr.) — wait a moment
wat maak ek nou? (Afr.) — now what do I do?
wat maak jy hier? (Afr.) — what are you doing here?
wat sê jy nou? (Afr.) — now what are you saying?
wie's jy daar? (Afr.) — who's there?
witblits (South African) — home-distilled spirits
witman (Afr.) — white man
witmense (Afr.) — white people

yebo (Zulu) — yes

Zuid-Afrikaansche Republiek (ZAR) — South African Republic (Transvaal Republic)